Before he could talk himself out of it, Lucas reached out and pulled her into his arms.

"I'm just so scared," she admitted. "Not for me but for Camden and you. For your family."

"No one is going to hurt Camden or my family," he assured her. Not that he was in a position to give that kind of assurance. Not with hired guns after them. Still, those hired guns would have to get past him, and since he was protecting his son, Lucas had no intention of making that easy for them.

Hailey looked up at him at the exact moment he looked down at her. He was so not ready for this. Well, his mind and heart weren't, but the rest of him seemed to think it was a good idea to kiss her or something.

Especially something.

The heat came. Memories, too. Vivid memories of Hailey naked and beneath him in his bed.

The very bed that was just up the hall.

RANCHER DEFENDER

USA TODAY Bestselling Author

DELORES FOSSEN

Previously published as *Lucas* and *Drury*

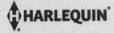

ISBN-13: 978-1-335-42724-3

Rancher Defender

Copyright © 2022 by Harlequin Enterprises ULC

Lucas
First published in 2017. This edition published in 2022.
Copyright © 2017 by Delores Fossen

Drury
First published in 2017. This edition published in 2022.
Copyright © 2017 by Delores Fossen

Recycling programs
for this product may
not exist in your area.

For questions and comments about the quality of this book, please contact us at CustomerService@Harlequin.com.

Harlequin Enterprises ULC
22 Adelaide St. West, 41st Floor
Toronto, Ontario M5H 4E3, Canada
www.Harlequin.com

Printed in U.S.A.

CONTENTS

LUCAS   7

DRURY   223

Delores Fossen, a *USA TODAY* bestselling author, has written over one hundred novels, with millions of copies of her books in print worldwide. She's received a Booksellers' Best Award and an RT Reviewers' Choice Best Book Award. She was also a finalist for a prestigious RITA® Award. You can contact her through her website at deloresfossen.com.

Books by Delores Fossen

Harlequin Intrigue

Mercy Ridge Lawmen

Her Child to Protect
Safeguarding the Surrogate

Longview Ridge Ranch

Safety Breach
A Threat to His Family
Settling an Old Score
His Brand of Justice

HQN

Last Ride Texas

Spring at Saddle Run

Visit the Author Profile page
at Harlequin.com for more titles.

LUCAS

Chapter One

Texas Ranger Lucas Ryland stared at the bed in the room at the Silver Creek Hospital.

It was empty.

He touched his fingers to the sterile white covers, already knowing they wouldn't be warm. According to the doctor, no one had been in that bed for at least the last fifteen minutes.

Maybe longer.

Mumbling something that Lucas didn't catch, Dr. Alfred Parton paced across the room. The doctor had already told Lucas that he wasn't sure how long the *patient* had been missing. That was one of the first things he had told Lucas when he called him. Of course, first Dr. Parton had dropped the bombshell.

Hailey Darrow is gone.

Lucas had rushed to the hospital to see for himself. And now that he had seen the empty bed with his own eyes, it didn't help with the jolt of adrenaline he'd gotten.

"How the hell did this happen?" Lucas demanded.

"No idea." Dr. Alfred Parton scrubbed his hand over his balding head, something he'd been doing a lot since Lucas had arrived. "I've asked everyone on the staff, and no one knows. But Hailey must have had some help. She wouldn't have been able to get up and just walk out of here."

No. Not after being in a coma for three months. She wouldn't have been able to stand on her own, much less get out of the bed and leave the building.

Of course, that only brought on a boatload of questions for Lucas—had she awakened and managed to talk someone into helping her leave? It was a valid concern, because the last time Lucas had seen Hailey conscious, she'd been nine months pregnant with their child and running. Not just from some guy who'd been chasing her.

But also running from him.

He'd found her, finally, unconscious from a car accident. She'd plowed into a tree, and a limb that'd come through the windshield had given her a nasty head injury. She'd also had a fake ID and enough cash for Lucas to know that she had planned on disappearing.

Even now, three months later, that felt like a punch to the gut, but a "punched gut" feeling pretty much described his entire relationship with Hailey for the year he'd known her.

"We have some security cameras," the doctor explained, "but none back here in this part of the hospital. They're at the front entrance, the ER and the pharmacy. We're still looking, but she's not on any of that footage."

Which meant she might still be inside the place. It wasn't a huge hospital, but there were clinics, storage closets and probably some unoccupied rooms.

"You think she'll try to go to the Silver Creek Ranch?" the doc asked.

Lucas cursed and yanked out his phone. He'd been

so shocked by the news that Hailey was missing that he hadn't even considered the next step of how this might play out.

But, yeah, if she was capable of moving, she would almost certainly try to get to his cousins' ranch, where Lucas now lived. Hailey would try to get to the baby.

Camden

His three-month-old son.

But he was Hailey's child, too.

And Hailey would go after him. Or rather, she would try. As far as Lucas was concerned, Hailey had given up her rights to their precious little boy when she'd gone on the run before Camden was born. Hailey had endangered herself and the baby in that car wreck.

"Search every inch of the hospital," Lucas ordered the doctor, though that was just the frustration talking because the staff was already looking for Hailey. "And let me know the second you find her."

Lucas headed out the door, hurrying, but he didn't call Camden's nanny because he didn't want to alarm her, yet. Instead, he called his cousin, Mason Ryland. Mason was a part-time deputy in Silver Creek, but since it was nearly 8:00 p.m., he'd already be home, and his house was just up the road from Lucas's new place.

"I'm not coming into the office," Mason said instead of a greeting. His cousin wasn't the friendliest of the Ryland clan, but he would protect Camden with his life.

Lucas prayed it didn't come down to that, though.

"Hailey's missing from the hospital," Lucas tossed out there. "I'm on my way home now, but make sure she doesn't get anywhere near Camden."

Mason cursed, too, and it was ripe enough that Lucas

heard Mason's wife, Abbie, give him a scolding about saying such things in front of their two young sons.

"You can explain when you get here," Mason said. "I'll head over to your place now."

Lucas thanked him and hoped he did indeed have something to explain—like Hailey's whereabouts and how she'd managed to escape. Right now, he didn't know nearly enough.

He ran out of the building and across the parking lot to his SUV. The November wind swiped at him, but he didn't duck his head against it. Lucas kept watch around him. A habit that had saved him a time or two while he'd been a Texas Ranger. But nothing seemed out of the ordinary.

The moment he was behind the wheel, Lucas started the engine. However, before he could throw the SUV into gear, he caught the movement from the backseat. Lucas whirled around, already reaching for his gun.

But it was too late.

Hailey was there.

She was sitting right next to the baby's empty car seat, and thanks to the security lights, he could see that she had a gun pointed right at him. *His* gun. The one he kept as a backup in the glove compartment. Since he hadn't seen her when he first approached the vehicle, it likely meant she'd ducked down out of sight. Hiding from him so she could—well—do whatever the heck she was doing.

"Leave your weapon in your holster," she ordered, and it was indeed an order.

That was a hard look Hailey gave him. But the hardness didn't mesh well with the beads of sweat on her forehead. It was chilly, definitely not warm enough weather for sweating, so this must have been from exertion. There was no color in her cheeks. She looked weak, and no doubt was, but she didn't need much strength considering the gun she had in his face.

Lucas had no idea if she'd actually shoot him, because she clearly wasn't thinking straight. Couldn't be. Or else she wouldn't have him at gunpoint. Then again, she had run from him three months ago, so it was obvious she hadn't trusted him.

Still didn't, apparently.

The head injury that had put her in the coma had healed with the exception of a thin scar near her scalp. Her blond hair was pushed back from her face now so the scar was easier to see, but in another month or two, it'd be practically gone. No signs of the trauma that had nearly killed her and the baby.

No visible signs, anyway.

Lucas would always remember. *Always.*

"Start driving," Hailey insisted. "We can't stay here."

Because the hospital staff would look in the parking lot. But that didn't explain why she was hiding and clearly trying to escape.

Hell, it didn't explain a lot of things.

Lucas did drive. Not far, though, and only after he hit the child safety button to lock all the doors so that Hailey wouldn't be able to get out. He drove out of the parking lot and went two blocks up before pulling over.

He purposely didn't choose a spot in front of any businesses in case something went wrong when he wrestled that gun away from her. Instead, he stopped in front of the town park. Since it was already dark, the park was empty.

"All right. Now talk." Lucas had a string of questions but went with the easiest one first. "How'd you get from your room to my SUV?"

"I walked."

"Impossible," Lucas fired back. He glanced around to make sure someone wasn't out there ready to help her with more than just getting out of that hospital bed. "People who've been in a coma for three months just don't get up and walk."

She nodded. Dragged in a thin breath. That's when he noticed she was shaking. "I've been out of the coma for nearly a week now, and I've been exercising my legs when no one was watching."

Nearly a week.

Damn.

"And none of the medical staff noticed?" he snapped.

"I was never in a vegetative state, just a deep coma, so the monitor already showed plenty of brain activity for me. The activity increased when I woke up, but I tampered with the machine so that it looked as if it malfunctioned. I kept doing that, and the staff thought they had faulty readings."

A nurse had indeed told him about the readings, and the hospital had called in someone to repair the machine. The Silver Creek Hospital wasn't big or modern by anyone's standards so they hadn't had another monitor to use on Hailey. That's why the nurses had been keeping a closer watch on her. Obviously, they hadn't watched nearly close enough.

"How'd you know how to tamper with the monitor?" he pressed.

She glanced away. "I'm good with computers and such."

This was the first Lucas was hearing about that, but

it didn't matter. Not when there were so many other things they needed to talk about.

"When I was trying to regain my strength, I made sure no one else saw me," she added.

Obviously. Just as she'd made sure he hadn't noticed her before he'd gotten in his vehicle.

Her gaze dropped to her stomach for just a second. "I listened to try to find out if I'd had a boy or a girl, but no one mentioned it. Not even you when you visited me on Monday."

Clearly she'd known he was there. Lucas had indeed visited her, something he did a couple of times a week. Why, he didn't know, because he couldn't get answers from a woman in a coma. It riled him to the core, though, that she'd been awake during that visit and hadn't said anything.

But what had he said?

Lucas wasn't even sure—maybe nothing—but he'd almost certainly glared at her. He still was glaring now.

"So, you faked being in a coma for the last week, built up your strength, and just walked out of the hospital?" he asked, going through the probability of that as he said it.

He was skeptical.

Hailey nodded. "I ducked into a supply room, and when I heard the doctor call you, I knew you'd be arriving soon. I made my way to the parking lot and hid behind some shrubs."

"And then you broke into my SUV," Lucas snarled.

"The back door was unlocked," she answered as if that was something she did all the time. To the best of his knowledge, she didn't, but then, he really didn't know much about this woman.

The mother of his child.

"Why didn't you let me know you'd come out of the coma?" Lucas demanded.

Hailey stared at him a long time. "I'll tell you that if you'll tell me what I had—a boy or a girl?"

He debated bargaining with her. Even with that gun aimed at him. But it was probably best to give her the information so they could move on to something else. Something that involved his ripping that gun out of her hand.

"You had a boy," he finally said. "He was born three months ago."

"Three months?" she repeated. It sounded as if she had to choke back a sob. "That long."

Yeah, that long. "The doctors had to deliver him by C-section because you weren't conscious when you went into labor."

She shook her head, her breath shuddering. "I don't remember."

"Comas are like that," he said, and he didn't bother to sound even marginally sympathetic. "I named him Camden David. But I have sole custody of him," Lucas added.

Not a lie, exactly. He did have custody of him and had tried to make it permanent, but the judge had refused on the grounds that Hailey might come out of the coma and her parental rights could be reinstated.

Could be.

Lucas would make sure that didn't happen.

Something went through her pale green eyes, and Hailey made a sound, part groan, part gasp. At first he thought maybe the reaction was due to his custody comment, but the tears proved otherwise. It was the reaction of a woman who'd just learned she had a son.

But she was a mother in name only.

"And he… Camden's all right?" Hailey asked, still blinking back those tears. "There were no problems with the delivery?"

"Yeah. No thanks to you."

"Is he safe?" she asked before Lucas could finish what he was about to say.

"Of course he is." Lucas couldn't stop himself from cursing. "What the hell were you thinking when you went on the run like that? And what happened to you? Were you driving too fast? Is that what caused the accident—and that?"

He pointed to her scar, but Lucas didn't pull back his hand. He knocked the gun away from her, and it fell on the front passenger's seat. Hailey immediately scrambled to retrieve it, but Lucas was a whole lot faster. He dropped it on the floor, well out of her reach.

"Don't make me draw my gun," he warned her and took hold of her wrist in case she was about to try to get out the door.

But she didn't try to escape.

A hoarse sob tore from her mouth, and Hailey eased away from him. Just in case she had another weapon back there, Lucas leaned over the seat and did a quick check around her. He frisked her, too. Since she was wearing a pair of loose green scrubs, a thin sweater and flip-flops, there weren't many places she could conceal a weapon.

Still, after what'd happened three months ago, Lucas looked.

His hand brushed against the side of her breast, and she made a soft sound. Not the groan she'd made earlier. This one caused him to feel that tug deep within his body. But Lucas told that tug to take a hike.

Their gazes connected. Not for long. Lucas finished the search and found nothing.

"Now, keep talking," he insisted. "Tell me what happened to you. Why did you go on the run, and why didn't you tell anyone before now that you were out of the coma?"

She opened her mouth and got that deer-in-the-headlights look. What she didn't do was answer him.

"Enough of this," he mumbled.

He took out his phone to call Mason and then the sheriff, but as he'd done with her earlier, Hailey took hold of his hand. "Please don't tell your cousins. Not yet."

Since most of his Ryland cousins were cops, that wasn't what he wanted to hear. "Did you break the law? Is that why you were on the run?"

"No." She closed her eyes and shook her head. Her head wasn't the only thing shaking, though. She started to shiver, the cold and maybe the fear finally getting to her. "But I'm in trouble. God, Lucas, I'm in so much trouble."

He was about to curse at her for stating the obvious, but something else went through her eyes.

Fear.

"It won't take long for word to get out that I'm awake," Hailey said, speaking barely louder than a whisper. "And he'll find out."

"He?" Lucas snapped.

Hailey's voice cracked. "There's a killer after me."

Chapter Two

Hailey closed her eyes a moment, hoping it would help with the dizziness.

It didn't.

It was hard to think with her head spinning, the bone-deep exhaustion and the muscle spasms that kept rippling through her body.

Hard to think, too, with Lucas glaring at her as if she were the enemy. Of course, in his eyes, that's exactly what she was.

He obviously didn't believe her. Didn't trust her, either, but somehow Hailey had to make him understand. First, though, he had to take care of what was most important—the baby.

"Are you sure Camden is safe?" she asked.

That caused a new slash of anger to go through his eyes. Probably because he believed she was dodging the news she'd just dropped on him.

There's a killer after me.

"He's safe," Lucas finally said, but he spoke through clenched teeth. "Now, tell me why you need to make sure of that. Does it have something to do with the so-called killer?" He didn't give her a chance to say a word, though. "Or are you trying to lie your way out of why you ran from me three months ago?"

"It's not a lie." She wished it was. "But I didn't tell the truth about some other things."

That tightened the muscles in his jaw even more. "Start from the beginning, and so help me, there'd better not be any lies this time."

Hailey nodded but glanced around them. Since it was Tuesday and a school night, Silver Creek wasn't exactly teeming with activity, but she did spot someone jogging in the park. She kept her attention on him until he disappeared around the curve of the tree-lined trail. Maybe it was nothing. Maybe the guy was just that— a jogger—but he could have been someone after her.

"We need to find a better place to talk," Hailey told him.

Lucas gave her a flat look. Cursed. "I'm not taking you to the Silver Creek Ranch."

That was no doubt where the baby was.

Camden.

Hailey mentally repeated that, something she'd been doing since Lucas had first mentioned her precious son's name. Learning something—anything—about her baby caused her heart to ache. It felt as if someone was squeezing it hard.

Mercy, she'd lost so much already. Three months. And there was a lot more she could lose. Thank God the baby was okay, but it was up to her to make sure he stayed that way.

"I can't see Camden," Hailey answered. Saying it aloud added an even deeper pain. "Not until I'm sure it's safe."

"You won't see him at all," Lucas snapped. He spewed

out more of that profanity. "You don't have a right to see him."

No, in his eyes, she didn't. But if and when this was over, she would see her son. Even if she had to push her way through an army of Ryland lawmen. No one would keep him from her.

Since it was obvious Lucas wasn't going to budge, Hailey tried to figure out the fastest way to convince him that it wasn't safe for her to be out in the open like this.

That meant starting from the beginning.

"I'm not who you think I am," she said.

A burst of air left his mouth, but it wasn't a laugh. "Obviously. You slept with me and then sneaked out, leaving me a note saying you couldn't see me again."

Hailey didn't need a reminder of that. She could have recited the note word for word.

Lucas, I'm sorry, but this was a mistake. I can't get involved with you.

"That was the truth," she continued. "I shouldn't have let things get so...intimate between us."

"But you did, and you got pregnant."

Yes, she had. Since they'd used a condom, the pregnancy definitely hadn't been something Hailey had been expecting. But that hadn't stopped her from wanting the child right from the start.

"Mistakes aside," Lucas continued, "you had no right to run away from me while you were carrying my baby." He cursed again. "If you hadn't had that car accident, I might have never found you. Of course, that was probably the plan, wasn't it? To run away so that I'd never be able to see my child?"

Hailey didn't even have to think about that answer. "No. That wasn't the plan."

He didn't believe her, but it was the truth.

"I was trying to stay alive, trying to keep the baby from being hurt," Hailey explained.

He tapped his badge. "I'm a Texas Ranger." That was probably his way of saying that if something was wrong, she should have gone straight to him.

But Lucas had been in danger, too.

Something he didn't know.

Yet.

Figuring she would need it, Hailey took another deep breath. "Two years ago, I was employed as a computer systems analyst in Phoenix for a man named Preston DeSalvo. I found out he was working with someone in the FBI. A dirty agent. And they were selling confiscated weapons. I went to the cops, DeSalvo was eventually arrested, and after I testified against him, I was placed in witness protection and given a new identity. The marshals relocated me here to Silver Creek."

She paused, giving him a few moments to let all of that sink in, but Lucas didn't take the time. He whipped out his phone again, and before she could stop him, she saw him press the contact for one of his cousins.

Sheriff Grayson Ryland.

"Don't tell him I'm with you," Hailey insisted. "The sheriff's office could be bugged."

She saw the debate Lucas was having with himself, but he didn't stop the call. He did put it on speaker, though, and it didn't take long before Grayson answered.

"I heard about Hailey," Grayson said right off the

bat. "I've sent two of the deputies to the hospital to help look for her."

"Thanks," Lucas said. And he paused. A long time. "Can you look up info on a guy named Preston De-Salvo?"

Grayson paused, too. Hailey knew the sheriff well because she'd worked for him as an emergency dispatcher shortly after her arrival in Silver Creek. Grayson had a lot of experience as a lawman and was probably suspicious.

"Is DeSalvo connected to Hailey?" Grayson asked, though she could hear the clicks of his computer keys.

"Maybe."

More keyboard clicking sounds. "Well, Preston De-Salvo was sent to prison about eighteen months ago. He's dead. Killed in a fight at a maximum security prison in Arizona a little over three months ago."

"Why was he in prison?" Lucas pressed.

"A laundry list of charges, including murder, extortion and gun running. An employee, Laura Arnett, testified against him, and she's in WITSEC." He huffed. "Now, what does this have to do with Hailey?"

"Maybe everything. I'll call you back when I know more. In the meantime, can you make sure the ranch is on lockdown?"

"Already have. Mason called and said you'd asked him to go to your house. You think Hailey could be headed there?"

"I'll call you back," Lucas repeated, probably so that he wouldn't have to lie to his cousin.

But the stalling wouldn't last long. Soon, very soon, his cousins would be demanding answers. Especially Grayson, since he wasn't just the sheriff but also the head of the Ryland clan. However, Lucas would be demanding them first.

"Laura Arnett?" Lucas repeated. "That's your real name?"

She nodded. "I haven't thought of myself as that since all of this happened. I'm Hailey Darrow. For now, anyway. But I'll have to come up with another identity. DeSalvo's dead, but no one knows who his partner was," she added.

"The dirty FBI agent," he spat out like the profanity he tacked onto that. "And you believe he's after you?"

"I know he is. Well, one of his henchmen, anyway."

She glanced around again, praying that one of those thugs wasn't nearby, looking for her.

"I don't know how he found me," Hailey continued. "Maybe he hacked into the WITSEC files, or he could have bribed someone to give him the info. But three months ago, I found an eavesdropping device in my house here in Silver Creek, and I knew my identity had been blown."

"You should have come to me." His jaw muscles were at war with each other again. "Or since you were in WITSEC, you could have called your handler."

"I didn't get a chance. Before I could do anything, a hired gun showed up at my house. I hid, but he yelled out that if I didn't give myself up, he'd go after you and use you to get me to cooperate."

The skepticism was still written all over his face. "Cooperate with what?"

Oh, he was not going to like this. "I have some computer files that I didn't turn over to the cops. Files that incriminate Preston's son, Eric. Nothing as serious as murder, but it would have put him away for a few years."

"I'll want to see those files." And it wasn't a suggestion.

She nodded. "It'll take a while to access them. I put them in online storage with some security measures. I set it up so the files won't open until twelve hours after I put in the password."

"Clever," he mumbled, but Hailey didn't think that was a compliment. No. Lucas was silently cursing her for not bringing this to him sooner.

"I let Preston know I'd leak the files if anything happened to me," Hailey explained, "and that his son would head to prison right along with him. It was my insurance, a way of making sure he didn't send his hired thugs after me."

Lucas lifted his shoulder. "But he sent them anyway?"

"No. Preston was dead by then. I think the person who sent the thugs is the dirty agent. First, though, he wants those files."

"Or it could be his son who's after you," Lucas quickly pointed out.

"Maybe. But I didn't personally mention anything to Eric about having incriminating info on him."

Of course, that didn't mean Eric hadn't found out. Eric hadn't visited his father in prison. Not once. But Preston could have said something to one of his lackeys, who in turn passed the info on to Eric. Which wouldn't have necessarily been a bad thing. Because it could have kept Eric off her back, too, had he ever decided to come after her.

"How did you get away from that hired gun?" Lucas asked a moment later.

"I sneaked out the back of the house. I had a car,

some cash and new identity papers in a storage unit." Hailey huffed. "I'll answer all your questions. I promise. But we can't stay here. In fact, you can't be with me."

He looked at her as if she'd just sprouted wings. "You think I'm going to dump you out here on the street?"

"No, but I was hoping you'd arrange to get me a car. Or let me use this SUV for a couple of hours."

"That's not going to happen. But I am taking you somewhere—to the sheriff's office."

"No." She couldn't say it fast enough, and Hailey went to the edge of her seat so she could take hold of his arm again. "Didn't you hear me? The office could be bugged. My hospital room was. That's why I didn't say anything to any of the medical staff. I wasn't sure who'd put it there or if I could trust any of them."

Lucas had already put the SUV in gear to drive away, no doubt to head toward the sheriff's office, but that piece of information stopped him. He turned, studying her, probably to decide how much of this was the truth.

Before he could make up his mind, his phone rang, and again she saw Grayson's name on the screen. She doubted Lucas would keep her secret much longer. He would spill everything to the sheriff.

And that meant she had to get out of there—fast.

But how? Lucas had all the doors locked, and she wasn't nearly strong enough to break the windows.

"We might have a problem," Grayson said when Lucas answered, and he put the call on speaker. "Dr. Parton called, and he said right after you left, a man showed up looking for Hailey. He claimed he was her brother."

Oh, God. "I don't have a brother," she mouthed.

"Doc Parton got suspicious," Grayson went on. "And

he just sent me the surveillance footage of the guy coming in through the ER entrance. I put his photo into the facial recognition program and got an immediate hit."

Lucas groaned, no doubt because he knew what that meant. If the guy was in the system, he had a record. "Who is he?" he asked the sheriff.

"Darrin Sandmire. A low-life thug." He paused. "Sandmire often works as a hit man."

Her heart slammed against her chest. It was happening. Her worst fears. The killer wasn't just after her. He was here in Silver Creek.

"Sandmire left the hospital before the security guard could stop him, so he could be anywhere in town. Now, you want to tell me what this is all about?" Grayson demanded.

"Yeah. I'll be at the sheriff's office in a few minutes." Lucas paused. "Hailey's with me."

The panic shot through her, and she tried the door handle even though Hailey knew she was trapped. If Lucas took her to the sheriff's office, she might be putting not only herself in danger but also all of them. Lucas put the SUV in gear again, but something must have caught his eye, because his attention zoomed to the driver's side window.

To the park.

Hailey saw it then, as well. The jogger she'd spotted earlier. But this time, he wasn't on the trail. He was coming straight toward the SUV.

And he had a gun in his hand.

Chapter Three

"Get down!" Lucas shouted to Hailey.

His first instinct was to draw his gun and take aim at the man running toward them. But Lucas didn't want to get into a gunfight on Main Street where innocent bystanders—or Hailey—could be hurt.

Lucas wasn't sure he believed everything she'd just told him, but it was obvious she had someone after her. Later he'd find out who that was, but for now he wanted to put some distance between this armed man and them. He hit the accelerator.

Just as the guy took aim.

And fired.

The bullet slammed into the side of the SUV, missing the window and Lucas by only a couple of inches.

"I need a gun," Hailey said, climbing over the seat to get to the passenger side. She started to fumble around for the weapon that he'd knocked away from her.

"Stay down," Lucas warned her, but her search took care of that. Hailey crawled onto the floor.

At least, it took care of it for a couple of seconds. Once she had the gun, she got back in the seat and took aim out the back side window.

She fired.

The sound blasted through the SUV, causing Lucas to curse. He hadn't actually expected her to shoot. Too bad she missed, because the gunman sent another bullet their way.

Lucas sped off. The thug got off one more shot before Lucas took the first turn he reached He wasn't driving in the direction of the sheriff's office, but he could double back.

Lucas tossed Hailey his phone. "Call Grayson and tell him there's an armed man near the park at the intersection of Main and Everett Road."

Hailey made the call, but she kept watch behind them, making sure that goon wasn't in pursuit. The moment Grayson answered, she rattled off the information. Then she hit the end call button. No doubt because she didn't want to answer Grayson's questions. That was okay. For now.

But as soon as they reached the sheriff's office, Hailey had better come clean about everything.

Lucas took another turn. Then another, meandering his way back to Main Street. That particular part of the park was only about seven blocks away from the sheriff's office, so it wouldn't take Grayson long to get a pair of deputies there to catch the guy.

"Do you know if that was Darrin Sandmire?" Lucas asked her.

"I have no idea. But I'm pretty sure that was the same man who came after me three months ago."

Hell.

Lucas had to rein in the anger that sliced through him. That was the SOB who'd put Hailey—and therefore, Camden—in danger. Too bad Lucas hadn't managed to shoot him. But then he rethought that. He didn't want the guy dead, not until he had answers from him.

Like who hired him.

Thugs like Darrin Sandmire always worked for bigger thugs. Maybe DeSalvo's son, Eric. Maybe that unidentified rogue agent. Soon, Lucas intended to find out who'd paid this killer to come after Hailey.

Lucas took another turn, the tires squealing against the asphalt. The moment he was on the side street, he saw something he didn't like.

A truck.

It wasn't right in the middle of the road, but the front end was jutting out from the parking space in front of a motorcycle repair shop.

Lucas hit his brakes.

"You think someone's inside the truck?" Hailey asked. Her voice was shaking like the rest of her.

Lucas didn't know, and it was next to impossible to see inside the truck's cab. There was a streetlight and a lit sign for the motorcycle shop, but the tint was so dark on the windshield that he couldn't tell. He pulled up a little farther though so he could get a better look at the front license plates.

"Out-of-state plates," he mumbled under his breath.

Maybe that in itself meant nothing, but Lucas got that feeling in his gut. The feeling that told him to get the heck out of there.

He threw the SUV into Reverse.

But the second he did that, the truck door opened, and a man bolted out.

The guy had a rifle.

"Get down," Lucas repeated to Hailey. "And this time, stay there."

Whether she would or not was anyone's guess, but he didn't want to have to worry about her being shot. He hit the gas, the SUV speeding backward. But he didn't get out of the path of that rifleman fast enough.

The bullet slammed into the windshield.

Since this wasn't the vehicle he used for work, the glass wasn't reinforced. The shot tore through the safety glass, the bullet exiting out the back.

Great. Just great.

Now he had two thugs after them, and Lucas had no choice but to go back in the direction he'd seen that other shooter in the park. Maybe the guy was long gone by now. Or better yet, maybe one of the deputies had managed to capture him.

When Lucas reached the side street, he spun the SUV around so he could drive forward. He definitely didn't want to head right into the middle of an ambush, so he headed for a better lit area.

"The truck's coming after us," Hailey said.

And that's when he realized she'd lifted her head and was looking out the side window.

Lucas pushed her right back down. "Don't make it easier for them to kill you," he snapped. Yeah, it was harsh, but Hailey was clearly the target of some very determined attackers.

Whoever was in the truck fired another shot at them, this one slamming into the rear end of the SUV. A second shot quickly followed.

Then a third.

"There must be two of them," Hailey muttered. She hadn't figured that out by looking at them, though. She was still on the floor.

But Lucas knew there had to be two, as well. Those

shots were too well aimed for someone who was trying to negotiate the turns and dodging the cars parked
along the street.

"Hang on," Lucas told her a split second before he
turned onto another side street. He was thankful he'd
grown up here and knew these streets like the back of
his hand.

His phone buzzed, and since Hailey still had hold of
it, she answered it and put it on speaker.

"Where are you?" he heard Grayson immediately
ask. "Someone just called about shots being fired near
Henderson's Motorcycle Shop."

"Someone in a blue pickup is shooting at us. We're
on Bluebonnet Street, coming up near the Corral Bar."
It was a risk since there'd be customers still inside, but
Lucas didn't plan on stopping or even slowing down.
"I'll turn back on Main Street and head in your direc-
tion. Please tell me you found the first shooter."

"Not yet. But I'll send Dade and Josh your way to
help," Grayson said, and he ended the call.

Good. Dade and Josh were both cousins, both deputy
sheriffs, and maybe having backup would cause these
thugs to quit firing.

The parking lot of the Corral Bar was lit up better
than the rest of the street, and Lucas glanced in his side
mirror at the truck. Definitely two men. And the one on
the passenger side was doing the shooting.

"I can return fire," Hailey insisted, already climbing
into the seat and lowering the window. "Please don't
stop me. This is all my fault, and I have to do something to stop them."

"No way." And he meant it. It might indeed be partially her fault for not coming to him sooner, but she wasn't sticking her neck out to fire any shots.

Hailey didn't get a chance to argue with him. That's because the sound of sirens stopped anything she was about to say. In the distance, behind the truck, Lucas saw the flashing blue lights of a police cruiser.

Dade and Josh, no doubt.

The driver stopped following Lucas and took a very quick turn off a side street. A street that would lead them straight to the highway.

No, hell, no.

Lucas didn't want these clowns getting away, but it wasn't smart to go in pursuit with Hailey in the vehicle. Besides, Dade and Josh went after them, and Lucas could only hope they'd catch them.

"Keep watch for the other shooter," Lucas told Hailey.

He hated to rely on her for help, but with the glass in the front, back and side windows cracked and webbed, they had reduced visibility. That would make it hard for them to see the guy hiding between one of the buildings where he could shoot at them as they drove by.

Lucas held his breath, going as fast as he could, and he didn't release that breath until he made it back onto Main Street. Definitely no sign of the shooter, so he headed for the sheriff's office.

"Can you run?" he asked her.

"I'll try," she assured him. Which meant she couldn't. "I had to use a cane to walk to your SUV."

Definitely couldn't.

The SUV squealed to a stop directly in front of the door to the sheriff's office, but he didn't get out. Lucas waited until Grayson hurried to the door and threw it open.

"I'm carrying you in," Lucas insisted, and he didn't leave any room for argument.

He scooped her up in his arms and rushed her inside the building, with Grayson locking the door behind them. But Lucas didn't stop there. He hurried her past the squad room to the hall that led to Grayson's office and the break room. That way, if someone did come in with guns blazing, she'd have some protection.

"Dade and Josh are in pursuit," Lucas told Grayson. "Arizona plates, but there was something covering the numbers. Mud, I think." Probably not an accident.

"Arizona?" Hailey repeated.

Lucas knew the reason for her concern. DeSalvo had been from Arizona, which meant his son, Eric, likely was, too. So, had Eric sent those goons after Hailey?

Now that they weren't in the SUV, Lucas got a better look at her. Especially a better look at the fear in her eyes. And the fact that she was having to grip the door to steady herself.

"As soon as it's safe, I'll have the doctor come over to see you," Lucas told her.

But she was shaking her head before he even finished. "I can't trust Dr. Parton. Or anyone in the hospital. Someone planted that bug on the table next to my bed."

Lucas certainly hadn't forgotten about that. The device needed to be checked, but that would have to wait, because Grayson no doubt had every available deputy on this manhunt for the shooters.

"When there's time, Hailey will need to give you a statement," Lucas told Grayson.

Grayson nodded. He still had his gun drawn, was

still keeping watch on the area just outside the building. "Is she in WITSEC?"

"Yes," Hailey answered. "But I don't want the marshals to know I'm here."

Grayson mumbled something Lucas didn't catch, but he didn't need to hear the words to know that Grayson wasn't pleased about all this going on right under his nose.

"Hell, you worked for me," Grayson added.

She nodded. "I figured it was a way to keep an eye on what was happening in town, just in case something went wrong." Hailey paused. "And something did go wrong."

Yeah. And Lucas wondered if sleeping with him was in that something-gone-wrong category.

"I'll call Mason and give him an update," Grayson said after he shot Hailey a glare.

Hailey dropped back a step, holding onto Grayson's desk. Lucas was volleying his attention between her and the outside. However, she got his complete attention when she made a soft gasp.

Lucas hurried to her, following her gaze to the computer on the desk. It was obviously the security feed that the doctor had sent Grayson. In the shot, the tall, lanky man was coming through the glass doors of the ER. Grayson had paused it and zoomed in on the man's face.

Darrin Sandmire, no doubt.

Lucas had no trouble seeing the renewed fear in Hailey's eyes. "That's definitely the man who came to my house three months ago. And the man who ran me off the road that night."

Lucas hadn't needed to hear anything else about the

guy to know that he wanted him caught, questioned and punished.

Hailey touched the screen to get the security feed moving again. Darrin disappeared from view when he walked past the camera and to the hall. Since it would have taken him several minutes to get to her room, Lucas sped up the footage, watching for Darrin to re-emerge.

He did.

But the man wasn't alone.

There was a woman with him, walking right by his side, and it was obvious they were talking. The woman was a blonde, and she kept her head down. Right until she was close to the camera.

Now Hailey's gasp wasn't so soft.

"I know her. That's Colleen Jeffrey."

The name meant nothing to Lucas, and he didn't recognize her, either. "Who is she?"

There were tears shimmering in Hailey's eyes when she looked up at him. "My half sister."

Damn.

Lucas was about to assure her that maybe this was a coincidence. But it didn't look like that to him. He needed to get this woman in for questioning right away.

He heard the footsteps. Hurried ones, and they put Lucas right back on alert again. Though he hadn't exactly been relaxing.

"We've got a problem," Grayson said, stepping into the doorway. "Someone tripped the security sensor near the back fence at the ranch. One of the ranch hands spotted a gunman."

Chapter Four

Hailey's breath froze. She wanted to scream, to shout out for Lucas to hurry to the ranch so they could protect their son, but the words and sounds were wedged there in her throat.

No. This couldn't be happening. This monster couldn't get to her baby.

Even without her warning, Lucas thankfully understood just how dangerous a situation this could be, because he took off running toward the front of the building. Hailey followed him. Or rather, she tried.

Lucas must have remembered she was still hobbling, because he spun around, scooped her up in his arms and hurried toward his shot-up SUV still parked just outside the door.

"We need to use a cruiser," Grayson called out to them. "Because this could be a trap to lure you into the open."

Lucas stopped, and while everything inside Hailey wanted to move, to hurry to the ranch, she knew Grayson was right.

"Wait right here for me," Grayson insisted. "I'll bring the cruiser around to the front."

Hailey didn't want to waste precious minutes while

he did that, but they didn't have many options here. Lucas and she waited, the time crawling by slower than a snail's pace, and it seemed to take an eternity for Grayson to drive up. Even before the cruiser came to a stop, Lucas and she jumped into the backseat, and Grayson took off again.

"I'll call the ranch and get an update," Lucas said.

As much as she wanted to know what was going on, Hailey didn't want anyone there distracted right now. She wanted all the focus on protecting the baby.

Camden.

The name seemed foreign to her. Probably because she'd yet to see her son, but maybe that would change soon. Maybe they'd get to the ranch and put an end to the danger.

"Tillie," Lucas said to whoever answered his call.

"One of the nannies," Grayson provided to Hailey, but he didn't even glance back at her when he spoke. He looked all around, no doubt in case someone was trying to follow them.

Or attack them again.

Hailey couldn't hear what the nanny was saying, but since Lucas's arm was pressed against her, she felt his muscles relax just a little. "We'll be there as fast as we can." He paused. "Hailey's with me."

The nanny perhaps hadn't even heard she was out of the coma, so this could be a real shock. An unwanted one. Hailey didn't know Tillie, but she doubted she was going to get a warm reception from anyone at the Silver Creek Ranch. It wouldn't matter that she thought she'd done the right thing.

Still did think that.

But a family of lawmen wouldn't see it that way.

They would believe she should have trusted them. However, maybe they could see now that all the trust in the world wouldn't have put an end to the danger.

Oh, mercy.

That reminder came at her hard, like a heavyweight's fist. The reason she'd tried to escape was to avoid this. To keep her child safe. And now he wasn't safe because of her.

"Whoever's behind the attacks will use Camden to get to me," Hailey said under her breath.

She hadn't intended to say that aloud, and it stung even more when Lucas made a sound of agreement. He'd finished his call with the nanny and now was keeping watch. Along with glancing at her.

"That doesn't mean you're going to try to take him and disappear," Lucas snapped. There wasn't a shred of gentleness in his tone. In fact, it was the same tone he likely used with criminal suspects.

"It's too late to take him and hide," Hailey agreed. "Too late for me to disappear, as well. Because now that they know I'm awake, they won't stop, and they'll try to use the baby to come after me."

That meant she needed to find out who *they* were. And fast. For that to happen, she needed to rely on Lucas.

Something that wouldn't please him.

It didn't please her, either, but no one would work harder than Lucas to keep Camden safe. Of course, once that happened, and this snake was captured and behind bars, Lucas and she would have another battle to fight.

For custody.

But that was a fight that would have to wait for another day. Right now, Hailey had enough to deal with.

"The fences are all rigged with security alarms?" she asked.

"Yeah," Grayson and Lucas answered at the same time. It was Lucas who continued. "There are also sensors on the grounds. Cameras, too. Since this clown tripped a sensor, the ranch hands and my cousins will be able to pinpoint his exact location before he can get near one of the houses."

Good. But pinpointing him wasn't the same as stopping the threat.

"Hurry," Hailey said to Grayson. She was speaking purely out of frustration, because he was going as fast as he safely could.

The rural roads that led to the ranch weren't exactly straight. Plenty of sharp curves and turns, and it certainly wouldn't help them if Grayson wrecked.

Something she knew all too well.

Hailey couldn't quite choke back a gasp when the cruiser tires squealed around one of those turns and it felt as if Grayson was losing control of the vehicle. All the memories of that other night came flooding back.

The frantic rush to get away from the person trying to kill her. The adrenaline and the fear. Even the feeling of the impact.

The pain.

But more intense than the pain and the fear had been the sickening dread that she'd failed.

"Flashbacks?" Lucas asked.

She nodded. "I remember that you're the one who found me that night. If it hadn't been you…"

Hailey didn't finish that thought. No need. Lucas had found her, and while it hadn't made things perfect, it had allowed her to deliver the baby safely.

Grayson took the final turn, and Hailey saw the ranch come into view. To say it was sprawling was an understatement. It'd been huge, but now that the Ryland cousins were buying up the adjacent land and building their own homes, the place stretched out for miles and miles.

They'd also added more security since the last time she'd visited. There was now a large security gate, and she saw several men near it. Ranch hands, probably, since she didn't recognize any of them.

"Get down," Lucas told her as they approached the gate. He lowered the window. "Anything?" he asked the men.

"Yep. Just a few seconds ago Sawyer called to say he shot at a guy who'd crossed over the fence. He and two of the other hands are chasing him."

Hailey sucked in her breath. Sawyer was his cousin as well as an FBI agent. "Did Sawyer have to fire shots anywhere near the houses?"

The guy volleyed glances among Lucas, Grayson and her. Maybe he was trying to figure out if it was okay if he answered since he probably didn't even know who she was.

"No, the shooting happened in the back pasture," the guy said after Lucas gave him a go-ahead nod. "Mason said, though, that y'all should wait down here until they've made sure there's only one."

Oh, mercy.

As hard as that was to hear—and it was even harder for her to stay put—Hailey knew he was right. The attacker might not be alone. Heck, he could have brought an entire army with him, and it was best to aim that army at her rather than launch an attack near the houses.

Still, waiting was hard.

Even if she lifted her head, something Lucas wouldn't like her to do, Hailey couldn't see Lucas's house from this part of the road, but she knew it was less than a half mile away. She knew because he'd taken her there for the one night they'd been together. The night she'd had a serious lapse in judgment and gotten way too personal with a man she should have avoided. Or so it'd seemed at the time. But without that night, she wouldn't have her son, and despite everything that'd gone on, the one thing she was certain of was that she loved her baby.

Lucas didn't seem to be having an easier time waiting than she was. He put the window back up, mumbled some profanity and took out his phone. This time she saw that he was calling the nanny again.

"Just checking to make sure everything is okay," Lucas said when Tillie answered.

Hailey automatically scooted closer so she could hear what the nanny had to say, but that only earned her a scowl from Lucas. He put the call on speaker, her cue to inch away from him. She did.

"The baby's fine," Tillie assured Lucas. "He went straight to sleep after his bottle. And Mason's still here just in case."

Just in case everything went from bad to worse. Hailey hated that it was a possibility, but Mason was another lawman, so it was good to have him there. She prayed, though, that he wouldn't be needed and that the danger would end soon. With this idiot intruder not just in custody but also willing to tell them the name of the person who'd hired him.

"You said earlier that Hailey was with you," Tillie

went on. She paused. "Is, uh, everything okay? Did that man try to get onto the ranch because of her?"

"Yeah," Lucas admitted. Now he was the one who paused. "I'll need to take the baby someplace safe. Will you be able to come with us?"

"Of course," Tillie quickly agreed.

Hailey was shaking her head before the nanny even answered.

The head shaking caused Lucas to scowl again. "I'm going to protect my son," he snarled as if she didn't want the same thing.

She did. More than anything, she wanted him safe. Lucas and his family, too. "But I want to see him."

That got Lucas's muscles tightening again. "And then what?"

It was a good question. Hailey didn't have anything resembling a good answer. "I don't know," she admitted. "I need some answers, and I think the place to start is with my sister."

"I agree," Lucas said without hesitation. "I'll want her contact info and anything recent you have on her. I'll especially want to know why she could want you dead."

"I don't know any of those things," Hailey had to admit. "I haven't seen or heard from Colleen since I've been in WITSEC."

Lucas huffed, clearly not pleased that she hadn't given him something to go on. "You two were close?"

"Once." But that was another round of bad memories. "We were both working as computer systems analysts for Preston DeSalvo's company. I testified against him, but Colleen didn't. She claimed she didn't see the incriminating evidence that I found."

Lucas jumped right on that. "She lied?"

"Maybe. But I can't believe she'd be the one behind this. I'm still her sister."

He gave her a flat look. "Cain and Abel were brothers, and you know how that ended."

Yes, with one murdering the other, but Hailey had to hang on to something, and that something was that her only sister hadn't betrayed her like this. Still, she wanted to talk to Colleen and get this all sorted out.

She nearly reached for his phone to make a call, but there was no one who came to mind that she could trust. Well, no one other than Lucas.

"I'll bring Colleen in for questioning," Lucas said as if reading her mind. He didn't get a chance to add anything else because the sound got their attention.

A shot.

Even though it was in the distance, it still caused Hailey's heart to slam against her chest. She held her breath, waiting, and even though she tried to steel herself for whatever would happen next, she still gasped when Lucas's phone buzzed.

"Mason," he said looking at the screen before he answered it and put the call on speaker.

She hadn't thought her heart could beat any faster, but she'd obviously been wrong. Mason was with the baby, and if he was calling then maybe that meant the shot had been fired close to the house.

Or in it.

Hailey pressed her fingers to her mouth and listened, praying.

"Sawyer fired the shot," Mason said. "The guy's alive for now."

"Is he talking?" Lucas asked.

"No, but I just called an ambulance, so maybe he'll

say something on the way to the hospital. Sawyer has a way of getting dirt to talk."

Good. But that didn't mean this was over. "Are there any other attackers out there?" Hailey pressed.

Just as the ranch hand had done, Mason hesitated. "No. Nothing else is showing up on any of the security feeds, either. It looks as if this clown came alone. And I don't think he came here to kill anybody. He had surveillance equipment on him."

So there could be others on the way. It was too much to hope that this guy's injury and arrest would get the person behind this to back off.

"It's safe for you to come to the house," Mason continued. "If you want to come, that is."

She knew what he meant by that. Mason was giving his cousin an out in case Lucas didn't want her to see the baby. Hailey was about to insist that happen when Lucas gave Grayson the go-ahead to get moving.

Toward the house.

Hailey sat back up, keeping watch around them, but she was also looking for the house. It finally came into view since it was the first building on the ranch road. All of the interior lights were off, probably as a safety precaution, but there were security lights on all four corners of the property. Enough for her to see the barn and corral that hadn't been there a year ago.

Lucas was making this place a home.

Part of her was thankful for that. Their son deserved it. But she was betting there was no place in this home for her.

Grayson pulled to a stop directly in front of the porch, and the door opened. Mason. Yet another unfriendly face, but then, Mason usually looked unfriendly. As he'd done at the sheriff's office, Lucas got her in—fast. This time, though, he didn't carry her. He looped his arm around her waist to steady her, and the moment they were inside, he moved away from her.

Hailey immediately looked around for the baby. But there was no sign of him or the nanny. She was about to demand to see him, but Mason stepped in front of her.

"Just got a text from Sawyer," Mason said, his voice low and dangerous. "The guy he shot is drifting in and out of consciousness, but this is what the guy said."

He held his phone screen up for her to see, and the words there caused her to drop back a step.

Hailey Darrow paid me to take the kid.

Chapter Five

Lucas didn't know who looked more shocked by the accusation that the wounded gunman had just made. He or Hailey.

"I didn't," she said, her gaze firing between Mason and him. "I only left the hospital a couple of hours ago."

Mason didn't seem convinced. "You were conscious for a week. You could have called someone and set this whole thing up."

The anger flared through Hailey's eyes, and she opened her mouth as if ready to return verbal fire, but she was obviously spent. Heck, so was Lucas, and while part of him hated to defend the woman who'd tried to run from him, he couldn't see how this would have played out.

"There was no phone in her hospital room," Lucas explained. "And yes, she could have borrowed one from someone on the staff, but that kind of thing doesn't stay a secret very long."

Lucas could have gone on and mentioned the part about Hailey not having touched her bank accounts since she'd been in the coma, and it wasn't as if she'd had wads of cash lying around the hospital to pay someone to carry through on something like this.

Even Lucas's own explanation didn't seem to convince Mason. "You trust her, then?" Mason asked.

"No," Lucas readily admitted. "But if Hailey intended to take the baby, she wouldn't have done it this way."

At least, he hoped like the devil that she wouldn't. The baby and other members of his family could have been hurt by the thug who'd trespassed onto the ranch.

"Thank you," Hailey said to him.

For some reason, that riled Lucas. Maybe because he didn't want to do anything for her that would cause her to say something like that.

"So, who did hire the *lying* sack of dirt?" Mason asked.

Hailey shook her head, but it was clear from the way she was looking around that her attention was elsewhere. She obviously wanted to see the baby, and Lucas tried to remind himself that if their positions were reversed, he would have wanted the same thing.

Of course, their positions would never be reversed because he would have never gone on the run from the law.

"I'll question Hailey's sister, Colleen, and Eric DeSalvo in the morning." Lucas tipped his head to the hall that led to the bedrooms. "Is Tillie in the nursery?"

Mason lowered his phone and nodded. Even though he didn't voice his disapproval as to what was about to happen, it was on his face. "I'll wait here until I get the all-clear from Sawyer."

Lucas thanked him and made a mental note to thank all the others who'd pulled together to keep Camden safe. For now, though, he had to focus on getting through this. And *this* was having Hailey see the baby.

From the moment Camden had been born, Lucas had

known it might come down to this. But as every day had passed with Hailey in a coma, he'd also considered that she might never wake up. That she might never have a claim on their child. Now, here she was, and Lucas was having to face one of his worst fears.

That he might lose his son.

Not to a kidnapper, either. But to Hailey. She wouldn't be able to get full custody of Camden. No way would Lucas allow that, but she would be entitled to visitation rights. Considering she was in WITSEC, that was going to be tricky. And not very safe for any of them.

Moving ahead of her, Lucas led her down the hall. She caught onto the side of the wall to steady herself, and she was probably moving as fast as she could go.

When they reached the nursery, Lucas stepped in, his gaze immediately connecting with the nanny's. There was just as much concern in Tillie's expression as there had been in Mason's. But she stepped aside so that Lucas—and Hailey—had the crib in their direct line of sight.

Where Camden was sleeping.

"I'll be in the living room if you need me," Tillie said, but her offer seemed to be a question, as if maybe he wanted her to stay.

Lucas nodded, giving her the go-ahead to leave, but Hailey didn't wait for Tillie to be out the door before she hobbled her way to the crib. The sound that left her mouth crushed at his heart. Part moan, part sigh.

All love.

It was a sound and a look that Lucas felt all too well because he got that same punch of emotion every time he was near his son. And even when he wasn't.

"He's so beautiful," Hailey whispered, touching her fingers to the wispy strands of dark brown hair.

Lucas had to agree with her, but he was certain that was the reaction of most parents. Certain, too, that Hailey would want to do more than just touch his hair. She looked back at him, as if waiting for permission. She didn't wait long, though, before she scooped Camden up in her arms.

She made that sound again and kissed his cheek. Even though Camden stirred a little, he went right back to sleep. Good. Even though his son was too young to know what was going on, Lucas didn't want to risk Camden being upset by having his sleep interrupted. He also didn't want to risk Hailey falling with the child, and since her legs were obviously still wobbly, he helped her to the nearby chair.

"Is he healthy?" she asked.

"Yeah." It was hard for him to talk about something so—well—normal. "He's right on target for his height, weight and milestones."

She nodded and looked up at him, and that's when he saw the tears in her eyes. "I was so scared that he'd been hurt in the accident."

"He could have been," Lucas quickly pointed out, but then instantly regretted the jab. It was the truth, but stating the obvious didn't make him feel any better.

"I know. I'm so sorry. When I ran, my only thought was to keep him safe."

Lucas nearly went for another jab by reminding her that the safe thing to do would have been to come to him, but that ship had already sailed. They were here now and had to deal with this. Not just the danger, either. But all those old feelings.

He'd been attracted to her once and vice versa. That's what had landed them in bed in the first place. And while there were still some lingering traces of the attraction, it wouldn't play into this. He hoped the bitterness he felt over what'd happened wouldn't, either. Right now, bitterness wouldn't help.

He was about to question her more about the night of the accident, to see if she remembered any details that would help them find out who was responsible for the attacks, but Hailey spoke before he did.

"Tell me about the delivery," she said.

Lucas paused, not because he intended to hold anything back, but because remembering that night still felt like a punch to the gut.

"I was scared," he admitted. "We didn't know if there'd been trauma to the baby, and since you were so close to your due date, the docs did a C-section on you. But everything turned out okay. Everything except that you were in a coma," Lucas added.

She, too, paused. Then nodded. "I've heard that some people remember and hear things while they're in comas. I didn't." She brushed another kiss on Camden's cheek. "I wish I could remember seeing him as a newborn. He's already so big."

Camden was, but while Hailey had indeed missed a lot, the baby wasn't old enough to have noticed that his mom hadn't been around.

Hailey looked up at Lucas again, those tears still shimmering in her eyes. "I know this is hard for you. You haven't had to share him with anyone for the past three months."

Lucas wasn't sure how to respond to that and didn't get a chance to say anything anyway, because Mason appeared in the doorway. One look at his cousin's face and Lucas knew something else had gone wrong. Apparently so did Hailey, because she slowly got to her feet, her attention nailed to Mason.

"The gunman died on the way to the hospital," Mason said.

Hell. Lucas had wanted him alive so they could get answers. But maybe they could still do that. "Did he have a phone on him? Maybe his boss's number is in his contacts?"

Mason nodded. "Grayson will check for that, but there's more." He paused. "The ranch hands did a thorough search of the fence line in that back part of the ranch, and it appears the dead thug didn't come alone. There were enough tracks back there for three people."

Lucas bit back the profanity that he nearly blurted out, something he'd been training himself to do now that he was a father. Still, it was hard not to curse about that. "Any other signs of the men?"

"No. They're apparently gone. For now, anyway."

That didn't mean they wouldn't be back. Maybe even tonight, since the darkness would give them an advantage for an attack.

"I've got men patrolling the entire ranch," Mason went on. "I also called everyone and told them to lock down and stay inside."

By "everyone" he meant his brothers and their cousins. No one would be leaving and coming onto the ranch unless Mason gave the okay. Which he wouldn't do until he was certain it was safe. And Lucas knew what that meant.

This time he wasn't able to stop himself from cursing.

Because it meant Hailey would have to stay there.

Of course, he probably wouldn't have been able to talk her into budging since she'd want to be near the baby, but Lucas had planned on having her sleep far away from the Silver Creek Ranch. Far away from Camden, too.

"I'm so sorry," Hailey whispered. Maybe she was apologizing again for the danger. But one look in her eyes and Lucas knew the reason for this "I'm sorry." She had also figured out what the sleeping arrangements would be.

"You can stay in the guest room," Lucas growled. It was at the end of the hall, as far away as he could get her while still having her under the same roof.

Hailey mumbled a thanks, and while Lucas thought part of her looked relieved, that was still fear he saw in her eyes. Worry, too. Especially worry when she looked at Mason again. His cousin wasn't budging. Mason continued to stand there, his hands bracketed on the doorjamb.

"What else happened?" Hailey asked Mason. Her voice was shaky again, probably because she knew they were about to get another dose of bad news.

"Grayson tried to get in touch with Colleen, so he could bring her in for questioning." Mason paused again. "But there's a problem. Colleen is missing."

HAILEY HOPED THIS medical exam wasn't a mistake.

She wasn't certain about the ER physician, Dr. Parton, but Lucas had assured her that Parton wasn't the one who'd planted that bug in her hospital room, that the doctor was trustworthy. So, that's what Hailey was going to do—trust him. Besides, she needed to make sure she was okay. Not just for her sake but to soothe some of the concern on Lucas's face.

Of course, she had plenty of her own concerns, too.

There were so many things for her to worry about, and that's what she'd done through the night and now the morning. The constant threat of an attack. Her missing sister. The obvious tension between Lucas and her. Between her and his family, too.

But it was hard for Hailey to focus solely on all of that when she was looking at her son's face while Lucas was holding him.

For the entire time she'd carried him, she had considered how he might look. Considered as well the love she would feel for him, but she'd way underestimated that love. She couldn't believe how deep it was for this child, and even though it crushed her heart, she knew that same feeling of love was the very reason that Lucas would do everything to hang on to his child.

Everything, including attempts to exclude her.

Those attempts wouldn't work, of course. Or maybe they wouldn't. If they couldn't stop the threat of another attack, then she might have no choice but to disappear. She'd do that if it meant keeping Camden safe.

She'd started that process by using Lucas's laptop and putting in her password for the storage cloud for the files she'd gathered on Eric DeSalvo. It'd be a few more hours before she could open them, but once Lucas had a chance to go over them, maybe he could find something he could use to arrest Eric. It might not put an end to the attacks, but at least it would get him off the streets for a while.

"Follow the light with your eyes," Dr. Parton instructed her.

Hailey did, though it meant taking her attention off her son. And Lucas. Lucas was feeding the baby his bottle while he had his phone sandwiched between his shoulder and his ear. She wasn't sure who was on the other end of the phone line this time, but Lucas had obviously adapted to juggling his work with fatherhood.

"From what I can tell, you're fine," the doctor said, stepping back from her. "You'll need a thorough exam, though, and some tests that I can do only at the hospital. Any idea when it'll be okay for that?"

It was the million-dollar question, and Hailey didn't have a clue what the answer was. She shook her head. "We're waiting on some information." Information that would ideally lead to an arrest.

The doctor didn't seem especially pleased with an indefinite delay to those tests, and Hailey knew why. There could be brain damage. And damage to her legs. The muscles felt a little stronger, but she was nowhere near a hundred percent and might need physical therapy to regain all her strength. No way could she risk going to PT or taking those tests now, though, and she didn't want to speculate how long it would be before that happened.

The doctor gathered his things and headed to the door, where Mason was waiting to escort him back to town. They left, leaving Hailey to sit there and watch as Camden finished his bottle. As if it were the most natural thing in the world, Lucas put the bottle aside and moved the baby to his shoulder to burp him.

A year ago, if someone had told her that the tough cowboy cop would be the doting father, she wouldn't have believed it. Lucas likely wouldn't have, either.

Tillie came out of the kitchen and made eye contact with Lucas. "You want me to take him?" Tillie mouthed.

"No, thanks. I'm finished with my call." He put away

his phone and looked at Hailey. "That was Grayson. Still no word on your sister, but Eric DeSalvo should be arriving at the sheriff's office any minute now."

Good. Hailey figured the best place to start with getting those answers would be with Eric. And Colleen. It sickened her to think that her sister might be involved in this.

"What about the other gunmen who were around the ranch last night?" she asked. "Any signs of them?"

"No. And the dead guy, Darrin, was using a burner cell phone and didn't have any contacts stored there. In fact, the phone hadn't been used, so there's nothing to trace."

Another dead end. Literally. Since Darrin had lived only long enough to accuse her of hiring him.

"Grayson had the medics take Darrin's picture," Lucas went on. When he reached to take his phone from his jeans pocket, it caused the baby to move, and Camden stirred, lifting his head just a little.

Hailey figured Camden was too young to see her from across the room, so she went closer. Lucas didn't scowl, exactly, but it was close. He took out his phone and handed it to her.

"Take a look at the picture Grayson sent, and see if you recognize Darrin. Is he the same man who went after you the night you were trying to get away?"

She took the phone, her fingers brushing against his. Lucas noticed. Noticed, too, that she was volleying glances between the baby and him. He pulled in a long, weary breath.

"Sit down," he growled. "You can hold Camden while you tell me about the picture."

Hailey moved as fast as she could, making her way

back to the chair. Lucas went to her, easing the baby into her arms.

There it was again. That punch of emotion.

Though it was hard to focus with Camden staring up at her, Hailey studied the photo. It wasn't the best shot since the man's face was twisted with pain, but Hailey picked through the features.

And remembered.

She sucked in her breath so fast that she nearly got choked. "He definitely looks like the man who ran me off the road."

Other memories came flooding back. The car following her. Her frantic attempt to get away. Then the crash.

"He rammed into the back of my car, forcing me into a ditch," she explained. "That's when I hit my head."

Thank goodness she'd been wearing a seat belt. That had prevented her from being thrown from the car, but it hadn't stopped the tree limb from coming through the windshield and hitting her.

Lucas stared at her, clearly waiting for more details. Hailey had more, but she had to fight the panicky feeling rising in her again. It wasn't that night, but it suddenly felt as if it was.

"After I crashed, Darrin came to the side of the car," Hailey continued. "He looked at me." But then she stopped, her attention going back to Lucas. "Why didn't he just kill me then? I was helpless, barely conscious."

"Maybe he didn't want you dead," Lucas said. "He probably wanted those computer files and would have been willing to torture you to get them."

Yes. That had to be it. "But he didn't get a chance to kidnap me, because that's about the time you drove up. Did you see Darrin leave?"

"I saw his SUV speeding away. I couldn't go in pursuit."

That's because she had needed medical attention ASAP. Lucas had saved her life. Camden's, too, by staying with them. Lucas didn't seem any more comfortable thinking about that night than she did, and he looked relieved when Tillie came back into the living room.

"Is Camden ready for his bath?" the nanny asked, her voice tentative, probably because she knew that Hailey wanted to continue holding him.

Lucas nodded. "Best if he sticks to his routine," he told Hailey. "Plus, we need to do reports for the attack."

Yes, paperwork. Necessary, but she still hated having to hand her son over to the nanny. She'd gotten so few minutes holding him. Of course, a lifetime would be too few.

"You can watch," Tillie added, glancing at Hailey. "That way, you'll know how to do it." She also glanced at Lucas, and Tillie seemed to ignore the slight scowl that was on his face.

Maybe a scowl because it would mean a delay in doing those reports, but also because Tillie was including her.

Hailey didn't give Lucas a chance to veto Tillie's offer. She stood, following the woman as best she could to the bathroom just across the hall from the nursery. Lucas followed, too. Good thing, because just before Hailey reached the door, she stumbled and would have fallen flat on her face if Lucas hadn't caught her.

And just like that, she was in his arms.

The memories came. No way to stop them. Not with Lucas and her being body to body. Hailey got some flashes of even more body contact. Of when they were naked in bed.

Mercy, that caused the heat to flood through her again. Worse, Lucas noticed, and he looked as if he wanted to curse again. He didn't. He moved her away from him. Well, he moved so that her breasts were no longer pressed against his chest, but he looped his arm around her waist to steady her.

"You should be resting," he grumbled.

"Would you rest if you were in my shoes?" she countered.

That only deepened his scowl. Both knew the answer to that—no, he wouldn't.

Lucas kept his arm around her when they went to the doorway, but it was obvious that he was trying to touch as little of her as possible. Hailey soon didn't notice it because her attention was on the baby. Or at least, it was until Lucas's phone buzzed. She was close enough to see Grayson's name on the screen.

She felt the muscles in Lucas's arm tense. Probably because this could be bad news. He stepped back into the hall, answered the call and put it on speaker.

"Is Hailey there?" Grayson said without even issuing a greeting. Yes, this was bad news. Hailey could tell from his tone.

"I'm here," she answered.

"San Antonio PD found your sister," Grayson continued.

"Where is she?" Hailey immediately asked.

"The hospital. She's hurt, and she's asking to see you. Colleen says she knows who's trying to kill you."

Chapter Six

A car accident.

That's what had put Colleen in the hospital. And not just any ordinary accident, but one that'd happened on the same stretch of road where Hailey had nearly been killed. Lucas figured that was either an eerie coincidence or someone was trying to send them a message.

If it was a message, Lucas hadn't needed it. He knew just how much danger they were in. That's why it was almost certainly a mistake to take Hailey off the ranch and to the hospital, with the threat of an attack still hanging over their heads. But he also knew this meeting with Colleen could give them critical information to put an end to the danger.

Maybe an immediate end.

If Colleen confessed to helping Darrin when he tried to run Hailey off the road.

Lucas doubted that would actually happen, but he wouldn't rule it out. Heck, he wasn't ruling out anything right now. After all, he'd sworn that Hailey would never be under his roof again, and she'd not only spent the night there but also was back in his arms. Sort of. As he'd done earlier, he had to help her out of the cruiser, and that involved touching her.

He didn't have to remind her to hurry, and she did. As much as a hobbling woman could hurry. Lucas only hoped all this moving around wasn't doing anything to harm her leg muscles. The sooner he put some physical distance between them, the better, and that started with her getting back to a hundred percent.

Lucas believed her story about someone trying to kill her. And he felt a little sorry for her. But he wasn't ready to welcome her back into his and Camden's lives.

There was a deputy at the door to the hospital. Another inside. Since his cousins Dade and Gage had escorted Lucas and Hailey to the hospital, that meant Grayson had three other lawmen plus himself tied up with this.

"Thank you for not saying it was a stupid idea for me to come here," Hailey whispered as they made their way down the hall.

Lucas glanced at her from the corner of his eye. "Just because I didn't say it doesn't mean I agree with this. You could have demanded that Colleen tell you everything over the phone."

She glanced at him, too. "I did demand," she reminded him.

Yeah, but Hailey hadn't stood her ground when Colleen had insisted that she speak to her sister in person. This felt like a trap, and while the baby wasn't in danger at the moment, Hailey clearly was.

When they reached the patient ward of the hospital, Lucas spotted yet another lawman cousin. Josh. But he wasn't alone. There was a lanky, dark-haired guy in a black suit standing next to him. Judging from their scowls, neither Josh nor the suit were happy.

Hailey had an equally unhappy reaction to the man.

She sucked in her breath. "That's Brian Minton. He was one of the FBI agents who worked on the DeSalvo investigation."

Even though they were only a few yards from Minton, Lucas stopped. "You don't trust him?"

The question was valid, considering Lucas could feel Hailey's suddenly tight muscles. She hadn't exactly been relaxed on the trip over, but the tension was even worse now.

"I don't trust anyone involved in that," Hailey answered without taking her attention off Minton. "Remember, Preston DeSalvo had a dirty agent on his payroll. I'm positive of that."

No way could Lucas forget it, especially now that he'd read the file about it. The problem was, there'd been at least a dozen agents involved in that case and countless others who might have distanced themselves from it just so there'd be no obvious connection to the DeSalvo family.

"Any proof that Minton's dirty?" Lucas pressed.

"No," Hailey readily admitted, and she got moving again. "What are you doing here?" she asked the agent.

"I've asked him the same thing," Josh provided. "I've also told him he's not getting into Colleen's room until I get the okay from the sheriff. I haven't gotten that okay," he added, directing his glare at Minton.

Minton tapped his badge. "I'm here to interview two witnesses—Colleen and Laura—or, rather, Hailey, as she's going by these days. This investigation belongs to the FBI."

"How do you figure that?" Lucas said, but he didn't wait for an explanation. "Hailey is in WITSEC, and the marshals are in charge of that. As for Colleen, she was in a car accident in the jurisdiction of the Silver Creek Sheriff's Office."

Minton gave him a blank stare and huffed. "You and I both know this is connected to the DeSalvo family."

Lucas almost hoped this guy was dirty just so he could arrest him. "I know no such thing. I'm just bringing Hailey here to visit her sister."

"A sister who could have information I need," Minton countered.

Welcome to the club, but Lucas was first in line to question Colleen.

"Who ran Colleen off the road?" Minton asked, volleying his gaze between Hailey and Lucas.

Lucas shrugged. "Don't have a clue. Yet. How about you? Do you know who did this?"

"Probably the same thug who caused Hailey's accident."

"That thug is dead," Lucas said. "He died last night. From what I understand, Colleen's accident happened hours later."

Judging from the startled look in Minton's eyes, he hadn't known that. Or else he was pretending not to have known. "Eric could be behind this," Minton added after a long pause.

Yes, he could be. Or Colleen. Or even Minton himself. Lucas kept his speculations to himself to see if Minton would continue. He did.

"Whoever did this had a chance to kill you that night," Minton reminded Hailey. "He might have had the same chance to kill Colleen. But he didn't take it." He paused. "Why?"

Hailey shook her head. "I don't know."

No more startled look in Minton's eyes, but the comment seemed to rile him. "There are rumors that you have some files. Files that could incriminate Eric. If you have something like that, it's illegal to withhold them."

Hailey didn't back down from the agent's suddenly lethal stare. "It's illegal only if I know about the files. I don't. Truth is, I have huge gaps in my memory."

Normally, Lucas hated lying and liars, but in this case, the lie was warranted. His gut told him to hold off on giving Minton anything until they'd sorted all of this out. The *sorting* began with Colleen.

"Once you get approval from the sheriff, I'll let you in to see her," Lucas said to Minton.

Minton protested, of course, but Josh blocked his way while Lucas ushered Hailey inside. Josh wouldn't let the agent in without a fight, but just in case that happened, Lucas stayed near the door. That meant letting go of Hailey while she stepped around him and turned toward her sister.

"Thank God you came," Colleen said.

Lucas had never met the woman, but he recognized her from the hospital surveillance tapes. Colleen was a blonde, and despite the fact that there were cuts and bruises on her face, she looked as if she'd recently combed her hair and put on some lipstick. That sent an uneasy feeling up his spine. People who'd just had a brush with death didn't usually think about their appearance.

Of course, maybe Colleen had faked the accident to make herself appear innocent.

"Laura, it's been so long," Colleen added.

"Hailey," she automatically corrected her. "I don't use Laura anymore." Hailey limped closer until she was finally able to catch onto the end of the bed for support. "Has anyone been in here who could have planted a bug in the room?"

Colleen's eyes widened, and then she shook her head. "Only the doctor and some nurses have come in to check on me. I would have noticed if they'd planted something."

Maybe, but just in case, Lucas took a look around. When he didn't find anything, he went back to his guarding duties.

"Did Minton leave?" Colleen asked, and it took Lucas a moment to realize she was talking to him. Since she hadn't asked for introductions, she likely knew who he was.

"He's still in the hall. The sheriff will stall him, but eventually he'll get in here to see you. Is that a problem?"

"Of course." Colleen didn't hesitate, either. "I don't trust any of the agents who helped put Preston behind bars."

Preston.

Interesting. Colleen certainly didn't say the man's name with the venom that Hailey did.

"Preston's dead," Colleen went on. "And Minton is one of the people responsible for that."

"Preston was killed in a prison fight," Lucas pointed out. "Are you saying that Minton arranged to have him killed?"

Colleen opened her mouth but then closed it just as quickly. "I don't know. But there was a lawman involved in the dirty stuff Preston was doing, and if I trust the wrong person, I could end up like Preston."

Yes, she could. So could Hailey, and it might happen even if she withheld that trust.

Hailey went a few more steps toward the bed and looked surprisingly steady. Maybe because she was trying to look strong for what was no doubt about to be a confrontation with her sister.

"Aren't you even going to ask me if I'm all right?" Colleen asked before Hailey could speak.

Hailey paused a long time. "Are you okay?"

"No," her sister snapped. "Someone tried to kill me." And she stared at Hailey as if she were somehow responsible for that.

"Are you going to ask me if I'm all right?" Hailey fired right back. Heck, she sounded stronger, too. "After all, I was in a coma, and not long after coming out of it, someone tried to kill me, too."

And she waited for Colleen to respond to that.

Lucas watched Colleen's expression and her body language, but the woman seemed clueless as to what was going on. Again though, she could have been playing dumb like the agent outside the door.

"The hospital surveillance footage," Lucas finally prompted her. "We saw you on it with the man who tried to kill Hailey."

Colleen gasped and pressed her fingers to her lips. "That man tried to kill my sister?"

"Not once but twice," Hailey confirmed.

Colleen gasped again and frantically shook her head. "He said he was a marshal, and he showed me a badge. It looked real."

"It was fake," Lucas told her. "And he was a hired gun. Any idea who he was working for?"

More head shaking from Colleen. "I honestly thought he was a marshal and that he was here to protect Hailey."

Hailey drew in a long, weary breath and sank down onto the foot of the bed. "Start from the beginning. We need to know everything about him, everything that he said to you."

There were tears shimmering in Colleen's eyes now, and while Lucas wasn't immune to those tears, he wasn't fully buying them just yet. The woman could be crying because she'd just gotten caught and could be arrested.

"The marshal called me yesterday," Colleen started. "He said his name was Donald Silverman."

"It was Darrin Sandmire," Lucas corrected her.

"Was?" Colleen questioned.

"He's dead. Killed in a shoot-out with one of my cousins while he was attempting to get to Hailey."

Colleen pressed her fingertips to her mouth for a moment. "I didn't know. I swear I didn't," she added, her attention shifting to Hailey.

Like Lucas, Hailey still didn't look convinced. "This man asked you to meet him at the hospital?"

She nodded. "He said you were in danger, and that he needed my permission to access your personal things, like your computer."

So that he could get those files that Hailey had hidden. Files that Lucas needed to know more about as soon as they were finished here with Colleen.

"I told him that I didn't know where the rest of your personal things were," Colleen went on. "That the only things I had were what was collected from the car the night of your accident."

"It wasn't an accident," Hailey said. "That man ran me off the road and put both my baby and me in grave danger."

Colleen blinked back the tears, and her expression changed a little. Not so much alarm on her face but concern. "You're not suggesting that I was working with this snake?"

Hailey stayed quiet a moment. "I only need to find out the truth. So we can keep Camden safe."

"Camden?" Colleen asked.

"My son. That's what Lucas named him, and I will make sure no one, including you, does anything to harm him."

That didn't do much to ease Colleen's alarm. "You think I was together with him on this," she concluded. "I'm your sister."

"Yes, but we haven't always seen eye to eye in the past. You refused to testify against Preston."

Colleen's alarm turned to something else, and Lucas was pretty sure that something else was anger. It flashed through her eyes. "Because as you well know, I didn't witness the crimes you said he did."

There it was. Not just her words but Colleen's tone. Yeah, there was bitterness. Maybe because Colleen had been personally involved with the man? Or maybe she'd been doing more than only IT work for him.

"Why would Darrin want you dead?" Colleen came out and asked Hailey.

Lucas hoped she wouldn't mention those files, and she didn't. Hailey only shook her head. "Is it possible he was working for Preston and that Preston left orders to have me killed?"

"No," Colleen answered. Way too fast. She was definitely in the defensive mode when it came to her former boss. "Preston wouldn't have done that."

"How do you know that?" Lucas snapped.

Colleen volleyed some annoyed glances between Hailey and him. "Because I visited Preston in jail a few times."

Lucas rolled his eyes, took out his phone. "If I call the prison, I can find out exactly how many visits you made."

Her mouth tightened. "I saw him every week. And I'm not going to apologize for that."

"You should," Lucas argued. "Because even from behind bars, Preston could have arranged for the attacks against Hailey."

"He didn't," Colleen practically yelled. It took her a moment to regain her composure, and then she shifted her gaze back to Hailey. "You always believed the worst about Preston, but I believe it was the dirty agent who set him up. The same agent who's been trying to get into this room. Probably to kill me. Maybe he's the one who wants to kill Camden and you."

That was entirely possible. "You have any proof that Agent Minton is dirty?" Lucas asked her.

"No, but since you're a lawman, you should be the one getting that proof. Because someone put me in this hospital bed, and the next time, he might succeed in putting me in the grave."

Because that was possible, too, Lucas decided it was time to have a more thorough chat with Minton. Of course, that meant Hailey spending a little more time in the room with her sister, but Lucas could chat with Minton in the doorway. That way, he could keep an eye on Hailey.

Lucas opened the door, expecting to come face-to-face with the riled agent, but Minton wasn't there. However, Josh wasn't alone. There was another man standing in front of him. A man that Lucas recognized from the research he'd done the night before.

Eric DeSalvo.

Like Minton, Eric was wearing a suit. But he sure wasn't scowling. The man was smiling. A slick kind of smile that reminded Lucas of a snake oil salesman.

"You're supposed to be at the sheriff's office for an interview," Lucas immediately reminded Eric.

"I'm on my way there, but I decided to make a detour." His smile widened. "Lucas Ryland, Texas Ranger," Eric greeted him. Obviously the man had done his research as well. "I understand you think I'm guilty of all sorts of assorted felonies."

"Are you?" Lucas growled.

"No, but I think I can help you solve this." He tipped his head to the end of the hall, where Lucas saw Minton walking away. "Arrange a plea deal for me, and I'll give you what you need to put Agent Minton behind bars."

Chapter Seven

Hailey hadn't wanted to make this trip to the Silver Creek Sheriff's Office. She'd wanted to be back at the ranch with her son. But these interviews could be critical to helping Lucas and her make sure that Camden stayed safe.

Well, there was one official interview anyway— with Eric.

But since Agent Minton had shown up, Grayson would be questioning him, as well. Of course, that didn't mean Minton would answer anything. Especially anything that could incriminate him, but maybe he would spill something that would be helpful. For that matter, maybe Eric would do the same, and this nightmare would stop right here, right now.

"They're about ready to start," Lucas said, joining her by the observation window of the interview room. He handed her a cup of much-needed coffee.

Eric was already seated at the gray metal table, an attorney on each side of him, and even though he couldn't see Hailey through the one-way glass, he occasionally looked in her direction. And he smiled again.

No doubt to unnerve her.

There was certainly no love lost between them, and

after his father had been convicted, Eric had issued plenty of veiled threats to get to her. Not because he'd wanted to defend Preston. He hadn't.

Eric hadn't had much love for his father, either, but he hadn't wanted Hailey to do anything that would include him in the charges against Preston. Father and son still had plenty of business ties. Ties that Preston would have gladly continued because from all accounts, he'd wanted to protect his son.

Hailey now understood the lengths a parent would go to to protect a child. Even when that child—Eric—had done everything to distance himself from his father.

"Where's Minton?" she asked.

Lucas hitched his thumb to the hall. "In the other interview room, where Dade will question him. Let's just say he's not happy about being questioned by a *local yokel* deputy sheriff, and he's on his phone to his boss to find out if he can get out of it."

Maybe his boss would side with Grayson. And even if he didn't, perhaps they could get the information some other way.

She glanced back at Eric when he smiled at her again. "Any idea what kind of plea deal he wants?"

Lucas shook his head. "After dropping the bombshell at the hospital, he clammed up, claimed he didn't want to say anything else without his attorneys present."

That didn't surprise her. "Eric always hides behind his attorneys. So did his father. Not the same attorneys, of course. Preston would have shared, but Eric never trusted his father enough to mix his personal stuff with the family business."

Lucas stared at her. "After this, you should be able to access those files. Too bad you can't do that before

Grayson talks to Eric, because there might be something he could use for leverage. Just how much jail time would Eric get with what you have?"

"Not nearly enough. It's an illegal sale of some land. He paid off some officials one county over and got the land rezoned so he could in turn sell it to one of his puppet companies. There's also a sale of confiscated weapons."

That got his attention. He moved even closer. So close that his arm brushed against hers. It was just a slight touch, but she felt it head to toe.

"How many weapons?" he asked.

"Not nearly enough," she repeated after she gathered the breath to speak. Mercy, she had to figure out how to stop these flutters when she was around Lucas. She also had to focus since this was an important conversation. "It's a felony, but since he's got a spotless record, he might not get more than a year."

Lucas's forehead bunched up. "Yet it was enough to keep his father from coming after you."

"Preston loved him. Despite everything."

"Exactly what is *everything*?" he asked.

Because he was looking her straight in the eyes and because he was so close to her, it took Hailey a moment to realize they were still talking about Eric. And not this attraction between them.

"I don't know all the details," Hailey explained, "but Preston was a widower since Eric was a little boy, and Eric always blamed his father for his mother's death."

"Was Preston to blame?"

"I don't know, but she did die in a car accident. The cops did investigate it. Nothing concrete turned up, though."

Lucas made a sound, one of skepticism. A sound that Hailey totally understood. "Three car wrecks, and I know mine wasn't an accident," she said. "Perhaps the others weren't, either."

"You think Colleen's telling the truth about that? About any of this?" he asked.

Hailey drew in a long breath. "I want to believe her. But things have sometimes been—well—tense between us. She was three when her father married my mother, and I think once I was born a couple of years later, she thought our parents doted on me more than her. And maybe they did when I was little. Then our mother died of breast cancer, and my father ended up abandoning us. Colleen blamed me for that, too."

She stopped and realized she'd never told anyone that. "Sorry," Hailey said. "Didn't mean to dump all of that on you."

"No. I wanted to hear it because it's motive. People have certainly killed for a lot less, and coupled with her disapproval over you testifying against Preston, maybe Colleen decided she'd had enough."

That turned Hailey's stomach. Because *enough* nearly cost her Camden.

"What happened to Colleen and you after your father left?" Lucas continued.

"Foster care. That's when we got closer. I think because we only had each other."

And now Colleen might be trying to kill her. Of course, her sister wasn't their main suspect. That person was sitting on the other side of the observation mirror, and Eric smiled again when Grayson finally came into the room.

Lucas reached over to turn on the audio so they could

hear the interview, and again his arm brushed against hers. The other time he hadn't noticed. Or at least, he'd pretended not to notice. But this time their gazes met.

And held.

He mumbled some profanity and looked away. "This isn't going to happen," he said, but she wasn't sure if he was trying to convince her or himself.

No way did he want to get involved with her. She totally understood that, but the attraction was undeniable. The heat was still just as strong as it had been the night she'd gone to his bed. Thankfully she didn't have to keep remembering it, because Grayson got her attention when he spoke.

"Tell me about this plea deal you want," Grayson demanded.

Eric looked directly into the mirror. "I've heard that Hailey might have something she believes could be incriminating about me. It'll be all fake, of course, but I need the chance to clear my name."

"You said you thought that Eric didn't know about those computer files," Lucas reminded her.

"I didn't think he did. The only one I personally told was Preston."

Lucas stayed quiet a couple of seconds. "Is it possible Preston told Colleen?"

Hailey sighed. Nodded. Yes, it was possible. "But why would Colleen have told Eric?"

Lucas didn't get a chance to answer because Grayson continued. "What kind of incriminating info?" Grayson pressed. He knew all about the computer files they'd soon be able to access, but he no doubt wanted to hear Eric's take on this.

"I'm not positive, but I think it's supposed to be about illegal arms. It could be anything since it's fake."

Grayson just stared at him. "And you think Hailey manufactured this?"

Eric shrugged. "Probably not her, but my father could have."

"From everything I've heard, your father cared about you. In fact, I heard he'd do pretty much anything to prevent you from going to jail."

"That's what he wanted everyone to believe, but as a lawman, you certainly know what he was capable of. It's not much of a stretch to think he'd come up with something to keep me in line."

Oh, mercy. Was it false evidence? "It looked real," she said to Lucas. "And besides, if it were fake, why wouldn't Preston have sent someone after me? He hated me for testifying against him."

"Maybe even Preston didn't have the stomach for murdering a woman in a coma. Still…the latest attacks didn't happen until after he was dead."

True. And that led them right back to Eric.

"All right," Grayson continued. "You want a look at these so-called files. What are you offering in exchange?"

"Some files of my own," Eric said without hesitation. "They won't be admissible in court, but they're recordings that my father made when people visited his office."

Judging from Eric's smug look, there was something critical on the recordings. Judging from Grayson's scowl, he wasn't pleased about it.

"Any reason you didn't turn these recordings over to

the authorities when the investigation was going on?" Grayson snapped.

Eric's smug look went up a notch. "Because I only recently found them. Yesterday, in fact."

Hailey groaned. He was lying. He'd probably had them all along. But why had he held on to them?

"Eric's up to something," Hailey mumbled.

Lucas made a sound of agreement, but before he could say anything, the door to the observation room opened, and she saw Dade and Minton standing there.

"I've played along with this fiasco long enough," Minton snarled. "I'm an FBI agent and won't be treated like this."

"Let me guess," Lucas said to his cousin. "The interview went well." His voice dripped with sarcasm.

"No, it didn't." Minton's tone was full of sarcasm, too. "I don't know anything that can help you end whatever the hell's happening to Hailey. And I won't know until you tell me everything that's going on." He glanced at the mirror. "Including what's going on with that piece of slime."

Hailey wanted to tune Minton out and focus on Eric's conversation, but Grayson, the lawyers and the DA had moved on to the details of the plea deal, and from what Hailey could tell, Eric was asking for immunity from prosecution.

Which meant there was likely something incriminating him on those recordings or in the files Hailey had.

Hailey hadn't intended to bring up anything to Minton about what Eric had just said, but Lucas obviously had something different in mind.

"Eric claims he has recordings that he got from his

father's office," Lucas tossed out there. "He's working out a plea deal now."

And Hailey soon knew why Lucas had done that. He pinned his attention to Minton, clearly looking for a reaction.

He got one.

Minton charged toward the window to have a closer look. "Any recordings come under the jurisdiction of the FBI."

Lucas huffed. "You seem to keep forgetting that this isn't an FBI matter. The recordings could be evidence in the recent attacks against Hailey. Attacks that happened right here in Silver Creek." He glanced at Dade. "Did anyone here in the sheriff's office request FBI assistance? Because that's the only way Minton could be involved in this."

Dade pretended to think about that. "Nope. No one here made a request like that. Grayson said if we needed help, we'd call in the Rangers. Of course, we won't have to call very loud since a Texas Ranger is standing right here in this room."

Minton's mouth tightened, but instead of verbal fire at any of the men, he turned toward Hailey. "I'm trying to keep you and your son alive." He nodded toward Eric. "You'll need all the help you can get with that piece of slime. He's dangerous. That's why you should give me copies of anything you have on him."

Lucas's huff was even louder this time. "This conversation is over." And he took Hailey by the arm and maneuvered her around Minton and Dade.

"It's not over," Minton insisted. "One way or another, I will get the evidence you have."

It sounded like a threat. Worse, it felt like one.

Hailey reminded herself that Minton could just be focused on the job, but if he was the dirty agent Preston had on his payroll, then she had two snakes to watch out for—Eric and Minton.

"I'll take you back to the ranch," Lucas said once they were out of earshot of Minton. "We'll wait there until you can get into the files. Maybe by then Grayson will have worked out something with Eric."

They went to the front where Lucas had left the cruiser, but before they reached the door, his phone buzzed. Hailey saw Josh's name on the screen. Since he was at the hospital, she instantly got a bad feeling.

Lucas obviously did, too, because he belted out some profanity under his breath. "A problem?" Lucas greeted his cousin.

"Yeah. Please tell me we have something to hold Colleen. Because if not, she's about to leave the hospital."

Hailey released the breath she'd been holding. She'd braced herself for something worse, like an attack. "Did the doctor say it was okay for her to go?"

"No. But she's leaving anyway unless we've got grounds to hold her."

"She was on the surveillance tape with a hit man," Hailey reminded Lucas.

But Lucas shook his head. "Not enough since she had an explanation for that, and there's no proof that she knew who he was. Can Colleen hear me talking right now?" he asked Josh.

"No," Josh repeated. "She's in her room getting dressed, and I'm in the hall."

"Good. Then let her leave, but I want a tail on her. Tell me where she goes and who she sees. Because if she's behind this, she might try to meet with her hired thugs."

True. Hailey hated to think Colleen would do that, but this might be a way to be sure.

"Will do," Josh said. "Hold on while I send a text to the reserve deputy who's in the parking lot. He's dressed in plain clothes."

Maybe Colleen wouldn't notice the man and would do whatever it was she was setting out to do. Part of Hailey wished, though, that her sister had had no part in any of this.

"Colleen's coming out of her room now," Josh added a moment later.

Josh said something else, something that Hailey didn't catch. Ditto for whatever her sister said to the deputy.

"Colleen just handed me a note that I'm supposed to give to Hailey," Josh finally explained.

"A note?" Hailey asked. "Why didn't she just talk to me?"

"Don't know. You want me to unfold it and read it to you?"

"Yes," she answered as fast as she could.

Hailey heard the rustling around on Josh's end, and a moment later he mumbled some of the same profanity that Lucas had just used. "It says, 'I'm sorry, Hailey. I know you'll never understand, but I did what I had to do.'"

Chapter Eight

"I did what I had to do."

Lucas hoped Colleen was referring to checking herself out of the hospital, but he had a bad feeling in the pit of his stomach.

It certainly hadn't helped when Colleen had managed to ditch the tail they had on her. Now she was in the wind. Could have been anywhere. Heck, she could have been out there planning another attack. Colleen had a lot of questions to answer, but first they had to find her and somehow force her to tell them the truth.

Of course, in addition to Colleen, Lucas had plenty of other things adding to that bad feeling. Minton, Eric.

And Hailey.

Hailey, though, was a bad feeling of a different kind.

Once again, he had no choice but to take her to his house at the ranch. It was either that or spend more time at the sheriff's office, and neither of them wanted that. In fact, Hailey had jumped to say yes when he suggested they go.

Hailey had *jumped* yet again when they'd arrived home and Tillie had offered to show her how to give Camden his bottle. Now Lucas was supervising that while he waited for updates on both the plea deal and Colleen.

"He really is a little miracle," Hailey said, smiling at Camden while she burped him.

Of course, Hailey was in heaven over doing something as simple as feeding and burping their son. "You might not call him a miracle when he wakes up every three hours," Lucas joked, because he thought they could use some levity.

At least, he could use it, anyway. His muscles were knotted so tight that his back and shoulders were hurting.

Hailey smiled, and he got a knot of a different kind. This one in his stomach. He remembered that smile. It was one of the first things that had attracted him to her, and even now it stalled his breath in his chest. Then she chuckled when Camden let out a burp that sounded as if it'd come from a grown man drinking beer. Lucas didn't join her on the chuckling, but he'd had the same reaction the first couple of times it had happened.

His phone dinged with a text from Josh.

Lucas glanced at his watch. "You should be able to get into the storage cloud to retrieve those files." That would get his mind off her smile and back to what he should have been focusing on.

She nodded, her forehead bunching up. Obviously she didn't want to let go of the baby just yet, but Lucas needed to see exactly what Hailey had against Eric.

Hailey kissed Camden, and she waited for Tillie to come and take the baby before she got up from the chair. She made her way to Lucas's office just up the hall. It seemed as if each hour she was walking a little better, but she still caught onto the wall to steady herself.

And she also caught onto him when she eased into the chair.

"Sorry," she said. No doubt because she felt his muscles tense. "I know it bothers you for me to touch you."

Yeah, it did. But not in the way she was thinking. It bothered him because it reminded him of things he shouldn't have been remembering. Instead of mentioning that, though, Lucas just motioned for her to get busy on the laptop.

She nodded, looked disappointed that he hadn't addressed the elephant in the room—the attraction. Something he had no plans to address.

"It'll take a couple of minutes for me to get through the passwords and security questions," she said just as his phone rang.

Since it was Grayson's name on the screen and no doubt a call about the investigation, Lucas answered it on speaker. That way Hailey wouldn't have to lean too close to him to hear.

"We worked out a plea deal with Eric," Grayson said. "A limited one for both of us. He'll get immunity only if there's something of evidentiary value on the recordings. The second condition is that the immunity will cover only one criminal count. A count that doesn't include murder or accessory to murder."

Lucas looked at Hailey. "Any chance of Eric having murdered someone?"

"Not that I know of," she answered. "From what I learned, the DeSalvo family crimes seemed to be limited to money laundering and the sale of illegal arms. Of course, it's possible someone was killed during those deals, but the deals I had knowledge of were mainly Preston's, not Eric's."

That didn't mean Eric didn't have any side deals of his own. But then, if he had, there was no way the man would give Grayson evidence to incriminate himself for murder.

"What did you mean about the deal being limited for both Eric and you?" Hailey wanted to know.

"The recordings are on old compact disks, and Preston set it up so they can't be copied. Eric wants the disks to stay here in the sheriff's office, and that means I'll have to tie up some manpower to listen to them."

Eric had probably added that into the deal to make sure Minton and the FBI didn't get their hands on them. Or maybe Eric had another reason for doing that.

"Did Eric give you any idea what was on the recordings?" Lucas asked Grayson.

"He says he hasn't listened to them all. Which I find hard to believe."

So did Lucas. Eric didn't seem like the sort to shoot himself in the foot by handing over anything that could be connected to him beyond the limits of the plea deal. Still, there might be something that Eric had missed.

"But what Eric did say," Grayson went on, "was that there are dozens of recorded conversations with his father and his business associates. Of course, he didn't get permission from any of these people. But there are names, he claims, that we can use to make some arrests if we can link those names to the crimes."

Yeah, because the recordings themselves probably wouldn't be admissible in court since Preston didn't get prior consent from at least one of the people he was recording. Then there was the problem of the tapes being in the hands of one of their suspects, one who could have doctored the conversations.

"I'll call you as soon as we have the recordings. Let me know what you find out from Hailey's files," Grayson added before he ended the call.

Lucas put away his phone and watched as Hailey accessed the site. Thankfully her fingers were working better than her legs. She had no trouble typing.

No trouble cursing, either.

That bad feeling in his stomach went up a couple of notches.

"The files are gone?" Lucas concluded, but he hoped he was wrong.

Hailey didn't answer him. She kept mumbling profanity. Kept searching through the storage cloud. Even though Lucas was far from a computer expert, he could see that all the files were empty.

Except one.

Hailey clicked on it, and when Lucas saw what was there, he was the one cursing. Not files to incriminate Eric. There was just a single document with one sentence written on it.

I did what I had to do.

It was the exact wording of the note Colleen had left with Josh, but in this case it didn't make sense.

"Why would Colleen want these files deleted?" Lucas asked. "From what I can tell, Colleen despises Eric."

Hailey groaned, obviously still dealing with the bombshell of what her sister had done. Or else what someone wanted them to believe Colleen had done.

"She does," Hailey confirmed. But then she shook

her head. "Or maybe that was all a pretense. I just don't know anymore."

Another groan, and she buried her face in her hands for a couple of seconds. When she lowered them, Lucas spotted the tears in her eyes.

Oh, man. Not tears. Not now. He was already feeling raw and exhausted, and he was a sucker for a woman's tears. Especially this woman. Because this was quickly turning into a very bad day for Hailey and this investigation.

She stood and looked around as if trying to decide what to do, but Lucas could see that there wasn't much fight left in her. "Colleen must hate me to side with a snake like Eric."

"Maybe she didn't have a choice. Maybe Eric has some dirt on her. Something that would send her to jail."

The tears continued. "Yes, but she knows those files are meant to protect Camden and me from Eric. Or from any of Preston's thugs who might be out there ready to carry out their late boss's dying wish to see me dead."

She was right. And Lucas had had enough of the tears. Before he could talk himself out of it, he reached out and pulled her into his arms. Of course, Hailey had been in his arms since she'd come out of the coma. It'd been necessary to keep her from falling.

This was different.

Lucas could feel it. And Hailey could feel it, too. She didn't go stiff as she had the other times they'd touched in the past twenty-four hours. She sort of melted against him.

"I'm just so scared," she admitted. "Not for me but for Camden and you. For your family."

"No one is going to hurt Camden or my family," he

assured her. Not that he was in a position to give that kind of assurance. Not with hired guns after them. Still, those hired guns would have to get past him, and since he was protecting his son, Lucas had no intention of making that easy for them.

Hailey looked up at him at the exact moment he looked down at her. Lucas silently said more of that profanity. He was so not ready for this. Well, his mind and heart weren't, anyway, but the rest of him seemed to think it was a good idea to kiss her or something.

Especially *something*.

The heat came. Memories, too. Vivid memories of Hailey naked and beneath him in his bed. The very bed that was just up the hall.

She didn't look away from him, and hell, he didn't look away, either. They just stood there with all those bad thoughts running through his head. Lucas was within a fraction of a second of acting on those bad thoughts by kissing her, but Hailey cleared her throat and stepped back.

"I'm sorry," Hailey said, rubbing her forehead and dodging his gaze. "I know that makes things worse."

It did, and Lucas didn't want her to clarify that. Or talk about it. Hell, he just wanted to concentrate on anything but this ache that was begging him to have sex with her right here, right now.

"You should try to call Colleen and ask her about this," he managed to say, and he handed her his phone.

Focus. He needed to deal with the problems of the investigation and not create new problems by having his body go rock hard with thoughts of Hailey.

She nodded. "I'm not sure if Colleen still has the same number. Until I came out of the coma, I hadn't been in touch with her since Preston's trial, and that was over eighteen months ago."

It was a long shot, but it was one that paid off. In a way. Colleen didn't answer, but when her voice mail greeting kicked in, Hailey and he got verification that her sister had kept the old number.

"Call me ASAP," Hailey said when she left the message, and there was a definite urgency in her tone.

But whether Colleen would phone her back was a different matter. After all, even though she'd been injured in that car accident, Colleen had still managed to elude the reserve deputy. Something Lucas wished he'd handled differently. He should have requested one of the regular deputies to follow her.

Hailey sank back down onto the chair and gave a heavy sigh. At least she wasn't crying, but this was obviously getting to her. Or rather, it was, until she looked up at him again, and there was something in her eyes. Not attraction this time.

"What if Colleen and Eric believe I have hard copies of everything that was in the online storage?" she asked.

It didn't take long, only a few seconds, for Lucas to figure out where this was going. And he shook his head. "You're talking about setting a trap. Definitely not a good idea, because it could send those hired killers after you again."

"The hired killers will come no matter what. I'm not sure why, but obviously the person behind this sees me as a threat. Or maybe the things that I know are what he or she considers the threat."

That was true, and it didn't rule out any of their suspects. Minton could want anything destroyed that could link him to being a dirty agent. Eric could be trying to save his butt from going to jail. And Colleen? Well, Lucas still didn't know why she was seemingly playing on Eric's side in this, but it was obvious she didn't want her sister to have any incriminating evidence about the man.

Or maybe the information in the file incriminated someone else? Like Colleen herself?

Too bad they didn't have the real files to examine.

"Just think this through," Hailey pressed. "We could leak that the computer files have been erased and that I'm getting the hard copies to give to Grayson. We could say that I'm getting them from a safe deposit box or something."

Lucas huffed. It would still put Hailey in immediate danger. Unless...

"Maybe we could get a cop to go in posing as you," Lucas said. "There's a reserve deputy, Kara Duggan, who has a similar height and build. We could arrange for there to be eyes on her and give her plenty of backup." But then he paused. "Of course, the gunmen might be expecting a trap and come here after you."

She pressed her lips together a moment. Clearly this thought had already occurred to her, but then Hailey's gaze drifted in the direction of the nursery. If the gunmen came here, Camden would be in danger.

"How about you and I go to the sheriff's office and then leak the info?" she suggested. "That way, if they do smell a trap, they'll go after me there and not come to the ranch."

Lucas went through all the things that could go wrong. And with hired killers, there was plenty that could go wrong.

"You know that none of our suspects will go after

the decoy, right?" he reminded her. "He or she will send a lackey."

Hailey nodded. "But if we have a lackey—alive—we might be able to find out who hired him."

True. Once they had the hired thug's name, then they could search for a paper trail or maybe work out a plea deal. Still, it wasn't without huge risks.

"You're sure you want to do this?" Lucas asked.

"I'm sure," Hailey said without hesitation.

Lucas hesitated, but he knew this was the only straw they had a chance to grab right now. He took out his phone, but it rang before he could call Grayson to set all of this up.

Dade's name popped up on the screen. "We got the recordings from Eric," Dade told Lucas. "They're actual disks. Dozens of them. He flagged one that we should listen to first. It's a conversation between Preston and Colleen." He paused. "I really think Hailey should hear what her sister had to say. Then we can figure out what we need to do."

Chapter Nine

Hailey didn't know what she was dreading more—this return trip to the sheriff's office to hear the recorded conversation that Dade had said she'd definitely want to hear, or leaving Camden.

Still, it was necessary. Not just for the recordings but also because they needed to work out the final details for the trap to lure out whoever was behind this. She hated that the reserve deputy would be in possible danger, but Hailey was hoping that Lucas would be able to set it all up so they could minimize the risks.

"Maybe this won't take long," Lucas said as they got into the cruiser.

They weren't alone. Josh and one of the armed ranch hands, Avery Joyner, were with them. Josh was behind the wheel with Avery riding shotgun. Lucas and she took the backseat.

"And I'm still not sure this is a good idea," Lucas added.

She'd lost count how many times he'd said a variation of that, and Hailey agreed with him. She wasn't sure it was a good idea, either, but at the moment they didn't have a lot of options as to how to put an end to the danger. Plus, she really did want to listen to those recordings. Of course, she could have had Dade play the conversations for her over the phone, but from the sound of it, there'd need to be some follow-up action when it came to her sister.

"Colleen or Preston must have said something bad for Dade to have called," Hailey remarked.

Lucas made a sound of agreement, but what he didn't do was take his attention off their surroundings. Like Avery and Josh, his gaze was firing all around them, watching for anyone who might attack them. "Not a surprise, though. After all, she's the one who likely deleted those computer files."

True. But there was something about it that didn't feel right. People with solid computer skills could have hacked their way in and then set up her sister to take the blame.

"What the hell?" Josh mumbled, and he slowed the cruiser.

Hailey followed his gaze to the end of the road, where someone had parked a black car. The road was barely a few yards off Ryland land, which was probably why the security system hadn't detected it, but there were also two ranch hands armed with rifles. They weren't pointing the rifles at their visitor, but Hailey figured they would if he tried to get on the ranch road.

"You know that man?" Avery asked Lucas.

And that's when Hailey spotted Minton stepping from the car.

"Yeah," Lucas answered. "That's FBI Agent Brian Minton."

Both Lucas and she groaned. She definitely didn't want to deal with the agent today. Especially since he was one of their suspects. But from the way Minton had parked, they wouldn't be able to get around him without speaking to the man. Judging from the way Lucas was cursing, the *speaking* wouldn't be friendly.

"Wait here, and I'll see what he wants," Lucas said to Hailey. He drew his gun, reached for the door but then glanced back at her. "And I mean it about waiting inside the cruiser. If Minton's behind the attacks, he could have snipers in the area."

That caused her heart to jump to her throat, and Hailey caught onto his arm. "If there are possible snipers, it's too risky for you to go out there."

"I won't be long," Lucas insisted, as if that made everything okay. Hailey wanted to remind him that it took only a split second for someone to gun him down, but he was out of the cruiser before she could even gather her breath.

Josh opened his door, as well. So did Avery. And they drew their guns while continuing to watch around them. Hailey tried to do the same, but it was hard not to focus on Minton and Lucas. Thankfully, with the front doors open, she could hear Minton when he *greeted* Lucas.

"These men wouldn't let me onto the ranch," Minton complained.

"Because they're smart and following orders. *My* orders. No one's getting onto the ranch unless you live or work here. Neither applies to you."

In addition to hearing them well enough, Hailey had no trouble seeing Minton's steely expression. "We're fellow peace officers. You'd think we could cooperate long enough to bring someone to justice. Especially since that someone is obviously after Hailey and now you since you're trying to protect her. They'll kill you to get to her."

"Cooperate? Right. You and I have a different notion about what that means. You want me to give this investigation to the FBI, and it's not mine to give. Sheriff Grayson Ryland is in charge."

"Well, he shouldn't be," Minton snapped. Every muscle in his face was tight, but he said something under his breath. Something she didn't catch. And then it appeared he was trying to rein in his temper. "I just need the information, that's all. I need to know what Hailey has. Eric, too. Especially Eric, because he could have altered those recordings." Minton paused. "I think Eric's trying to set me up."

"And how and why would he do that?" Lucas asked.

"I'm investigating him, and I think I'm close to giving him a dose of the justice he deserves. He'd obviously do anything to stop me, and that includes doctoring the tapes that he claims he just found. Eric's got the money and resources to do something like that."

Interesting. Maybe Minton was trying to do some damage control beforehand just in case there was anything in those conversations about him.

"Did you and Preston have conversations in his office?" Lucas pressed. He was still keeping watch around them, and while Hailey knew this chat could be important, she didn't want Lucas out there any longer.

Minton nodded. "A couple of them, in fact. Remember, I was investigating both Eric and him, and I interviewed Preston. Anything I said could be altered or taken out of context, and I just don't want my name sullied because of a snake like Eric."

"I get that, but it still doesn't mean you can listen to the recordings. Eric worked out a plea deal, and we have to abide by that." Lucas glanced around again. "If you want to keep up this little chat, then call the sheriff's office and make an appointment." With that, he headed back to the cruiser.

Obviously Minton didn't like being dismissed that way, because the flash of anger returned on his face. "Not cooperating with me is a huge mistake," the agent snarled, and he, too, turned back toward his car.

He didn't get far.

Because a shot slammed through the air and smashed right into the front end of Minton's car.

HELL.

Lucas had known right from the start that something like this could happen, but he'd hoped he would get lucky. Apparently not, though.

He was still a few yards from the cruiser and started to run so he could dive in, but the next shot stopped him. It didn't go toward Minton's car but right at Lucas. He had to drop to the ground, and it wasn't a second too soon.

Because if Lucas hadn't, the next shot would have hit him.

"Get in!" Hailey yelled.

He had no trouble hearing her and the fear in her voice, but Lucas hoped like the devil that she was staying down. The windows in the cruiser were bullet-resistant. That didn't mean, though, that these shots wouldn't eventually tear their way through the glass and reach her.

Another shot came.

This one landed near Minton again, and like Lucas, the agent had no choice but to go to the ground and use his car as cover. The ranch hands outside took cover, as well. They scrambled into the ditch.

Good.

Lucas didn't want them in the line of fire, but he also needed the attack to stop. Because they weren't the only ones in danger. Anyone else on the ranch could be hit if this idiot trying to kill them had a long enough range.

Judging from the sound of the shots, they were coming from a heavily treed area across the road. The oaks were huge there and would make the perfect catbird seat for a sniper. But that wasn't all that Lucas realized. There was more than one gunman.

"Can you see who's shooting?" Minton called out to him.

"No. But I think they're at your eleven and one o'clock."

Lucas only hoped there weren't more, but considering the other attacks, there was no telling how many the sick person behind this had sent after them.

The two gunmen were clearly working together to keep all five of them pinned down while also keeping watch on the cruiser. When Josh tried to open the door, no doubt to return fire, one of the gunmen sent a bullet his way. Definitely not good because it didn't stop with just one shot. A barrage of bullets went into the cruiser, each of them with the possibility of being deadly.

Lucas had to do something *now*.

"Minton, somehow you need to get in your car and move it," Lucas ordered.

Because until he did that, they wouldn't be able to move the cruiser forward and get the heck out of there. There was no way Lucas wanted to go in reverse and have these hired guns just follow them onto the ranch.

Minton did try to move. He made it a few inches

before the shots turned in his direction, and he had to scramble to the ground again.

By now, someone had called for backup, and even though there were several of his lawmen cousins on the grounds, they wouldn't be able to get to them right now without putting themselves in grave danger.

The shots shifted again. Some went in the direction of the ditch. No doubt because Avery had tried to fire. Since the hands were armed with rifles, they would stand a better chance of putting an end to this than Lucas would with his handgun. It was obvious, though, that the thugs weren't going to give the men a chance to shoot.

Lucas glanced over at the cruiser to make sure Hailey was staying put. She wasn't. She was by the door nearest him, and she was opening it as wide as it would go. Of course, that caused the gunmen to fire at her.

"Get down!" Lucas told her.

He didn't want her risking her life, but he was thankful about the door maneuver. It would make it easier for him to get back into the cruiser if he could just get a break from the gunmen. Even then, though, he'd still need Minton to get the devil out of the way.

"I'll create a diversion," Lucas said to Minton. He didn't shout and hoped his voice didn't carry so the gunmen would hear him. "When they start shooting at me, get to your car."

Minton nodded. Lucas had to admit that the man looked just as concerned about this as Lucas was. Maybe that meant Minton wasn't a dirty agent after all. But then, this could all be a ruse to make him look innocent, especially since no one had actually been shot. The gunmen would have had ample opportunity to do that when Minton and he had been talking out in the open.

Anything that Lucas did at this point was a risk, but doing nothing was even riskier, so he got into position the way a sprinter would at the start line, and after saying a quick prayer, he bolted toward the cruiser.

"No!" Hailey shouted when Lucas started moving.

But he was already doing that diversion that he hoped would work. It did. The shots started coming right at him, each of them smacking into the ground and kicking up bits of asphalt right at him. Still, Lucas didn't stop. He barreled to the cruiser and jumped inside.

"You shouldn't have done that," Hailey cried out. She grabbed him and pulled him into her arms.

Lucas could feel her shaking. Could feel the relief, too. Relief he understood because he was feeling it as well. But he couldn't think about that right now. Instead, using the cruiser door for cover, he took aim and started shooting in the direction of those gunmen. They were perhaps out of range, but it might distract them enough to buy Minton a little time.

Avery joined Lucas, and both of them fired. For the first time since this attack had begun, the gunmen stopped shooting. It was just enough time for Minton to dart around to the side of his car and get in.

"Put on your seat belt," Lucas told Hailey.

He didn't have to tell Josh to get ready to move because his cousin had already put the cruiser in gear. Thankfully it didn't take long for Minton to start his car engine, and as soon as he'd done that, he hit the accelerator.

Josh did the same.

Minton sped out onto the main road, turning toward

town. The majority of the bullets followed him, slamming into the back of his car. But some of the shots came at the cruiser, too.

"Don't go the same direction as Minton," Lucas instructed Josh.

His cousin didn't question that, probably because he already knew that Lucas considered Minton a suspect. Josh went in the opposite direction. That would also get them to town. Eventually. But it was a longer route. Still, as long as it got them out of the path of those shots, Lucas didn't mind the extra miles.

Well, provided he could keep Hailey safe by going that extra distance. Lucas didn't want to be near Minton, but he also hoped they weren't heading straight for another attack.

"I've already called Mason," Josh explained. "He heard the shots and was already putting the ranch on lockdown. Grayson's sending someone to find those snipers."

Lucas figured they wouldn't be easy to find. They'd probably had a darn good escape route mapped out before either of them ever pulled their triggers. Still, that didn't mean they wouldn't leave some kind of evidence behind.

"Is anyone following us?" Avery asked, looking around.

Lucas was looking, as well, but he didn't see anyone. Not at first, anyway. And then, just ahead, he spotted the black SUV that had pulled into an old ranch trail. Josh no doubt saw it, as well, because he muttered some profanity under his breath.

No way could it be the shooters because they wouldn't have had time to leave those trees and make it to this point. But Lucas doubted that it was a coincidence that someone happened to be on this rural stretch of the road at the same time someone had been trying to kill them.

"Turn around," Lucas said to Josh. He kept his attention pinned to the vehicle while he pushed Hailey down onto the seat. "Go back in the other direction."

It was dangerous, but he didn't want to risk driving past that SUV in case someone started shooting at them again. Best to get Hailey to safety, and then he could have the deputies go on the search for the SUV.

"Don't stop by the ranch," Lucas added. "Just keep driving to the sheriff's office."

Josh hit the brakes, and even though the road was barely wide enough to do a U-turn, his cousin managed it by using the gravel shoulder of the road. He got the cruiser headed in the other direction. But not before Lucas caught a glimpse of the people inside the SUV.

"No," Hailey said under her breath. And Lucas knew from her tone and her gasp that she'd seen them, too.

There was a man behind the wheel. Someone that Lucas didn't recognize, but he sure as heck knew the person in the front passenger seat.

Colleen.

Chapter Ten

One minute Hailey felt numb from the spent adrenaline, but the next minute she wanted to scream. Yet another attack could have killed them.

Attacks perhaps orchestrated by her own sister.

It turned her stomach to relive the image of Colleen in that SUV. Less than a half mile from those snipers at the ranch. Had she been sitting there, staying close to her hired thugs? Because she certainly didn't look like a hostage.

From the glimpse that Hailey had gotten of her, she'd seen no restraints on Colleen, but her sister had looked surprised to see her. Maybe because Colleen had figured they'd be heading toward town and not her direction.

The one good thing in all of this was that Camden and the rest of the people at the ranch were safe. Their attackers hadn't tried to get onto the grounds to continue their rampage there. Even more, Mason had sent additional armed ranch hands to guard Lucas's house. Of course, they wouldn't be able to go outside, but that was better than putting themselves in harm's way.

"Are you okay?" Lucas asked her.

Hailey didn't even try to pretend she was. She just

shook her head and hoped the truth didn't worry him too much. There was already enough worry on his face without her adding more.

Josh pulled to a stop directly in front of the sheriff's office, and Lucas quickly ushered her in. She'd already prepared herself that Minton would be there, and he was. He was also glaring at them.

"I blame you two for this," Minton snapped. "I could have been killed because of you."

Lucas returned the glare. "How do you figure that?"

"You should have already called in the FBI on this. Obviously this is too big an investigation for the locals to handle."

Now that got Grayson glaring, but it was Lucas who took up the argument with Minton.

"And by calling in the FBI, you mean *you*?" Lucas challenged the man. He huffed. "I didn't have a lot of reasons to trust you before this latest fiasco, and this didn't improve things."

"You think I had something to do with this?" Minton howled. He didn't wait for Lucas to answer. "I didn't, and because you're so stubborn about handling this yourself, you put Hailey right back in danger. Is that what you want, huh?"

"I've had enough of him," Hailey managed to whisper. She was barely hanging on by a thread, and she needed a moment to compose herself. Maybe during those moments she'd figure out how to put an end to all of this.

That's all she had to say to Lucas to get him moving. He still had his arm around her waist from when he'd ushered her in from the cruiser, and now he got her moving toward the hall, heading to the break room.

"I'm sorry," she added. "I should have just stood up to him—"

"No, and we shouldn't have stayed in the squad room for as long as we did. It could have been a ploy to keep us near the windows so that the snipers can finish us off."

Mercy. She hadn't even considered that, but she should have. She needed to be thinking clearer because the stakes were sky-high.

"I need to call Colleen again," she said, figuring that Lucas would hand her his phone to do that.

He didn't. He took her into the break room, had her sit on the sofa. "Grayson can talk to Colleen. In fact, he'll bring her in for questioning."

Yes, because her sister was more than just a person of interest. She'd been in the vicinity of a crime scene and had likely deleted those storage files. Grayson no doubt had lots of questions for her. Anything Colleen said at this point should be part of the official investigation. Still, Hailey needed to hear what her sister had to say, and if Grayson couldn't get her in soon, then she'd try again to call her.

Lucas handed her a bottle of water that he took from the fridge. "This will have to do for now, but you probably could use something stronger."

She could indeed use it. And she got it when Lucas dropped down next to her and pulled her into his arms. It was such an unexpected gesture that Hailey went stiff for a moment. Lucas noticed, too.

He eased back a little, glanced down at her. "I know. This isn't a smart thing for me to be doing, but you look ready to drop."

"I am," she admitted. "And you're right about it not being a smart thing."

It brought back the memories of when they'd been lovers, and Hailey didn't have the energy to fend off those old images. Or the heat, which wasn't old at all. Anytime she was around Lucas, that heat flared up with a vengeance. Now was no different.

"I'm also scared," she admitted. "For Camden. For you. For all of us."

He didn't try to dismiss those fears. He couldn't. Because they were real. The danger just kept coming at them.

Lucas made a sound of agreement and eased his hold on her a little. Hailey was certain he would just pull away. But he didn't. He stayed there right next to her, and he slowly turned his head to look at her again. Since she was already looking at him, their gazes met. Held.

The air was suddenly so still it felt as if everything was holding its breath, waiting. Hailey certainly was. She had no idea where Lucas was going to take this, but she knew what she wanted.

She wanted him.

Hailey saw that want in Lucas's eyes. Saw the storm that was brewing there, too. He hadn't forgiven her for what she'd done. Probably didn't completely trust her, either, but that didn't stop this attraction.

He cursed. His voice hardly had any sound. And she saw the storm get much stronger as he lowered his head and touched his mouth to hers. It was barely a kiss, but it caused that fire inside her to blaze out of control. A simple kiss from Lucas could do that.

And then he did more. Much, much more. His mouth

came to hers again, and this time it was for more than just a touch. He kissed her. Really kissed her.

His taste was a reminder of all those memories and images she'd been battling since she'd come out of the coma. A battle she was losing because the memories came flooding back and mixed with this new firestorm that the kiss was creating.

A sound rumbled in his chest. Definitely not one of agreement this time. It was one of protest and a reminder of a different sort. He didn't want to be doing this, but like her, he seemed helpless to stop it.

The kiss lingered on a moment. Then two. And just when Hailey was ready to pull him even closer Lucas stopped.

"I think I've complicated things enough for one day," he grumbled.

That made her smile even though there wasn't anything to smile about. What he'd said was the truth. The kiss had complicated things. Heck, being together upped the complications, as well, but until they found a way to put an end to the danger, they were joined at the hip.

And afterward…well, Hailey wasn't ready to go there just yet, though she knew a future without danger also meant a future in which Lucas and she had to work out a custody arrangement for Camden.

There was a knock at the door, and a moment later Grayson opened it. He stared at them, and even though he didn't say anything about how close they were sitting, he probably noticed that they looked as if they'd just been doing something they shouldn't have been doing.

"Everything okay?" Grayson asked.

"I was about to ask you the same thing." Lucas got to his feet. "Bad news?"

Grayson lifted his shoulder. "Josh filled me in on the details of the attack. Two of the deputies just arrived in the area where those snipers were. They're not there, of course, but there are tire tracks. It's a long shot, but CSI might be able to get a match from them if they were driving a custom vehicle. The gunmen might have left prints or trace evidence behind as well."

That seemed like such a long shot, but everything was at this point. "What about the black SUV?" Hailey asked.

Grayson shook his head. "No sign of it, either. I don't guess either of you got the license plate numbers?"

"No," Lucas and she said in unison.

Hailey added a sigh. Again, she wasn't thinking straight. The shock of seeing her sister had prevented her from looking at the plates. Plus, Josh had been so fast at turning the cruiser around that she'd barely managed a glimpse of Colleen, much less any specifics about the SUV.

"Any luck getting in touch with my sister?" Hailey wanted to know.

"No. I've left her a message, and San Antonio PD will go out to her place and see if she's there."

She wouldn't be. In fact, Colleen was likely on the run right now, and there was no telling when she'd surface.

"Minton finally left," Grayson went on. "But we haven't seen the last of him."

"No, we haven't," Lucas agreed. "Either he's the most persistent FBI agent in the state or else he's dirty."

Yes, too bad they didn't know which. Because if

Minton was clean, then he might truly be able to help them with this investigation.

"I know you wanted to lure out the person who's doing all of this, but we'll have to put the trap on hold for a little while," Grayson added. "I need all the reserve deputies out looking for that SUV and dealing with the snipers."

Understandable. He had a new crime scene to process.

"Is Eric still here?" Lucas asked.

"No. He's at the DA's office getting a copy of the plea deal." Grayson paused, looked at Hailey. "If you're feeling up to it, you need to come to my office. We have Preston's recordings set up in there, and we listened to something else that you should hear."

LUCAS CERTAINLY HADN'T forgotten about the recordings that Eric had given Grayson. After all, that was one of the reasons Hailey and he had been on their way to the sheriff's office.

The other reason they had come was to set that trap that was now on hold. No way did Grayson have enough manpower to cover protecting the reserve deputy, and there'd been enough people put at risk today without adding that.

"You're sure you're steady enough to do this now?" Lucas asked her as they made their way to Grayson's office.

She nodded, didn't stop walking. He suspected Hailey was nowhere near *steady*. Not so soon after nearly being killed. But it was clear she was going to steel herself up and listen to what he hoped would give them information they could actually use. As opposed to information that would just make Hailey feel worse than she already did.

Grayson had two laptops in his office, and Josh was listening to one with headphones. Since there were hours of recordings, there was no telling how long it would take to go through them all.

"I've loaded the recordings into audio files that we can access from several computers," Grayson explained, and he hit the play button, motioning for Hailey and Lucas to sit. "This is the first conversation that's connected to you," he added, looking at Hailey. "It was recorded about two weeks before the start of Preston's trial."

It didn't take long before Lucas heard a man's voice. Preston, no doubt. "We need to do something about your sister," he said.

"I could talk to Laura." It was Colleen who responded. Lucas recognized her voice from the phone conversation she'd had with Hailey.

"Talking won't help," Preston snapped. "She could send me away for life. Is that what you want?"

"No. Of course not." Colleen paused for several seconds. "What do you want me to do?"

Preston, however, didn't hesitate. "Find something I can use against her, something to neutralize her."

"There wasn't anything to find," Colleen insisted. "Nothing illegal, anyway."

"Then make Laura believe that I'll hurt you if she doesn't back off. She loves you. She'll protect you. If that doesn't work, plant something that'll get her to stop."

"Plant what?" Colleen asked.

"Anything illegal. I don't care what, just something

to make the cops think she's trying to cover up her own crimes by pinning them on me. You're a whiz with the computer, so hack into hers and see what you can do."

Grayson hit the pause button and turned to Hailey. "I'm guessing this is the first you're hearing of any of this?"

Hailey nodded. "I knew Colleen didn't want me to testify against Preston, but she never said anything about this false threat of making me think he would hurt her."

"Maybe because Colleen thought something like that wouldn't work with you?" Grayson pressed.

"No. It might have worked." Then Hailey groaned softly. "But I wouldn't have just stopped pursuing Preston. I would have just figured out a way to keep Colleen safe."

Lucas hoped Hailey would have done that by going to the cops. She didn't know him then. They hadn't met until after Preston's trial and after she'd entered WITSEC, but she'd obviously been working with some cops that she'd trusted.

"As far as I know," Hailey continued, "Colleen didn't plant anything illegal on my computer." She took a deep breath as if to steady her nerves. This was no doubt only adding salt to the wounds, but Lucas knew this wasn't the last of the things she probably wouldn't want to hear.

"Preston and Colleen sound *friendly*," Lucas commented. "Just how friendly were they?"

"I don't know for sure, but since Colleen didn't do what Preston wanted her to do—I mean, by planting something to frame me—then maybe they weren't as friendly as Preston seems to think they were."

Lucas latched right onto that. "You think Colleen was afraid of him?"

Another headshake from Hailey. Then a shrug. "Maybe, but Colleen never gave any indication of that."

"Of course, we haven't had a chance to listen to all the recordings," Grayson said. "But so far there's nothing about Colleen being afraid. Nothing about the specific nature of Colleen and Preston's relationship, either." He paused. "In fact, I'm betting that the recordings have been edited with parts cut out."

"You think Eric did that?" Lucas asked.

"Maybe. But it could have just as well been Colleen or Preston. The CSI lab is analyzing the originals to see if there have been any alterations. If not, it makes the second recording—well—all the more interesting. It's the last one, made the final day of Preston's trial. He was out on bond, but since he was convicted just a few hours later and put in jail, he didn't have a chance to go home again."

Grayson pressed the play button again, and like on the other recording, Lucas immediately heard Colleen's voice. "It's true. Hailey does have something incriminating on Eric. I'm not sure exactly what, but she won't use it against him. She wants to hold it over your head to make sure you don't go after her."

Preston cursed. "If I end up behind bars, you need to fix that for me. Swear that you will."

"I will," Colleen answered without hesitation.

"You'll also need to pay your sister back for what she's doing to me," Preston continued. "Understand?"

Again, Colleen didn't hesitate. "I understand."

Even though Hailey didn't make a sound, Lucas could see her body tense, and he put his hand over hers.

It must have felt like a punch to the gut to hear her sister basically say that she would get revenge for Preston. Was that what the attacks were all about? Payback?

Colleen didn't say anything else because Preston's phone rang. "I need you to step out while I take this call," he told her. He didn't continue for several seconds, probably until Colleen had left. "How's my favorite FBI agent?" Preston said to the caller. There was plenty of sarcasm in his voice. "Have you tied up the loose ends for me?"

Lucas moved closer to the computer so that he wouldn't miss a word. This had to be the dirty agent.

"Please tell me that Preston gives us a name during this conversation," Lucas said to Grayson.

"Sorry, there's no mention of a name, but there's other info that might be able to help us ID him."

Good. Lucas kept listening.

"If the worst happens and I'm convicted," Preston continued, "go to my bank in San Antonio and destroy everything in the safe deposit box."

Too bad they couldn't hear how the agent responded to that, but Lucas knew what Grayson meant about that *other info*. "You're getting surveillance footage from Preston's bank?"

Grayson nodded. "It'll take a while, though, because I need a court order." Which he would get for something like this. Eric might have been telling the truth when he said the recordings could help them arrest Minton.

"One final thing," Preston said to the caller. "If Colleen doesn't take care of the situation, I want you to kill Laura."

Lucas didn't think it was his imagination that Hailey became even paler than she already was, and he did more than hold her hand this time. He slipped his arm around her. Yes, she already knew someone was trying to kill her, but it was hard to hear it spelled out like that. But Hailey eased out of his grip and reached for the phone.

"I'm calling my sister," she insisted, snatching up Grayson's desk phone and putting it on speaker.

No one stopped her, mainly because Lucas didn't expect Colleen to answer. But she did. She answered on the first ring.

"I just heard proof that Preston asked you to kill me," Hailey said without issuing a greeting. "Don't bother to deny it. What I want to know is if you're carrying through on his wishes."

"No." Colleen's voice was shaky, and she didn't jump right into an explanation. She took several moments. "I couldn't go through with it."

"You're sure about that?" Lucas snapped. "You were near the ranch today when there was another attack."

"I was lured there." Colleen paused again. A long time. "I thought I was meeting someone who could give me information. But it turned out to be a hoax."

"What kind of information?" Hailey demanded.

More hesitation. "About this nightmare that's happening. Hailey, I'm so sorry, but I'm not behind the attacks. Things haven't always been good between you and me, but I'm not a killer."

"Then who is?" Hailey pressed. "Who's the dirty agent who was working for Preston? Is it Minton?"

"Maybe." Colleen gave a heavy sigh. "I wish I could say it's him, but I'm not sure there is an agent. Not a real one, anyway. I think it could have been one of Eric's henchmen posing as an agent."

Interesting. This was the first Lucas was hearing of this possibility. "Why would you say that?"

"Some things just aren't adding up, and I think Eric duped Preston into believing he had an agent on the take. I also believe Eric might have used that fake agent to spy on his father. I'm so sorry," Colleen repeated.

Lucas heard something in her voice. Guilt maybe. Maybe fear.

It wasn't fear, though, that he saw on Hailey's face. It was pure frustration. Something he felt as well. Because Colleen was stalling, and he wanted to know why.

"Why did you erase the files that Hailey had on Eric?" Lucas demanded.

"I swear, I didn't have a choice."

Lucas huffed. "That's not an answer. Why did you do it?"

Colleen hesitated again before a hoarse sob tore from her mouth. "Because it was part of the ransom demand."

Lucas looked at Hailey to see if she knew what the heck Colleen was talking about. Clearly she didn't.

"A ransom?" Hailey questioned.

Colleen sobbed again. "For my baby with Preston."

And with that, Colleen ended the call.

Chapter Eleven

A baby.

Hailey sat there for a moment, stunned with the news her sister had just dropped on them, and then she pressed Redial. Colleen didn't answer. The call went straight to voice mail.

"Colleen could be lying," Lucas pointed out.

Yes. This could all be some kind of ploy to make them believe that her sister was being manipulated into doing these things. But it was also possible.

"Preston and she could have had an affair." Hailey was talking more to herself than anyone specific, but it prompted Grayson to take out his phone.

"I'll have someone run a search of birth certificates," Grayson explained. "Any idea how old a baby would be if it exists?"

Even though the thoughts were racing in Hailey's head, she forced herself to think. "Preston went to prison eighteen months ago, so unless he had conjugal visits, the baby would have to be at least nine months old. But possibly older. Colleen never said anything about being pregnant, though."

Not exactly surprising, because Colleen and she

hadn't been on the best terms when Hailey had entered WITSEC.

"If there really is a baby, then Eric could have kidnapped it to get Colleen to cooperate," Lucas suggested. "*If*," he emphasized.

Yes, that was a big if. But even if Colleen did have a child, that didn't mean it was Preston's. She could have gotten pregnant by someone else after he went to prison.

Grayson was still on the phone, but Hailey heard a familiar voice coming from the squad room. And she groaned. It was Minton, and she didn't want to go another round with him today. Obviously, though, that's what was going to happen, because he was demanding to see Lucas and her.

"I'll handle this," Lucas said, getting to his feet.

It was tempting to let him do just that, but Hailey got up as well so she could see what had prompted this latest visit from one of their suspects. Of course, he was no longer at the top of her list because Colleen was now in that particular spot.

"I'm getting a court order for those recordings," Minton informed them the moment he caught sight of them. "My boss will be here any minute with it. You need to turn over copies of those recordings Eric gave you along with the files you have on Eric. And I want them now."

"We'll just wait for that court order if you don't mind," Lucas answered. "Even if you do mind, we'll wait."

Hailey had no idea if there really was a court order or if this was a bluff on Minton's part. But she could clear up one thing for him now. "My sister hacked into my online storage and erased the info I had on Eric."

Minton's eyes were already narrowed, and they stayed that way. "You expect me to believe that?"

She lifted her shoulder. "I don't care what you believe, but it's the truth."

Now Minton cursed. "No way would Colleen help Eric."

Not voluntarily. But Hailey had to rethink that, too. With all the possible lies being bantered about, Hailey had no idea if Colleen even despised Eric.

"Why would Colleen have done something like that?" Minton pressed.

Hailey looked at Lucas to see if he had an opinion on how much or how little she should say, and he took the lead from there.

"Colleen perhaps had a child who's been kidnapped. You know anything about that?" Lucas asked.

Hailey carefully watched Minton's reaction, and now his eyes widened in disbelief. Or perhaps he was faking that response. Because if someone had indeed taken Colleen's child, it could have been Minton. Yes, Eric had a stronger motive, but Minton could have done it to force Colleen to do whatever was necessary to make sure his crimes weren't revealed.

Anything, including those attacks to murder Hailey.

"This is the first I'm hearing of a child," Minton answered. "It's true?"

"We're trying to confirm it now," Lucas assured him.

Minton took out his phone. "I want to talk to Colleen. Where is she?"

Hailey shook her head. "Your guess is as good as mine."

It didn't surprise her that Minton had Colleen's number in his phone. After all, her sister was part of the investigation into Preston. And now Eric. It also didn't surprise her when Colleen didn't answer.

"I'll have someone from the bureau look for her," Minton said, and he fired off a text.

Finding Colleen still wasn't within the FBI's jurisdiction, but at this point Hailey just wanted her sister found so she could be brought in for questioning. She only hoped that whoever Minton had contacted wasn't as dirty as he possibly could be.

"What do you know about this so-called kidnapping?" Minton continued when he'd finished the text.

"Not much." Lucas took out his own phone. "But let me talk to someone who might know."

Hailey wasn't sure who he was going to call. When Lucas put the phone on speaker, though, the DA's office answered, and he asked to speak to Eric.

"Tell me about Colleen's baby," Lucas said the moment Eric came on the line.

"What baby?" Eric snapped.

He seemed as surprised as Minton had been. Of course, it was possible neither man had had much personal contact with her sister, so their reactions might have been genuine.

"Colleen claims someone kidnapped her baby with Preston," Lucas explained. "Was it you?"

Eric's profanity was even worse than Minton's had been earlier. "She's lying. She's doing this to get money from Preston's estate. Well, it won't work. He left everything to me in his will."

Hailey figured that was true, and maybe that was her sister's motive for this. Of course, if Colleen truly had been having an affair with Preston, then he'd probably arranged to have her receive some money before he was killed in prison. At least Hailey hoped that was the case. No way, though, would Eric want Colleen or anyone else, for that matter, to have a dime of his father's money. Eric hated Preston, but he loved the big bucks and trust fund that came with the family name.

"I want to talk to Colleen," Eric practically shouted.

"Welcome to the club," Lucas grumbled, and without even saying goodbye, he ended the call.

Minton jabbed his finger toward Lucas's phone. "That doesn't prove Eric's innocent. No way would he admit to kidnapping his half sibling. If a baby really exists, that is."

"A baby does exist," Grayson said as he came out of his office. For four little words, he got everyone's attention. He came into the squad room before he continued. "According to Texas Vital Statistics, Colleen gave birth to a daughter eleven months ago. Her name is Isabel."

The emotions flooded through Hailey. She had a niece. Colleen had been telling the truth. About that, anyway.

"And the father?" Hailey asked.

Grayson shook his head. "No name's on the birth certificate. In Texas, Colleen would have needed written consent to include the father's name."

Maybe because it would have been too much trouble to get the consent with Preston in jail. Or perhaps Preston wasn't the father after all.

"So, where's the baby?" Minton asked, his attention volleying among Grayson, Lucas and Hailey.

None of them had an answer. Only Colleen could give them that information, and they had to find her first. But if her niece had indeed been kidnapped, Hailey wanted to help. Especially now that she was a mother herself, she couldn't stomach the thought of a baby being taken.

"I'm sorry," Lucas said to her, his voice a soothing whisper. So was the slight touch on her arm.

She looked up at him, their gazes connecting, and the look he gave her was comforting, as well. For a second or two. Then he must have remembered that it wouldn't take much for the comforting to turn to something more.

The fire.

No, it wouldn't take much at all, and now wasn't the time for that. Maybe there'd never be time. Because, like now, Lucas would continue to fight this attraction. No way did he want to go another emotional round with her, especially since she wasn't in any position to renew a relationship.

Hailey cleared her throat, hoping that would clear her head, as well. "I'll try to call Colleen again. If she doesn't answer, I can leave a voice mail so she'll know I found out I have a niece."

She turned to go back into Grayson's office to do that, but the sound of the door opening stopped her. Hailey braced herself for another visit from Eric, but it was a bulky, dark-haired man she didn't recognize. Apparently neither did Lucas, because he instantly stepped in front of her and drew his gun.

But their visitor had a gun, too. And a badge.

"You can put your weapon away," Minton insisted. "This is FBI Agent Derrick Wendell."

Judging from the now smug look on Minton's face, this was someone he wanted to see, and it didn't take Hailey long to figure out why.

"Sheriff Ryland?" Agent Wendell asked, looking at Grayson. When Grayson nodded, Wendell took a paper from his pocket. "This is a court order. You're to turn over the recordings and all evidence that's connected to Eric DeSalvo."

Grayson mumbled some profanity under his breath and took the court order to read through it. However, Hailey figured it was legit.

"The FBI has been conducting a long-time investigation into Eric and his business operations," Wendell continued. "We have reason to believe some of these operations have crossed into other states, making it a federal case."

Lucas looked at her, and even though he didn't say anything, Hailey knew what he wanted to ask her. Did she know about any of Eric's illegal interstate deals? She didn't.

But that didn't mean there weren't any.

She shook her head and was about to tell Minton and Wendell that, but Wendell's attention went to her next. "Hailey Darrow." He didn't wait for her to confirm that. "I'm here to take you into custody."

"WHAT THE HELL do you mean by that?" Lucas growled.

Even though Lucas glared at the agent, Wendell only shrugged as if the answer were obvious. It wasn't. Not to Lucas, anyway.

"Miss Darrow is a material witness in this federal investigation. Plus, someone's trying to kill her. One of Eric's henchmen, no doubt. The FBI intends to put her in custody and keep her safe so she can testify against him."

"She's already in protective custody—mine," Lucas argued. No way was he letting Hailey go with this clown. "There's proof on the recordings that Preston was dealing with a dirty agent. How do I know that agent isn't you? Or him?" he added, tipping his head to Minton.

Judging from the way Minton's face went red, he didn't appreciate that. Apparently neither did Wendell, because he scowled. But it was going to take a lot more than riled FBI agents to get Lucas to hand her over.

"I'm not dirty," Wendell insisted. "And you haven't done a good job of protecting Hailey so far."

"I'm alive." She stepped out from behind Lucas. "I'd say that's a good job, considering that someone's been trying to kill me from practically the moment I came out of a coma."

No, he hadn't done a good job. Because if he had, Lucas would have already found the person responsible for the attacks. Though he did appreciate Hailey standing up for him. But part of him didn't like it, either.

Hell. They were on the same side of this argument, and that was tearing down more barriers between them. Barriers that Lucas wanted in place until he'd worked out a whole lot of things with Hailey. Including her intentions for custody of Camden.

"Hailey can't go with you," Grayson told the agents. "I haven't even interviewed her about the attacks."

"Again, our jurisdiction," Minton argued right back.

"Possibly," Grayson said. "But the attacks might not even be related to Eric. Or the dirty agent. This could be connected to some other things that went on in Silver Creek prior to Hailey's coma."

"What things?" Wendell challenged.

"I'm not at liberty to discuss that with you right now. But it's not federal."

Grayson was sticking up for them. Sticking his neck

out, too, since he could be hit with obstruction of justice if the agents could prove he was stonewalling them. Which Grayson was. But he was also buying Hailey some time. She'd already been through hell and back and definitely didn't need to be around someone who might be trying to kill her.

Minton huffed, put his hands on his hips. "Then go ahead. Interview her. Do what you need to do, but she'll be coming with us when you're done."

Grayson shook his head. "Not anytime soon." He glanced at the court order. "This applies only to the recordings, which you can have. But there's no mention of Hailey being forced to be in your *safekeeping*." There was plenty of sarcasm on that last word.

The muscles in Minton's jaw stirred, and he turned toward his fellow agent. "Get the paperwork for Hailey. I'll get the recordings."

Wendell didn't jump to leave. He glanced at all of them as if trying to figure out how to resolve this without attempting to convince a judge that it was a necessity for him to take Hailey into forced custody. But he must have realized this wasn't an argument he could win with the Ryland lawmen, because he issued a terse "I'll be back" and headed out.

"Give me the recordings now," Minton said the moment Wendell was gone. "But Hailey doesn't leave the building until Wendell gets back."

Grayson nodded, headed to his office to get them. Giving up the recordings was no big deal since Grayson had made copies of them, but Lucas needed to make sure that Wendell didn't find a judge to do Minton and Wendell's bidding. He took Hailey by the arm and led her to the break room.

Lucas called one of his fellow Rangers and asked him to keep an eye on Wendell for him, and once he'd done that, he saw to Hailey. Who was obviously even more shaken up.

"Please don't let him take me," she said, her voice with hardly any sound.

"I won't." But Lucas only hoped it didn't come to a legal showdown between them and the FBI.

He sat on the sofa next to her, and because he thought they could both use it, he made a FaceTime call to the nanny. It was something he did often while away on business so he'd be able to see his son—if not in person, then at least on the screen.

"Is everything okay?" Tillie asked the moment she answered.

"Fine," Lucas lied. Of course, Tillie must have known it was a lie, but she managed a smile.

"Camden's sleeping," she said, whispering, "but I'll carry the phone to the nursery so you can get a peek."

Hailey moved closer to him, her attention glued to the screen, and she was holding her breath. A breath she released when Camden came into view.

The baby was sleeping, all right. He was on his side, a blue blanket draped over him. Tillie moved the phone closer to his face so they could have a better look.

Hailey touched her fingers to her lips for a moment. "I wish I were there to hold him."

Yeah. So did Lucas. Being away from his son created a horrible ache in his chest. "Maybe soon," Lucas told Hailey, and he hoped that was true. He didn't want this mess with the FBI to drag on so they'd be stuck here in the sheriff's office.

Even though Camden wasn't moving and certainly

nowhere near being awake, Hailey and he continued to watch him for several minutes.

Lucas thanked Tillie before he ended the call. "We'll check in again with her in a couple of hours, when Camden will be awake," he added to Hailey.

She nodded, and he figured she was trying to look a lot braver than she felt. "You're being nice to me," she said.

He wasn't sure how to respond to that, so Lucas didn't say anything. Big mistake. Because his silence caused Hailey to look up at him. Normally her looking at him wouldn't be a big deal, but they were close. Side by side. Arms touching. With their emotions running sky-high, something as simple as a look could become a trigger for this attraction.

And it was.

Lucas felt the slam of heat go through him, and before he could remind himself that kissing Hailey would be a dumber-than-dirt sort of thing to do, he lowered his head and put his mouth to hers.

He'd thought that the attraction between them couldn't get any hotter, but he had been wrong. It did, and along with the fire came the need. A need that his body remembered only a couple of seconds into the kiss. That fire and need were what had started this whole ordeal with Hailey. Apparently the ordeal was going to continue, too. Because he certainly didn't stop kissing her.

Hailey didn't stop, either. In fact, a soft sound rumbled in her throat. A sound filled with the same need and heat that Lucas was feeling. She slipped her hand around the back of his neck, pulled him closer. Not that he needed much encouragement for that, because Lucas was already moving in on her.

He deepened the kiss, took hold of her shoulder and dragged her against him. Great. Now they were body to body with the kiss raging on and on until finally he had to stop just so they could catch their breaths.

She looked at him again, silently questioning whether this was a good idea. It wasn't. But that didn't stop Lucas from going back for a second kiss. It didn't help, of course. But this time he stopped not because of air. If he didn't stop, he was going to drag her upstairs. There was an apartment up there. With a bed.

Definitely not good.

Kissing had already added too many complications to this mix, and sex would spin those complications out of control.

He was about to apologize to her, but Grayson opened the door to the break room. Hell. One look at his face and Lucas knew something was wrong.

"The FBI isn't taking Hailey," Lucas jumped to say.

Grayson shook his head. "Not yet, anyway. No, this is about Colleen."

Hailey slowly got to her feet. "What happened?"

"There's something you need to see." Grayson motioned for them to follow him, and he led them to his office.

Thankfully, Minton wasn't there. He was still across the hall in the squad room, pacing, and judging from his expression, he was riled about something other than not getting his way about taking Hailey.

"If that's something that pertains to the FBI's investigation," Minton called out, "then I want to see it."

"It's not about the investigation," Grayson assured him. "This is a family matter." Once Hailey, Lucas and he were inside the office, Grayson locked the door, no doubt to stop the agent from barging in.

Josh was no longer in the room listening to those recordings. Or rather, the copies of the recordings. Grayson had no doubt put him in one of the interview rooms.

"What's going on?" Lucas asked, but he was almost afraid to hear the answer.

Grayson tipped his head to his desk. There was a padded envelope, opened, along with several papers. "This just arrived by courier," he explained. "There's no name on it, but I've already called the courier's office and asked them to tell me who sent it."

Lucas went closer, Hailey following right behind him, and he saw the first piece of paper. It appeared to be test results.

"DNA," Grayson supplied. "According to the person who sent it, this proves that Isabel is Colleen's baby."

"Does the test really prove it?" Hailey immediately asked.

Grayson lifted his shoulder. "This sort of thing can be faked, but it looks real. It has both the baby's DNA and a sample apparently retrieved from Colleen. Josh is calling the lab to verify." He wore a plastic glove when he moved aside the test results to show them what was beneath.

A photo.

Of a baby girl.

Hailey leaned in even closer, her gaze combing over the picture. She nodded. "The baby definitely resembles Colleen."

Of course, they'd known Colleen had a child, but Lucas figured all of this was leading to something bad.

It was.

"This was the final thing in the envelope," Grayson said, showing them another piece of paper. "It's a ransom demand—for a quarter of a million. But there's another demand. The kidnappers say if Hailey doesn't personally turn over everything she has on the De-Salvo investigation, then Colleen will never see the child again."

Chapter Twelve

Hailey heard every word of what Grayson said. Saw it, too, written in the ransom demand. But it still took a moment to sink in.

Mercy.

If this was real, then her niece could be in grave danger. It didn't matter that she'd never seen the child. Hailey still loved her and wanted to protect her.

"No," Lucas said before Hailey could speak. "You're not going to do this."

Since she was about to tell him that she would indeed do it, he'd obviously known what she was thinking. "I have the money in savings. It's from my father's life insurance. I've never spent any of it, and it's in a bank in San Antonio."

"The money's not the problem," Lucas argued.

Yes, she knew what he meant. It was the *personally* part of the demand. Someone wanted her dead, and this could be a trap to lure her out into the open.

"But we can't just let them disappear with the baby," she snapped. What she felt was pure frustration because Lucas and she were both right. She couldn't go out to deliver anything, but she also couldn't just give up on getting back the baby.

"Just sit," Grayson suggested to her. "We'll work this out somehow."

His phone buzzed, and he lifted his finger in a wait-a-second gesture. Since the caller had gotten Grayson's full attention, Hailey figured it had to be about the kidnapping.

"Eric or Minton could have taken the baby," Hailey tossed out there.

Lucas nodded. "Or this could be something Colleen concocted. We don't know what her real motives are."

True, but it sickened her to think that her sister might be using her own child to do whatever it was she was trying to do. Plain and simple, maybe this was about the money.

"Even though my mother adopted Colleen, she didn't leave Colleen any money from her life insurance," Hailey told Lucas. "She and my mother were on the outs at the time of her death, and she left it solely to me. I offered to share it with Colleen, but she was so angry at being cut out of the will that she refused."

"Was Colleen angry enough to do something like pretending to kidnap her own daughter?"

Hailey had to shrug. "Colleen was always angry about a lot of things. Still…this doesn't feel like something she'd do."

Of course, she'd been wrong about Colleen before. She hadn't thought her sister would delete those files she'd stashed away about Eric. Which was a reminder that she didn't have a key part of what the kidnappers were demanding.

"If we can work out a deal with the kidnappers so I don't personally have to deliver their demands, I'll need to put together some fake files to give them."

Lucas didn't give her his opinion on that because Grayson finished his call and turned to them. "That was the agency for the courier who delivered the package. The person paid in cash, and according to his driver's license, his name is Eldon Silverton. It's fake," Grayson quickly added.

Hailey didn't even bother to groan because it had been such a long shot, anyway. She seriously doubted that the kidnappers would have used someone who could be identified and therefore linked back to them. Or rather, linked back to the person who'd orchestrated all of this.

"What about security cameras?" Lucas asked. "Does the courier agency have them?"

Grayson shook his head. "I think we've struck out with the courier. With the lab, too, because it was Darrin Sandmire who ordered the lab results."

Darrin was the man who'd tried to kill her the night she'd been put in a coma. According to Colleen, he'd been behind the attack shortly after Hailey left the hospital.

Darrin was also dead.

So, yes, that meant they had indeed struck out since they couldn't question Darrin about it. But something about that didn't make sense.

"Why would the person behind the kidnapping use Darrin for this?" she asked. "Why not just use someone with a fake ID?"

"It was to convince us that this is real," Lucas answered, and it prompted Grayson to nod. Thankfully, Lucas continued with his explanation, because Hailey wasn't following this. "We know Darrin's a thug. *Was* a thug. The kidnappers wanted us to understand that a thug like this was involved. That way, we could be sure the baby was truly in danger."

All of that made sense, but it also tightened the knot in her stomach. Because if a snake like Darrin had been involved, there was no telling who had the baby now.

"Let me take care of Minton," Grayson said. "And then we'll try to contact Colleen again. From now on, any conversation with her needs to be recorded."

And Hailey knew why. Her sister might be involved in this crime in some way, and anything Colleen said might lead them to the truth.

When Grayson unlocked the door and threw it open, Minton was standing right there. It was possible he'd heard some or even all of what they'd said, and he clearly wasn't happy about being excluded.

"You need to leave," Grayson ordered him before Minton could get out a word. Lucas went to his cousin's side. "Until you have papers putting Hailey in FBI custody, you have no right to be here," Grayson added.

Minton had never been a happy-looking person, and Grayson's words only made it worse. "I'm an FBI agent."

"Which gives you no right to be here. This is the sheriff's office, and last I checked, I'm the sheriff. You're leaving, and that's not a request. You can come back when and only when you have something to convince me to turn over Hailey to you."

Minton still didn't budge. He threw glances at all of them, his glare lingering on Hailey for a few long moments.

"You'll regret this," Minton said, and it sounded like a threat. He turned and stormed out.

Grayson and Lucas stood in the doorway and watched the man leave, and they didn't move until Hailey heard the front door slam.

"Make sure he doesn't come back," Grayson told one of the deputies.

He returned to his desk, handed Hailey the phone and put the recorder right next to it. Hailey pressed in the number, and it rang. And rang.

Her heart dropped when it went to voice mail.

"Colleen, I need to talk to you right away," Hailey said once she was able to leave a message. "We got a ransom demand from the kidnappers of your baby. Please call me back ASAP."

She was about to put the phone away, but it rang before she could do it. Hailey answered it as soon as Grayson hit the record button again, and she immediately heard her sister's voice.

"The kidnappers got in touch with you?" Colleen asked. "How? When?" She certainly sounded like a mother who'd had her child taken.

"A package was delivered to the Silver Creek Sheriff's Office," Lucas answered. "There's a demand for a quarter of a million and any info Hailey has on the DeSalvo family. They want her to deliver everything to them herself. Now, who's behind the kidnapping?"

"I don't know. I swear, I don't. But I'll pay them whatever it takes to get back my baby. Where and when do they want Hailey to make the drop?"

Colleen made this sound as if it were a done deal, that Hailey would indeed be involved in the exchange, but Hailey figured no way would Lucas let that happen.

"We'll go over all the details with you," Lucas said. "But only if you come here to the sheriff's office. I have some questions for you."

Hailey guessed that Colleen would come up with an excuse as to why that couldn't happen. After all, she'd stonewalled them practically from the start of this nightmare. And her sister did hesitate for a couple of seconds.

"All right," Colleen answered. "I'm just up the street and can be there in a few minutes. But please come out and watch for me. Draw your gun, too. Because when I come out in the open, they'll try to kill me."

"Who's trying to kill you and why?" Lucas snapped. But he was talking to himself, because Colleen had already hung up.

Hell. It didn't make sense that someone was trying to kill Colleen. Especially not the kidnappers. They'd probably want her alive so she would push Hailey to pay the ransom.

Maybe.

And maybe the idea was to kill Hailey when she delivered the money and files. Then, also murder Colleen so that anything the sisters had learned about the DeSalvo family would die with them. Of course, that theory worked only if Colleen was innocent. The jury was out on that. Still, Lucas couldn't risk her being gunned down if she was truly out to rescue her child.

"Wait here," Lucas warned Hailey.

She took hold of his arm. "It's too risky for you to go out there." The very thing she'd said to him when he was meeting Minton at the ranch.

That hadn't turned out so well, but Hailey must have realized they didn't have much of a choice about this, because her grip melted off him. "Just be careful," she added.

There was plenty of emotion in her voice, and Lucas didn't think all that emotion was related only to what was about to happen. No. That kiss was playing into this. It had deepened things between them. Had upped the stakes. And that wasn't good, because they were both already distracted enough without adding higher stakes.

"I mean it," Lucas warned her. "Stay put."

He headed toward the front door with Grayson following right behind him. Both drew their weapons. However, they didn't actually go outside. They stayed in the doorway, Lucas looking up one side of the street and Grayson the other. One of the deputies hurried to the window. All of them preparing for what might be another attack right on Main Street.

But there was no sound of shots. No sign of Colleen, either. Not at first, anyway, but then Lucas spotted someone on the sidewalk just two buildings up from the sheriff's office. Not Colleen, though.

Eric.

Lucas didn't like the timing of the man's arrival, and apparently Eric didn't like it much, either, when he spotted Grayson's and Lucas's weapons. He cursed as he got closer.

"Are the guns really necessary?" Eric asked.

"They're not for you," Lucas assured him. "There might be gunmen in the area."

That put plenty of alarm on Eric's face. Alarm that he could have been faking, but it still got him running toward them. Lucas considered not letting him in, but if Colleen was innocent and she saw Eric out front, that might send her back into hiding.

"Frisk him," Lucas told the deputy when Eric went into the reception area.

Lucas barely spared Eric a glance. Instead he kept his attention on Main Street, and he finally saw more movement. It was in the same area where Eric had just been. But the person wasn't on the sidewalk but rather peering around the corner of a shop.

Definitely Colleen.

Lucas motioned for her to come to them. She didn't. Not right away. She kept looking around. Not just up and down the streets but also on the rooftops. Colleen definitely seemed concerned about being gunned down. Lucas was concerned about that, as well, but if she was in danger, then that alley wasn't a safe place. Heck, nowhere out in the open was safe.

Colleen finally came out and raced toward them. She was limping, maybe an injury from her car accident, and judging from her expression, she wasn't just afraid but also in pain. The moment she reached the door, Grayson pulled her inside.

"What's he doing here?" she snarled, looking at Eric.

"I could ask you the same thing," Eric countered.

"Take Eric to an interview room," Grayson told the deputy who was still in the process of frisking the man.

"I don't want to be put away in an interview room," Eric protested. "I need to talk to Colleen."

Lucas was about to tell him, "Tough." But Colleen spoke first. "Did you kidnap my baby?"

Her voice was shaking. So was she. And that was no doubt what prompted Hailey to come out of Grayson's office and go to her sister. Something Lucas definitely didn't want her to do. Especially when Eric stepped in front of her. Eric wasn't facing Hailey, though, but rather Colleen.

"You really had a baby?" he demanded.

"Yes," Colleen snapped, "and someone took her. Was it you?"

Eric stared at her as if trying to sort all of this out. Of course, maybe he already had it sorted out if he'd been the one to kidnap the child.

"No. I didn't. Is there DNA proof?" Eric pressed. "Real DNA proof that hasn't been faked by you?"

"There is proof," Grayson verified. "Now, let's all move away from the windows." He pointed to Eric. "You either leave or go in the interview room."

Eric's chin came up. "I'm not leaving until I see solid evidence that I have a half sibling."

"Arrest him," Grayson told the deputy without hesitation. "He's obstructing justice."

Eric howled out a protest, moved out of the deputy's grip. He glared at all of them before he stormed out of the sheriff's office. Good. One less pain to deal with.

"What did the kidnappers send you?" Colleen asked the moment Eric was gone.

But Lucas didn't get a chance to show her. That's because his phone rang, and he saw Unknown Caller on the screen.

Usually not a good sign.

"Record it," Grayson said, and Josh hurried to get a recorder from his desk so that Lucas could do that.

Grayson's phone rang, too, and he stepped into the hall to take it. He motioned for Lucas to go ahead and answer his call. Lucas did, and he put it on speaker.

"Are you ready to talk?" the caller immediately said.

It was a man, but Lucas didn't recognize the voice. "About what?"

"The kids, of course. You want to get them back, right?"

Every muscle in Lucas's body tightened. "Kids?"

"Yeah. Colleen's girl and your boy. We have them both."

Chapter Thirteen

The panic slammed through Hailey so fast that she couldn't speak, couldn't breathe. But she could feel, and what she was feeling was the sheer terror after learning that someone had taken her son.

Lucas didn't respond to the caller. He looked at Grayson, and Hailey could tell from his expression that something had gone wrong.

Oh, God.

"The ranch is under attack," Grayson said, confirming her fears.

"Do they really have Camden?" Lucas asked.

Grayson shook his head, then cursed. "They're sorting that out now. An SUV armed with gunmen broke through the gate. Mason and the others responded, but it's chaos there."

"Told you," the caller taunted.

"They might not have him," Lucas tried to assure her. But he didn't look convinced of that any more than she was.

Hailey wanted to know how in the world this had happened. She wanted to scream, run outside, find the nearest vehicle and hurry to the ranch. Lucas must have known what was going through her mind, because he took hold of her arm and had her sit at the desk next to Josh. No way could she stay put, though. She got up and started pacing.

"Let's just wait for a report from Mason," Lucas told her. He motioned to Josh who was at his desk, and Lucas mouthed, "Try to trace the call."

"Yeah, and Mason will soon tell you that we have the boy," the caller added. "And now it's time to talk about how you get both kids back."

"Prove to me that you've got him first," Lucas insisted. "You sent a picture of the girl, but I don't have anything to convince me that you truly have my son."

"Soon. I'll give you proof before our little exchange happens, and if you do what you're told, I'll give you the kids."

"I swear we'll do whatever you ask," Colleen blurted out. "Just please don't hurt them."

"Nobody will get hurt if you follow my instructions to a T."

Hailey didn't put much trust in a snake who would kidnap babies, but she moved closer to the phone so that she wouldn't miss a word of those instructions. It was so hard to focus, though, with the tornado of bad thoughts going on in her head.

"The price is now a half million," the man said. "All because there are two of them now. Go ahead and start gathering the money. I'll give you an hour—"

"That's not enough time," Lucas interrupted. He was almost certainly stalling the kidnapper to give Josh more time to trace the call. "The money has to come from a bank in San Antonio. It'll take a while for them to pull together that kind of cash."

"All right, you have until morning. And no, don't ask

for more time than that, because it's all you're going to get. Along with the money, Hailey's got to give us the files she has on the DeSalvos."

Files that she didn't have. Because Colleen had deleted them. Colleen opened her mouth, maybe to tell the kidnapper just that, but Hailey shook her head, stopping her. If this man learned that the files were gone, it might compromise the ransom and rescue. Hailey would just come up with some fake files to give them.

But there was something about this particular kidnapper's request that didn't make sense.

Hailey had assumed that Colleen had deleted the files to appease the person who'd kidnapped her baby. If she'd done that, though, then this man wouldn't be demanding them now, because he would know the files no longer existed.

"Hailey won't be delivering anything to you," Lucas argued. "You'll get the money and the files, but someone else will be doing the drop."

The kidnapper paused for several heart-stopping moments. If this man insisted she deliver the goods, she'd have to do it, of course. But it would be a suicide mission. Still, she'd go through with it if it meant Camden and her niece were safe.

"All right," the kidnapper finally said. "Not Hailey."

Hailey's breath swooshed out, but she certainly didn't feel any relief. She waited for the other shoe to drop, and it didn't take long.

"You and Eric DeSalvo will bring the money and the files." The kidnapper's words hung in the air.

Grayson and Lucas exchanged a glance, but she could see Lucas's answer in his eyes before he even spoke. "Why Eric?" he asked.

"Let's just say Eric will be bringing some cash of his own. For those files."

So Eric was being blackmailed. Or at least, according to this man he was.

Lucas huffed. "I'll have to work it out with Eric—"

"Just do it," the kidnapper snapped. "I'll call you back with the drop-off point. Have everything ready to go."

"I got the kidnapper's location from the cell tower," Josh said the moment the man ended the call. "It's coming from Sweetwater Springs. I'll get the sheriff to send someone out there."

Hailey latched onto that like a lifeline. Maybe the sheriff could find them and put an end to this.

While Josh contacted the Sweetwater Springs sheriff, Hailey went to Grayson to see if he'd heard anything about what was happening at the ranch. He had the phone pressed to his ear, and while she could hear someone talking on the other end of the line, she couldn't make out what the person was saying.

Lucas came closer to her, and he slipped his arm around her waist. Waiting. And no doubt praying, as Hailey was doing.

"I'll wait to talk to Eric," Lucas explained.

Yes, but it would have to be done. Well, it would unless they managed to end this kidnapping. But Eric would still have to be brought in to answer questions about whether or not he was being blackmailed about those blasted files.

"I didn't know you two were back together," Colleen said.

Hailey glanced at her sister, ready to explain that it wasn't like that between Lucas and her, but she didn't want to waste the energy. Besides, it seemed a strange observation to make when their children could be in grave danger.

Grayson pressed the end call button, his attention going straight to Lucas and Hailey. "Mason and the ranch hands are closing in on the trespassers. There are three of them. And we still don't know if they took Camden. It shouldn't be long, though, before Mason calls back."

A second was too long, and Hailey's legs suddenly felt ready to give way.

Josh finished his call and joined them just outside Grayson's office. "I know the timing for this is bad, but I found out something about that surveillance footage from the bank."

Hailey certainly hadn't forgotten about that. It was the security feed that was supposed to show the dirty agent Preston had sent to destroy whatever was in his safe deposit box.

"It was Eric," Josh said.

It took Hailey a moment to get what he was saying. "Eric?" she asked. "Why would he be on that footage?"

Josh shrugged. "He'll have to answer that. Have to answer, too, what was in the box, since there's no security footage for that."

Hailey tuned out the rest of what Josh was saying when Grayson's phone rang. The sound shot through the room, shot through her, too, and Grayson answered it as fast as he could. What he didn't do was put the call on speaker. Probably because he wanted to buffer any bad news that he got. But that wasn't a bad news kind of look on his face. He blew out a quick breath.

"Camden's safe," Grayson relayed.

Suddenly she was in Lucas's arms. This time, though, not because of a kiss but because they were both overcome with relief. Relief that Colleen wasn't sharing. She went back into the squad room and sank down into one of the chairs. Hailey hoped she was having that reaction simply because she was still terrified for her daughter and not because her sister had planned this failed kidnapping.

"Is everyone okay?" Lucas asked Grayson.

"Yes. The attackers didn't get into your house. Tillie's shaken up, of course, but she said Camden's too little to know what was going on. She hid with him in the bathroom."

Good. That was probably the safest place for her to have been, but it ripped at Hailey's heart to know that her precious son, the nanny and everyone at the ranch had been put in that kind of danger.

"One of the attackers is dead," Grayson went on. "The other two escaped, but Mason called in help to look for them."

She figured the men were long gone by now, but if they could get an ID on the dead one, it might lead them back to who'd hired him.

"I need to see Camden," Hailey insisted.

Lucas didn't even argue with that. He looked at Grayson. "Can you spare a deputy to go with us?"

"Josh can do it." Grayson didn't get to add more because Lucas's phone rang.

Unknown Caller was on the screen again. Lucas waited until Grayson turned on the recorder before he answered it.

"So, we didn't get your boy," the kidnapper said. It

was the same man who'd called earlier. "Not this time, anyway. But there's always tomorrow."

The muscles tightened in Lucas's jaw, and Hailey could tell he wanted to go through the phone lines and rip this guy to pieces. Hailey did, too. But more than anything, she just wanted to hold her baby and make sure he truly was safe.

"You'll still pay the ransom if you want your sister's kid back," the kidnapper insisted. "Get that money together. Those files, too, and I'll be in touch." And he ended the call.

"I'll have the call analyzed," Grayson volunteered. "To see if he's still in Sweetwater Springs. The three of you go ahead and leave."

"But what about my daughter?" Colleen asked, getting to her feet. "You can't just leave while that monster has her."

"Staying here won't help her," Lucas answered. He hooked his arm around Hailey, and along with Josh, they started toward the door. "When the kidnapper calls with drop-off instructions, I'll come back."

Hailey hoped not. Maybe they could work out a different deal. One that didn't include Lucas, her or anyone in his family. Perhaps Eric could do this solo.

There was a cruiser parked out front, and the three of them hurried to get in it. Josh took the wheel. She thought Lucas would ride in the front, but he got in the backseat with her. He brushed a quick kiss on her forehead. A kiss no doubt of relief, and he kept watch around them. So did Josh.

There was a storm moving in, and the sky was already getting dark, but Hailey hoped the rain would hold off until they made it to the ranch. She didn't want anything to slow them down.

Josh certainly wasn't moving slowly. He was speeding through town, and like Lucas, he was also keeping watch.

"You think Colleen could have been the one to arrange this attack?" Lucas asked. It was a question that hadn't been far from her mind.

"It's possible. But even if she wasn't the mastermind, she could have known about it. Getting Camden could have been part of the kidnappers' demands to her."

Of course, Colleen hadn't said a thing about a demand like that, but it still could have happened. If Colleen was truly desperate to get her daughter back, then she might be willing to do anything. That could include having Camden taken.

Because if the kidnappers had him, they had the ultimate bargaining tool to get Lucas and her to cooperate.

Josh had just made it out of town when Lucas's phone rang again. Hailey hoped it wasn't the kidnapper calling to give them an immediate drop for the ransom. But it was Grayson. Hailey felt a new slam of fear and prayed that nothing else had gone wrong at the ranch.

"Pull over and check the cruiser," Grayson said the moment Lucas answered the call.

"What's wrong?" Josh and Lucas asked in unison.

"It might be nothing, but a waitress from the diner across the street said about thirty minutes ago she saw somebody walking by the cruiser. A man she didn't recognize. She said at one point the guy appeared to drop something, and he stooped down out of sight for a couple of seconds."

"Hell." Lucas added some more profanity as Josh

pulled to the shoulder of the road. "Why didn't she tell you this sooner?"

"She got busy with some customers and just now got a break. Like I said, it might be nothing. I just want to be sure."

Judging from Lucas's and Josh's reactions, though, it could be some kind of tracking device. Or worse.

"I didn't see anyone around the cruiser," Hailey said.

But then, they'd had plenty of distractions with Minton, Eric and Colleen all there. Plus there'd been the calls from the ranch about the attack and those from the kidnapper.

"Stay inside the cruiser until I check it out," Lucas told Josh and her.

She hated that he was going out there again, but Grayson was right. They had to be certain no one had tampered with the vehicle.

Lucas already had his gun drawn, and he stepped out. Josh opened his door, too, no doubt in case this became an ambush. But there really was no place for attackers to hide on this particular stretch of the road. There were no trees, just flat pasture, and the ditches weren't particularly deep. She also couldn't see any vehicles either ahead of or behind them.

Hailey held her breath, waiting as Lucas went around the cruiser. He was moving quickly. Until he got to the rear of the vehicle. Because she was watching him so closely, she saw the instant alarm on his face.

"Get out now!" Lucas shouted. "There's a bomb."

LUCAS FELT HIS heart slam against his chest.

He didn't take the time to kick himself for not checking out the cruiser before hurrying Hailey into it. He should have gone over every inch of it before they left the sheriff's office. But they'd been so eager to get to the ranch and check on Camden, so he hadn't done it.

Now it might cost them their lives.

Josh was out of the vehicle within seconds, mainly because his door was already open, but Hailey was struggling with hers. Lucas threw it open for her, dragging her out, and he started running with her in tow. But they weren't moving nearly fast enough. They had to put some distance between them and the car, so he scooped her into his arms and raced toward the pasture.

They made it only a few yards past the ditch, though.

The blast ripped through the air, throwing them forward and onto the ground. Lucas scrambled to cover Hailey's body with his and hoped that the flying debris didn't kill them.

Chunks of the cruiser came crashing down. Most of the pieces were in flames, and the other jagged shards fell into the pasture all around them.

"Josh?" she said, no doubt checking to make sure he'd gotten out.

He had. Lucas's cousin was on the ground only about two yards away, and from what he could see of him, he didn't have any injuries. In fact, he was already calling for backup.

"Josh is okay," Lucas assured her.

But Hailey was a different matter. When she looked up at him, he saw the two small cuts on her forehead. Probably from the fall. Maybe she hadn't broken any bones or suffered any internal injuries.

He glanced back at the cruiser. What was left of it, anyway. It was now a fireball, and if they'd been inside when that bomb had gone off, they'd all be dead.

"We need to get into the ditch," Lucas told them.

The sound of the blast was still causing his ears to ring, and it was hard to think. However, he didn't need to think hard to know they shouldn't stay out in the open like this. Someone could be coming to finish them off.

He helped Hailey to her feet, and despite the ringing noise, he still heard the grunt of pain she made. She'd need to be checked out by a doctor. First, though, they needed to get out of here.

"Grayson's on the way," Josh relayed.

Good. They were so close to town that it wouldn't take him long to get there, but trouble could arrive ahead of him. Lucas figured whoever had planted that bomb was probably nearby so they could finish them off.

And he was right.

Within seconds after having that thought, he saw the SUV coming up the road from the direction of the town, and Lucas knew they didn't have much time. They had to take cover now. He ran toward the ditch, dropping down into it. It was shallow, too shallow, but it was the only thing they had right now.

"Stay down as far as you can get," he warned Hailey, and both Josh and he got into crouching positions so they could return fire if necessary.

The SUV screeched to a stop just about twenty feet from them. It was hard to see just how many were inside, though, because of the black smoke coming from the cruiser. The gas tank was already gone, so there probably wouldn't be a secondary explosion, but Lucas wanted Hailey to stay down just in case. That's why he cursed when he felt her put her hand in the waist of his jeans and take his backup weapon from his slide holster.

"You might need an extra hand," she insisted.

He didn't have time to argue with her. Didn't want to turn his attention from that SUV for even a second, but he hoped like the devil that she didn't do anything to get herself hurt worse than she already was.

"Can you see how many of them there are?" Lucas asked Josh.

His cousin shook his head and then scurried down the ditch, no doubt to get a better angle. While Josh was still in motion, though, the front passenger door of the SUV flew open. The barrel of a gun appeared.

And the shot came.

Like the explosion, it ripped through the air, and the bullet slammed into the asphalt just a few inches from Lucas and Hailey. He shoved Hailey back down, took aim and returned fire. His shot smacked against the door and sent the gunman ducking back inside the SUV.

But not for long.

The driver lowered his window and started shooting. Not just one shot, either. These came at them. A barrage of bullets that tore right through the mud and dirt in the ditch. Soon it would tear into them, too, if Lucas didn't do something.

He couldn't lift his head for long. Too risky. And if these thugs managed to kill him, then Hailey would be left as easy prey. So Lucas glanced up just long enough to get his aim. Then he lowered his head.

And he fired.

Lucas could tell from the pinging sound of the shots that he was hitting the SUV. Ideally he was hitting the gunmen, as well, but if so, that didn't stop them from continuing to fire.

"Grayson," Hailey said.

It took Lucas a moment to pick through all the noise from the gunshots to hear a welcome sound. A siren. Grayson certainly wasn't making a quiet approach, and Lucas was thankful for it. Thankful because the gunmen stopped firing.

But that wasn't the only thing they did.

Almost immediately, the driver threw the SUV into Reverse and hit the accelerator hard. He sped backward until he reached the dirt path at the edge of the pasture and then spun the SUV around so that it was heading in the opposite direction.

Lucas came out of the ditch and started firing, hoping to shoot out the tires. Just up from him, Josh did the same. But they were too late.

The gunmen were getting away.

Chapter Fourteen

Hailey held Camden close while he slept in her arms. She wasn't sure she would ever want to let go of him again. Lucas and she had come so close to losing him.

So close to making him an orphan, too.

But Hailey didn't want to think about that. She only wanted this time with her son. Of course, Lucas wanted time with him, as well, but he was on the phone, pacing and trying to get more information from Grayson about the attack. Especially more information about who'd been in that SUV.

Since they'd gotten back to his place, Lucas had learned that the camera at the bank on Main Street had captured some footage of the SUV used in the attack. The footage wasn't clear, but the CSI lab might be able to enhance it enough so they could see the license plate number or even their attackers' faces.

Outside, the storm was finally moving in, and the rain was starting to spatter against the windows. The air felt heavy and thick, almost as if it were bearing down on them. It didn't help that the house was nearly dark, too. Lucas had turned off all the lights when they'd gotten in. Probably so anyone watching them wouldn't be able to see their shadows and know where to aim.

Lucas finished his latest call and went to her, sinking down on the sofa next to her. He didn't say anything. He just looked at her. Or rather, he looked at the cuts on her face. Tillie had tended them after Hailey had showered and changed her clothes, but they were no doubt a clear reminder of what'd happened to them.

"I'm sorry this happened," Lucas finally said.

Hailey shook her head. "It's not your fault. Remember, we're in danger because of me."

Admitting it put a lump in her throat. Brought tears to her eyes, too. She blinked them back because it wouldn't do either of them any good for her to break down and cry. Still, she lost the battle fighting it, and tears spilled down her cheeks.

Lucas cursed under his breath, pulled her to him and kissed her forehead. She was almost positive he didn't want her in his arms. Or so she thought. Until their gazes connected again. Yes, he did want it. Even though he knew it was only breaking down more of those barriers between them.

"What about Colleen's baby?" she asked. "Have the kidnappers called back yet with the drop-off point?"

"No, but I suspect we won't hear from them until morning. I hope it's not sooner, because Grayson still hasn't convinced Eric to do the drop with me."

Hailey hoped the kidnappers changed their minds about that. She didn't want Lucas out there where he could be gunned down, and she especially didn't want him out there with Eric. If Eric was the person behind everything, then he could lead Lucas right into a trap and then use Lucas to draw her out.

And it would work.

No way would Hailey hide herself away and let Lucas be hurt or killed just to protect her.

"Grayson said there's no sign of the gunmen," Lucas continued after he looked away from her and stared at Camden. He touched his fingers to the baby's toes peeking out from the blanket.

She hadn't expected there would be, and Hailey already knew it would take the crime lab a while to get to the camera footage from the cruiser, especially since they had so many other things to process from this investigation. Which was a reminder about Eric showing up on the security footage from the bank.

"Has Grayson had a chance to talk to Eric yet?" she asked. It'd been a couple of hours since the attack. Maybe more than a couple since she hadn't been keeping up with the time. But she figured Grayson would make that a priority.

Lucas nodded. "Eric claims the only reason he went to the bank was that he listened to the recordings and wanted to get to the safe deposit box before one of his father's lackeys did."

It could be true. Could. But this was Eric, so there was no telling. "What was in the box?"

"According to Eric, nothing much. Just some records of illegal land deals and such that Preston had done over the years. He says he destroyed them since those were his father's last wishes."

Since Eric hated his father, she seriously doubted he would care a flying fig about carrying out Preston's wishes. "There must have been something in the box to incriminate Eric."

Lucas made a sound of agreement. There was no way to prove that, though. Maybe Grayson could go after

Eric for destroying possible evidence, but with everything else he and his deputies had on their plates, that probably wouldn't happen soon, either.

"Minton came by the sheriff's office again," Lucas continued. "Of course, he says this latest attack is yet another reason for you to be in his protective custody." He paused. "If that's what you want—"

"No." And Hailey didn't even have to think about it. "I want to be here with Camden and you."

Lucas stayed quiet a moment, just long enough for her to know something was wrong. It was also plenty long enough for the feeling of panic to start spreading through her.

"Please tell me I don't have to go with Minton," she said.

"No. Well, not unless he manages to get a court order, which hasn't happened. Even then, I think we could fight it."

Good. But something else was obviously wrong, because his forehead bunched up. "Grayson and I talked about Camden, and we don't think it's a good idea for him to be here. Those attackers could try to come after him again. The ranch is secure, but he'd be better off at the main house."

The place where Mason and his family now lived. It was in the center of the ranch, which would make it harder for kidnappers to get to Camden. Still, there was a problem.

"If the kidnappers have us under surveillance, they might see that we're taking him there," Hailey pointed out.

Lucas nodded. Hesitated again. "The kidnappers want Camden only to use him to get to you."

Because Hailey was fighting the spent adrenaline and the new wave of panic, it took her a moment to figure out what he was saying. "You don't want me to be with Camden."

Another nod.

Oh, mercy. That felt like a punch to the stomach, and it caused a fresh round of tears to fill her eyes. It broke her heart to think of not having Camden close to her.

But Lucas was right.

Her baby was much safer without her around. Plus, Lucas's house was close to the main road. Too close. It would be the first place that gunmen reached if they stormed the ranch.

"How soon would Camden have to leave?" she asked.

"Soon," Lucas said. "Now would be better. I already talked to Tillie about it when you were in the shower, so she's ready. Sawyer and two ranch hands are outside patrolling, but they'll drive Tillie and Camden to the house."

That punch felt even harder, and she saw Tillie peer out from the kitchen, where she was almost certainly waiting for Lucas to break the news. The nanny gave her a sympathetic look, but Tillie was probably ready to put some distance between her and Hailey. After all, Tillie was in danger, too, simply by being around her.

"I'll take good care of him," Tillie assured her.

Hailey knew she would, but it was still hard to let go of the baby. She gave him a kiss on the cheek. Added several more. And she handed him to Lucas so he could take him to Tillie. Once he'd done that, he sent a text. No doubt to Sawyer or one of the hands, because it wasn't long before Hailey heard the sound of a vehicle pulling directly in front of the house.

"We'll come up in the morning to see him," Lucas told the nanny.

When visibility would be better, and it would be easier to spot any attackers who were trying to get close to the ranch. Of course, the visibility wasn't that good right now, which only made her fears skyrocket.

"What if they start shooting when Tillie and Camden go outside?" Hailey asked.

"There's nothing to be gained from them hurting Camden," Lucas assured her. "They want to take him, but they can't do that if he's at the main house."

It felt like a horrible loss to have these next hours taken away. But maybe Lucas and she could use that time to figure out a way to put an end to the danger. They could still set the trap using the reserve deputy to try to lure out the culprit with the promise of getting those files that Colleen had deleted.

"Stand back," Lucas told her. "I don't want you by the door when it's opened."

Yes, because it might prompt the gunmen to fire shots at her. That would put everyone, including the baby, in harm's way.

Hailey tried to hold it together but failed miserably when Lucas disarmed the security system so he could get Tillie and Camden out of the house. They didn't spend but just a couple of seconds out in the open before Sawyer got them in a cruiser. He took off with them as soon as they were inside.

Two other ranch hands stayed behind, no doubt to keep guard. Lucas did his part in keeping them safe, as well. He locked the door and reset the security system.

As fast as she could, Hailey went to the windows

on the same side of the house as the road and opened the curtains. She watched as Sawyer sped out of sight.

"That's not a safe place to stand," Lucas said. He not only moved her back but also closed the curtains again. Shut off the lights, too. "You should try to get some rest," he added. "I'll call Grayson and see if there are any updates."

Hailey had every intention of moving toward the guest room where she'd been staying, but her feet suddenly seemed anchored to the floor. Her eyes seemed out of her control, too, because she started to cry again. She hated the tears. They wouldn't help anything, and in fact, they clearly made Lucas uncomfortable, because his forehead bunched up.

Lucas gave a heavy sigh and went to her. He pulled her into his arms. "It's just temporary," he reminded her.

She got the feeling he was talking about more than just Camden. He probably meant her being here in his house.

In his arms.

They stood there in the darkness with only the sound of the rain and their breaths. She could feel his heartbeat since his chest was against hers. At the moment Hailey could feel everything about him. Feel everything about herself, too.

Especially the heat.

It came, of course. It always came when she was anywhere near Lucas. It was especially there now because they were coming down from the nightmare of the attack and having to be separated from Camden.

"I'm okay," she told him, giving him an out so he could back away.

But Lucas didn't budge. "I always swore that I'd never go another round with you."

That stung, but it was exactly what she expected him to say. "Understandable. I made mistakes with you. Not the sex," Hailey quickly added. "That wasn't a mistake because we got Camden. But I messed up pretty much everything else."

A sound that could have meant anything rumbled in his chest. "I still don't think it's a good idea for us to get involved. Not like this." He glanced at the close contact between them.

Because she thought they could use some levity, she smiled. "Are you trying to convince yourself?"

"Yeah," he admitted.

The levity vanished. So did what was left of her smile. Now, that was not what she'd expected him to say. Lucas was the sort of man who kept his feelings, and his pain, close to the vest. She'd hurt him by not trusting him, and it would take him a long time to get over that.

Or maybe not.

"I'm not doing a good job of convincing myself," he added. "In fact, I'm sinking fast here. I'm trying to come up with a damn good reason why I shouldn't just strip you naked and take you to my bed."

That robbed her of what little breath she had. And it fired up every inch of her.

"I hope you can't think of a reason," she whispered.

There. She'd given him the green light that he probably didn't want. Probably wouldn't take, either.

But she was wrong.

He lowered his head, kissed her. Not a gentle I'm-still-thinking-about-this kind of kiss. It was the real deal. Long and deep. It didn't do anything to cool down her body. Just the opposite.

The kiss went on for so long that Hailey staggered a little because she couldn't breathe. Lucas caught her, tightening his grip around her, and he pulled back so they could take in some air.

He also cursed himself. And he looked down at her. Despite the darkness, she could still see a storm of a different kind brewing in his eyes. Fire mixed with the bitterness of the past.

The fire won out.

Because Lucas scooped her up in his arms, kissed her again and headed in the direction of his bedroom. He stopped along the way to kiss her again. Maybe to make one last-ditch effort at rethinking this, but they were obviously past the point of no return.

Later there'd be consequences.

But Hailey didn't want to think about those now.

She wanted only to feel, wanted to let Lucas take her to the only place she wanted to go. A place with no tears, no gunmen. It was just the two of them, giving in to the heat that had been blazing since they'd first met.

He carried her to the bed, eased her onto the mattress. He was being too gentle with her. Probably because she didn't have her full strength, but she didn't want gentle. Not with this ache starting to throb inside her.

Hailey caught onto him, dragging him closer, and ideally letting him know that she wasn't fragile. Also letting him know that there was already a need to finish what they'd started. In case he didn't get the message, she put her hand over the front of his jeans.

Yes, he got the message, all right.

He lowered the kisses to her neck. Foreplay. Definitely not overrated when it came to Lucas, though there really was no need to fan these flames any higher.

She was wearing a loaner dress that had been in a stash that some of the Ryland wives had sent over. It was loose, so Lucas had no trouble pushing it up, and she felt his hand on her bare skin. His mouth, too, when he took those kisses to her breasts. Then her stomach. He lingered there a moment before he stripped off her bra and panties.

And he kept kissing her.

Hailey didn't want to be the only one naked, though, so she went after his shirt. Not an easy task, though, since Lucas was still wearing a holster. He had to put the kisses on hold to help her with that, and the battle started up again. Hailey wanted his clothes off *now*, but Lucas was back to the kisses.

Which kept going lower.

If they continued in that direction, he was going to make her climax. Something she desperately wanted. But not like this. She wanted him inside her.

Hailey caught onto him, pulling him back up. The movement created an incredible sensation with his body sliding over hers. That made her reach for his zipper. She fumbled around and cursed, causing Lucas to smile. As he'd done with the shirt, he helped her get off the rest of his clothes.

But then he stopped. And moved away from her.

She could have sworn her heart stopped, too, but then she realized he was only getting a condom from the nightstand drawer. It brought back the memories of the other time they'd been together.

The memories got a whole lot better, though.

Lucas came back to her, and once he had on the condom, he gathered her into his arms again. Kissed her. And entered her slowly, easing into the heat of her body. Hailey hadn't thought she'd wanted gentle and easy, but this was working just fine for her. He took his time, building the fire even hotter.

It didn't last.

Couldn't.

The need soon took over, and slow and easy was done. Now it was all about finishing this. And he did. Lucas moved in her, the pace as frantic and deep as the need. Until both of them went flying right over the edge.

Chapter Fifteen

Lucas tried to get some sleep. Hard to do, though, with a naked Hailey right next to him. Especially hard to do with the thoughts racing through his head. Thoughts of tomorrow's ransom drop and of the danger to his son.

Thoughts, too, of what'd happened between Hailey and him.

He figured he should regret the sex. And in some ways he did. It was a distraction that he didn't need at a time when he should have been focused on the investigation. Still, it was hard to regret something that'd been damn good.

At least she was sleeping now. That was good. But he figured her body hadn't given her much of a choice about that. Hailey had been running on adrenaline since coming out of the coma, and she needed to rest. Because tomorrow would be a hellish day for her, as well.

Lucas only hoped he could get back Colleen's baby without anyone getting hurt or killed. While he was hoping, he added that Eric would cooperate and do the drop with him. So far, he hadn't agreed, which meant Lucas would have to convince him or else renegotiate with the kidnappers.

Maybe Colleen wouldn't do something stupid before then.

Shortly after Hailey had fallen asleep, Lucas had gotten a text from Grayson telling him that Colleen had refused to stay at the sheriff's office any longer. Grayson
hadn't had any grounds to hold her, and even though
he'd reminded her that the kidnappers could be watching the place, Colleen had left anyway. At best, she was
just going somewhere else to wait for the ransom drop.
At worst, she was in grave danger. And Grayson didn't
have the manpower to send someone out to make sure
she didn't get herself into trouble.

Right now, the Rylands had enough trouble on their
hands.

Lucas glanced at the laptop that he'd brought into the
bedroom after Hailey had fallen asleep. It was on the
nightstand next to him, and it showed the feed from the
security cameras positioned all around the ranch. No
doubt several of his cousins were watching the cameras,
too, as was the head ranch hand. All of them looking to
make sure someone didn't try to sneak onto the grounds.

So far, so good.

It was a bad night, though, for any kind of sneaking
around outside. The rain was steady and heavy, and
there was the occasional jag of lightning in the sky.
Maybe the storm would be enough to keep the thugs
from another attempt to take Camden or Hailey.

With a few strokes on the laptop keyboard, Lucas
pulled up the feed from another camera. This one was
in the nursery at the main house. Tillie had set up the
camera so that they could see Camden. And there he
was, sleeping in a crib. He was sharing the room with
Mason's son, Max. Tillie was in the guest room just

up the hall and would no doubt have a baby monitor next to her bed so she'd be able to hear the babies if they woke up.

As if she'd sensed what Lucas was doing, Hailey stirred, her eyes opening and her attention going straight to the screen. She smiled. Sat up.

"It's not the same as having him here with us, but it's still nice to see him," she said.

Yeah. It was. But the *us* gave Lucas some hesitation. She'd said it so easily, as if it were normal. It wasn't. And Hailey must have realized her slip, because she muttered an apology under her breath.

Lucas hated that she felt the need to apologize. Hated even more that he felt as if he should have one. Because despite the fact that she was in his bed, they were a long way from getting to the *us* stage.

Once he'd taken care of the danger, they could start working on that. And Lucas refused to believe he couldn't put an end to the attacks, because if he couldn't, it would mean Hailey and Camden going to a safe house. Or her even returning to WITSEC, but this time she would have to take Camden with her since as long as he was out there, the snake behind this could use the baby to get to Hailey.

"Colleen left the sheriff's office," Lucas told her. "Grayson couldn't talk her out of it."

Hailey gave a heavy sigh. "No, he wouldn't have been able to do that. Did Colleen say where she was going?"

Lucas shook his head. "But unless she manages to get her hands on the money, she can't do the ransom exchange." And he hoped she didn't even attempt it.

She looked at Camden again. Then Lucas. "You're

no doubt thinking we messed things up big-time," she said. "And yes, I'm talking about the sex."

He let that hang in the air for a couple of seconds. Then lifted his shoulder. "Well, yeah, when I mess up, I aim for big."

She laughed, but it wasn't exactly from humor. More nerves. Something he understood. Reality was quickly settling in, and there was no way they could go back to where they'd been just hours earlier. There was no such thing as casual sex when it came to Hailey.

The silence settled between them. And it wasn't exactly comfortable. Hailey fixed her attention to the laptop and on Camden. As much as he wanted to continue looking at their son, though, he had to switch the camera back so he could help watch the security feed. That didn't do much to ease the discomfort between them.

"Just how bad do you think it'll get tomorrow?" she asked.

He considered lying and saying "not bad at all," but he couldn't make that kind of guarantee. He looked at her, though. Saw the worry on her face again, so Lucas decided to go with a half guarantee.

"I'll make it work," he assured her and brushed a kiss on her cheek.

Of course, that sparked the attraction again, along with sparking another kiss. This time not on the cheek but her mouth. Hailey moved right into the kiss, too, sliding closer and touching him.

Not good since they were naked.

That didn't stop him, though, from deepening the kiss and hauling her right against him. However, then something stopped Lucas.

It was just a soft beep, barely audible because he

had the sound turned down on the laptop, but it was a sound that went through him like the lightning bolt that slashed outside.

Because it meant something or someone had triggered one of the dozens of sensors positioned all around the ranch.

The laptop was showing six different cameras, the ones positioned on the most vulnerable points of the ranch. The fence lines and the road. He looked at each of them but didn't see anything.

"Does that sound mean what I think it means?" Hailey asked. She moved away from him, her attention back on the screen.

"It could be nothing," Lucas tried to assure her. "Sometimes animals trigger the sensors. The storm could, too, if the wind knocked down a tree branch or something."

Lucas held on to that hope, but it was hard not to think the worst. Hard to stave off the knot that was already tightening in his gut. A knot that got even tighter when his phone buzzed, and he saw Mason's name on the screen.

"Any idea why the alarm went off?" Lucas immediately asked him.

"No. I'm looking through the camera feeds now, all of them, and I don't see anything. You?"

"Nothing." Lucas put the phone on speaker so he could get dressed, but he also tapped the keyboard to scroll through some of the other security feeds. "But I'll keep watching."

"Yeah, be ready just in case," Mason said, ending the call.

That sent Hailey scrambling from the bed. There

were no signs of the heat and attraction on her face now. Just the fear as she grabbed her clothes and started putting them on. Fear that Lucas needed to rein in right now, because this could be a long wait to find out if anything was truly wrong.

"No one can get near the main house," he reminded her. "Not without going through a dozen ranch hands and plenty of other houses."

Since those places all had lawmen inside them, Lucas was pretty sure Camden was safe. But "pretty sure" didn't ease the knot in his stomach. He wanted a hundred percent guarantee when it came to his son, and it didn't matter where Camden was. He wouldn't have that guarantee until the person responsible for the attacks was dead or behind bars.

Hailey finished dressing—obviously she was preparing herself in case they had to go outside, but Lucas was hoping that didn't happen.

Lucas put back on both his weapons, and even though it was hard to force himself to sit down, he did for Hailey's sake. So that she'd sit, too. She did, right beside him, and they both watched the screen as he scrolled through all the feeds.

She shook her head. "I still don't see anything."

Neither did he, but it was dark, and even with the security lights, there were still plenty of shadows. Plenty of places for someone to hide, too, what with all the fences, trees and outbuildings. But if someone was out there and that person moved, then the sensors would pick him up, and the alarm would ding again.

The seconds crawled by, turning into minutes, and just when Lucas was ready to try to level his breathing, he saw something. Movement not near the fence line but near the road. It was just a blur of motion, barely in camera range and not actually on ranch land.

"What?" Hailey asked. She'd obviously noticed that he'd tensed.

"Maybe nothing," he repeated.

Lucas clicked on that specific screen, enlarged it and zoomed in on the area where he'd seen the motion. He was hoping it was a deer or an illusion caused by the rain.

But it wasn't.

It was a man dressed all in black. And he had a rifle aimed right at Lucas's house.

HAILEY COULDN'T STOP herself from gasping when she saw the man. He was lurking behind one of the trees directly across the road from the ranch.

"Oh, God," she said, and she scrambled to get the gun from Lucas's nightstand.

He took hold of her hand and had her sit next to him again. He also adjusted the view of the camera so that she could see the truck that was parked at the end of the road. Unlike the man with the rifle, the truck was actually on the ranch.

"Two of the hands are in the truck," Lucas explained, and he took out his phone and fired off a text. No doubt to warn them that there was definitely a problem.

Lucas went back to the camera angle so they could see the man, and Hailey realized he wasn't alone. There was another armed guy directly behind him.

The skin crawled on the back of her neck. Because she knew what those men wanted.

They wanted her.

And they'd try to use Camden to get her

"Get down on the floor," Lucas instructed.

She did as he said, and he grabbed the laptop to bring it to the floor with him. The difference was he had her lie all the way down while he stayed in a sitting position. Probably so he'd be better able to respond if things turned bad in a hurry.

Hailey tried not to panic. Hard to do, though, when all she could feel was the panic and fear. Both went up a significant notch when she saw the headlights of an approaching car on the screen. The vehicle no doubt carried more thugs arriving to launch a full-scale attack.

Both the hands in the truck opened their doors, and they put out their rifles. Ready to return fire.

She gasped again when the dinging sound shot through the room. But it wasn't a security alarm. It was Lucas's phone to let him know he had a text. She saw Mason's name on the screen.

"Mason's on the line with the hands at the road," Lucas said when he read the text. "He's sending them backup right away." He cursed. "But I need to stay here."

She knew the profanity wasn't for her but the situation. He wanted to be down there helping the hands, but all of this could be designed to have him do just that. So that she'd be alone and an easy prey.

The car came to a stop directly in front of where the hands were parked. Hailey saw another vehicle, too. A cruiser barreling down the ranch road toward the hands, the two armed men and the newly arrived vehicle. A moment later, another cruiser followed the first. So there were plenty of lawmen responding to what was no doubt about to become the scene of another attack.

"What the hell?" Lucas said, moving closer to the laptop screen.

Hailey watched as the driver of the car got out. Colleen. And her sister lifted her hands into the air as if surrendering. Colleen said something to the ranch hands, but since there was no audio, Hailey had no idea what.

But this couldn't be good.

Either her sister was part of the oncoming attack, or else she was going to be right in the middle of it.

Even though it was pouring rain, Colleen stayed outside the car, and after a very short conversation with the hands, she took out her phone. A moment later, Lucas's own phone rang. He answered it and put it on speaker.

"Hailey?" Colleen asked. Her voice was frantic. As was her expression. "You have to tell these men to let me onto the ranch."

Hailey debated how to answer that. But Lucas had no such debate with himself. "Did you bring those gunmen with you?" he asked.

"What gunmen?" Colleen's gaze began to slash all around her.

"The ones across the road."

A sob tore from Colleen's mouth, and she ducked back into the car. "No, I didn't bring them, but I think they want me dead."

"If they wanted that, you already would be," Lucas pointed out. "They had a clean shot and didn't take it."

And it wasn't as if the men had left. Hailey could still see them on the corner of the screen. Could see the approaching cruisers, too. They pulled to a stop behind the ranch hands' truck. The doors opened, and four of Lucas's cousins—Dade, Sawyer, Josh and Gage—all took aim at the gunmen while they used the doors of the cruisers for cover.

"You're just going to let me stay out here?" Colleen protested.

Hailey was torn about what to do. Her instincts were screaming for her to protect her sister, but her instincts were even stronger to keep Camden safe.

"Answer me!" Colleen practically shouted.

"I can't let you near my son," Hailey said. "Leave and go to the sheriff's office. You'll be safe there."

That brought out some vicious profanity from Colleen. "I stopped Preston from having you killed. You owe me!"

That chilled her to the bone, but then Hailey reminded herself that it might not even be true. It could be Colleen who wanted her dead. Or even Colleen just carrying through on Preston's old wishes.

Colleen added some more profanity, but Hailey shut her out when Lucas's phone dinged, indicating he had an incoming call.

Unknown Caller popped up on the screen.

"I have to put you on hold," Lucas said to her sister, and he answered the other call.

"I know I said I'd be in touch in the morning," the man said by way of greeting, "but I just couldn't wait." It was the kidnapper, the same one who'd been communicating with them.

"Where are you?" Lucas asked.

"Nearby but out of range of all those pesky cameras you got all around the ranch. You might be able to see a couple of the fellas I brought with me, though."

"I do, and you probably see that there are six men with guns aimed right back at them."

"Yeah, they know. None of us want a gunfight. Especially not Hailey and you. Not with your boy and all those Ryland kids and babies so close. Somebody might get hurt."

Instead of ice in Hailey's blood, that sent some hot rage through her body. How dare this snake threaten not only her son but also everyone else on the ranch? She nearly yelled at him and wanted to use some of those same curse words that her sister just had, but Lucas spoke before she could say anything.

"If you don't want a gunfight, what do you want?" Lucas asked the man.

"I thought you'd like to see who's with me," he said, obviously not answering Lucas's question. "I'm sending you a pretty picture now."

Almost immediately, Lucas's phone dinged with a text. Again from Unknown Caller, and it did indeed have a picture attached. It took a moment to load.

Hailey's heart went to her knees.

Because it was a picture of Colleen's baby. Not alone. Minton was holding her in the crook of his arm.

And there was what appeared to be a bomb strapped to Minton's chest.

Chapter Sixteen

Hailey snapped to a sitting position, and she practically snatched the phone from his hand so she could get a closer look of the photo that the kidnapper had just sent them.

But Lucas didn't need a closer look. He'd already seen more than enough.

"It could be fake," Lucas reminded Hailey. "Minton could be their boss, and he could have set all of this up."

She gave a shaky nod, repeated that last part. But he wasn't sure she was buying it. Her breathing was already way too fast, and she was no doubt having to battle the panic that had to be crawling through her. Lucas felt some of that same panic, too, but he had to rein it in so he could focus on what exactly he was seeing.

And how to fix it.

"Let me speak to Minton," Lucas told the kidnapper.

"Thought you'd want to do that. I'll put him on the line, but for just a few seconds. After that, you and I will have a little chat about what you need to do for this to turn out good for all of us."

Lucas didn't have to wait long before he heard Minton's voice. "They hit me with a stun gun when I was going into my office," Minton said, his voice a snarl.

His expression in the photo matched the snarl, as well. Either he was one unhappy camper or he was pretending to be one. "Now I have a bomb on me, right next to the baby."

"Yes, I saw the photo. Is it real?" Lucas came out and asked.

"Hell, yes, it's real!" Minton's shout must have startled the baby, because she began to cry.

Not good. Hailey's nerves were clearly already frayed enough, and the baby's cries only added to the urgency of this situation.

"How do you know the bomb is real?" Lucas pressed. "Do you have personal knowledge of explosive devices?"

"Yes, I do, but not in the way you're insinuating. I didn't put this bomb on myself. These idiots did after they kidnapped me. And I don't know who they're working for, but if you don't do as they say, they're going to start the timer. After that, I'd have only two minutes before this kid and I get blown to bits."

Lucas glanced at the photo again, at the placement of Minton's hands, and he saw that they were literally tied around the baby. Two minutes probably wouldn't be enough time to get out of those ropes and remove the bomb. Especially since it was possible the kidnappers were also holding Minton at gunpoint and wouldn't give him a chance to escape.

"Well?" the kidnapper said, coming back on the line. Lucas could still hear the baby crying, so obviously the little girl and Minton weren't too far away. "Convinced that we mean business?"

"I was convinced of that before you put an innocent

baby in danger. Get the baby away from that bomb and then we'll talk."

"We'll talk now," the man snapped.

"All right," Lucas snapped right back. "You want the baby alive to collect the ransom. Well, you're risking a half million dollars by keeping her that close to the explosive."

"There's no real threat to her," the kidnapper said. "Not at this moment, anyhow. You gotta do something, though, to keep it that way. You can have the baby in exchange for Hailey. And before you go all cowboy cop on me, this isn't your decision. It's Hailey's. I'll give her five minutes to decide."

Lucas was about to tell him that he didn't need a second of that five minutes, that the answer was no. But the kidnapper hung up.

"You're not going out there," Lucas insisted.

She moved as if ready to get up, but he caught her arm to force her to sit back down. He needed to convince her to stay put, but he also had to keep watch on the security screens in case those gunmen started firing.

"These men want you dead," Lucas reminded her. "And along with two of our suspects, Colleen and Minton, there are gunmen. Going to meet them won't get the baby rescued. It will only get you killed."

She stopped struggling to get away from him, and even in the darkness, Lucas saw the tears shimmer in her eyes. "I have to do something to help that baby. She's my niece."

Lucas got that. Hell, he had a niece, and he would have done anything to keep her safe. But a suicide mission wasn't the way to go, especially since it was possible the child wasn't even in any real danger.

"So, what do we do?" Hailey asked.

He looked at the screen again. Still no movement from the gunmen. Lucas panned around, trying to get a glimpse of the vehicle holding Minton and the baby, but he didn't see anything.

Hell.

The kidnappers could have the baby anywhere, including out of the state.

"Let me see first if Colleen stayed on hold," he said.

Though Lucas wasn't sure what to tell Hailey's sister. It didn't seem a good idea to mention the bomb. However, it turned out he didn't have to make that decision, because Colleen was no longer on the line. Her car was still at the end of the road, though.

But it didn't stay there.

Colleen backed out the car, turned onto the main road and hit the accelerator. Lucas thought she had decided to leave, and he adjusted the camera angle to see if she was heading back to town.

She wasn't.

Colleen turned her car directly at the white wooden fence that fronted the ranch, and she bashed right through it. Her car went straight into the pasture. Too close to Lucas's house.

Hailey gasped. "What is she doing?" she said under her breath.

Lucas hated to think the worst, but he did. Colleen could be coming to kill them.

Dade and Gage got back into their cruiser and went in pursuit. Mason was no doubt sending someone, too, but there wasn't a lot of help to send. Most of the men were already tied up guarding the houses and the other fences, especially the back, where it would be easier for someone to launch an attack.

Colleen's car didn't make it far, though. The rain had obviously soaked the pasture, and she made it only about a hundred yards before her tires bogged down in the mud and grass. That didn't stop her, though. She barreled out of the vehicle and started running.

Directly toward Lucas's house.

He hadn't even been sure that Colleen knew which house was his, but she must have done her homework, because she was headed their way on foot.

And not alone, either.

Before Dade could get the cruiser turned around, another vehicle came up the road. A black SUV. And it looked like the same one with the attackers who'd tried to kill Hailey, Josh and him after the bombing.

"Those men are after Colleen?" Hailey asked.

Lucas didn't know the answer. Not at first, anyway. But he soon got one. The SUV didn't go after Colleen. Nor did it bog down. The driver came to a stop, and his passenger opened his door.

And the guy aimed something at Lucas's house.

It was too big to be a regular firearm, and Lucas had to zoom in on it to figure out what it was. A tear gas gun. At least, he hoped it was that and not a grenade launcher. Either way, Hailey and he had to get the heck out of there now.

Lucas closed the laptop, tucking it under his arm, and he took hold of Hailey to get her moving. It was chilly and raining, but Lucas was pretty sure there wouldn't be enough time to grab any raincoats or umbrellas.

And he was right.

There was a crashing sound of breaking glass in the

living room, the side of the house that faced those thugs. Followed by another sound of the canister plinking to the floor. A couple of moments later, another canister came flying into the house.

"We have to hurry," Lucas warned her. He handed her the laptop so he could draw his gun.

Time was up, because tear gas started to spew through the entire house. Lucas ran with her to the back door and prayed he wasn't carrying Hailey right into an ambush.

HAILEY WAS MOVING as fast as she could, but it wasn't fast enough. The tear gas was on them before Lucas and she could get to the back door.

She started to cough, the gas cutting off her breath along with burning her throat and eyes. It was no doubt doing the same thing to Lucas, but he still managed to get the door open. He already had his weapon drawn when he stepped out onto the porch and looked around. He must not have seen anyone because he pulled her out of the house.

"We can't stay here," he said.

A moment later, she realized why. Another canister came bashing into the house. Then another. It wouldn't be long before the tear gas was so thick back here that they would be coughing too hard to run.

But where?

If they ran outside, they could be gunned down.

She could see Lucas's gaze darting around while he was trying to figure that out. They had a couple of choices. They could try to make it to the side of the house where he'd parked his truck. The problem with that was it was also the side where those canister-shooting thugs were positioned.

It was where she'd last seen Colleen, too.

So that probably wasn't a good direction to go. That left the barn, a detached garage and a storage building. Beyond that was open pasture, where one of those riflemen would be able to pick them off.

"We'll run to the garage," Lucas told her. "I have another truck there we can use to escape. Stay as low as you can and move fast."

Hailey wasn't sure she could go fast. Not with her legs so wobbly, and now that she couldn't breathe so well, it would be even harder. Still, they didn't have much of a choice.

Lucas took her hand and led her off the porch and down the steps. When they reached the yard, there was no more awning, so the rain and wind came right at them. Even though Hailey had on the hoodie, it wasn't nearly thick enough, and it didn't take long before she started to shiver. Still, she ran until Lucas pulled them behind a large oak.

Not a second too soon, either.

A shot blasted through the air and slammed right into the tree.

It wasn't just the rain that was raw and bitter. Suddenly the fear was, too. Not because the shot had come so close to hitting Lucas and her, but because she didn't want bullets being fired anywhere near Camden and the others.

More shots came, but these didn't slam into the tree. That only made the fear worse because Hailey couldn't immediately figure out where those men were shooting.

Then she realized they were aiming at the cruiser that Dade and Gage were trying to get closer.

Mercy.

The shooters were no doubt doing that to stop Lucas's cousins from helping them. At least the cruiser was bullet-resistant, but she figured sooner or later, either Dade or Gage would step out so they could return fire.

Hailey considered taking out the laptop to see if she could check the security cameras, but she needed to be ready to move. Plus, she didn't want to risk getting it wet. Right now, it was still under her arm where it was semiprotected. Once they were in the garage, then she could check and make sure none of these hired killers were heading for the main house. Maybe she'd also be able to find her sister. If Colleen was innocent, then she was in grave danger out in the open with those bullets flying.

Lucas's phone buzzed, and he took it from his pocket and handed it to her. Probably so he could keep his hands free. When Hailey saw Mason's name on the screen, she answered it right away.

"Is everyone all right?" she immediately asked.

"Fine for now. I want to keep it that way. Dade told me about the bomb, the baby and Minton. As soon as Dade can, he'll move in to help. In the meantime, our other cousins, Nate and Landon, are trying to work their way to the pasture. If they get a clean shot, they'll stop the gunmen."

That was good. Hailey hoped that would happen. It wouldn't get back her niece, but it would end the immediate danger. At least, it would if these men didn't set off that explosive. But she figured they were going to use Colleen's baby as the ultimate bargaining tool to get to her.

"What about my sister?" Hailey asked. "Where is she?"

"I lost sight of her, but the last I saw her, she was moving in the direction of Lucas's barn."

Then that was all the more reason for Lucas and her not to go in there. "What about the car with Minton and the baby?"

"Still nothing on that. Grayson's coming in from town, and he'll look along the way."

Maybe they'd get lucky and could spot it. Of course, in the dark and rain, it would be hard to do.

"I can see Lucas and you," Mason went on a moment later. "Make your way to the main house when you can. You're too damn close to these dirtbags."

Yes, they were. And while Hailey desperately wanted to see Camden, she was also terrified of having these men shoot at them if they went in that direction. Plus, Lucas and she had to get to the garage first.

"I'll have the ranch hands fire at the dirtbags," Mason added. "That should keep them occupied a couple of seconds so that you and Lucas can get moving."

"But what about the shots going to the main house?" she asked.

"The ranch hands are positioning themselves so that won't happen," he assured her.

She thanked him and added, "Just keep Camden and everyone else safe." Maybe Mason and the others would be able to do that.

She relayed the information Mason had given her to Lucas, but before she even finished, Hailey heard the shots. These weren't coming from the hired killers but rather from the ranch hands. As Mason had said, it created a distraction because the gunmen were now shooting at the hands.

"Let's move," Lucas told her.

They started running. There weren't any trees or anything else right by they could use for cover, so Hailey held her breath while they were out in the open. It seemed to take an eternity to go the fifteen or so yards. The rain certainly didn't help, either, and her shoes sank down into the boggy ground.

The moment they reached the garage, Lucas took her to the side door and threw it open. He stepped in first, his gaze slashing from one side to the other. What he didn't do was turn on the lights. Probably because it would alert the gunmen to their position. Maybe the men had been so involved with the gunfight distraction that they hadn't seen Lucas and her make their way there.

"Stay right next to me," he warned her.

She did, and while he continued to look around them, he inched his way to a truck parked at the front of the garage. The back was a workshop and storage area and was filled with shelves, tables and equipment. It would give someone places to hide. Not exactly a reminder to soothe her already raw nerves.

"I need to check and make sure no one tampered with the truck," Lucas added. "Keep watch around us."

That didn't help her nerves, either. Hailey just wanted to get out of there, but after what'd happened with the cruiser, they had to take precautions.

Lucas stooped down, and using the light from his phone, he began to make his way around the truck. She followed him while keeping watch, but Hailey didn't see anyone, thank goodness.

But she heard something.

Lucas must have, too, because he quickly stood and moved in front of her. They waited, listening. Hard to hear, though, what with the shots continuing outside, but Hailey was almost certain she'd heard something move. Or maybe it was just the wind and rain.

No, it wasn't.

There was another sound, and this time Hailey was able to pinpoint it.

Someone was in the truck.

Chapter Seventeen

Hell. What now?

Lucas pivoted and took aim in the direction of the truck cab. He didn't see anyone, but he was positive someone was in there.

He had known it was a risk to come into the garage, but it would have also been a risk for them to stay in the yard with heaven knew how many hired thugs now on the ranch. However, they might have gone from the frying pan right into the fire.

"Come out or I'll shoot," Lucas warned the person. But it was a warning he hoped like the devil that he didn't have to carry out. Because he didn't want to shoot in cramped quarters with Hailey.

Definitely didn't want to start a gunfight.

And he also didn't want to alert the armed thugs that Hailey and he were in the garage. That would only cause them to open fire. Or maybe launch another tear gas grenade.

"It's me," someone said.

Colleen.

Lucas groaned and definitely didn't lower his gun. "Put your hands where I can see them," he ordered.

"I'm not the one trying to kill you." Colleen added a sob. "When will you believe me?"

"I might start to believe you when you get out of the truck, hands up."

Other than another sob, Colleen didn't respond, and the seconds crawled by before she finally lifted her head. Lucas could see then that she'd been down on the seat. She lifted her hands, too.

"Satisfied?" Colleen snapped.

"Not yet. Step out, keep your hands in the air and don't make any sudden moves. Get behind me," he added to Hailey. "And try to keep watch around us in case she's not alone."

Because Hailey's arm was right against his, he felt her tense even more. He hated that he was having to put her through this, but they couldn't get in the truck until Lucas figured out what the heck Colleen was up to.

Colleen stepped from the truck, and Lucas could see she didn't have anything in her hands. She also didn't appear to be carrying a weapon. Like Hailey, Colleen wasn't wearing a coat. The rain had soaked her jeans and top, and they were clinging to her. Still, Lucas motioned for her to turn around, and when she did, he made sure she didn't have a weapon tucked in the back waist of her jeans.

She didn't.

"I told you I wasn't trying to kill you," Colleen said.

Just because she wasn't armed didn't mean she wasn't behind this attack. "Why are you in here? *How* are you in here?" Lucas amended.

"I just started running when my car got stuck. This was the first place I reached. I knew I needed to try to get to my baby, but I couldn't find the truck keys."

They were on a hook on the wall, but since Colleen hadn't turned on the lights, either, she would have had trouble spotting them.

"Do you know where the baby is?" Lucas asked.

"No." Colleen winced when there was another round of loud gunfire. "But I have to find her. I have to save her." She made a loud sob. "Is there anything you can do to make them stop shooting? Can you try to negotiate with them or something?"

Her fear seemed genuine enough, but after the hell Hailey and he had been through, Lucas planned on hanging on to his skepticism a while longer.

"I don't have any control over those gunmen," he told her. "But there are armed ranch hands out there, and they might get them to stop soon."

Colleen looked at Hailey. "Please help me get my daughter back. Please. Just think if it were your son and how hard this would be for you."

"I have thought about it," Hailey answered. "Those kidnappers want me in exchange for the baby."

"Then do it." Colleen didn't hesitate even a second, either. Maybe because she knew there was no danger for her. But there'd be plenty for Hailey. "I'd go if they would let me."

"Really?" Lucas pressed.

"Of course."

Then he was about to put that to the test. Without taking his gun off the woman, he passed his phone back to Hailey. "Hit Redial and see if the kidnapper will answer."

Colleen's eyes widened. "What are you going to do?"

Lucas didn't actually expect the kidnapper to answer

and was surprised when he heard the man's voice. "Are you ready to send out Hailey?" the man asked.

"No, but Colleen is here, and she's willing to meet with you."

And Lucas carefully watched Colleen's reaction. She didn't look annoyed or afraid. "Yes," she said. "I'll come right now. Just tell me where I need to go so I can get my baby."

"Guess Lucas told you about our little explosive device, huh?" the kidnapper taunted.

Colleen's gaze slashed to Lucas. "What is he talking about?"

"So he didn't tell you," the kidnapper continued before Lucas could speak. "Minton and your baby girl are real close to a bomb right now."

Colleen gasped. "Oh, God. Is it true? Is there actually a bomb?"

"There is. A bomb set to go off with just a flip of a switch. And if you want that to change, then convince your sister to come out and chat with us. You come, too. In fact, I insist both of you come."

Even though Colleen looked on the verge of a panic attack, Lucas blocked Hailey from going closer to her. If Colleen was truly innocent, then he'd owe her a huge apology, but for now his priority had to be keeping Hailey safe.

"What exactly do you want from the women?" Lucas asked the kidnapper.

"Any and all files they have about the DeSalvo family," he answered without hesitation.

"And then what?" Hailey added.

"Then, tomorrow morning you'll get that ransom money, and you'll get both the women and the kid."

Lucas seriously doubted it. Judging from the sound she made, so did Hailey. Colleen was the only one of them who was clearly eager to do this.

"Let me know if the women are coming out," the kidnapper said. "Once they do, the shots will stop on our part. You'll have to make sure the Rylands and the ranch hands stop, too." And he ended the call.

"Call him back," Colleen insisted. "Have him tell me where Hailey and I need to go to get my baby."

"That's not going to happen," Lucas assured her. "Not on Hailey's part anyway."

But what was his next move?

He wanted to get Hailey to the main house, where she'd be safer and with Camden. However, he couldn't just leave Colleen here, either.

"Call Mason," Lucas told Hailey. "Let him know that Colleen is here, and I'm trying to figure out what to do with her. I also want to know if the road is clear between my house and his."

"You don't need to figure out what to do with me," Colleen shrieked. "We have to get the baby." She snapped toward Hailey. "This is all your fault, anyway. You probably have all sorts of information stashed away on Preston and Eric. Information that could send me to jail, too."

"Are you admitting to some crimes?" Lucas immediately asked her.

"No! But Hailey always had it in for Preston. I figure Eric, too. And if she hadn't been so hell-bent on putting them in jail, none of this would be happening."

Maybe that was true, but in this case, being hell-bent was the right thing to do. "Preston was a criminal. He deserved to be behind bars." And that was all the breath he was going to waste on Colleen. "Call Mason," he repeated to Hailey.

"I really am innocent," Colleen continued while Hailey located the number. "Darrin forced me to go to the hospital. He said it was the only way to get my baby. But he lied. And then he tried to kill me when he ran me off the road."

If that was true, then it was another reason Lucas was glad that Darrin was out of the picture. Hailey made a sound of agreement, probably because she felt the same, and she finished making the call to Mason. She also put it on speaker.

"What's the latest on the gunmen?" Lucas asked the moment his cousin answered.

"Pinned down, for now. But they're not budging, and I can't have the hands, Dade or the others go in any closer."

So they were at a stalemate. Well, in a way. Hailey was still in danger.

"Grayson called," Mason went on. "He spotted a vehicle just up the road from the ranch, and he's going to do a quiet approach to see if Minton and the baby are there. One of the deputies is with him."

"Tell the sheriff to be careful," Colleen blurted out.

"Who the hell is that?" Mason asked.

"Colleen. I'm in my garage with Hailey and her. Colleen was hiding in here."

Mason cursed. "And your plans?"

"Still debating that. How safe would it be for me to drive Hailey to the main house and then come back here to wait with Colleen?" That was just in case she was innocent and therefore in danger.

But Hailey was shaking her head before Lucas even

finished his question to Mason. "That's too risky for you," she insisted.

"Hailey's right," Mason agreed. "When the gunmen spot your truck, I figure they'll start shooting at it."

Lucas wasn't giving up just yet on this particular plan. He wanted some distance between Colleen and Hailey. Between Hailey and those shooters, too. "Maybe the hands could continue keeping them occupied?"

"They could, but why don't you stay there for a couple more minutes. That'll give me time to hear from Grayson. If the baby is in that vehicle, I'll need to send him some help. Plus, I'd rather the gunmen not have any reason to get to the main house."

No way could Lucas disagree with any of that, but he definitely didn't like the idea of staying put, either. Maybe he tempted fate with that thought, because he heard a sound. Not one of the normal gunshots. This was more of a blast. One that he'd heard four other times before.

It was the sound of another gas canister being fired.

And this time it didn't smash into the house. It hit the garage door, and from what he could tell, it bashed into the wooden part of the door and not the glass inserts just above it. However, that didn't stop the gas from spewing in around the sides and bottom.

Mercy. Lucas definitely hadn't wanted things to go this way, but they had to move. That was especially true when the next canister came crashing through the glass.

"In the truck, now," he told Hailey and Colleen. He grabbed the keys from the wall hook.

They were already starting in that direction anyway. First Colleen. Then Hailey, who got in the middle. They were already coughing, too, and he hoped the tear gas didn't water his eyes so much that he wouldn't be able to see.

The moment Lucas started the engine, he hit the remote control to open the door, and once he had enough clear space to get out, he gunned the engine.

Driving right into that cloud of tear gas.

But that was just the start of their troubles. Because the gunmen started shooting at them.

HAILEY TRIED TO clear her eyes and throat so she could help Lucas get them to safety. If that was possible. The shots were coming at them so fast that it was like being trapped in a hailstorm.

The bullets tore through the windshield, and Hailey took hold of Colleen and pushed her lower on the seat. She got lower, as well, but Lucas couldn't while driving.

Lucas cursed. "Hell, they shot into the radiator."

No doubt to disable the vehicle. But how had they even known Lucas, Colleen and she were in the garage in the first place? Hailey hoped it was a guess on their part and they didn't have some insider information from Colleen. Her sister could have called or sent those thugs a text when she saw them come into the garage.

"Where are we going?" Hailey managed to ask Lucas even though she was having to fight for every breath. And she was shaking from the wet and cold. She had such a tight grip on the laptop and Lucas's phone that she was afraid they might shatter.

"Away from those shots. Away from the main house, too."

Good. As much as she wanted to get to safety, it was too risky to go in that direction. Too risky to stay put, too, and Lucas didn't speed toward the road but rather across the backyard and to the side of his own house. That put an instant buffer between them and the gunmen. What it didn't do was get rid of the lingering tear gas.

Probably because the thugs sent two more canisters their way.

The gunmen were trying to flush them out, trying to force them out into the open, where they'd be easier targets.

"Watch Colleen," Lucas said to her. A reminder that he didn't trust her sister. Neither did she, and her alarm went up a significant notch when Colleen threw open the glove compartment.

"I need a gun," her sister insisted.

Hailey wanted that, too, but she hoped there wasn't one for Colleen to find. There wasn't. But Lucas took out his backup weapon, and when he handed it to Hailey, she had to shift the laptop under her arm so she could take it. Hailey put it in her pocket.

Giving her the gun earned Lucas and her a glare from Colleen, but Hailey didn't care. She preferred not to be in a closed vehicle with one of their armed suspects.

She lifted her head enough so she could adjust and pull out the laptop. She opened it and prayed the Wi-Fi signal was strong enough outside the house.

It was.

She pulled up the security camera screens so she could help Lucas keep watch. After all, the gunmen could sneak around the front of the house and attack. Hard to see much of anything, though, with the darkness, the tear gas and the rain, but at least the rain was washing away some of the gas. That should make it easier for them to breathe and see.

Despite the nightmare going on around them, Lucas's gaze met hers. For just a couple of seconds. She wanted to tell him how sorry she was that this had happened again.

She wanted to say a lot of things to him.

But since it wasn't the time or the place, Hailey went back to keeping watch. Right now, that was the best thing she could do for all of them. Too bad she didn't see something on the screens that would help Dade and the others close in on the gunmen. She switched the angle.

Nothing.

Then she switched it again, and that's when Hailey saw the movement. With the thick rain, it was just a blur, but someone had definitely moved up behind the two gunmen.

Another man dressed all in black. This one, though, was also wearing rain gear—a coat with a hood.

Hailey wasn't sure how he'd gotten there, but it was possible he'd come from the vehicle that had crashed through the fence. That SUV was only yards away from the other thugs.

"There's a third gunman," she relayed to Lucas.

And it made her wonder if there were others in the SUV. It tightened her stomach even more to think that there could be enough of them to overrun the ranch. Plus, there were the two across the road with the sniper rifles who had pinned down Josh and Sawyer.

"If any of the gunmen move," Lucas said, "let me know."

The words had no sooner left his mouth when the newcomer did move. He hurried behind a tree.

Coming closer to the ranch.

Closer to Lucas's house.

More movement caught her eye, and when she adjusted the camera angle, she saw the guy aim the tear gas launcher. No, not again. But he fired. Not one but two canisters.

Except these were different.

The gas coming from them was thicker, and it was milky white.

Hailey turned the laptop so that Lucas could see it, and he cursed. "Smoke bombs."

Hailey knew the reason for his profanity. As bad as the tear gas was—and it was *bad*—the smoke bombs could be worse. Because they could conceal the gunmen trying to move closer to the house.

And that's exactly what was happening.

The smoke began to spread, and it continued when the men fired off several more.

"Keep watch as best you can," Lucas advised her.

She would, but it was next to impossible to keep track of the men now. Maybe the rain, though, would work in their favor and quickly wash the smoke away as it was dissipating the tear gas.

A buzzing sound shot through the truck, and Hailey's heart jumped to her throat. At first she thought it was their attackers, but it was only Lucas's phone. With all the chaos going on, she'd forgotten that she was still holding it.

"It's Grayson," she relayed, looking at the phone screen. She answered it right away and put it on speaker.

"Please tell me you found my baby," Colleen jumped to say.

"No, but I'm close enough to the car to see inside.

There are two men in the front seat and an infant carrier in the back. The person I don't see is Minton. Any idea where he is?"

Hailey quickly scanned through all the camera angles. Even with the smoke, she could see Dade and the others pinned down. She couldn't see the gunmen, though, who'd been shooting and launching that tear gas and the smoke bombs.

But there was no sign of Minton.

"I don't know," Hailey told Grayson. "According to what the kidnapper showed us, he was in the car with the baby earlier."

"Yeah, but he's not there now, or if he is, he's down on the floor where I can't see him."

"Does that mean the bomb isn't there, either?" Colleen blurted out.

"I can't tell. But I'm going closer as soon as I have the backup that Mason's sending." Grayson paused. "Do I want to know how bad things are at the ranch?"

"The gunmen haven't gotten to the houses," Lucas answered.

What Lucas didn't say was—they hadn't, *not yet*. But there was always the possibility that they would unless the Rylands and ranch hands figured out a way to stop them.

"I'll call you back when I can," Grayson said before he hung up.

Hailey hoped he could get the baby out of there. That would be one less worry on their minds. Because even if Colleen was guilty, Hailey still wanted her niece far away from this dangerous situation.

"Where's the third gunman you saw?" Lucas asked her.

That sent Hailey's attention back to the computer

screen. As she'd done before, she panned around the camera angles, looking at the tree where she'd last spotted him. But even when the smoke cleared a little in that area, there was no sign of him now.

Sweet heaven.

Because she'd gotten so preoccupied with Grayson's call, Hailey had lost sight of him. That could turn out to be a fatal mistake. Especially considering the gunman could be hiding in one of those smoke clouds that were drifting toward Lucas's house.

"Any chance the third gunman could be Minton?" Lucas added.

Hailey went back through what she'd seen of the man, but she had to shake her head. "I never saw him standing fully upright, so it's hard to know how tall he is. Plus he was wearing a hood, so I couldn't see any part of his face. But it's possible it's Minton. Or Eric."

However, it was just as likely that it was another thug who'd been hired to kill her.

"Grayson has to get to my baby," Colleen said.

Obviously she wasn't thinking about the third gunman. Maybe not even thinking about who was responsible for this. Her focus seemed to be solely on the baby. And she was crying.

Hailey was definitely affected by those tears, and it tore at her heart to think how much her sister could be suffering right now. She slid her hand over Colleen's, causing her sister to flinch. At first. Then Colleen gave her hand a gentle squeeze.

"No matter what happens," Colleen said, "I'm sorry for the way things have turned out."

Hailey was about to ask her exactly what she meant by that. But she didn't get a chance to say anything.

That's because the passenger door flew open, and before Hailey could even register what was going on, someone latched onto Colleen and dragged her from the truck.

That someone put a gun to Colleen's head.

Chapter Eighteen

Lucas whipped his gun in Colleen's direction. But it was too late. The man already had her before Lucas could do anything to stop it.

However, Lucas could do something to keep Hailey safe. He crawled over her, putting himself in front of her. He didn't lower his weapon. He kept it aimed at the guy. He also watched Colleen's reaction.

She called out for help, tried to get away, but the man only jammed the gun harder against her head. It seemed convincing.

Seemed.

But Lucas reminded himself that this could all be part of the ploy to get to Hailey. A ploy he hadn't been able to prevent because he hadn't seen the guy sneaking up on the truck.

Behind him, he could hear Hailey's breath gusting, and he knew she had to be scared. Lucas hoped, though, that she would continue to keep watch around them, because heaven knew how many hired guns could be coming at them.

"Let Colleen go," Lucas demanded, though he figured this would get zero results.

And it didn't.

The guy laughed. He was wearing a tear gas mask that covered the lower part of his face, but Lucas could see enough of him to know that this wasn't Minton or Eric. He was likely just another hired gun.

"Sorry, can't let her go," the man finally said. "Got my orders, and I'm to keep this gun on her."

"Who's giving those orders?" Lucas snapped.

"It's not my place to tell, but you'll know soon enough. The boss is on the way. He should be here any minute now, and then things will get real…interesting."

Hell. Lucas had figured as much, but it was gut-tightening to hear it spelled out for him.

"Keep an eye on the security feed," Lucas told Hailey, but he wasn't even sure there was enough room for her to maneuver the laptop around so she could look. There hadn't been a lot of time when he'd moved in front of her, and she was literally jammed against him, the steering wheel and the door.

"Don't let him kill me," Colleen begged while she stared at Lucas. "*Please.* I don't want my daughter to be an orphan."

Neither did he, but Lucas wasn't sure yet how to put a stop to this. Especially when the guy shifted the gun and took aim at him. Hailey must have seen that, because she came over his back, putting her head in front of his.

Lucas cursed at her, tried to get her to move back, but she fought him.

"He won't kill me," Hailey insisted. "Not until he's sure I've given him everything I have on the DeSalvo family. But he'll kill you."

"The little lady's right," the gunman verified. "And since I can't risk a bullet going straight through you and into her, then I have to settle for just telling you to toss out that gun."

One of the last things Lucas wanted to do was surrender his gun. But he didn't want to risk Colleen and Hailey being shot, either. So he tried to reason with this guy.

"Whatever you're getting paid, I'll double it," Lucas offered. "I can make the call now and have the funds transferred to your bank."

"That sounds real nice." The sarcasm dripped from his voice. "But doing something like that would get me killed. Besides, I'm getting paid pretty good for this. Now, throw out that gun."

Lucas felt something against his back. Hailey's hand. And it wasn't empty. She had hold of his backup weapon, no doubt a reminder that he could use that. But the problem was that once Lucas didn't have a visible weapon, this thug might change his mind about shooting.

And yes, the bullet could go through him and kill Hailey.

Even if it didn't, it could kill him, and then this thug would be able to do whatever he wanted with Colleen and Hailey.

"Time's up," the guy said without warning.

The shot blasted through the air.

Followed by Colleen's piercing scream.

Lucas felt as if someone had slugged him, and he had to fight his instincts to move away from Hailey and leave her unprotected. But it also sickened him to hear Colleen make sharp sounds of pain.

And to see the blood.

"Oh, God," Hailey said, and she would have come over Lucas if the thug hadn't pointed his weapon right

at her. She stopped, freezing, but she kept repeating,
"Oh, God."

"I only shot her in the arm," the man said as if that
was some huge concession. Which, in a way, it was.
Because he could have just as easily killed her.

The blood spread quickly across Colleen's arm, and
she looked at Lucas, silently begging him to help her.
He'd wanted proof that Colleen was innocent in all of
this, and the gunshot was it. He seriously doubted that
she would have agreed to a henchman shooting her as
part of the deal.

In the distance, Lucas heard another blast from the
launcher. More smoke bombs, no doubt.

"No more warnings," the gunman said to Lucas.
"Toss out the gun or I shoot her again. This time I
might not be so careful where I aim."

He wasn't bluffing, so Lucas had no choice but to
throw his gun out of the open truck door. Now he only
hoped he could get to his backup weapon when he
needed it. And he would need it. He was certain of that.

"Now what?" Lucas snapped.

"We wait." The guy glanced at the back of the house,
where the smoke was still the thickest. He also peeled
off his gas mask. Probably because the rain had rid them
of the tear gas. Lucas's eyes were still burning, but the
sensation wasn't nearly as bad as it had been.

Hailey still had his phone, and Lucas heard it buzz.
Mason or Grayson was probably calling. But the thug
shook his head. "Let that go to voice mail."

Hailey did, and she eased the backup weapon to Lucas's side. Ideally the gunman didn't see what was going
on, but he had his attention nailed to them.

"Help me," Colleen said. She was shaking now.

Maybe going into shock. And she needed medical attention. However, the only way she was going to get that was for Lucas to get rid of his thug so they could call for an ambulance.

"When I move, get down," Lucas whispered to Hailey.

He felt the muscles in her body tense. Clearly, she didn't like the idea of him moving. Probably because she knew what the outcome could be. But thankfully Hailey didn't argue with him.

Lucas got ready to launch himself at the gunman. Maybe he'd be able to knock both him and his gun to the ground. Of course, Colleen would be in the middle, and Lucas prayed she didn't get hurt any worse than she already was, but if he didn't do something fast, they'd all be dead.

His phone buzzed again, distracting him for a moment. Something bad was probably going on. Maybe that bad thing didn't include Camden, but even if it did, Lucas had to put it out of his mind and try to finish this.

He didn't get far

Lucas hadn't even started moving when he saw something out of the corner of his eye. Someone was coming toward the back of the truck. Maybe one of his brothers or a Ryland cousin.

But it wasn't.

The gunman smiled, and while he still had hold of Colleen, he moved away from the truck door, making room for their visitor.

"Told you it wouldn't be long," the gunman taunted. "The boss is here."

LUCAS SHIFTED HIS body so that it was hard for Hailey to see. He did that so he could reach the gun she was trying to give him, but it also meant she didn't know who had just arrived. She had no trouble recognizing his voice, though.

"Finally," he said.

Eric.

She hadn't known which of their suspects would be coming at them through the smoke, but Eric certainly wasn't a surprise. But was he working with Minton? Or had he come up with this all on his own?

Whatever *this* was.

"Can we leave now?" the thug asked Eric.

Eric shook his head. "Soon, though. I'm getting another vehicle up here since your idiot comrades shot out the radiator of Lucas's truck. Not very smart, and they'll pay for that."

So Eric was planning on using it to escape. But she doubted that he and his hired gum would be leaving alone. No.

Eric would try to take Colleen and her with him, and that meant Lucas would try to stop it. He could be hurt or killed in the process.

Hailey put aside the laptop so her hands would be free in case things were about to get worse than they already were. Lucas took the gun, but there was no way he could lift it without causing Eric and the thug to shoot first. Both had their weapons aimed at Hailey and him.

"You bastard," Colleen spat out. "You took my daughter, and now you had your hired gun shoot me. And why? I erased all those files. I did everything you told me to do."

"You knew it was Eric?" Lucas asked, and he didn't sound pleased that Colleen might have withheld that from them.

Colleen shook her head. "No. But I suspected it. He knew Preston had left me money, and taking my baby was the only way to get it back."

Eric lifted his shoulder. "You didn't deserve a penny of DeSalvo money just because you slept with my father."

"I had his child!" Colleen practically shouted, but the outburst combined with the blood loss must have drained her, because she sagged against the gunman holding her. He shoved her back up, jamming the gun against her head again.

"You think that matters to me?" Eric didn't wait for her to answer. "Because it doesn't."

Hailey saw the anger rise on Eric's face and knew she couldn't let his short fuse and horrible temper come into play here. "Why did you do all of this?"

"Isn't it obvious? I don't want to die in jail like my father. You have files and information that could put me behind bars."

True, but it wasn't for anything serious.

"You made the deal with the DA," Lucas reminded him.

"It included only the recordings from my father's office." He glanced around, no doubt looking for the vehicle that was coming for them.

Lucas's phone buzzed again. The third time someone had tried to call them in the past couple of minutes. It was no doubt important. Maybe even about Camden. But Hailey didn't answer it.

"When the FBI, CSIs or some other agency with initials analyzes the voice on those tapes, they might be able to identify Melvin here." He tipped his head to the gunman. "Melvin has worked for me for years. He has a record, and it wouldn't take much to connect him to me if they were able to match his voice."

"There was no dirty agent," Lucas concluded. "But you let your father believe there was."

"You'd be surprised what I learned from the old man when he thought he was talking to an actual agent. I made lots of money on deals where my father gave the fake guy some insider information. Of course, I had to share some of that cash with Daddy to make him think he was running things."

Yes, but Preston wouldn't have known his own son was working behind the scenes to milk him of family funds. It was all so senseless since Eric would have inherited most of it anyway.

At least, he would have, unless there'd been another child.

Oh, mercy.

"What are you going to do with your half sister?" Hailey blurted out.

That put some new alarm in Colleen's face. Probably because she'd pieced it together, as well. Eric wouldn't want any competition for the DeSalvo estate, and it was possible that the baby—and therefore Colleen—would have a claim.

"Yes," Eric said, looking at Hailey. He'd obviously seen the realization in her eyes. "And of course, you have to go, too. You know too much. Plus, I'm betting you have some dirt on me squirreled away."

Hailey was about to say that she didn't have anything else now that Colleen had deleted the files. But she changed her mind and went with something that might save them.

"If anything happens to me, the files I have will be sent to every news agency in the state," she lied.

Eric laughed, but the laughter stopped just as quickly

as it'd started. "Where are the files?" he snapped. His temper was definitely showing again.

"I'm not telling you. Not until you get Colleen an ambulance and you and your hired killers are off Ryland land."

Eric's mouth tightened. "Nice try. But you're all dying. Including him." His glare slashed to Lucas. "Thanks to Hailey including you in this, she's signed your death warrant."

"Hailey didn't involve me," Lucas said, his voice low and dangerous. "*You* involved me when you tried to kill her and put my son in danger. How the hell do you possibly think you're going to get away with this?"

"Easy. I plan on pinning all of this on Minton. He's an idiot. And soon he'll be dead like the rest of you."

Sweet heaven. If Minton was anywhere near the baby, then she could be hurt, too. Or worse.

Hailey heard the sound of a car approaching from the back of the house. A moment later she saw the black SUV, the one that had brought in the gunmen. Had no doubt brought Eric, too.

"All of you will come with me," Eric insisted. "And that way I'll have some leverage to make sure Hailey gives me everything that she possibly has on me."

By leverage he meant they would become his hostages.

Eric would no doubt torture Lucas and Colleen to get Hailey to give him something she didn't have. Once he figured that out, he would indeed kill all of them. Probably Minton, too.

"Let's move," Eric said, and he used his gun to motion toward the approaching SUV.

Hailey knew that time was up. They had to do something now even though Lucas didn't have a clean shot. Eric was staying behind Colleen and his hired gun.

And Lucas did something, all right.

He sprang from the seat, barreling out of the truck, and he crashed into Colleen, Eric and the gunman.

They all went to the ground.

But the only sound Hailey heard was the shot that one of them fired.

THE SHOT WAS DEAFENING, but Lucas prayed that it hadn't hit Hailey, Colleen or him. It was hard to tell because the impact of slamming into the ground had knocked the breath out of him, and the pain spiked through him when his jaw collided with the hired gun's Glock.

Lucas hadn't wanted things to play out this way, but Eric hadn't given him much of a choice. If they'd gotten into that SUV with him and his hired killers, Colleen, Hailey and he would have soon been dead.

Colleen screamed when they fell, but Lucas still didn't know if she'd been shot again. That's because the fight started almost immediately. The thug slammed his gun against Lucas's head so hard that it probably gave him a concussion.

That didn't stop Lucas from fighting, though. The stakes were too high for him to lose. He still had hold of his gun, but it was too risky to get a shot off now. He had to get Colleen out of the way first, and that wouldn't be easy since she was trapped between Eric and him.

Eric spewed out a string of profanity, and for a guy who didn't work with his hands, he was fighting hard. He was also trying to shoot Lucas. Eric brought up his gun, but Lucas managed to knock it away in the nick of time.

Eric's shot blasted into the ground right next to Lucas.

Hailey yelled out something. Something that Lucas didn't catch, but he hoped she would stay back.

She didn't.

He saw her out of the corner of his eye. She had gotten out of the truck and had picked up his gun. The one he'd thrown out of the truck. She was trying to take aim, but there was no way she'd have a clean shot.

But Eric did.

The goon was punching Lucas, but he still managed to see Eric lift his gun again. And this time he aimed it at Hailey.

"Get down!" Lucas shouted to her.

He wasn't sure if she did—not in time, anyway—before Eric pulled the trigger again. Lucas didn't look to see where the shot had gone. Instead he shifted his weight, shoving Colleen out of the way so that he could pin down Eric.

Melvin was obviously looking out for his boss, because he walloped Lucas in the head again. More than anything, Lucas wanted to shoot the guy, but he couldn't let go of Eric to do that.

Someone fired, though.

Hailey.

She'd shot into the ground. Maybe to distract Eric and Melvin. If so, it worked in a bad way. Melvin looked at Hailey.

And he took aim.

That meant Lucas had to release Eric so he could dive at Melvin. Melvin still managed to pull the trigger, but Lucas was able to throw Melvin enough off balance that he didn't shoot Hailey. But Melvin had come darn close to doing just that.

Too close.

Lucas couldn't tell her that now because he was fighting for their lives, but later he wanted her to know that she should never take a risk like that again. Because she could have been killed. He could have lost her.

Colleen scurried away from them, and while she was holding her injured arm, she ran to Hailey. Maybe because Hailey didn't see it coming, Colleen wrenched the gun from her hand. Colleen pointed it at the men.

"Give me back my daughter, Eric," Colleen shouted. "Or so help me, I'll kill you right now."

Lucas prayed she didn't shoot, because the way she was shaking, there was no telling who Colleen might hit. His cousins were likely nearby, and a stray shot could kill one of them. It also caused his heart to slam against his chest when he saw that Hailey was trying to get the gun back from her sister. No way did he want Hailey in a struggle—any kind of struggle—where there was a gun involved.

Since every second this went on was another second when someone could get killed, Lucas threw his own gun aside so he could latch onto Melvin's. Of course, Eric took full advantage of that. He tried to take aim again, but Lucas stopped him by slamming his elbow into Eric's jaw. Eric howled in pain and dropped back down to the ground.

A shot cracked through the air.

Lucas's breath stopped, and despite being in a fist-fight with Melvin, he glanced at Hailey to make sure she was all right. She wasn't. She was seemingly frozen with both Colleen's and her hands on the gun.

Melvin cursed, and he froze as well.

Lucas looked on the ground beside him and saw Eric.

Bleeding. The shot that Colleen had fired had hit him in the stomach.

"You're gonna pay for that!" Melvin yelled, and he tried to turn his gun on Colleen.

Lucas didn't let that happen. He used the new surge of adrenaline that he got to grab Melvin's gun. Of course, Melvin didn't just give it up. He kept trying to aim it at Colleen. But instead, Lucas turned the gun on the hired killer.

Just as Melvin pulled the trigger.

The bullet went into his chest. Since the shot was at point-blank range, Melvin didn't even draw another breath. It killed him instantly.

Lucas didn't waste a second on the gunman. Instead, he took the guy's weapon and aimed it at Eric. He also kicked Eric's gun from his hand and took aim at him in case he tried to move. He did, but it was only to clutch his stomach and his chest.

And he laughed.

"You think this is over," Eric said, looking at Colleen and Hailey. "It's not."

That's when Lucas realized that Eric wasn't just holding his hand to his gunshot wound. He pressed something on his chest. A small box that resembled a remote control on a garage.

A split second later, Lucas heard a sound he definitely didn't want to hear.

An explosion.

Chapter Nineteen

"No!" Colleen yelled.

Lucas didn't yell, but he frantically looked around to see if he could find the source of the explosion. It hadn't come from the area where the tear gas had been launched. No. This was further away. Just up the road from the ranch.

In the same area where Grayson had said he'd spotted the kidnapper's vehicle.

Colleen must have realized that, too, because despite her injury, she turned and started to run in that direction.

"Stop her," Lucas told Hailey. Though he hated to give an order like that since Colleen was still armed. It was obvious she was hysterical, and there was no telling what she might do.

Lucas checked first to make sure there were no weapons near Eric. He was bleeding, maybe dying, but that didn't mean he wouldn't be able to shoot them. It would be the ultimate way to get his revenge.

Hailey hooked her arm around Colleen's waist but didn't have a solid enough footing and her sister slung her to the ground. That meant a change of plan. Lucas scooped up one of the guns and handed it to Hailey.

"Make sure Eric doesn't get up," he told her, and he took off running after Colleen. There were possibly some of Eric's hired guns still in the area, and he didn't want Colleen shot for a second time tonight. The next bullet just might kill her.

Might kill him, too.

Lucas only hoped they didn't get caught in the middle of a gunfight.

He had to tackle Colleen, dragging them both to the ground again. This couldn't be good for her injury since she was still bleeding. But despite that injury, she fought like a wildcat.

"I have to get to my baby!" she shouted.

Yeah, Lucas understood that, but he shook his head and got in her face. "You can't go down there. It's a good quarter of a mile away, and you'll be killed."

Logic wasn't going to work here, so he just pinned her to the ground with his body and wrenched the gun from her hand. Colleen kept fighting him, punching his chest with her fists, and Lucas just let her do it while he kept watch to make sure they weren't about to be ambushed.

He looked back at Hailey. Even from a distance he could see that she was shaking, but she still had the gun aimed at Eric. Eric wasn't saying anything, wasn't moving, either. Lucas had rarely wished someone dead, but he hoped in this case that Eric was so that he would no longer be a threat to Hailey and Colleen.

But there were other threats out there.

Colleen finally quit fighting, her hands dropping to the ground, and she sobbed. The tears came, mixed with the rain on her face, but Lucas could deal with the tears as long as she didn't run out into the path of those possible gunmen. Now that he knew Colleen was innocent in all of this, he definitely wanted to make sure he kept Hailey's sister alive.

He got up, pulling Colleen to her feet, and he took her to the truck, pushing her into the middle so Hailey could get in, as well. He wouldn't be able to drive the truck, but at least being inside it was better than having them stay in the open.

Hailey had such a fierce grip on the gun and her muscles were so rigid that it took Lucas a moment to get her moving. When he finally did, she sagged against him.

"The baby," she said.

Lucas figured she was praying that her niece was okay. He was doing the same and adding some extra prayers for Camden and the rest of his family.

"Both of you stay down," Lucas told them once he had Hailey in the cab of the truck.

She nodded, took out his phone and showed him the screen with the missed calls. All three were from Mason. Lucas certainly hadn't forgotten about them, but he wanted to keep his hands, and his attention, free in case they were attacked again.

Hailey must have understood that, because she hit the redial button and put it on speaker. Mason answered on the first ring.

"What the hell was that explosion?" Mason immediately asked.

"I'm not sure." Lucas didn't want to spell out his worst fears. "Have you talked to Grayson?"

"He's not answering his phone, and he's nowhere near any of the security cameras. Please tell me he wasn't near that bomb when it went off."

Lucas didn't know, and again he didn't want to guess.

Grayson was smart, so maybe he'd made it out of there with the baby.

"The reason I called you earlier was to warn you about Eric," Mason went on. "I saw him on one of the cameras. Is he dead?"

"Not yet. Can you call an ambulance for Colleen and him?" Lucas asked.

"Already done, and they're on the way. Dade and the others have cleared the gunmen so the medics can get through. I'll send a cruiser down to pick up Colleen, Hailey and you. Colleen is innocent, right?"

Lucas glanced back at her. "Yeah." Innocent and shaken to the core. Also still losing some blood. Hailey had peeled off her hoodie and was using it as a make-shift tourniquet.

"Good," Mason answered. "Then the three of you can come here. I'll have Dade or someone wait with Eric. Let me know the moment you hear anything from Grayson."

"I will." Lucas looked around the yard again. "Are you sure the gunmen are all out of commission?"

"All the ones on the ranch grounds. The ones across the road, too." He paused. "Don't know about Minton, though."

Yes. Lucas hadn't forgotten about him, either. Eric had claimed there was no dirty agent, and that should clear Minton's name. If Eric was telling the truth.

Lucas heard the sound of an approaching car coming from the main part of the ranch, and he automatically pivoted in that direction with his gun aimed and ready. But it wasn't one of Eric's thugs. It was Sawyer and Josh. Josh hurried out of the cruiser toward them

"I drew the short straw," Josh said. "Go ahead with Sawyer. I'll make sure Eric doesn't go anywhere."

Lucas hated to put this on his cousin, but one look at Hailey and Colleen and he knew he had to get them out of there. He thanked Josh, and because he didn't want the women out in the open any longer than necessary, he scooped up Colleen and took her to the cruiser. He would have gone back and done the same for Hailey, but she was already trailing along behind him. He put Colleen in the front seat. Hailey and he took the back.

"I'm okay," Hailey said to him.

It was almost certainly a lie, but Lucas latched onto it. He also latched onto her. He pulled her into his arms, probably with a lot harder grip than either of them had been expecting.

The relief came. She was alive and in one piece. No thanks to Eric. That fight could have played out a dozen different ways, and in any one of the scenarios, Hailey could have been hurt or worse.

Colleen, however, wasn't faring as well. She was sobbing now, hunched over and probably in a lot of pain. Maybe it wouldn't be long before the ambulance arrived, though Lucas was worried that she might not go to the hospital until they got news about the baby.

It wasn't a long trip to the main house, but it certainly felt like one. Lucas kept watch the whole way, but thankfully he didn't see any signs of danger.

Only the aftermath.

He spotted one of the gunmen, dead, in the pasture. Not far from where they'd launched the smoke bombs and the tear gas. The goon and his fellow hired thugs had turned the Silver Creek Ranch into a war zone.

That twisted at Lucas's gut. But it was also something he had to push aside.

For Hailey's sake.

Heck, for his own peace of mind.

Because he thought they could both use it, he brushed a kiss on Hailey's forehead. Then her cheek. Yes, they both needed that. Needed the real kiss that followed, too. It wasn't nearly long enough, but Lucas figured he could do better later. Later, he wanted to do a lot of things. Like tell Hailey that he had died a thousand times tonight worrying about her, and that it had driven home to him just how important she was to him.

"I'm in love with you," Hailey blurted out.

Judging from the startled look in her eyes, she hadn't intended to say that. Nor did she have time to add more, because Sawyer pulled to a stop directly in front of the main house, and that was their cue to get moving. Sawyer helped with Colleen, but before they even made it up the steps, Lucas heard two welcome sounds.

The ambulance sirens.

And his son.

Camden was fussing, and while it was obvious he wasn't happy about something, just hearing him eased the knot in Lucas's stomach.

Despite her limp, Hailey hurried in ahead of them. And Lucas let her. She looked around the massive foyer. No sign of Camden there, but he was in the adjacent family room with Tillie and Mason's wife, Abbie. Tillie was pacing while rocking Camden, obviously trying to get him to sleep. Hailey went to him and pulled him into her arms.

Camden stopped fussing right away and studied her face. Hailey was still pretty much a stranger to him, but that didn't stop his boy from smiling. He smiled even more when he looked in Lucas's direction.

Everything suddenly seemed all right with the world.

Well, almost everything. His phone buzzed, and when he saw Grayson's name on the screen, Lucas knew this was a call he had to take.

"Is it about the baby?" Colleen asked. Sawyer was trying to get her to sit, but she batted away his hands and went to Lucas.

Lucas figured it was indeed about the baby, but he wasn't sure it would be good news. No way to buffer it from Colleen, though, since she was right next to him. Because she would probably be able to hear every word anyway, he went ahead and put it on speaker.

"I have the baby," Grayson immediately said.

Lucas could feel the relief go through the room, and Hailey went to her sister to give her a hug. Colleen broke down again, crying, but Lucas figured these were happy tears.

"Is she okay? Was she hurt?" Colleen blurted out.

"She's fine," Grayson answered. "I'm bringing her to the ranch right now. The ambulance is ahead of me."

Which meant Colleen wouldn't have much time with her daughter before being whisked away to the hospital. She wouldn't care much for that, but Colleen needed medical attention ASAP. She also clearly needed to see her daughter right away, because she started toward the door and would have hurried out, no doubt to watch for Grayson. But Lucas stopped her. He didn't want any one of them outside just yet.

"What about the explosion?" Hailey asked.

"The bomb detonated after the baby was already out of the car," Grayson answered. "Minton killed the kidnapper, but he couldn't disarm the bomb, so he took the baby and ran. When I'd looked in the SUV earlier with the binoculars, I thought she was still in the vehicle, but it was only her car seat that I saw."

Good. Lucas hated that the baby had even had to go through a nightmare like that, but at least she wasn't near the blast.

Thanks to Minton.

"Where is Minton?" Lucas pressed.

"With me."

Lucas felt no regret about that whatsoever and hoped all of Eric's hired thugs were dead or arrested. And speaking of Eric, he needed to give Grayson an update on the idiot who'd done his best to make their lives a living hell.

"Minton won't be staying," Grayson continued. "He wants to borrow a vehicle to get him back to his office, so once I'm at the house, I'll let him use my truck."

Even though Minton was innocent and had helped them by saving the baby, Lucas could understand why the agent didn't want to hang around. He hadn't exactly been friendly to Hailey and the rest of them. Plus, like Grayson, he probably had reports to write up about the attack.

"If Eric's still alive, he'll need to go to the hospital, too," Lucas said.

"Yeah. I got a call from Dade. Eric died a couple of minutes ago. The ME will come out and take care of the body. The bodies of the other gunmen, as well."

Lucas thanked him. He definitely didn't want any of his cousins or their families waking up to a giant crime scene, so maybe the bodies and the debris could be cleared out by morning.

Grayson had been right about the ambulance, because Lucas heard the siren as it made the turn toward the main house. He wished he could talk Hailey into going to the hospital, too, to be checked out, but judging from the grip she had on Camden, that wasn't going to happen.

"Maybe I can ride with the baby and Colleen in the ambulance?" Tillie suggested. Lucas wanted to kiss the woman for making the offer. "Unless Hailey and you need me here for Camden, that is."

"No," Hailey and Lucas said in unison. They'd be just fine now that the danger had passed.

Well, maybe it had passed.

"Are we sure there are no more hired killers?" Lucas asked Grayson.

"The hands and deputies are doing a final search now, but there's no one shooting. Just in case one's hiding, Sawyer and Josh are going to do a sweep with infrared. Mason's still in his office checking the security cameras."

Hailey closed her eyes a moment, nodded. She was obviously thankful for these extra security measures. It would help everyone get some sleep for what was left of the night. Everyone except Colleen. But he figured she wouldn't mind. She was alive, and her baby had been rescued.

Grayson ended the call just as the ambulance pulled to a stop in front of the house, and this time Lucas wasn't able to hold Colleen back. That's because Grayson had said he was right behind the medics. And he was. He didn't waste any time getting out and bringing the baby to Colleen.

There were more tears, of course, and Colleen hugged her daughter as tightly as Hailey was hugging Camden.

"You should go," Grayson prompted Colleen. Apparently he'd already given his keys to Minton, because the agent drove away.

Colleen managed a shaky nod, but despite the fact she was bleeding, she carried the baby toward the ambulance. Tillie was right behind her.

"Call me when you can," Hailey told her sister. "And if the doctors keep you at the hospital overnight, I'll be there first thing in the morning."

Despite everything that had gone on, Colleen managed a weak smile and a thank-you. Maybe this was the start of a better relationship between the sisters.

"Tell Mason I'm taking his cruiser," Grayson said to Abbie. "If anyone needs me, I'll be with the ME and then at the office."

Lucas felt guilty since Grayson had a long stretch of work ahead of him. And he'd help. But not tonight. Tonight he needed to be with Hailey and Camden.

"Do you want me to take Camden?" Abbie asked.

Lucas certainly hadn't forgotten about Mason's wife being there, but he didn't understand her question. No way did he want Camden out of his sight. But Lucas looked at Hailey. Then himself. They were soaking wet, covered in mud, blood and heaven knew what else.

"You can use the showers in the guest rooms," Abbie suggested.

"In just a couple of minutes." Hailey kissed Camden's cheek, and despite the fact that he was right up against her wet clothes, he didn't seem to mind.

Abbie must have decided they needed some alone

time, because she disappeared down the hall. Probably to check on her own sons.

Hailey got a few more kisses and then passed Camden to Lucas so he could do the same. It was pure magic. Somehow, just holding his son could melt away most of the misery from the past couple of days.

But misery wasn't the only thing that'd happened tonight.

"You said you were in love with me," Lucas reminded Hailey.

She made a soft sound of surprise. "Yes, *that*." Then she dodged his gaze and opened her mouth to say something that Lucas realized he might not want to hear.

"You can't take it back," he growled, and then frowned when he heard the tone of his own voice. He hadn't meant to make it sound like an order. "Please don't take it back," he amended.

Hailey didn't make another sound of surprise, but judging from the way her eyes widened, she certainly hadn't been expecting that from him. Well, Lucas hadn't expected it, either. Nor was he sure when he'd wanted Hailey's "I'm in love with you," but he definitely wanted it.

With Camden in the crook of his left arm, Lucas slid his right hand around Hailey's waist and pulled her closer. He kissed her. Not some gentle, everything-will-be-all-right kind of kiss, either. This was long and deep. Just the way he liked his kisses when it came to Hailey.

The kiss stirred the heat between them, but it did more than that. It made things crystal clear for Lucas.

"I fell in love with you shortly after we met," he said with his lips still against hers. "That hasn't changed.

Never will. I want you in my bed…my life. Our lives," he added, glancing down at Camden.

And Lucas pulled back so he could see her reaction. He expected her to be stunned. Maybe even have a run-for-the-hills kind of look in her eyes.

She didn't.

Hailey smiled, slow and easy. A smile that lit up her whole face, and she pulled him right back to her for another kiss. "Good. And you can't take it back."

Lucas had no intentions of ever taking it back. Ever. He gathered Hailey and his son into his arms and held on.

* * * * *

DRURY

Chapter One

Special Agent Drury Ryland pulled into his driveway, his truck headlights slashing through the curtain of rain. Rain that nearly caused him to miss the movement behind his detached garage.

Nearly.

But Drury managed to catch a glimpse of someone darting out of sight.

He groaned because it wasn't exactly the hour or the weather for a visitor. Or the place. He was home, in one of the nearly dozen houses on the sprawling Silver Creek Ranch, and all those houses were occupied by lawmen. Anyone who'd come here to break in was a couple of steps past being stupid.

Of course, it might not be a break-in.

Because Drury's arm was still throbbing from the six stitches he had just gotten, he had no trouble recalling the encounter he'd had three hours earlier. A thug had knifed him during an FBI sting operation. Drury had managed to arrest him, but the guy had sworn on his soul that he would get even with Drury. No way could the soul-swearing guy have gotten out of jail yet, but he could have sent one of his buddies to do his dirty work.

Drury brought his truck to a stop, eased his hand

over his gun and tried to pick through the darkness and rain so he could get another glimpse of the guy. Nothing. But Drury knew he was there.

"I'm Agent Drury Ryland," he shouted. "Come out so I can see you."

The guy didn't. And not only didn't he come out, he fired a shot. Before Drury could even react, the bullet slammed into his windshield.

The next two shots went straight into his truck's engine. One must have hit the radiator because steam started spewing into the air.

Drury cursed. There went his way to escape. If he wanted to escape, that is. He didn't. He wanted to confront this moron and make him pay for starting a gunfight on Ryland land.

Since the sound of the shots would no doubt alert his cousins and brothers, Drury sent a quick text to one of those cousins, Sheriff Grayson Ryland, and requested backup. However, Drury was hoping he could put an end to the situation before backup even arrived.

Drury threw open his truck door, and using it for cover, he took aim at the shadowy figure that kept peering around the garage. He couldn't just start pulling the trigger, though. It had to be a clean shot because Drury didn't want it to ricochet and risk hitting a ranch hand or someone inside one of the nearby houses.

The shooter obviously didn't have that concern because he fired off another round at Drury. Big mistake. Because he had to lean out from the garage, and Drury took the shot.

And hit the guy.

Not a kill shot, though. He must have hit him in the shoulder because the gunman took off running. A few seconds later, Drury heard the sound of an engine.

No.

He didn't want this clown getting away. Drury had to find out why the heck he'd just tried to kill him.

A dark-colored SUV sped out from behind the garage. Not coming toward Drury. But rather the driver went on the other side of the house, through the yard and onto the road. Since there weren't any houses at this angle, Drury emptied the clip into the SUV.

Drury was certain he hit the guy again, but he kept going, speeding away from the house. He was about to jump in his truck and try to go in pursuit, but then Drury saw Grayson's cruiser approaching. Grayson was not only the sheriff of Silver Creek, but he lived the closest and that's why Drury had texted him.

When Grayson reached Drury, he put down the window, and Drury saw he wasn't alone. Grayson's brother Mason was with him.

"Any idea who's in that SUV?" Grayson asked.

Drury had to shake his head, but he lifted his arm to show them the fresh bandage. "Maybe a friend of the person who gave me this."

"We'll go after him," Grayson said. "Keep watch. Make sure he doesn't double back."

Since Drury's place was the first house on the road that led to the ranch, that wouldn't be hard to do.

When Grayson drove off in pursuit, Drury had a look around the grounds. He didn't see anyone else, though. And if his attacker had left any blood by the garage, the rain was washing it all away. That made it even more critical for Grayson to find him so Drury could get some answers.

He went to his back porch and cursed when he found the door unlocked. It was possible he'd just forgotten to lock it. Just as possible, though, that someone had broken in.

Especially after what'd just happened.

Drury got his gun ready and kicked open the door that led into his kitchen.

"Don't shoot," someone said.

A woman.

Because she'd whispered that order, Drury didn't immediately recognize her voice, but he certainly knew who she was when she stepped closer.

Caitlyn Denson.

The kitchen was dark, but there was enough illumination coming from the hall light that he had no trouble seeing her long brown hair and her face.

And the blood trickling down her forehead.

Drury didn't know what shocked him the most. The blood or that she was even there at all. They weren't exactly on friendly terms and hadn't been in a long time.

He had so many questions, and he wasn't sure where to start. But his lawman's instincts kicked in, and he checked her hands for weapons. Empty. And the pale yellow dress she was wearing was wet and clinging to her, so he knew she wasn't carrying concealed.

Still, he didn't lower his gun. He kept it aimed at her. And he maneuvered himself so he could watch out the large bay window in the living room while still keeping an eye on Caitlyn.

"I heard you'd built a house here on your cousins' ranch, and your name is on the mailbox. I parked behind your barn," she said, as if that explained everything.

It didn't, not by a long shot.

"Did you have anything to do with that?" Drury

tipped his head to the side yard where the shots had just been fired.

Caitlyn's eyes widened for just a second, and a thin breath left her mouth. "I think he was here because he's looking for me. I swear, I didn't know he'd follow me."

Well, it was an answer all right. But it only led to more questions. "You're going to have to give me a better explanation than that. And start with how you got that cut or whatever the hell it is." He grabbed some paper towels with his left hand and gave them to her.

She nodded and pressed the towels to her head. "I didn't break in, by the way. The door was unlocked, but you should know that I would have broken in if necessary. I needed a place to hide." She staggered, caught the back of the chair.

Drury cursed and went to her, holstering his gun so he could help her get seated and have a look at the wound that was causing her to bleed all over his kitchen floor. His stomach knotted when he saw the wound close-up.

"Did someone club you on the head?" he asked.

Caitlyn nodded, lightly touched the wound and grimaced when she saw the blood on her fingertips. "I'm not certain who did it. I didn't get a look at his face. But it could have been the same man who shot at you."

And if so, the thug had come to finish what he'd started, and Drury had gotten caught in the middle. Caught only because she'd come here. But why?

"You're sure you don't know who he is?" Drury pressed.

Even though he didn't spell it out, she obviously got what he meant. Was this connected to her late husband, Grant Denson? Grant had been dead for nearly two years now, but he'd been involved in some nasty illegal stuff when he was alive that might now have come back to haunt Caitlyn.

Of course, when you sleep with snakes, you should expect to get bitten.

Was that what had happened now?

"I honestly don't know the man's name," she explained. "But I know why he's after me." Her voice broke, and a hoarse sob tore from her mouth. "God, Drury, I'm so sorry. I didn't have anywhere else to go, and I didn't think he'd come here."

All right. That got his interest. Because she had a mother-in-law, Helen, who was loaded, not just money-wise but with all sorts of resources, including but not limited to thugs who could take care of the person who'd clubbed Caitlyn on the head.

"Start from the beginning," he demanded.

Caitlyn didn't exactly jump to do that, but she did nod again and then took a couple of seconds to gather her breath. "The year before Grant was killed, we were trying to have a baby, and we went to the Conceptions Fertility Clinic in San Antonio."

Everything inside him went still. He was well aware of the clinic because of the shady things that'd happened there just a month earlier. Specifically, embryos had been stolen and implanted in surrogates so that the former clinic manager could then "sell" the babies to the biological parents.

Ransom, extortion and black-market babies all rolled into one. Nasty business.

"All the babies were recovered and given to their parents," Drury reminded her.

Caitlyn paused a heartbeat. "Not all."

"Are you saying…?" But he stopped. "What the hell are you saying?"

"Day before yesterday I got a call from a man who said a surrogate had given birth to mine and Grant's daughter and that if I wanted the child, then I'd have to pay him a million dollars. He sent me a swab with the baby's DNA, and I had it analyzed. The man was telling the truth."

DNA could be faked. So could test results.

"And?" Drury questioned. "How did you get Grant's DNA to do a comparison?"

"From a comb I found in his things that I'd boxed up."

Drury made a circling motion for her to continue.

"I arranged payment, draining nearly every penny from Grant's estate, but when I went to get the baby, she wasn't there. Instead, the man demanded even more money."

Drury groaned. "Let me guess. They told you not to go to the cops or that you'd never see her again?" He waited for her to confirm that with a nod. "That's what criminals tell marks like you. Hell, they might not even have the baby. Or there might not be a baby at all. Even if the DNA appears to prove it's your child, they could have gotten the DNA from an embryo sample stored at the clinic."

Other than a soft moan, she didn't get a chance to respond because Drury's phone rang. "It's Grayson," he said, glancing at the screen.

That got her back on her feet, and Caitlyn shook her head. "Please don't tell him I'm here. Not yet. I'm not sure who I can trust."

"Well, you can't trust me," he snapped.

But that was a lie. He was a lawman and would do whatever it took to protect her or any other bleeding woman who showed up at his house.

"Please," she repeated, sounding just as desperate as she looked.

Drury wasn't going to let that *please* or desperation sway him. He intended to tell Grayson everything because while she might not trust his cousin, Drury darn sure did.

"We found the shooter," Grayson said the moment Drury answered the call. "He'd crashed his SUV into a tree about three miles from the ranch. He's hurt but alive."

"Who is he?" Drury asked.

"No ID, and the vehicle is registered to a woman in Austin."

Maybe that meant the SUV was stolen. Of course, Drury already knew this guy was a criminal capable of murder. "Did he happen to say why he fired shots at me or what he was doing at my place?" Drury pressed.

Caitlyn moved closer. Too close. No doubt trying to hear the conversation.

"He's not saying much of anything. He's groggy, slipping in and out of consciousness," Grayson added. "We'll get him to the hospital, but I did find something in the SUV that was, well, disturbing. Some rope, a ski mask, duct tape and rubber gloves."

No baby. Though Drury hadn't expected there would be. Caitlyn had likely been the victim of a scam, and now that they couldn't milk any more money from her, this thug had been sent to get rid of her.

"I'll head to the sheriff's office now," Drury insisted.

"You need a ride? When I drove by earlier, I saw your truck was messed up."

"Yeah. That thug shot the radiator. But I have a car in the garage. I'll also have someone with me who can shed some light on this."

Caitlyn was shaking her head before he even finished.

"Who?" Grayson asked, but he continued before Drury could respond. "Gotta go. Ambulance is here. You can tell me when you get to the office. See you in a few."

"No," Caitlyn said, still shaking her head when Drury ended the call. "You shouldn't have done that. You shouldn't have told Grayson you were bringing someone in."

And she took off. Not toward the door but rather into the living room.

"What the heck do you think you're doing?" Drury asked.

She didn't answer that. Caitlyn hurried to the side of the sofa, and she grabbed something from the floor. Even though the room was dark, Drury had no trouble seeing the bundled-up coat.

And the stun gun.

Caitlyn picked up both, and with the coat clutched to her chest, she started running, headed to the back door this time.

Drury stepped in front of her, blocking her path, but Caitlyn tried to dart around him. He didn't want her to get a chance to use that stun gun on him, so he caught onto her arm and knocked the stun gun from her hand.

"I have to go," she insisted. "It's not safe."

Maybe it wasn't, but that didn't mean Drury was just going to let her head out. He pulled her closer and had a better look at the coat.

Damn.

In the middle of that bundle, Drury saw something move. And that something was a baby.

Chapter Two

Caitlyn hadn't expected Drury just to let her walk out of there, but she also hadn't thought this insanity would go from bad to worse.

This definitely qualified as worse.

Now that he'd seen the baby, there was no way he'd willingly let her leave.

"The baby's yours?" he snapped.

"Maybe."

She'd figured Drury wasn't going to like that answer, and he didn't. He groaned. Then cursed.

"But I believe she's mine," Caitlyn went on. "And the man said she was. I figured I could have her tested later, but for now I have to go. That man who shot at you wants to kill me and take the baby."

"Yeah. I got that. According to Grayson, he had rope, tape, a ski mask and gloves in his SUV. All the makings of a felony or two."

Oh, God. Her stomach dropped. Even though Caitlyn had known the man didn't have good intentions, it sickened her to hear it spelled out like that. It also confirmed what she'd felt in her heart.

That he had no intention of giving her the baby.

had some answers. Maybe not even then. That meant she had to get away at the first chance she

"I took her from th

now

dizzy because

"Look, I know you

said. "But let me leave."

An understatement about the favors.

And the sound Drury made let her know that he didn't owe her a thing. Not after she'd walked out on him four years ago. He'd been in love with her. *Then.* Definitely not now, though. There wasn't a shred of love between them at this moment.

However, Caitlyn could still feel the tug of attraction. The one she'd had for Drury the first time she'd laid eyes on him. That attraction was all one-sided now, on her part. Drury's glare proved it.

"Please just help me by letting me leave right now," she begged.

It seemed to take him a couple of seconds to get his jaw unclenched so he could speak, and he didn't look at her when he did it. He volleyed his attention between the baby and the window. Drury was no doubt looking to see if the thug had indeed sent someone else to come after her.

Good.

Because Caitlyn was looking, too.

"How'd you get the baby?" Drury asked.

She huffed. There wasn't time for all this talk, but it was obvious he wasn't going to let her leave until he that man," Caitlyn said, blinking back the tears that were burning her eyes. Her voice, like the rest of her, was trembling. "I really don't know who he is, and I didn't see his face. He was wearing a ski mask."

"Keep talking," Drury insisted when she paused again.

"I was meeting him to deliver another payment, but this time I brought a stun gun with me."

Mercy. It was hard to relive this. The memories were still so fresh and raw. The fear, too.

"When I handed him the money," she went on, "I reached for the baby. He smashed me on the head with his weapon, but I was able to hit him with the stun gun. He fell to the ground. I grabbed the baby and got away."

No groan this time. Drury cursed again instead. "You could have been killed."

"I could have lost her," Caitlyn pointed out just as quickly. "Even if she's not my daughter, she belongs to someone, and I had to get her away from that monster."

Drury didn't seem swayed in the least by that. "You should have involved the cops."

"I couldn't because the man said he'd know if I brought anyone with me." In addition to the tears and trembling, Caitlyn had to fight the sudden tightness in her chest. "He said he would hurt the baby if I wasn't alone. I couldn't risk it."

She must have looked ready to fly into a million little pieces because Drury huffed. Then did something surprising. He touched her arm. It barely qualified as a pat, but she'd take it.

Too bad he didn't offer her a hug, or she would have taken that, too.

The touch didn't last long. Drury looked at her, his gaze lingering for a moment before it also slipped away.

"During any of your conversations, did this clown say if he was working for someone or how he got the baby in the first place?" Drury asked.

"No. But I'm not sure he's connected to anyone at Conceptions Clinic." She hesitated about adding the next part. Not because it wasn't true.

It was.

But it wasn't going to shorten this conversation.

"I think the man might be working for Helen Denson."

There, she'd said it aloud. Her worst fear. Or rather, one of them. She had plenty of others at the moment, but at the top of that list was that her dead husband's rich, manipulative mother could be the one who'd orchestrated this nightmare.

Caitlyn could almost see the wheels turning in Drury's head, and he was likely trying to work out why she'd just accused her former mother-in-law of such a heinous crime.

"Helen hates me," Caitlyn explained. "And she was furious when she found out Grant left his entire estate to me. I think she would do anything, including something like this, to get back the money."

Of course, that could mean the baby wasn't hers. After all, Helen could have used any baby to carry out a scheme like that.

"Why would Helen be upset about you inheriting what belonged to your husband?" he asked.

This was another long explanation, one she didn't

have time or energy to give him. Caitlyn went with the short version. "Grant and I were separated when he was killed in that car accident. I was already in the process of getting a divorce."

He pulled back his shoulders just slightly. Surprised by that. Later, if there was a later, she would tell him more. For now, though, she had to remind him of the urgency of her situation.

"That man who had the baby wasn't working alone," she continued. "When I made the first payment, there were two of them, and I'm pretty sure they had a lookout or someone nearby because one of the men had a communicator in his ear, and he was talking to someone. I can't stay here because they'll come back."

"Come on," Drury said. He still had a firm grip on her arm. "We'll go to the sheriff's office and get this all straightened out."

"They'll look for me there if they don't attack us along the way first. The baby could be hurt. You, too." She almost added that she couldn't live with that, but it was an old wound best left untouched.

"If you didn't want me involved, then you shouldn't have come here," he grumbled.

"I swear I didn't know the man would follow me. I mean, he was out from the stun gun, and he didn't have his partner with him this time. Didn't have the communicator in his ear, either." A heavy sigh left her mouth. "I guess he had a lookout after all."

Caitlyn figured Drury would ignore everything she'd just told him and demand once more that she leave with him.

But he didn't.

His gaze volleyed from her to the baby. "Whose coat is that?" he asked.

She had to shake her head. "It was right next to the baby on the seat of the kidnapper's SUV, and I grabbed it to cover her from the rain."

"Put the baby on the sofa," Drury instructed, and his tone and body language sent a chill straight through her. "It could have a tracking device—or something worse—in it."

Sweet heaven.

Caitlyn hurried to the sofa, easing the baby onto it. The little girl was still sleeping, thank goodness.

"I checked her after I brought her into your house," she explained. "No cuts or bruises." It sickened her, though, to think there could have been.

Drury didn't respond. He moved in front of the newborn, eased back the sides of the coat.

The baby was wearing a pink drawstring gown with little ducks on it. There was even an elastic headband with a bow holding back her dark brown curls from her face, and she had a thin receiving blanket around her. She was clean. Her diaper appeared to have been changed recently, and since she wasn't crying, that probably meant she'd been fed. Whoever had her had at least taken care of her.

Probably so they could protect their *investment*.

Something twisted inside Caitlyn at the thought.

She almost hated to feel this kind of anger. This kind of love for that precious little girl. Because the baby might not even be hers.

Caitlyn repeated that to herself.

It didn't seem to stop the flood of feelings that poured through her, and that love could mean she would

be crushed if she had to hand over the baby to someone else.

"Lift her up," Drury said, still searching every inch
of the coat. "Gently."

That gave her another jolt, and she prayed there
wasn't anything on or near the baby that could hurt her.

Caitlyn eased the newborn into her arms. Of course,
it wasn't the first time she'd held her, but without the
coat around her, she could feel just how tiny and fragile she was.

Drury went through the coat pockets, coming up
empty each time, and he turned his attention to the bow
on the baby's headband.

"Hell," he mumbled.

Caitlyn watched as he gently slipped off the headband, and she saw it then.

"It's a tracking device," he said. "That's how the man
was able to follow you."

Caitlyn shook her head. "I should have noticed it.
Drury. I'm so sorry."

"Save it." He tossed the headband onto the coffee
table. "In case I missed something, don't use the blanket to wrap her." He pulled a throw off the back of the
sofa and handed it to her. "Use this."

"Where are we going?" she asked, draping it over
the baby.

"Away from here. And fast." He took out his phone
and sent a text. Probably to Grayson. "I don't want any
other hired guns coming to the ranch. Every one of my
cousins has wives and kids, and they're all right here
on the grounds."

That didn't help steady her heartbeat.

Drury led her to the back door, grabbing a remote

control from the kitchen counter. He used it to open the detached garage, and he stepped out onto the porch to look around.

The rain was still coming down hard, but the porch was covered so the baby was staying dry. However, she was starting to squirm, maybe because Caitlyn's dress was damp and it was cool against her. She needed dry clothes. Baby supplies.

And a safe place to take her.

But where?

The sheriff's office certainly didn't seem like an ideal location since the man's partners could go looking for her there.

"Wait here in the doorway, and I'll pull the car up to the steps," Drury said. He'd already started to walk away but then stopped and turned back around to face her. "So help me, you'd better not try to run."

Since she was indeed thinking just that, Caitlyn wondered if he'd read her mind. Or maybe he could just see the desperation on her face.

Because she didn't know what else to do, Caitlyn did wait. And she prayed. She trusted Drury, but her trust wouldn't do a darn thing to protect him or the baby.

He hurried to the garage, and it took only a few seconds before she heard the engine turn on. Only a few seconds more before he pulled the car to the steps with the passenger's side facing her.

The moment Drury threw open the door and frantically motioned for her to get in, she knew something was wrong.

"Someone's coming," Drury said.

Caitlyn saw the headlights then. There was a car on the road. And it was speeding right toward them.

Chapter Three

Drury cursed himself for not getting Caitlyn away from the house any sooner. But he'd delayed because he hadn't been sure what was going on.

Still wasn't sure.

But he couldn't wait around and find out if whoever was in that car had friendly intentions. Judging from the tracking device he'd found, his guess was no. No friendly intentions here. That vehicle was likely carrying more shooters who'd come after Caitlyn and the baby. And being inside the house wouldn't necessarily help them if these morons opened fire.

Caitlyn ran down the porch steps, and Drury reached across the seat to pull her inside. The moment she was in, he gunned the engine to get them the heck out of there.

"You're not going to drive toward that car, are you?" she asked. The fear was right back in her voice. Not that it'd completely gone away, but there was a triple dose of it now.

It was raining, they didn't have a car seat and bullets might start flying at any second.

"We're not going toward the car," he assured her, and he bolted out of the side of his yard and headed not for the highway, but toward the main house.

It was a risk, but there were no completely safe options here.

Drury tossed her his phone. "Text Grayson and tell him what's going on. And climb in the back with the baby. Get all the way down on the seat and stay there."

She gave a shaky nod, and with the baby cradled in her arms, Caitlyn scrambled into the back. Drury heard her typing the text, but he kept his attention on the other car. Even though he hadn't turned on his headlights, the driver of the vehicle must have seen him because he came after them.

Hell.

He had hoped the guy would just back off when he saw where Drury was headed. No such luck.

Drury drove toward the main house, but he certainly had no intentions of stopping. There was a security gate just ahead, and like everybody else on the ranch, he had the remote to open and close it. He started pushing the remote button the moment it came into view, and the metal gates dragged open.

It seemed to take an eternity.

And that car behind him just kept getting closer and closer.

"He's got a gun," Caitlyn said, and that's when Drury realized she'd lifted her head and was looking out the back window.

"Get back down," he warned her.

Yeah, the guy had a gun all right. Drury had no trouble spotting it because the passenger lowered his window and stuck out his hand, trying to take aim.

The moment the gates were open, Drury gunned the engine and flew through them, hitting the remote to close them.

It worked.

The gates closed before the shooter could get through. The driver hit his brakes, slamming into the gate, but the gates held.

Thank God.

Drury kept going, and he sped past the houses that dotted the ranch. He didn't dare stop because the gunman might have a long-range rifle in the car, and Drury didn't want to give the guy any reason to keep firing.

"Grayson says his brothers and the ranch hands have been alerted," Caitlyn relayed after getting a response to the text she'd sent.

Good. Though he doubted that gunman would get out of the car and go in pursuit on foot, it was better to be safe than sorry.

Especially since Drury was already sorry enough for this fiasco.

He stayed on the road that coiled around the pastures, and once he was past the exterior security lights, it was too dark for him to see. Drury had no choice but to turn on his headlights.

"Where are we going?" she asked.

Some place she wouldn't like. "The sheriff's office. And before you remind me that these goons can follow us there, they can follow us anywhere. At least if we're at the sheriff's office, the deputies and I can protect you, and it'll get these idiots away from my family.

"Don't say you're sorry," he added, his voice a little harsher than he'd intended.

Drury had caught a glimpse of her face in the mirror and could tell from the tears that she was about to apologize again. Well, it wouldn't help. Nothing would right now except getting her and that baby to safety.

His phone rang, the sound cutting through the other sounds of his heartbeat drumming in his ears and the wipers slashing at the rain.

"It's Grayson," Caitlyn said. She passed him the phone, but since Drury still had hold of his gun, he pushed the speaker button and dropped the phone on the seat next to him.

"Where are you?" Grayson asked. "And what the heck's going on?"

"I'm at the back of the ranch on one of the trails and about to come out on Miller's Hill. The car with the gunmen didn't get past the gate."

"No," Grayson agreed. "Gage had eyes on the car, and he said the driver turned around and sped off. He got the license plate numbers, but they're bogus. Gage and Dade went in pursuit."

Both men were Grayson's brothers. And his deputies.

"I'll take the back roads to get to the sheriff's office. I should be there in about twenty minutes." Drury paused. "Caitlyn Denson is with me."

Grayson paused, too, and then cursed. A rarity for him since he was the father of a five-year-old son and had cut way back on his bad language.

"Caitlyn?" Grayson repeated like the profanity he'd just used. "You're not involved with her again, are you?"

"No, not like that." And Drury couldn't say it fast enough.

"Good. Because the last time you hooked up with her…"

Grayson didn't finish that. Didn't need to finish it. Because Drury remembered it well enough without any reminders. Caitlyn had been a CPA in those days. A

CPA who'd been helping Drury investigate the crime family that had employed her.

At least Drury had believed she was helping him.

However, he'd been wrong. Because Caitlyn had ended up marrying the very man whose family Drury had been investigating. But those were old memories, and he didn't have time for them now.

"So, why is Caitlyn with you?" Grayson pressed. "And are those gunmen after her?"

"They're after her." That was the easy question to answer. The first one, not so much. "There might be another baby from Conceptions Clinic."

He gave Grayson a moment for that to sink in.

"Caitlyn and Grant Denson's baby," Grayson concluded.

"Yeah. At least that's what a man told Caitlyn." Drury could still see her in the glimpses that he was making in the rearview mirror, and she was hanging on to every word. "According to her, a man demanded a ransom. She paid it, but he reneged."

Grayson mumbled some profanity. "Where's the baby now?"

"In the backseat of my car with Caitlyn. She was waiting inside my place when I got home." He figured it wouldn't take Grayson long to fill in the blanks.

And it didn't.

"Caitlyn came to you for help."

Drury settled for another *yeah* and didn't miss Grayson's disapproval about that. Well, Drury wasn't so happy about it, either.

"I don't know for sure, but the guy you caught is probably the same one who had the baby. He should have stun-gun marks on..." Drury looked back at her so she could provide that.

"The left side of his neck."

Grayson made what sounded to be a weary sigh. "I'll have the doc check for it. I got a name on the guy already. Ronnie Waite. He was in the system not because he had a record but because he used to be a prison guard."

Interesting. Drury would have bet his paycheck that the guy had a record. But then maybe whoever was behind this had made sure to use someone who was clean.

"Ronnie Waite," Drury repeated to Caitlyn. He turned onto another road and glanced around to make sure they weren't being followed. "Do you know him?"

Caitlyn repeated the name, then shook her head. "Is he in charge of this or just a lackey?"

"Don't know yet," Grayson answered. "How did Ronnie or anyone connected to this contact you?"

"Only one man contacted me," Caitlyn answered, "and he always called. I used the internet to do a reverse number lookup, but it wasn't listed."

Probably because the phone had been a burner or disposable prepaid cell. No way to trace that. But if Ronnie still had the phone on him, Grayson would have it checked.

"Does Caitlyn, or the baby, need to see a doctor?" Grayson asked.

"Yes," Drury said at the same moment that she answered.

"No. I mean, I want the baby checked out, but I'm fine. And I don't want to be in the hospital while Ronnie is still there."

"Caitlyn's not fine," Drury argued. "She might have

a concussion. But I agree about not going to the hospital. She shouldn't be there until we're certain Ronnie can't get near her."

"I'll have a medic come to the office then." Grayson paused. "We'll get into all of this once you're here, but I'll need you to think of anyone who could have hired this man."

"Helen," Drury and Caitlyn said in unison.

"All right. I'll get your former mother-in-law here for a chat," Grayson agreed without hesitation. "I'll also see if there's any way to connect her to Ronnie."

"There has to be a surrogate out there, too," Caitlyn added. "I'm not sure how to find her, but she might be linked somehow to Ronnie."

"I can question Ronnie about that. And check for a Jane Doe DB who might have recently given birth."

DB as in *dead body.*

Caitlyn made a slight gasping sound. Probably because she'd just realized what Grayson was saying—that the surrogate could have been murdered after she gave birth. Whoever was behind this wouldn't have wanted to keep a surrogate alive unless, of course, the surrogate was in on the plan.

"I'll have Mason call the lead investigator who handled the Conceptions Clinic case," Grayson went on, "but if Helen's the one who did this, would she have had access to the embryo? In other words, could someone at the clinic have legally given it to her?"

"No. Not legally." Caitlyn drew in a long breath. "In fact, when Helen found out that Grant and I had visited the clinic, she tried to bribe one of the nurses to get info about what we were doing. When I found out,

I had our counselor put a note in my file that no information should be given to the woman."

"That doesn't mean Helen played by the rules," Drury reminded her. In fact, he'd be surprised if she had. But there was someone else in that scummy family who was also a rule breaker. "What about Grant's brother, Jeremy?"

Drury couldn't be sure, but he thought Caitlyn shuddered. "Jeremy wouldn't have done that. And yes, I'm sure. The last thing Jeremy would want is another heir to share the inheritance he'll get from his mother."

"Okay," Grayson said, "this is enough to get things started. How far out are you now?"

"About ten minutes. No one's following us, but when we get to the sheriff's office, I want to get Caitlyn and the baby inside ASAP."

"No problem. Park right in front of the door."

Drury hit the end-call button and took another glance back at her. "I know you don't want to go to the sheriff's office, but you can trust Grayson. If there's anything to link Helen to this, he'll find it."

And so would Drury. He hadn't especially wanted to get involved with Caitlyn, but this wasn't about her. It was about that baby in her arms.

"You think I'm a fool for getting involved with Grant," she said. "But I swear, I didn't know what Grant was when I married him."

"You should have. You knew what his family was, knew that I was investigating them."

"Yes," she whispered. And she repeated it. "His family but not him." She paused. "I think Jeremy might have been the one who killed Grant."

"Killed? I thought he died in a car accident."

"He did. One that Jeremy could have arranged." Though she shook her head right after saying that. "I don't have any proof, and knowing Jeremy, there won't be proof to find. But I meant what I said about Jeremy not wanting any competition for his mother's estate."

The last time he'd tangled with the Densons, he hadn't fared so well. Drury had ended up with a black mark on his reputation for getting involved with Caitlyn, a woman who'd clearly double-crossed him and had almost certainly been sleeping with him to get info about his investigation.

Of course, that hadn't stopped Drury from trying to go after the Densons again. Until his boss had finally gotten him to back off when Helen had threatened a lawsuit for harassment. Drury hadn't wanted to hurt the Bureau for what had essentially become a personal vendetta on his part.

"I hate being drawn back into the viper pit." He hadn't intended to say that loud enough for Caitlyn to hear.

But she heard. Because she gave him another "I'm sorry."

He kept the next comment to himself. Was she sorry she'd dumped him for Grant? Or sorry that she hadn't gotten that safe fairy tale that she wanted?

Drury wanted to tell her that she couldn't create "safe." The cut on her head and baby in her arms were proof of that. Still, he couldn't fault her for trying. After all, she'd seen her own father—a Texas Ranger— gunned down right in front of her when she was only eight.

Hard to get past memories like that.

Drury took the final turn toward town, and he tried

to shut out everything so he could focus on their surroundings. It was late, nearly midnight, and with the rain there wasn't anyone out and about. Still, those thugs could be waiting on a side street, watching for them.

He held his breath and didn't release it until he saw the sheriff's office. And Grayson in the doorway. The moment Drury had brought the car to a stop, Grayson hurried Caitlyn inside, and Drury followed right behind her. He got her away from the windows—fast. Even though they were bullet resistant, he didn't want to take any chances.

After everything that'd gone on, Drury hadn't expected a warm greeting from Grayson and Mason. And he didn't get one. Mason was on the phone, scowling. But then, that was something Mason did a lot.

However, Grayson was scowling, too.

At Caitlyn

"Is there any part of your story you want to rethink?" Grayson asked her.

That put some alarm in her eyes, and Caitlyn shook her head. "No. Why?"

"Because I just got off the phone with the doctor who's patching up Ronnie Waite, and Ronnie says that's his daughter and that you kidnapped her. He's demanding a warrant for your arrest."

Chapter Four

Caitlyn felt as if someone had knocked the breath right out of her. She shook her head, tried to deny what Ronnie had claimed, but the words were trapped in her throat.

"Is it true?" Grayson snapped.

It was more of an accusation than a question, and Caitlyn was thankful it had come from Grayson and not Drury. Still, that didn't mean Drury believed she was innocent. He was staring at her, clearly waiting for her to say something.

"Everything happened just the way I told you," she insisted.

Drury just kept staring, but Grayson made a sound, one to let her know she was going to have to do a whole lot better than that if he was to believe her.

"The baby isn't his," Caitlyn tried again. "I paid him one ransom, and he demanded a second one. Since I figured he wasn't just going to hand over the baby, I hit him with a stun gun and took her from him."

"I don't suppose you recorded any of that encounter?" Grayson, again. And he used the tone of the lawman in charge. Which he was. He also made this sound, and feel, like an interrogation.

Mercy. If she couldn't convince him of her innocence, he might take the baby. He might arrest her. That couldn't happen because if she was behind bars, she wouldn't be able to protect the baby.

"He clubbed me on the head," Caitlyn added, and she looked to Drury for help. She held her breath, hoping that he would back her up, and he finally nodded.

"When I found Caitlyn in my house, she was scared. And bleeding."

Grayson lifted his shoulder, and even though he didn't say the actual words, his expression was a reminder that she'd fooled Drury before. That's the way the Rylands would see it anyway. But she hadn't fooled him so much as she'd been fooled.

By Grant.

But that was an old wound of a different kind.

"Think this through," Caitlyn continued because she clearly had some more convincing to do with Grayson. "Why would I steal a baby and run to Drury?"

Grayson stayed quiet, probably because there was no scenario he could come up with where she'd do that. Because she wouldn't.

"So, the baby is really yours?" Grayson asked.

Caitlyn hated to hesitate, but she didn't want to withhold anything. Considering her track record with the Rylands, it would be hard enough to get them to trust her if they caught her in a lie.

She looked down at the newborn. At that precious little face, and she got that same deep feeling of love that she'd gotten the first time she saw her. Of course, she'd been wrong about her feelings before, but Caitlyn didn't think that was the case right now. In fact, she would stake her life on it.

"Other than the test I had run on the DNA sample the kidnapper sent me, I don't have any proof," Caitlyn admitted, "but she looks like the pictures of me when I was a baby."

Grayson groaned, an almost identical reaction to the one Drury had had when she'd first told him.

"I can get the proof," she insisted. "I can have her DNA tested again and compared to mine and Grant's. I just need time." She stepped closer to Grayson and looked him straight in the eyes. "But I'm not going to give her to you so you can hand her over to the very man who tried to kill us."

Grayson's attention shifted to Drury then. "You believe her?"

Drury didn't answer for several long moments. "The guy shot at me when I pulled up in front of my house. If he was truly just after Caitlyn to get his child back, then why go after me like that?" He tapped his badge. "I identified myself, and he still shot at me. Plus, he had those items in his vehicle."

No head shake from Grayson this time. He nodded. Apparently, that was enough to convince him that Ronnie was lying.

"I'll post a deputy outside his hospital room and keep digging into his background to see what turns up," Grayson said. "Why don't you two wait in my office while I call the doctor and get him down here?"

Caitlyn wasn't sure she could trust the doctor. Any doctor. But her options were limited. She couldn't just go running out into the rainy night with the baby, and she didn't even have any supplies.

"Could you please have someone get the baby some formula and diapers?" she asked.

Another nod from Grayson, and he got started on that while Drury led her to Grayson's office. It wasn't the first time she'd been there. Once when she'd still been seeing Drury, he'd brought her here to meet his cousins. Of course, they had been a lot friendlier to her than they were now.

Because her legs felt ready to give way, Caitlyn sank down into one of the chairs and looked up at Drury. "Thank you."

He huffed, clearly not meant to convey "you're welcome" because he probably hated her for getting him involved in this. Maybe soon she could convince him that she truly was sorry along with making plans to put some distance between them.

But how?

She didn't even have a phone, and besides even if she had one, Caitlyn wasn't sure who to call. Maybe a bodyguard, but at this point, she didn't even know who she could trust.

Other than Drury, that is.

And that trust was on shaky ground. Yes, he would protect her because he was an FBI agent and it was his job, but she'd already put him in danger once and didn't want to risk doing that again.

"Can you help me arrange for a safe house?" she asked.

A muscle flickered in his jaw, and he pulled a chair from the corner and sat where he was facing her. "Yes, I can do that, but I want you to do something for me. Tell me everything—and I mean everything—about who could be part of this."

Caitlyn was certain she looked confused. Because she was. "You mean about the baby?"

"For starters. You didn't have anything to do with what went on at Conceptions, did you?"

That put a huge knot in her stomach. Not because it was true. It wasn't. But because he would even consider she'd do something like that.

"No. I gave up on having Grant's baby months before he died." And she made the mistake of dodging his gaze.

Drury noticed.

He put his fingers beneath her chin, lifting it and forcing eye contact. "Explain that," he insisted.

Caitlyn hadn't wanted to get into all of this now, but it could be connected. *Could*. Still, it would mean reopening old wounds that still hadn't healed. Never would. Plus, it was hard to discuss any of this when she was holding the baby. Perhaps Grant's and her baby.

"When Grant was killed, he'd been having an affair," she said.

"Is that the reason you were divorcing him?"

"Among other things." Caitlyn paused. "The only reason I'm bringing it up now is because his girlfriend, Melanie Cordova, could be responsible for at least part of this."

Of course, he looked confused, and Drury motioned for her to continue.

Caitlyn did, after she took a deep breath. "Melanie was devastated after Grant's death, and it's possible she's the one who arranged for the baby to be born. So she could have some part of Grant."

"Even if that *part* meant the baby would be yours?" he questioned. "Because as a mistress, you'd think the last thing she would want around was her lover's baby with another woman."

"I know," Caitlyn admitted. Obviously, there were holes in her theory about Melanie's possible involvement. "But maybe Melanie was so desperate to have Grant's child that she didn't care if I was the biological mother."

Judging from the way his forehead bunched up, Drury clearly wasn't on board with this. "Then why would Melanie have demanded a ransom? Why even let you know that the child existed?"

Caitlyn had to shake her head. "Unless she just wanted the money to raise the baby. Of course, that doesn't explain why that thug Ronnie had her."

"Maybe that wasn't Melanie's choice. If she hired him to extort the ransom, he could have double-crossed her and kidnapped the baby."

Mercy. Caitlyn hadn't even thought of that. Maybe this was a sick plan that had gone terribly wrong.

"How long has it been since you've seen Melanie?" Drury asked. "Is it possible she carried the baby herself, that she's the surrogate?"

It was yet something else Caitlyn hadn't considered, but she had to nod. "I haven't seen her in over a year. For a few months after Grant died, she stalked me. Followed me, kept calling, that sort of thing, but that all stopped about a year ago."

Perhaps around the time Melanie would have been arranging for the procedure to have the baby.

Caitlyn didn't have to ask how Melanie would have gotten the fertilized embryo from Conceptions. She could have bribed someone in the clinic, possibly even the former clinic manager who'd orchestrated several births just so she could extort money from the babies' biological parents. Something that Drury knew all too well.

Since two of those babies were his twin niece and nephew.

The clinic manager was dead now, killed in a gunfight with Drury's brother Holden so she couldn't give them answers, but it was possible that Melanie could.

Drury stood. "I'll make some calls and get Melanie in for questioning."

He took out his phone, but before he could do anything, Grayson stepped into the doorway. One look at his face, and Caitlyn knew something was wrong.

"Ronnie called Child Protective Services," Grayson said. "He wants the baby in their custody."

That robbed Caitlyn of her breath, and she stood, as well. She also pulled the baby even closer to her. "It's some kind of trick. Ronnie probably figures it'll be easier to snatch the baby from foster care than from me."

Grayson made a sound of agreement. "But that won't stop CPS from taking her. They're on their way here now."

Caitlyn would have bolted for the door if Drury hadn't stopped her. No. This couldn't be happening.

"If I let them take the baby, it'd be like giving her back to Ronnie," Caitlyn pleaded. "I can't do that."

She braced herself for an argument, but one didn't come.

"Ronnie tried to kill me," Drury reminded Grayson. "Anything he does is suspect, and Caitlyn is right. He or one of his thug friends would have a much easier time getting the baby from CPS. In fact, the plan could be to kidnap her as soon as she's taken from the building."

Still no argument from Grayson, but he did stay quiet a moment. Before he nodded. "I don't trust Ronnie, either. Or rather I don't trust the person he's working for."

Grayson looked at Caitlyn. "That still doesn't mean I can give you a blank check on this. How much time will you need to prove she's your daughter?"

Caitlyn had to shake her head. "How much time for you to arrange another DNA test, one that would hold up against a court order?"

"Forty-eight hours, maybe even sooner, if we put a rush on it," Drury answered. "We'll need the lab you used to process Grant's DNA, though."

Yes, because she didn't want to take the time to try to find another hair sample. "I used Bio-tech in San Antonio. They'll have both Grant's and my DNA on file there."

She could see the debate Grayson was having with himself. He was a lawman. A good one, judging from everything she'd heard. And it likely didn't set well with him that this would essentially be an obstruction of justice since he was allowing Caitlyn to walk away with the baby rather than turning her over to CPS.

"All right," Grayson finally said. "Forty-eight hours. I'll get the DNA test kit. After that, go ahead and get Caitlyn and her out of here."

The relief was instant, and it left her just as breathless as the news of Ronnie calling CPS. She wasn't going to have to give up the baby. Not just yet anyway. But that didn't mean she had a safe place to take her.

"Where?" she asked Drury and hoped he had some idea.

"Don't tell me where you're going," Grayson quickly added. "I don't want to have to lie to CPS. Oh, and figure out how the baby can get a checkup from the doctor." He walked away, no doubt to get that kit.

She certainly hadn't forgotten about the checkup but didn't know how to make it happen.

"It's not a good idea to go back to my place," Caitlyn insisted before Drury could say anything. "Or yours."

"Agreed. But there's a guesthouse on the back part of the ranch. It's out of sight from the other houses, including Grayson's, and we can use it just for tonight. Since my cousins have lots of babies, it'll be easier for us to get supplies."

"It'll also make them a target if Ronnie and his goon friends attack again," she quickly pointed out.

"We can lock down the ranch, close the security gate and use some of the hands for extra protection."

Maybe, but Caitlyn still wasn't sold on the idea. *Think.* Where else could she go? And preferably some place that didn't put others in danger.

"It's just for tonight," Drury said as if he knew what was going through her mind. "The baby will need to be fed soon, and it won't be long before CPS arrives."

True. Still, Caitlyn didn't like it one bit.

"Are you, uh, okay with this?" But she immediately waved off her question. "Of course you're not okay. First thing in the morning, I promise, I'll start looking for bodyguards."

He didn't give her his opinion on that. "I'll pull an unmarked car to the back of the building."

Drury headed out as Grayson came in with the DNA test kit. He'd obviously done this before because he did the cheek swab in just a few seconds. The baby still stirred a little and made a whimpering sound of protest, but she went right back to sleep.

"I'll have this couriered to the lab," Grayson explained as he started toward the door again. But he stopped. "If the child's not yours, I'll expect you to turn her over to CPS. Got that?"

She nodded. Caitlyn understood that's what would have to happen. Well, she understood with her head anyway. It was her heart that was giving her some trouble because Caitlyn felt as if this baby already belonged to her. It would crush her to learn differently.

Caitlyn heard the footsteps in the hall and automatically tensed, but it was just Drury. He glanced at the DNA packet.

"I'll call you as soon as we have the results," Grayson assured them.

Drury took her by the arm and led her to the back of the building and through a break room. He paused at the exit, opening the door and glancing around. He also drew his weapon before he helped her out and into the backseat of the waiting unmarked car.

Which wasn't empty.

Drury's brother Lucas was behind the wheel.

"Lucas came when he heard about the attack," Drury said.

Since Lucas was a Texas Ranger, it made sense that he would know about the attack, but it surprised her that he would involve himself in this. Like most of the Rylands, Lucas disliked her, maybe even hated her, because of the nasty breakup between Drury and her.

Lucas didn't say a word to her, though he did spare her a glance in the rearview mirror. He took off as soon as Drury had shut the door.

Drury kept his gun drawn, and he looked all around them. No doubt for any thugs who might be watching for them to leave.

Suddenly, a new wave of fear crawled through her.

As bad as it'd been inside the sheriff's office, this was worse.

"Is the car bulletproof?" she asked, and she hated the tremble in her voice.

"Bullet resistant," Drury corrected.

She wasn't certain, but Caitlyn thought that meant they could still be shot. Drury was certainly aware of that possibility, too. And this had to be bringing back god-awful memories for him.

"I'm sorry," she said.

There was no way Drury could have known what the blanket apology meant. Or at least she hadn't thought he would know, but when he glanced at her, she saw it in his eyes. The memories.

Or rather the nightmare.

Of his wife. Lily. She'd been killed by a gunman's bullet in a botched store robbery, and while Caitlyn didn't know all the details, she knew Drury had still been grieving her loss when they'd met. Heck, he probably still was.

And she hadn't helped with that.

Just as Drury had started to risk his heart again, she'd stomped on it. It didn't matter that she thought she had a good reason. Several of them in fact. No. It didn't matter.

Drury's phone buzzed, and Caitlyn prayed this wasn't another round of bad news. However, that wasn't a bad news kind of look on Drury's face when he looked at the screen.

"Don't say anything," he warned her. He pressed the answer button and put the call on speaker.

It didn't take long for her to hear the caller's voice. "What the hell did you do?" the man asked.

Caitlyn immediately recognized the voice, and it only tightened the knot in her stomach. Because it was her former brother-in-law and one of her suspects.

Jeremy.

"Well?" Jeremy snapped when Drury didn't immediately answer.

"Well what?" Drury snapped right back.

"You know. You damn well know."

Drury huffed. "I'm giving you one more chance to make sense, and if you don't, I'm ending this call. Then you can bother someone else. What is it that you think I did?"

"You sent those men after me," Jeremy insisted.

Drury looked at Caitlyn, no doubt to see if she knew anything about this, but she shook her head.

"What men?" Drury questioned.

"The men who want money. A ransom, they said. They want me to pay them for Grant's kid."

It took Caitlyn a moment for that to sink in. Had the kidnappers really contacted Jeremy? If so, they'd probably done the same to his mother, too. Of course, that was assuming that Jeremy was telling the truth, but Caitlyn didn't trust him. Trusted his mother even less.

Drury cursed. "Start talking, and tell me everything," he ordered Jeremy.

"I've already told you everything. Two men showed up at my office a couple of minutes ago. Or rather the parking lot at my office. They accosted me, showed me a picture of some kid that they claimed was Grant and Caitlyn's."

"Who were the men?" Drury pressed. "And where are they now?"

"I don't know. Never saw them before in my life. But

they said something about the kid being born through a surrogate and if I wanted the kid that I was to pony up a million bucks. They said I had one hour to get the cash, and they left. They drove off in a black SUV."

"I'm still trying to figure out why you think I had anything to do with this," Drury said.

Jeremy made a sound to indicate that the answer was obvious. It wasn't. "The men told me to pay the money to you."

Because Drury's arm was touching hers, she felt his muscles tense. "Me?"

But Jeremy didn't jump to verify that. Instead, he cursed. "The men are back."

Caitlyn heard some shouts, one of them belonging to Jeremy. "Stop!" he yelled.

"Get someone out to Jeremy Denson's office," Drury told his brother. "Jeremy, are you there?"

No answer.

The line was dead.

Chapter Five

Drury waited. Something he'd been doing all night.

Patience had never been his strong suit, and that was especially true now. He wanted answers. Answers that he wasn't getting. Well, he wasn't getting the right answers anyway.

He'd certainly gotten a string of wrong ones.

No news on Jeremy. Nothing else on the kidnappers, either. Ronnie was sticking to his story about Caitlyn stealing his child. And CPS was pushing Grayson to disclose the location of the baby.

Grayson was staying quiet for now on anything about the baby, though he almost certainly knew that they were at the ranch. Drury wasn't sure how long Grayson's silence would last. Especially since CPS had said they would get protection for the little girl. If they did that, Drury wasn't even sure it was a good idea for Caitlyn and him to keep her.

Unless the child turned out to be hers, that is.

If the baby was indeed her child, then there was no way Caitlyn would give her up. A match wouldn't mean the baby was safe, though. Caitlyn, either. And that left Drury with another question for which he didn't have an answer.

What then?

The logical part of him was saying he should step away from this. That his past with Caitlyn was just that—the past. But the illogical part of him put up an argument about it. Drury figured it had plenty to do with the old attraction. The one that was still there.

He threw back the covers and got off the sofa where he'd spent the night. Not sleeping, that's for sure. The sofa was about six inches too short for his body, and the thoughts racing through his head hadn't exactly spurred a peaceful sleep. He could still hear the shots. Could still see that look of terror on Caitlyn's face.

Of course, the shooting had brought back the old memories. Of that same look of terror on Lily's face before she'd died in his arms. Memories that he pushed aside. Like the attraction for Caitlyn, he didn't want to cloud his mind with things from the past that he couldn't change.

Since he didn't hear Caitlyn stirring in the bedroom, he tried to be quiet when he went to the kitchen and made some coffee. The small counter was dotted with baby formula and other supplies. Something Lucas had managed to get for them before he'd left the guesthouse shortly after midnight. Later, Drury would need to thank him for helping. Grayson, too.

And that thanks would include them not mentioning that he shouldn't be under the same roof with Caitlyn.

Drury sipped his coffee, went through his emails on the laptop that Lucas had also provided. No updates since the last time he checked other than Grayson was going to have the deputy at the hospital talk to Ronnie again. Maybe the man would cave on his story so that there'd be no question about Caitlyn's innocence.

She already had enough strikes against her with his family of lawmen without adding that.

He heard a slight thudding sound in the bedroom, and Drury practically threw his coffee cup on the table and hurried to find out if anything had happened. Not that he had to go far. It was literally only a few steps from the kitchen. He drew his gun from his shoulder holster and threw open the door, bracing himself for the worst. But it wasn't the *worst*.

Caitlyn was standing there naked.

Almost naked anyway. She was putting on an over-size bathrobe, and he got a glimpse of her body before she managed to yank the sides together and tie the sash.

"Sorry," she whispered. Maybe an apology for the peep show. Or maybe because she'd clearly startled him. Caitlyn picked up the plastic baby bottle that she'd obviously dropped. "I'm on edge, too," she added.

No doubt, but at the moment she didn't exactly look on edge. Their gazes connected. Held. And he saw in her eyes something he didn't want to see. The old heat.

Drury looked away and reholstered his gun. Since he was already there, he also checked on the baby. There'd been no time to get a crib, so the little girl was sleeping on the center of the bed where she'd likely spent most of the night. The covers on the floor told him that Caitlyn had probably slept there.

"I was afraid of rolling onto her during the night," Caitlyn said. "She's so little." There was some fear in her voice, but he didn't think it was from the danger but rather because it was true. The baby really was tiny.

"Did she sleep okay?" he asked.

Caitlyn nodded, then shrugged. "I guess she did.

I don't really know how often a baby should be waking up."

Neither did Drury, but Caitlyn had gotten up twice in the night to warm bottles. Drury had asked if he could help. Especially since Caitlyn had had to walk right past him to get to the kitchen. But she'd declined his offer.

"Please tell me you have good news. *Any* good news," Caitlyn said.

It took Drury a couple of moments to come up with something that could possibly be considered good. "Grayson is bringing in both Helen and Melanie for questioning."

Caitlyn flexed her eyebrows. "I'm betting neither was happy about that."

"They weren't. Especially Helen. Grayson said she didn't seem too concerned when he told her about the call we'd gotten from Jeremy."

"She wouldn't be. Jeremy and she haven't been on friendly terms in years. Jeremy's a hothead."

Yeah, Drury had figured that out from the brief phone call. But the "hothead" was about to be labeled a missing person if they didn't hear from him soon.

"Someone had tampered with the security cameras in the parking garage where Jeremy made that call," he explained. "There's no footage for fifteen minutes before the call or for a half hour afterward."

She stayed quiet a moment. "You think Jeremy could have really been kidnapped?"

Drury had to lift his shoulder. "You know him better than I do. Would he fake a disappearance?"

"Yes," Caitlyn said without hesitation. "If it benefited him in some way. And this possibly could if he thought he was a suspect in the attack last night." But then she shook her head. "Of course, he wouldn't have had any part in her birth." She glanced at the baby.

"Because he wouldn't want to share his inheritance." Drury remembered Caitlyn mentioning that. "But if he's worried about splitting an inheritance, wouldn't he try to smooth things over with his mom?"

"Helen can't cut him out of the estate. That's in the terms of his late father's will. Jeremy will inherit everything unless Grant has an heir."

Drury figured the estate had to be worth millions. Still, it took a coldhearted SOB to go after a child because of money. If that's what Jeremy had done. Considering the bad blood between him and his mother, Helen might have used this as an opportunity to get rid of Jeremy, her sole surviving son.

Especially if the woman thought she had a new heir. Grant's baby.

"I was about to take a shower." Caitlyn fluttered her fingers toward the adjoining bathroom. "That's why I wasn't dressed when you came in. I was going to put her in the carrier on the bathroom floor, but could you watch her?"

Drury nodded. And hoped the baby didn't wake up. Unlike his cousins, he just wasn't comfortable holding a newborn.

"I won't be long," Caitlyn added, and she hurried into the bathroom.

He sank down on the edge of the bed and studied the little girl's face. He could see Caitlyn's mouth and chin. Or at least he thought he could. No resemblance to Grant, though, and it surprised him a little to realize that even if he had seen it, it wouldn't have made him uneasy. His beef had never been with Grant.

But rather Caitlyn leaving him to be with Grant.

Of course, it was his own stupid fault for handing Caitlyn his heart when he knew he was the wrong man for her. She'd told him right from the get-go that she couldn't get involved with a lawman. Not after her lawman father's violent death. Even after they'd started an affair, she had continued to tell Drury that it could never be more than temporary between them.

Too bad he hadn't believed her.

Caitlyn was right about not being too long. She stayed in the shower only a couple of minutes, and it took her even less than that to dress. She hurried out while combing her wet hair.

She smelled like roses.

The soap, no doubt, but it was something he wished he hadn't noticed.

"Thanks," she said.

Since it was time for him to get the heck out of the bedroom, Drury stood, but the moment he did, the baby squirmed a little and made a fussing sound. He stepped back so that Caitlyn could go to her and take her in her arms.

They made a picture together. And Drury had no trouble seeing the love for the child in Caitlyn's eyes.

"I know," Caitlyn said, following his gaze to the baby. "I shouldn't get so attached. But I've always wanted a child, so it's hard not to have deep feelings for her."

An understatement. Caitlyn had *really* wanted a child. Something she'd made clear when they were together.

Something that had driven a wedge between them, too.

Heck, it still made him take a step back now.

Too many memories. More of those old ones that he wanted to forget. But couldn't. Because he hadn't just lost his wife the day she'd been murdered. He'd lost the child that she'd been carrying.

"Will you still help me with a safe house?" she asked. "An unofficial one, of course. I don't think you want to use FBI channels."

Neither did he. "I'll help with the house." Hell, he'd ended up helping with plenty of things he didn't want to help with, but despite their past he was still a sucker for a damsel in distress, and at the moment Caitlyn was in a lot of *distress*.

She mumbled another thanks. "I was going to get started on contacting some bodyguards, and I was hoping I could use your laptop to get some phone numbers."

He nearly offered her a protection detail. But he was also toeing the line on the law. Heck, he'd probably crossed over that line, and he didn't want to bring any of his fellow agents or family into this.

"The laptop's on the table in the kitchen," he said.

She gathered the blanket around the baby and headed that direction. Drury followed, but before he even made it there, his phone buzzed, and he saw Grayson's name on the screen. He considered not putting the call on speaker, just in case this was more bad news, but he'd end up telling Caitlyn about the conversation anyway.

"You're on speaker," Drury warned Grayson right off, though he doubted that would change anything Grayson had to say.

"Good. Because Caitlyn needs to hear this. I've arranged for the doctor to examine the baby. Yeah, I know. It's a risk, but she needs to be checked out."

"I agree." A weary sigh left Caitlyn's mouth. "And it's something I should have remembered to do."

"You've had a lot on your mind lately." There was a touch of sarcasm in Grayson's tone. "I want you two to take the baby to the hospital. And don't worry, she won't be near Ronnie. The doctor will meet you in his private office to do the exam. I've arranged for Lucas and one of the deputies to escort you there."

Escort was a nice way of saying *back up* in case someone tried to gun them down again.

"Anything new from Ronnie?" Drury asked.

"Nothing. He's lawyered up and is refusing to cooperate with us. Not CPS, though. He's still pressuring them to give him the baby. Which they won't do," Grayson quickly added. "Not without DNA proof anyway, and it'll be tomorrow before we have that."

"The DNA will show that Ronnie's not the father," Caitlyn said like gospel, and Drury hoped that was true.

He didn't exactly relish the idea of handing over a child to someone who'd shot at him. Of course, that wouldn't happen anyway unless Ronnie was cleared of all charges.

"Ronnie said he can prove the baby is his," Grayson went on. "Because he can describe the birthmark on her ankle. Does she have a birthmark?"

"She does," Caitlyn admitted. "But Ronnie could have easily seen it when he had her."

"That was my theory, too. By the way, Melanie's on her way in," Grayson added a moment later. "Drury, if you want to be here for the interview, you could have Lucas or someone else stay with Caitlyn and the baby."

It was tempting. "When will she be there?" Drury asked.

"Within the hour." He paused. "I have plenty of questions for her now that I've read the police report for Grant's car accident. Melanie's purse was found in the vehicle."

Drury had read the report, too. Not recently. But shortly after Grant had died. Why? He didn't know. It was a way of picking at those old wounds, but he hadn't been able to stop himself. So, yeah, he knew about Melanie's purse.

Obviously so did Caitlyn. "Melanie claimed that Grant and she had been together that night, but when he dropped her off at her place, she forgot her purse." She frowned. "The police cleared her as a suspect, but you think Melanie could have had something to do with his death?"

"Do you?" Grayson asked right back.

She certainly didn't jump to deny it. Caitlyn took a moment and gently rocked the baby even though the little girl was no longer fussing. "Possibly. Jeremy is still my top suspect for that. If it wasn't an accident, that is. But I suppose Melanie could have been upset with Grant about something."

"You don't know?" Grayson pressed.

"No. By then Grant and I were separated. That's why I was a suspect at first, but I was cleared, too, because it was ruled an accident. Added to that, I had an alibi."

"A ruptured appendix," Drury mumbled.

Caitlyn's gaze raced to his, and she looked a little surprised that he knew that. When it came to her, Drury always seemed to know a little too much. Like that she'd nearly died herself that night and was in emergency surgery at the same time her estranged husband swerved off the road and hit a tree. Since there'd been other skid marks nearby, the cops had first thought someone had run him off the road, but the CSIs hadn't been able to prove that the marks were made the exact same time as the accident.

"I just want to know as much about Melanie as possible before I question her," Grayson went on. "Does she have any hot buttons?"

"Me," Caitlyn answered. "Until I filed for divorce, she was harassing me. She hates me. That's why I told Drury that I didn't think she had anything to do with the baby or Conceptions Clinic."

Grayson made a sound to indicate he was withholding judgment on that. "I'll let you know if I find out anything from her, and I'll have Lucas give you a call once he's on his way there. By the way, Lucas didn't tell me exactly where you were on the ranch, and I'd like to keep it that way."

So would Drury. The fewer people who knew, the better.

Drury ended the call, and since Caitlyn had said she wanted to use his laptop, he turned it in her direction. She glanced at the baby. Then at him.

"I'll get the carrier from the bedroom," she said, not giving him a chance to decline to hold the baby. Not that he would have. But Caitlyn must have realized that it wasn't something he wanted to do.

Several moments later, she came back into the kitchen, the baby already snuggled into the carrier, and she set the carrier on the table next to the laptop.

"For a bodyguard search, try starting with Sencor Agency in San Antonio," he suggested.

She muttered a thanks and got started on that just as Drury's phone buzzed again. Not Grayson this time but rather his brother Mason, who lived at the main house on the ranch.

"We have a visitor," Mason growled the moment Drury answered. "She's at the security gate pitching a fit. I didn't tell her either of you were here, but she's insisting on seeing Caitlyn."

Even though Drury didn't have the phone on speaker, either Caitlyn heard or else she noticed the alarm on Drury's face because she slowly got to her feet.

"Who is it? Melanie?" Drury asked.

"No. It's Caitlyn's mother-in-law, Helen. And along with demanding to see Caitlyn, she says she wants her grandbaby right now."

Chapter Six

Caitlyn squeezed her eyes shut a moment. This was the last thing she'd expected—for Grant's mother to show up at the Silver Creek Ranch.

"How did Helen know Caitlyn was here?" Drury asked, taking the question right out of her mouth.

Of course, Caitlyn had an even more important question. How had Helen found out about the baby?

"She said a man called her," Mason answered. "Ronnie Waite. He told her that Caitlyn would be here."

Caitlyn had to shake her head. "Why would Ronnie have done that? He's claiming the baby is his."

"Yeah, apparently your mother-in-law doesn't believe that."

"Former mother-in-law," Caitlyn automatically corrected.

Mason grumbled something that sounded like a *whatever*. "She's on hold on the house line if you want to have a little chat with her. If not, I'll have the ranch hands *escort* her off the property."

Helen wouldn't go peacefully. She didn't do much in life that qualified as peaceful. And Caitlyn didn't want the Rylands or their ranch hands to have to deal with the woman. Heck, she didn't want to deal with Helen, either, but the fastest way to get rid of her might be to take the call.

"I'll speak to her," Caitlyn volunteered.

"Not a smart idea," Drury snapped. "It'll confirm to her that you're here."

"I can tell her that I transferred the call to your location," Mason suggested. "I won't have to tell her where, exactly, that location is."

"Yes, please do that," Caitlyn said, ignoring Drury's huff. She picked up the landline phone and waited.

Despite Drury not agreeing to this, he used the laptop to tap into the ranch's security system. There were multiple screens, and he zoomed in on the one at the security gate. Helen was there all right, her phone pressed to her ear while she glared at the two armed ranch hands who were blocking her from getting past the gate.

Helen was aware of the camera because she was volleying glances between it and the ranch hands. The October wind had kicked up some and was rifling through her blond hair. Hair that was usually perfect. Ditto for her dark jacket, but she definitely looked a little disheveled this morning.

At least the baby had fallen back to sleep and Helen wouldn't be able to hear her, but just in case she woke up, Caitlyn would keep her voice soft. Also for the baby's sake, she would make this conversation short.

"Start talking," Caitlyn *greeted* Helen the moment the woman came on the line.

"No, you start talking. Tell these goons to let me onto the ranch so I can see the baby."

"We're not at the ranch," Caitlyn lied. "So, you need to leave before they arrest you. It's not very smart to go to a ranch with a family of lawmen and start making a scene."

"It's not right for you to withhold my granddaughter from me," Helen countered. "Did you think you could hide her?"

Caitlyn took a moment to consider her answer, but a moment was too long because Drury took the phone from her and put it on speaker. "What did Ronnie tell you?" he demanded.

"Special Agent Drury Ryland, I presume?" Helen spat out his name like profanity. "Ronnie said you'd be with Caitlyn, that you were helping her hide the baby."

"No, I'm helping her stay alive. Someone tried to kill the baby and her last night. What do you know about that?"

Helen gasped. Shocked, or else faking that she was. "The baby was in danger?"

"Not what you'd planned, huh?" Drury asked. "Did you tell Ronnie not to fire shots around the baby?"

Since Drury had just accused Helen of hiring a thug like Ronnie to get the baby and kill Caitlyn, it wasn't much of a surprise that her eyes narrowed to slits.

"I know what you're doing," Helen said. "You're trying to put the blame on me for this. Well, I didn't do it. Hell, I didn't even know I had a grandchild until this morning when he called me."

"And did he tell you that the child was his?" Caitlyn countered.

"He said it was possibly his. Or my granddaughter. But he said the odds are that she was Grant's daughter."

Caitlyn groaned. The man was playing both sides.

"What did he want in exchange for the information he was giving you?" Drury asked.

Helen paused. No, it was a hesitation. "He wants me to help him get out of any possible charges that might be filed against him."

"He shot at me, and I won't be giving him a get-out-of-jail-free card on that," Drury stated. "Now tell me everything you know about Ronnie and Conceptions Clinic."

Caitlyn expected the woman to launch into a verbal tirade and blast Drury for the order. She didn't. Helen pushed her hair from her face and sighed.

"I did go to Conceptions," Helen finally admitted. "Not recently, but I went there when Grant told me that Caitlyn was having her eggs harvested. I wanted to find out more about the procedure."

Caitlyn knew Helen well enough to know that she was leaving something out of that explanation. And she thought she might know exactly what.

"You tried to bribe someone into stopping the in vitro," Caitlyn said. Yes, it was a bluff, but she knew she'd hit pay dirt when again Helen didn't jump to deny it.

Helen glanced away from the camera, but her defiance quickly returned. "I knew your marriage to Grant wouldn't last. You weren't in love with him, and he was seeing another woman. That bimbo, Melanie."

Not defiance that time but anger. Apparently, Melanie and Helen had clashed. Or maybe Helen blamed Melanie in some way for her son's death.

"No one at the clinic would listen to me," Helen went on. "And then Grant died and I forgot all about Conceptions."

"Really?" Drury challenged. "You're sure you didn't arrange to use their stored embryo so you could have a grandchild?"

"No." Helen was adamant about it, too. "I had nothing to do with that. But someone must have seen this as a way to make some money. They did with others at Conceptions."

They had, and other than his niece and nephew, there'd been another child, as well. One not connected to the Ryland family or Caitlyn.

"You paid them a ransom," Helen snapped. "Didn't you, Caitlyn?"

It was probably a guess on her part, but Caitlyn saw no reason to deny it. "I did. And when Ronnie reneged on the deal, that's when I hit him with a stun gun and took the child." Caitlyn paused long enough to draw in a long breath. "Helen, if you hired him, tell me now because I need to know if there are others who'll try to kidnap the baby."

"I didn't hire him." No hesitation whatsoever. "But if my granddaughter is in danger, I can help."

"She doesn't need your help," Drury fired back.

Judging from the profanity that he mumbled, he hadn't intended to say that. Probably because it sounded as if he was volunteering to make sure she was safe. Caitlyn wouldn't hold him to that, though. As soon as she had a safe place to go, she and the baby would leave.

"You have no right to keep my granddaughter from me," Helen argued. She didn't wait for either of them to respond. "I know Caitlyn's always been in love with you, but you're not the baby's father. My son is."

Caitlyn tried not to react to that. Hard to do, though, when she felt as if someone had slapped her. It must have felt that way to Drury, too, because he stared at her, mumbled more of that profanity and looked away.

"You went to Conceptions to stop Caitlyn from having Grant's baby," Drury reminded Helen. "Now you want me to believe that you have a right to see a child that you never wanted to exist?"

Helen didn't fire off a quick answer that time. "My son is dead, and this baby is part of him. Part of *me*. You can't stop me from seeing her."

"I can and will if it means keeping her safe," Drury insisted.

"You can't mean that. You really want to protect Grant's child? Any child for that matter."

Caitlyn saw Drury's old wounds rise to the surface. Helen probably knew all about Drury's past. Knew that her comment would pick at those old wounds. And Caitlyn hated the woman for it.

"I'm an FBI agent," Drury finally said. "I'll do my job, and right now my job is protecting Caitlyn and the baby. A baby whose paternity doesn't matter to me because it won't stop me from protecting her. You won't stop me, either."

Helen flinched. "What does that mean? I told you that I want this child. I wouldn't hurt her."

"Then who would?" Drury snapped. "Who would hire a man like Ronnie to kidnap her?"

"I don't know."

"Then guess!" His voice was so loud that it startled the baby.

Drury mumbled an apology, and Caitlyn gently rocked the carrier so the baby would go back to sleep.

"Jeremy," Helen said.

It didn't take Caitlyn any time at all to realize that Helen had just accused her son of some assorted felonies. Or rather she'd *guessed* he was involved.

"You have proof?" Drury asked.

"No." The woman's shoulders dropped. "I'm sure

Caitlyn told you all about how much Jeremy hated Grant. I'm sure Caitlyn told you a lot of things. Pillow talk reveals lots of secrets."

Caitlyn had to bite her lip to keep from shouting out a denial that Drury and she were involved again. Besides, Helen wouldn't believe her no matter what she said, especially since Drury and she were under the same roof.

For the moment anyway.

"Why don't you tell me more about Jeremy?" Drury countered. "Is he really missing or did he fake his disappearance?"

"Who knows?" There was no concern in her expression or her tone. She could have been discussing the weather. "I gave up trying to figure Jeremy out a long time ago."

Drury made a sound of disagreement. "And yet you just accused him of attempted murder. Are you sure you're not trying to put the blame on your son so you won't look guilty?"

Helen glanced around, and when she looked back at the camera, Caitlyn could see new resolve in the woman's eyes. "I'm done with this conversation. If you don't let me see my granddaughter, then I'll call your boss and tell him exactly what you're doing."

"Call him," Drury responded.

Obviously, that wasn't the reaction Helen expected because she shot a glare into the camera. "This isn't over," Helen said, and she stormed back to her car, slamming the door once she was inside.

"She means it." Caitlyn eased the baby carrier back onto the table. "Helen will make trouble for you."

Drury kept his attention focused on the screen where they could see Helen driving away. "She'll try."

Yes, and Helen would keep trying until she got what she wanted. But she wouldn't just want the baby if it turned out that she was her granddaughter. Helen would want the baby without Caitlyn in the picture.

Drury glanced at her and no doubt saw that she was trying to blink back tears. "Don't apologize again," he warned Caitlyn.

She did anyway, but she doubted it would be the last of the apologies that she would owe him. Caitlyn sank down in the chair next to him.

"If you're going to talk about those things Helen just said about us, don't bother," Drury added. He dismissed it with a shake of his head.

However, it dismissed nothing for Caitlyn. "I was in love with you when we were together," she said.

Drury didn't dismiss that, but he did stare at her for a long time before he looked away. "Do you really want to dig up these old bones?"

No. But she couldn't seem to stop herself. "We didn't really talk when things ended between us." In fact, Drury hadn't said a word when she'd told him she was leaving. He wasn't saying a word now, either. "I left because I couldn't be there, not after what happened."

There was no reason for her to explain that. Because Drury hadn't forgotten that he'd nearly been killed just the day before she'd ended things. Nearly killed while doing his job.

A job he would never give up.

"I saw the pictures of the attack," she went on.

Again, she didn't need to add to that because he knew which pictures she meant. Drury had been caught in the middle of a gunfight while on a task force to arrest a serial killer, and there'd been bystanders around who'd taken photos that had appeared in every news outlet in the state. On social media, too.

Everywhere she looked, she'd seen Drury on the ground after taking a bullet to the chest. Thankfully, the Kevlar had prevented him from being killed, but he'd had several cracked ribs. Along with escaping death by only a couple of seconds. The killer had taken aim at Drury again, but Drury's partner had stopped him before he could pull the trigger.

In Caitlyn's mind, however, she saw the trigger being pulled. She felt the pain of losing yet another man she loved.

Drury's gaze came back to her. "Is there a reason you're going through all of this now?"

"Yes. I just wanted you to know that it wasn't you. It was me."

For a moment Caitlyn wasn't even sure he was going to acknowledge that. But then he huffed, got to his feet and went to the window.

"We were both in a bad place at that time," he finally said.

Yes, because he was trying to get over the loss of his wife and unborn child. Heck, he was no doubt still trying to get over that. Losing them wasn't a wound that was ever going to heal.

"Does that mean you can forgive me?" she asked.

"No."

Caitlyn had steeled herself up for that answer, but it still cut to the bone. Because it was true.

But Drury waved it off, spared her a glance. "I don't want to forgive you," he amended. "It's easier to hang on to the hurt than it is the pain."

She nodded, and while it wasn't exactly a truce, it was a start. A start that she would take.

His phone buzzed again, and Caitlyn automatically checked the computer screen to make sure Helen hadn't returned. Or that kidnappers hadn't shown up to storm the ranch. But other than the ranch hands, there was no one else at the gate.

"It's Grayson," Drury relayed.

Unlike some of the other calls, he didn't put this one on speaker, and since the air was practically zinging between them, Caitlyn didn't go closer. Best not to risk being so close to him when everything felt ready to explode.

Caitlyn couldn't hear a single word of what Grayson was saying, but she had no trouble interpreting Drury's response. He cursed.

Mercy, what had gone wrong now?

"How did that happen?" Drury snapped.

Again, she couldn't hear Grayson's response. Whatever it was, though, it didn't help Drury's suddenly tight muscles. It seemed to take an eternity for him to finish the conversation and another eternity before he turned to her.

"Ronnie's gone," he said.

"He escaped?" And her mind automatically thought the worst. That he'd gotten away and was coming after the baby and her. "We should leave now."

Drury shook his head. "He didn't escape. Two men sneaked into the hospital, knocked out the deputy and took him at gunpoint. According to several eye-witnesses, Ronnie's been kidnapped."

Chapter Seven

"I don't like being here," Drury heard Caitlyn say under her breath. She probably hoped that would make the doctor speed up the exam that he was giving the baby.

Drury hoped that as well, but Dr. Michelson sure didn't move any faster. Too bad because being in the hospital was an in-your-face reminder that only a couple of hours earlier, those gunmen had stormed in.

And kidnapped Ronnie.

Well, maybe that's what had happened. But Drury wasn't about to buy it just yet. It was just as likely that Ronnie's comrade-thugs had pretended to take him by force. Or maybe the person who'd hired Ronnie had done that. Not necessarily to rescue him, though, but to silence him after he'd failed to get his hands on the baby.

"There are two deputies outside the door," Drury reminded Caitlyn.

He hadn't figured that would erase the worry on her face. It didn't. Maybe because she remembered that a deputy had been outside Ronnie's room as well, and that hadn't stopped the attack. In fact, the deputy had been hurt. Not seriously. But it could have been a whole lot worse.

"Well, she appears to be fine," the doctor finally said. "Since you don't know the exact day of her birth, I'm estimating that she's at least a week old. She's been well fed, no signs of any kind of injury or trauma."

Caitlyn released the breath that she must have been holding. Of course, Drury had expected the child to be in good health since he hadn't seen any signs to indicate otherwise.

"Can you tell if she was born with a C-section?" Drury asked. "It might make it easier for us to find the surrogate who carried her."

"It's hard to say in her case. Her head is well shaped, which could mean a C-section delivery, but the surrogate could have also had a very short labor. Therefore, the baby wouldn't have been in the birth canal that long."

This seemed like way too much personal information. And it brought back the memories.

Always the memories.

His wife, Lily, had been only three months pregnant when she died, but she'd started reading books about pregnancy and delivery even before they'd conceived. What the doctor had just told him rang some bells. But Drury pushed those bells and memories aside and forced himself to look at the situation from a lawman's point of view.

Basically, the information didn't help at all because it didn't rule out any woman who'd given birth within the past couple of weeks. Plus, Drury figured whoever was responsible for this hadn't delivered the child in a hospital. Too much of a paper trail.

Caitlyn made a sharp sound, and it not only grabbed Drury's attention. It caused him to reach for his gun. False alarm. The sound was the doctor giving the baby a blood test. The baby didn't like it much and kicked and squirmed. Drury figured it was necessary, but he had to look away. Yeah, he was plenty used to seeing blood, but it was different when it was an innocent baby.

"I'll get this to the lab," the doctor said when he finished. Caitlyn immediately got up and scooped the child into her arms.

"I thought you said nothing was wrong with her," Drury reminded him.

"This is just routine, something all newborns have done." Dr. Michelson headed for the door but then stopped. "I won't put your name on it," he said to Caitlyn. "I'll just list it as Baby Ryland. There are enough of those around here that it won't raise any suspicions."

He was right about the sheer number of Rylands, but Drury figured it still might get some attention. The wrong attention, too. That's why Drury didn't want to stick around the hospital much longer. Even though they were in the clinic section, on the other side of the building from where Ronnie had been, that didn't mean someone didn't have the place under surveillance.

"How soon can we leave?" Drury asked the doctor.

"Soon. I just need to get the paperwork for Caitlyn to sign." He headed out, shutting the door behind him.

The baby didn't fuss for long. Probably because Caitlyn was rocking her and looking down at the baby's face with an expression he knew all too well. Love. She'd gotten attached to the child, and that could turn out to be a bad thing if the DNA tests proved the baby belonged to someone else.

But who else?

There'd been no reports of missing newborns in the area, and if the child had been kidnapped from her parents, someone would have almost certainly reported it. If they were still alive, that is.

Caitlyn glanced at him. "I'm sorry about the doctor putting *Ryland* on the lab test."

They were talking about those blasted memories again. The ones Drury didn't want to discuss with her. With anyone.

Instead he took out his phone to make a call about the safe house, but before he could do that, Caitlyn sat down beside him. "I really think you should just walk away from this," she said. "I know how hard this is for you."

Yeah, it was hard, but that pissed him off.

"Walk away? *Right.* I'm a lawman, and even if I weren't, I'm not a coward. There's someone after the baby. Someone who's free as a bird right now." He had to get his teeth unclenched before he could continue. "No, I won't walk away until I'm sure she's safe."

Drury hadn't intended to blurt all that out. Hadn't intended to make a commitment that would keep Caitlyn right by his side. And she would be. Because the baby and Caitlyn were a package deal. At least until the DNA results came back anyway and the person responsible for the danger was caught.

He looked at her and saw that she was staring at him. He also saw just how close they were to each other. Close enough for him to draw in her too-familiar scent. That scent had his number because it slid right through him. Silk and heat.

Apparently, this was his morning for doing things he hadn't planned on doing because he made the mistake of dropping his gaze to her mouth. He remembered how she tasted, knew how it felt to kiss her long and deep.

Worse, his body remembered it, too.

She took in a quick breath, and he saw the pulse

flutter on her throat. There was some of that heat in her eyes. Her body seemed to be remembering, as well.

Drury suddenly wanted to kiss her. Or maybe it wasn't so sudden after all. Kissing, and other things, had a way of coming to mind whenever he saw Caitlyn.

He was so caught up in the notion of that kiss that Drury nearly jumped when the sound of his phone startled him. Great. Talk about losing focus.

Grayson's name was on the screen, and Drury pressed the answer button as fast as he could. Maybe his cousin had found something to put an end to all of this.

"Are you still at the hospital?" Grayson asked right off.

"Yeah. But we're nearly finished."

"Good. How would you feel about leaving the baby with the deputies and coming here to the sheriff's office for a short visit?"

"I wouldn't feel good about it at all," Caitlyn answered, which meant she'd heard every word.

Drury put the call on speaker anyway. "What's going on?"

"Melanie's here, and she's in a very chatty mood. Well, up to a point anyway. She's been telling us about Helen's visits to Conceptions, and she claims she knows who Helen might have hired to steal Grant and Caitlyn's embryo."

"She has a name?" Drury quickly asked.

"Says she does, but she's insisting on talking to Caitlyn face-to-face. She says she has questions for her."

Drury didn't want to speculate as to what those questions might be, but he was plenty skeptical that Melanie had any information that would help.

"This could be a ploy to get Caitlyn out into the open," Drury reminded him.

"I know. I could give you a protection detail to get

here. A second detail for the baby so she can be taken back to the ranch. But I can't tie up that kind of manpower for long."

No, because that would include four deputies, and that was a third of the lawmen working there.

"You really think my seeing Melanie would help anything?" Caitlyn asked. "And what if CPS finds out I'm there?"

"I can't guarantee you that CPS won't show up, but if they do, I could stall them. As for whether or not Melanie can help, who knows? Right now, I'd like nothing more than to charge her with obstruction of justice for withholding possible evidence, but I doubt I could get the charges to stick. Melanie could just claim she doesn't have any real info and that she was bluffing so she could speak to Caitlyn."

Drury agreed, and it would also likely rile the woman to the point where she wouldn't give them any info.

"It's your decision," Drury told Caitlyn.

She glanced at the baby, then at Drury before she nodded. "Let's do it," Caitlyn said, getting to her feet.

Drury certainly didn't feel any relief over that decision. Even if Melanie did manage to give them something, it could come at a very high price.

"Go ahead and send the protection details," Drury told Grayson.

"All right… Wait, hold on a second."

Even though there wasn't any alarm in Grayson's voice, Drury went on instant alert. Caitlyn, too. And they waited for several long moments before Grayson finally came back on the line.

"This is apparently the day for surprises," Grayson said. "The cops just found Jeremy."

THE DAY FOR SURPRISES.

Caitlyn hoped Grayson's comment didn't come true in a bad sort of way. It sickened her to think of leaving the baby, even for a short period of time, but that wasn't even her biggest concern.

There could be another attack.

Not only on her, either, but someone could go after the baby while the protection detail was taking her back to the ranch. She hoped they were keeping watch as well as Drury was right now. Though Drury's and her ride was only a short distance, and the ranch was miles away.

"My cousins will protect the baby with their lives," Drury reminded her.

It was the right thing to say, and she believed him. The Rylands might not like her, but they were good lawmen and would do their jobs. Still, that didn't mean the worst couldn't happen, and besides, the visit could all be for nothing. Caitlyn was past the point of having second thoughts about this and had moved on to fourth and fifth thoughts and doubts. That didn't just apply to Melanie.

But to Jeremy.

She listened as Drury got a phone update on the man, and apparently Jeremy had wandered into San Antonio PD with a story about escaping from his kidnappers. Whether that was true or not remained to be seen, but at least now that the cops knew where he was, maybe they could keep an eye on him to make sure he wasn't planning another attack.

"Was Jeremy hurt?" she asked when Drury finished his call.

"Not a scratch on him, but his clothes were disheveled."

Which he could have easily done himself. "How did he *escape*?"

Drury shook his head. "SAPD's questioning him now, and after they're done, they'll send us a copy of the report. In the meantime, we'll deal with Melanie and then head back to the ranch."

That couldn't come soon enough for her. "I'm not even sure why Melanie wants to see me," she said. "If she's really got something dirty on Helen, why wouldn't she just give it to Grayson?"

It was a question she'd already asked herself a dozen times, and she still didn't have an answer.

"Maybe Melanie wants to bargain with you about something," Drury suggested.

She shook her head, not able to imagine what that would be.

"If the baby is Grant's," Drury continued, "maybe she thinks she can convince you to turn the child over to her."

Caitlyn hadn't intended to curse, but the profanity just came out. "No way would I give that woman a baby, any baby."

He lifted his shoulder, continued to glance around as they approached the front of the sheriff's office. "Melanie probably doesn't think too highly of you so she might think she can buy the baby from you."

"She doesn't think much of me, and the feeling's mutual." Caitlyn huffed. "But it does sound like Melanie believes I'd do something that despicable."

The deputy pulled to a stop directly in front of the door to the sheriff's office, and Drury quickly got her inside. He didn't stay at the front with her but rather headed past reception and straight to Grayson's office.

Grayson was there, seated at his desk, and he tipped his head to the room across the hall.

"Melanie's in there. Brace yourself," Grayson warned them. "She's a piece of work."

Caitlyn had firsthand knowledge of that, and she tried to look a lot more confident about this meeting than she felt. She wanted only to finish it so she could get back to the baby and complete the plans for a safe house and bodyguards.

When Drury and she walked in, Melanie was seated, her attention on her phone screen, and she barely spared them a glance before continuing to read a text.

"You took your time," Melanie grumbled.

The other times she'd crossed paths with Melanie, the woman had been wearing some high-end outfit suitable for the runway, but today she was wearing skintight jeans and a red top. The heels of her stilettos were no thicker than pencils.

"What did you have to say to me?" Caitlyn asked, and she didn't bother to sound friendly. "I understand you have something on Helen?"

Melanie glanced at her again. A disapproving glance, and as if she had all the time in the world, she got to her feet. With those heels and her height, she towered over Caitlyn and could practically meet Drury eye to eye.

"This is how this will work," Melanie said. "I'll give you some information, and in exchange you'll give me what I want."

Drury's hands went on his hips. "And what exactly is it you want?"

"To do a DNA test on the baby that Caitlyn believes is Grant's and hers."

So, this was about the baby. But Caitlyn certainly hadn't expected Melanie to demand a DNA test.

"What's this about?" Caitlyn pressed.

"It's about giving me a DNA test." She spoke slowly as if Caitlyn were mentally deficient.

Caitlyn had to stop herself from rolling her eyes. "Why don't you explain what you mean?" she asked at the same moment Drury had his own question.

"How did you know about the baby?"

Judging from Melanie's hesitation, that wasn't something she wanted to answer, but she must have felt she couldn't sidestep it. Not with Drury glaring at her like that.

"Helen," Melanie finally said. "She told me. But it doesn't matter how I found out. This is about what went on at Conceptions." Again, the tone was an attempt to make Caitlyn feel like an idiot. She didn't feel like one, but she was confused. "Helen went to Conceptions to stop Grant and you from having a baby."

"Old news." Caitlyn hoped her own tone made Melanie feel like an idiot. "Helen already admitted that."

Judging from the brief widening of Melanie's eyes, she hadn't expected that. "Did she also tell you that she succeeded, that she did stop it?"

"I stopped it," Caitlyn clarified. "When I filed for a divorce."

"But you think someone else started it again." Melanie wasn't smiling exactly, but it was close. The expression of a woman who had a secret. "Well, you're wrong. No one started it the way you think."

"What the hell are you talking about?" Drury snarled.

With that sly half smile on her face, Melanie sank down onto the chair. "I went to Conceptions, too. Not to stop Caitlyn and Grant's procedure. Grant had already promised me that he would put a stop to that."

Drury glanced at Caitlyn, no doubt to see if that was true, but she had to shrug. It possibly was. Near the end of their marriage, things hadn't been exactly rosy between Grant and her. Of course, Grant could have lied to his mistress, too.

"I didn't go to Conceptions until after Grant died," Melanie continued. "And I went there to have my eggs harvested. I paid them to use Grant's semen."

"That's illegal," Caitlyn pointed out, but just as quickly, she waved it off. It wouldn't have mattered to Melanie if it was illegal or not. Heck, judging from everything that'd happened at Conceptions, it wouldn't have mattered to them, either.

"I wanted Grant's baby," Melanie said as if that justified everything. "Not yours and his baby. Mine and his."

It took a moment for Caitlyn to find the breath to speak. "Are you saying you think the baby I rescued is yours?"

"Absolutely," Melanie answered without hesitation. "I paid Conceptions to implant mine and Grant's embryo into a surrogate. That's why I'm demanding a DNA test."

Caitlyn felt Drury slip his arm around her waist, and only then did she realize that she wasn't too steady on her feet. "Melanie could be lying," Drury reminded her.

Yes, she could be, but Melanie's smile made Caitlyn think otherwise.

"Why would you use a surrogate?" Drury asked the woman. "Why not just do artificial insemination and carry the baby yourself?"

"Because I have female problems. Not that it's any

of your business. Besides, I don't handle pain very well and didn't want to go through childbirth."

And she probably didn't want to risk stretch marks and such on her model-thin figure. In that moment, Caitlyn hated Grant for bringing Melanie into their lives. Hated even more that all of this could be true.

"What's the name of the surrogate?" Drury snapped.

"I don't know. I don't," Melanie repeated when that intensified Drury's glare. "The person at Conceptions told me that had to be kept confidential."

That didn't surprise Caitlyn. Some surrogates would have wanted to keep their identities a secret.

"Even if you paid Conceptions to do the procedure," Drury said, "there are no guarantees that they carried through on it. They were into all sorts of illegal activities and could have just taken your money."

"But there's a baby," Melanie argued.

"A baby that could just as easily be Caitlyn's. After all, the kidnappers contacted her for a ransom. Why wouldn't they have gone to you?"

The smile faded, and Melanie glanced away. "Probably because I'm not loaded like Caitlyn. She's the one who inherited all Grant's money. I didn't get a penny of it."

Yes, and Melanie was just as bitter about that as Helen was. "Did you use your own child to get ransom money from me?" Caitlyn came out and asked.

"No," Melanie practically shouted. But the volume and emotion did nothing to convince Caitlyn that it was true.

God, it could be true.

The baby might not be hers after all. Her stomach knotted and twisted until she felt as if she might throw up.

Drury stared at Melanie. "Let me guess. You think

if you have Grant's child that Helen will pony up lots of cash to get shared custody. Or maybe you plan to charge her for visitation rights?"

"That's none of your business. I have my DNA on file at several labs in San Antonio," Melanie went on. "But I don't trust you to tell me the truth. That's why I want you to bring the baby here so I can watch someone do the test."

"The baby is in protective custody because someone's trying to take her," Drury snapped. "A real mother wouldn't want to put the child in danger by demanding that she be brought here."

That caused Melanie's shoulders to snap back, and she opened her mouth, no doubt ready to argue. But she must have realized just how that would make her look—like the cold, calculating person she was. Plus, if Drury was right about Melanie using the baby to get money from Helen, she wouldn't want to risk her investment being harmed.

"My lawyer will be in touch to schedule that DNA test," Melanie said. "With witnesses. I don't want Caitlyn or any of your cowboy cops trying to pull a fast one on me."

With that accusation, Melanie waltzed out.

Drury kept his arm around her waist, and Caitlyn was thankful for it. Thankful, too, that he'd refused to bring in the baby for testing. Of course, he might not be able to refuse for long. If Melanie had any proof whatsoever that she was the child's mother, then she might be able to get a court order.

"I'll give you two a minute," Grayson said, stepping out and closing the door.

Caitlyn thought she might need more than a minute.

"You okay?" Drury asked her. "Dumb question, I know, but I'm in that gray area where anything I say could make it worse."

She could only shake her head. "Until the kidnapper called me with a ransom demand, it'd been a long time since I'd thought about having a baby. Now, it crushes me to think that I might lose her."

"Yeah." Without taking his arm from her, he stepped in front of her, reached out and touched her cheek. Except he was wiping away a tear. Caitlyn hadn't even realized she was crying until he'd done that.

"Just know that everything Melanie said could be a lie," he continued. "Her story doesn't make sense. She claims she doesn't have money, but she would have needed plenty of cash to bribe someone at Conceptions, plus pay for a surrogate. It's more likely that she tried to get Conceptions to go along with her stupid plan but didn't have the money to put the plan into action."

Caitlyn latched onto that like a lifeline. "Thanks for that."

He nodded but didn't move. Drury stayed put right in front of her. Too close. Well, too close for him anyway, but she wished he would pull her into his arms.

And that's what he did.

Caitlyn stiffened for just a moment from the surprise, but then she felt herself melting right into him. He seemed to do the same against her, and just like that, the memories returned. Good memories, and she had so few of those in her life that it was almost impossible to push them away.

She certainly didn't push Drury away.

Nor did he do any pushing.

He lifted his head a little, their gazes connecting.

He was so close to her that she could see the swirls of blue and gray in his eyes. Could see the muscles stirring in his jaw. Drury seemed to be having a fierce debate with himself about something, but Caitlyn didn't know what exactly.

Not until he kissed her, that is.

It barely qualified as a kiss. His mouth just brushed over hers, but his warm breath certainly made her feel as if she'd been kissed.

Now, he stepped back. Cursed. And shook his head. "I just complicated the hell out of this."

"It was already complicated," she assured him.

She figured that wouldn't get any better, either. Drury and she would always have this attraction between them, and because of the past, they would always feel the need to fight it.

"We should get back to the ranch." He didn't wait. Drury headed into the hall but then came to a dead stop.

That's when Caitlyn heard a too-familiar voice.

Jeremy.

He was in the reception area where one of the deputies was frisking him, and the moment she stepped into the squad room, her former brother-in-law spotted her.

"I figured you'd be here," Jeremy snapped. He pointed his finger at Caitlyn. "You want to explain to me why you had me kidnapped?"

Chapter Eight

Drury did not want to have to deal with this now, and he was pretty sure that Caitlyn felt the same way. However, it was clear they were going to have to at least address the stupid accusation Jeremy had just thrown at her.

First, though, Drury had his own issue to address. "Why are you here? Shouldn't you be at San Antonio PD?"

"Not that it's any of your business, but I walked out."

Grayson groaned and took out his phone. No doubt to call his brother Nate, who worked at SAPD, to find out what was going on.

Jeremy flung another pointed finger at Caitlyn. "Now, why did you have me kidnapped?"

"I didn't," Caitlyn answered. "And what makes you think I did?"

Jeremy gave her an annoyed look. "Because one of the kidnappers said you'd hired them."

Caitlyn gave him the look right back. "I didn't hire them, and why would you believe them? They're kidnappers."

"Well, someone kidnapped me, and since whatever's happening seems to be centered on you, that made it easier to believe. That and you hate my guts."

Caitlyn certainly didn't deny the hate part, but she looked at Drury, gave a weary sigh. "Can we leave now?"

Drury nodded and looked at Gage. "Could you bring the car around to the back?" That way, they wouldn't have to go past Jeremy.

Gage returned the nod and headed out of the building. It wouldn't be a fast process, though, because Gage would have to check and make sure no one had planted any kind of tracking device on the vehicle.

"You're not leaving," Jeremy said to Caitlyn. "Not until you tell me who came after me and why."

Caitlyn gave another sigh. "I don't know. The man who tried to kill Drury and me escaped or maybe was taken from the hospital, so I don't have any more answers than you do."

Jeremy disputed that with some ripe profanity. "Then why was that idiot Melanie just here?"

"To be interviewed," Drury stated. He didn't give Jeremy any more info, something that caused his eyes to narrow.

"Did Melanie have me kidnapped?" Jeremy snarled.

"Maybe. With your personality, I'm surprised half the state doesn't want to kidnap you. Or just shut you up. Now, why would you think Caitlin is involved?" Drury demanded. "And if you're going to make any accusation, I'd like some facts and proof to go along with it."

"She's a gold digger. What more proof do you need?"

"Something that'll hold up in court," Drury flatly answered.

"Something like phone records," Grayson added the moment he ended his call. Drury hadn't heard Grayson's conversation, but apparently he'd learned something.

Judging from Jeremy's expression, it wasn't anything good, either.

Grayson turned to Drury. "SAPD examined Jeremy's phone records and discovered four calls from our missing kidnapper, Ronnie."

Yeah, definitely not good for Jeremy. "Want to explain those calls?" Drury demanded.

"I didn't know who he was, all right?" The volume of Jeremy's voice went up a notch. "He said he was interested in investing in one of my business ventures. I had no idea he was into anything illegal."

Maybe, but Drury wasn't going to take the man's word for it. "Did SAPD get anything else?" Drury asked Grayson.

"Only that Jeremy was uncooperative and unable to give any details whatsoever about the people he claimed kidnapped him."

"They wore ski masks!" Not only did his voice get louder, the muscles in his face had turned to iron.

Obviously, Jeremy had a temper, and he wasn't saying or doing a thing to convince Drury that he hadn't been the one to orchestrate this plan to ransom the baby and attack Caitlyn and him. Of course, Melanie and Helen were still on his suspect list, too, and the three were going to stay there until the person responsible was caught.

"Did you have anything to do with what went on at Conceptions Clinic?" Caitlyn asked Jeremy.

Jeremy threw his hands up in the air. "So, now you're accusing me of that, too?"

"Did you?" she pressed.

"Of course not." He spat out some more profanity. "From what I've heard, Grant could have a kid out there because of the mess at Conceptions. You really think I'd have any part in creating an heir?"

"No," Caitlyn agreed. "But you might have had a part in trying to make sure that heir didn't exist."

Jeremy's eyes narrowed. "I'm sick and tired of you making me out to be the devil in all of this. Why don't you go after my mother?"

"You'd love that, wouldn't you? Because with your mother behind bars, you'd control the estate."

Jeremy shrugged, clearly not denying that.

Drury had seen and heard more than enough from this clown, and the timing was perfect because Gage came in through the back exit. "The car's ready," Gage said.

That was all Drury needed. Apparently Caitlyn, too, since they both got moving.

"That's it?" Jeremy called out to them. He tried to follow them, but one of the deputies blocked his path.

Drury ignored him. "Is someone else going with us?" he asked Gage.

Gage nodded. "Someone I found in the parking lot." He opened the door, and that's when Drury saw Lucas in the front seat.

"Worried about me?" Drury joked when Caitlyn and he got into the backseat. Gage took the wheel. The moment they were all buckled up, he took off, heading onto Main Street.

Lucas glanced at him. Then at Caitlyn. Even though there was no way Lucas could have known about that near kiss earlier, his brother could no doubt see that the attraction was still there.

"Yeah, I am worried about you," Lucas admitted,

but he didn't spell out what that worry included. However, Drury figured Caitlyn was part of that concern.

Lucas took out a photo from his pocket and handed it to Drury. "Either of you recognize her?"

Caitlyn leaned closer to Drury to have a look. Drury studied it, too. A young woman in her early to mid-twenties. Brunette hair and slight build.

Drury and Caitlyn shook their heads at the same time. "Who is she?" Caitlyn asked.

"Nicole Aston."

Drury repeated the name under his breath to see if it would trigger any kind of recollection, but it didn't. "Should we know her?"

Lucas flexed his eyebrows. "I think she might have been the surrogate."

That certainly got Drury's attention. Caitlyn's, too. "How do you know that?" she asked.

"I ran a search on recent female missing persons in the state and found out that Ms. Aston was a college student. According to her friends, she was a surrogate. And she disappeared a week ago."

Bingo.

Caitlyn studied the photo a moment longer before she handed it back to Lucas. "I don't think I've ever seen her before. But I doubt Conceptions or whoever's behind this would have wanted me to cross paths with the surrogate."

Lucas made a sound to indicate he agreed with that. "I just thought maybe she would try to get in touch with you. Especially if she suspected anything illegal was going on at Conceptions. Of course, maybe the powers that be made sure she didn't get suspicious."

Even though this conversation was important, Drury

continued to keep watch around them. So did Lucas and Gage. Now that they were out of town, it was a little easier since there weren't many buildings. Just some ranches and a lot of open farm road.

"Do Nicole's friends and family have any idea where she could be?" Caitlyn asked.

Lucas shook his head. "Both her parents are dead. No boyfriend. Her *friends* are pretty much just her classmates who said she kept to herself a lot."

Which might have explained why Conceptions would have wanted her for a surrogate. Still, there was another possibility. "Nicole could have given birth and then changed her mind about giving up the baby. She could be in hiding."

Lucas agreed fast enough that Drury knew that he had already considered it. "Her bank account hasn't been touched in a week, though. Prior to that, there were monthly deposits of fifteen hundred dollars. I've put a tracer on the deposits, but it was wired in, probably from an offshore account."

In other words, the tracer was a long shot. It also meant someone had tried to cover their tracks. Most people who hired a surrogate didn't need to have their tracks covered like that.

Drury was so caught up in what Lucas had just told him that he hadn't realized some of the color had drained from Caitlyn's face. "Someone could have killed her to silence her."

Yeah. Drury decided not to confirm that out loud. Besides, Gage made a sound that had his attention shifting in that direction.

"What the hell?" Gage grumbled.

Drury followed his gaze and asked himself the same thing. There was something on the road just ahead.

Gage slammed on the brakes, and Lucas and Drury automatically drew their weapons. That's because they got a better look.

That *something* was a body.

Caitlyn didn't get a long look at the person in the middle of the road. Drury had pushed her down onto the seat. All three lawmen kept their guns ready, obviously bracing for some kind of attack.

But nothing happened.

"I'll call Grayson," Lucas volunteered, and a moment later she heard him doing that.

The car also started to move again. Slowly. Gage was no doubt trying to get even closer to see if the person was truly dead or if this was some kind of ruse. After everything that had happened in the past twenty-four hours, none of them was in a trusting sort of mood, and Drury's gaze was firing all around them. No doubt searching for anyone who might be lying in wait.

"Blood," Drury said under his breath. "Anyone recognize him?"

Caitlyn lifted her head, just long enough to have a look at the man. He was belly down on the pavement, his face turned toward the car, and while his eyes were open, they were lifeless. Fixed in a blank stare.

For a moment she thought it was Ronnie since the man had the same hair color and a similar build, but it wasn't him.

She also glanced around at their surroundings. There were no houses. No other vehicles, either. Just miles of flat pastures stretching out on each side of them. Thankfully, there were only a few trees, and the ones that were nearby weren't wide enough to hide a gunman.

"Grayson's sending an ambulance and some deputies," Lucas relayed when he finished his call. "He'll be here in less than ten minutes." He tipped his head to the body. "Anyone else thinking it'd be a really bad idea to go out there and make sure the guy's dead?"

"Agreed," Drury and Gage said in unison.

"As soon as the deputies arrive to secure the scene, we're out of here," Drury told her. Then he turned back to Gage and Lucas. "Keep an eye on the ditches," he added.

Caitlyn's heart was already racing, and that certainly didn't help. Some of the ditches could be quite deep on the farm roads. Deep enough for someone to use to launch another attack.

The seconds crawled by, and it felt like an eternity. An eternity where Caitlyn had too much time to think, and her thoughts didn't go in a good place.

Oh, God.

"This could be a diversion so kidnappers can go after the baby," she blurted out.

None of them dismissed that, which only caused her to panic even more, and Drury took out his phone. "I'll call the ranch," he said.

Even though she was close to both Drury and his phone, Caitlyn couldn't hear what he said to the person who answered. That's because her heartbeat was crashing in her ears now, but she watched for any signs on Drury's face that he'd just gotten bad news.

More of the long moments crawled by before he finally said, "Everything's okay there. The place is on lockdown. Two of the deputies are with the baby, and the ranch hands are all armed."

Good. Of course, that didn't mean all those measures wouldn't keep the kidnappers from trying to take her again.

"Someone's coming," Lucas said, getting their attention.

Caitlyn had another glimpse over the front seat, and she saw the red truck approaching from the opposite direction. It wasn't a new model, and it appeared to be scabbed with rust. It definitely didn't look like the sort of vehicle that their attackers would use. Plus, this road led to several ranches, so it could be someone just headed into town.

Lucas, Gage and Drury lifted their guns anyway.

The truck slowed as it neared the body and their car, but because of the angle of the sun and the tinted windshield, Caitlyn wasn't able to see who was inside. She especially wasn't able to see when Drury pushed her back down on the seat.

Not a second too soon, either.

She got just a glimpse of the passenger in the truck. He threw open the door and aimed an Uzi at them.

A hail of bullets slammed into the car.

The sound was deafening, and the front windshield was suddenly pocked with the shots. The glass held. For now. But this wasn't just ordinary gunfire. The rounds were spraying all over the car, and even though it was bullet resistant, that didn't mean the shots wouldn't eventually get through.

"Hold on!" Gage told them.

That was the only warning they got before he threw

the car into Reverse and hit the accelerator. The tires squealed against the asphalt as he peeled away.

The shots didn't stop, though. The gunman continued to fire into the car, and it didn't sound as if he was getting farther away. Because he wasn't. She glanced out again and saw that the driver of the truck was coming after them. The shooter was leaning out the window to fire at them.

Gage cursed and sped up, but he was driving backward, and the shots had taken off his side mirror.

"Stay down," Drury warned her.

She did, but Caitlyn wished she had a weapon. Judging from the last glimpse she'd gotten of the truck, it was going fast, and if it was reinforced in some way, the driver could ram into them and send them into the ditch. If so, they'd be sitting ducks.

"Backup's on the way," Drury reminded her. Probably because she looked terrified. And she was.

But Caitlyn was also furious with the gunmen and with herself. Here, once again, she'd put Drury and his family in danger, and she still didn't know who was responsible for this.

Jeremy and Melanie both knew Drury and she had been at the sheriff's office, and it wasn't much of a stretch for them to figure out that they'd be heading to the ranch. Of course, Helen could have known that, too. Any of the three could have sent these thugs to try to kill them.

And there was no doubt that's exactly what they were trying to do.

This wasn't a kidnapping attempt. No. Those bullets were coming one right behind the other, each of them tearing into the car and windshield.

"Enough of this," Gage growled.

He hit the brakes, and for several heart-stopping moments, Caitlyn thought he was going to get out and make a stand. However, he backed the car into a narrow side road. In the same motion, he maneuvered the steering wheel to get them turned around. He darted out right in front of the truck. So close that it nearly collided with them.

Gage sped off.

"We'll lead them straight into backup," Drury said. He took out his phone, no doubt to let Grayson know. "We need to take them alive," he reminded the others.

Yes, because it was the fastest way for them to get answers.

"Hell," Drury mumbled.

She wasn't sure why he'd said that, but the shots suddenly stopped. Caitlyn followed his gaze, and he was looking back at the truck. She lifted her head just a fraction and peered over the seat to see that the truck was turning around.

Mercy.

They were going to try to get away.

She could only watch as the truck U-turned in the road. And that's when she got a look at the driver. It was someone she recognized.

Ronnie.

Chapter Nine

Drury figured he should be feeling some relief right about now. After all, he had Caitlyn safely back at the ranch, and other than the unmarked car being shot to pieces, there'd been no other damage.

Well, not to Caitlyn, him or his family.

But a man was dead. They didn't have an ID on the guy yet, but he'd almost certainly been murdered to get them to stop in the road so they could be gunned down. It was a high price to pay.

Caitlyn was paying a high price, too. She wasn't crying or falling apart. Not on the outside anyway. However, she had the baby in her arms and was rocking her as if that were the cure for everything. It had certainly soothed the baby. She was sacked out, and maybe just holding the little girl would soothe Caitlyn, too.

As much as she could be soothed considering she'd come close to dying.

"Grayson will question all of our suspects again," Drury reminded her. He was at the front window, volleying glances between Caitlyn and Lucas. His brother was outside the guesthouse and was pacing across the porch while he talked on the phone.

No doubt pushing to get any updates on the attack.

Drury was thankful for his help because he didn't exactly want to have those phone conversations in front of Caitlyn. Not with that shell-shocked glaze in her eyes.

"Ronnie," she said under her breath.

She didn't add any profanity, but Drury certainly had whenever the man's name came up. He'd never believed Ronnie's story that he was the baby's father and innocent in all of this, but the attack proved it. Ronnie had definitely been behind the wheel of that truck.

So, who'd hired him?

Drury checked his laptop to see if there'd been any breaks on finding a money trail. Breaks on anything else for that matter. But nothing.

"There's an APB out on Ronnie," Drury told her. "Everyone will be looking for him."

That wasn't a guarantee that they'd find him, but the APB was a start.

She nodded, and he thought the shell-shocked look got even worse. He also noticed that not all the rocking was actually rocking. Caitlyn was trembling. Probably feeling pretty unsteady, too, because she eased the baby into the carrier that was on the coffee table directly across from her.

Drury glanced out the window again. In addition to Lucas, two other armed ranch hands were out there. The front gate was locked, and the perimeter security system was on. That meant things were as safe as they could possibly be, so he left the window, went to the sofa and sank down beside her.

Caitlyn squeezed her eyes shut a moment. Groaned softly. And she eased against him, her head dropping onto his shoulder.

"I can still hear the gunshots," she said.

Yeah, so could he. He didn't want to tell her that she would hear them for the rest of her life. But she would. So would he. And he would remember that look of terror on her face.

There wasn't really a way to comfort her right now, so Drury just slipped his arm around her and hoped that helped. It seemed to do that. For a couple of long moments anyway. Until she lifted her head, and her eyes met his.

Any chance of comforting her vanished. A lot of things vanished. Like common sense because just like that, Drury felt the old attraction.

"I don't know how to stop this," she said. Her voice was a whisper, filled with her thin breath.

She wasn't talking about the danger now.

It would have been safer if she had been.

Before he could talk himself out of it or remember this was something he shouldn't be doing, Drury lowered his head and kissed her. There it was. That kick. He'd kissed her plenty of times, but he always felt it. As if this was something he'd never tasted before.

And wanted.

He hated that want. Hated the kick. Hell, in the moment he hated her and himself. But that didn't stop him from continuing the kiss.

This would have been a good time for Caitlyn to pull away from him and remind him just how much of a bad idea this was. She didn't. She moaned, a sound of pleasure, and she slipped her hand around the back of his neck to pull him even closer.

She succeeded.

The kiss deepened. So did the body-to-body contact, and her breasts landed against his chest. He felt another kick. Stronger than the first one, and even though he knew it would just keep getting stronger and stronger, he kept kissing her.

It didn't take long for things to rev up even more, and if Drury hadn't heard the sound, the heat might have taken over. But the sound was the front door opening, and that caused Caitlyn and Drury to fly apart as if they'd been caught doing something wrong.

Which they had been.

Kissing Caitlyn not only complicated things, but once again he'd lost focus.

Drury reached for his gun, but it wasn't necessary. Lucas came in, and yes, he'd seen at least a portion of the kiss. Or maybe he'd just caught the guilty look on Drury's face.

Lucas spared them both a glance, but his attention settled on the baby. He went closer, looking down at her, and he brushed his fingers over her toes that were peeking out from her pink gown.

His brother was certainly a lot more comfortable with the baby than Drury was. With good reason. Lucas was a father himself to a two-month-old son, and he was raising him alone since the baby's mother was in a coma.

Bittersweet.

Much the way Drury felt about this baby. He'd been protecting Caitlyn and the little girl, so that created a bond between them. But the old wounds were still there. Always would be.

"Grayson got an ID on the dead guy," Lucas said, sitting on the coffee table next to the baby. "His name was Morgan Sotelo. A druggie with a long record. No known family or address."

Which was probably why he'd been killed. No one would have missed him. Drury doubted the guy was actually involved in the attacks, and that sickened Drury. He'd been killed so that Ronnie and his henchmen could kill again.

"Nothing on Ronnie?" Caitlyn asked.

Lucas shook his head. "But the dashcam on the car recorded the whole attack, so we might be able to get an ID on the shooter since he wasn't wearing a mask. Sometimes, an ID leads to an address and friends or neighbors who might rat out his location."

A location that wouldn't be easy to find because the snake had no doubt gone into hiding. Temporarily, anyway. If Ronnie and the thug got another chance to attack, they would.

"Why do they want me dead?" she asked. "And why do they want her after I paid them the ransom?"

Drury had been giving that a lot of thought, and it wasn't a theory Caitlyn would like hearing. "If Melanie's behind this, she could want you out of the way, and then she could sell the baby to Helen."

Caitlyn's forehead bunched up and she nodded. "And the same could be true for Jeremy. Neither one of them would care if they put the child in danger, either, but Helen… Why would she risk something like that?"

"Maybe she hadn't. That still doesn't mean I'm taking her off the suspect list, though. After all, the men who attacked us are low-life scum. Even if Helen gave them orders to keep the child safe, that doesn't mean they followed those orders."

There was also a fourth possibility. That the low-life scum had gone rogue and were trying to cash in on a much bigger chunk of the money. After all, if they killed Caitlyn, Helen would rightfully be granted custody, and they could possibly milk a huge ransom from Grant's mother.

The baby whimpered, snagging their attention, and even though she did that a lot, this time she didn't go right back to sleep.

"She probably needs to be changed." Caitlyn got to her feet and lifted her out of the carrier so she could head to the bedroom.

She gave Drury a glance, and even though she didn't say anything, he saw the fresh concern in her eyes. Not for the attack this time. But because Lucas had witnessed that kiss.

Lucas watched her leave, no doubt waiting to discuss a subject that Drury didn't want to discuss. However, his brother didn't start that unwanted discussion. He just sat there, staring at Drury. Waiting. This was a brother's game of chicken.

"What?" Drury finally snapped.

Lucas kept staring. "I didn't say anything."

"You don't have to speak to say something."

The corner of Lucas's mouth lifted for just a second. The smile faded fast. "If you stay, you'll have to forgive her."

In the grand scheme of things, forgiving her would be the easy part. "Caitlyn told me right from the beginning that she didn't want to get involved with a lawman."

Lucas nodded. "Because of her dad." He paused. "Last I checked, you're still a lawman."

"Yeah. The badge didn't stop us from landing in bed four years ago."

"And it won't stop you now," Lucas reminded him.

"But maybe the notion of a heart-stomping will. You really intend to go through that again?"

Now, here was why he wished he could avoid this discussion. Because the answer was obvious. He didn't want to go through that again. Coming on the coattails of losing Lily, it had nearly broken him. And that's why somehow, some way he had to stop it. That started with finding the sick jerk who was behind the attacks.

He stood, ready to head to his laptop and get to work. That would also cue his brother that it was not only the end of this chat but also that he should be getting back to whatever he was supposed to be doing. However, before Drury could even take a step, his phone buzzed.

Grayson again. Since this could be an important update on the case, Drury answered it on the first ring.

"The lab just called," Grayson greeted. And he paused. "They put a rush on the test and got the DNA results for the baby."

CAITLYN TOOK HER time changing the baby so that Lucas and Drury would be able to have the talk that she could tell Lucas was itching to have. Lucas was no doubt out there right now lecturing Drury about the kiss he'd witnessed.

She was lecturing herself about it, too.

Of course, it wouldn't help. For whatever reason, she seemed to be mindless whenever she got within twenty feet of Drury. Just the sight of him could break down the barriers she'd spent a lifetime building. The trick would be continuing to build them, and that wouldn't be easy to do as long as Drury and she were under the same roof.

There was a knock at the door. A second later it opened, and she saw Drury standing there.

"What happened?" she asked, getting to her feet. She left the baby lying on the center of the bed. "Did Lucas chew you out for kissing me?"

When Drury didn't jump to confirm or deny that, she knew that this wasn't about his brother but that there was some kind of new information about the case.

"The baby's DNA results are back," he said.

Caitlyn sucked in her breath so fast that she nearly choked. "This soon?"

He nodded. "The baby is yours and Grant's."

Even though Caitlyn didn't have any trouble hearing what Drury had said, his words just seemed to freeze there in her head. For several seconds anyway. Then the relief came.

Sweet heaven.

This was her daughter.

She wasn't Melanie's. Not Ronnie's, either. Her child.

Drury went closer, took her by the arm and had her sit. Good thing, too, because the emotions came flooding through her. So fast and hard. The shock, yes. But there was something much, much deeper.

The love.

Caitlyn had felt the love the instant she'd seen the baby, but it seemed much stronger now. And complete. She was the mother of a child she'd always wanted.

Even though the baby had gone back to sleep, Caitlyn scooped her up and kissed her. She woke up, fussing and squirming a little, but Caitlyn continued to hold her. This time, though, she looked at her through a mother's eyes.

Yes, the love was overwhelming.

"Are you okay?" Drury asked.

Caitlyn managed a nod. She was more than okay. For

a couple of seconds anyway, and then she remembered the danger. That was suddenly overwhelming, too, now that she knew someone had not only created her baby, they wanted to steal her back.

Drury sank down on the edge of the bed next to her. Not so that he was touching her, though, but it was still close enough to get the baby's attention. The little girl opened her eyes, and she stared at him as if trying to figure out who he was. The corner of her mouth hitched up in a little smile.

Caitlyn had read enough of the baby books to know that the smile wasn't a real one, but it certainly felt real. It must have to Drury as well because he returned the smile before his attention went back to Caitlyn.

"Grayson is letting Child Protective Services know so they'll stop pursuing temporary custody," Drury explained.

Good. That was one less thing on her list of worries. "And what about Melanie?"

"Grayson will let her know, too. Since no one has contacted her with a ransom demand, I think it's safe to say that Grant and she don't have a child."

Caitlyn had to agree. "The more I think about it, Melanie's baby claim made even less sense. The only thing Grant and I had stored at Conceptions was the embryo. There wasn't any of his semen for them to create an embryo for Melanie."

Drury nodded, and since he didn't seem surprised, maybe he'd already considered that.

"What about the safe house?" she added. Because it suddenly seemed more critical than ever to get her out of harm's way.

"It's ready."

She immediately heard the *but* in his tone.

"After what happened on the road earlier, I'm not sure it's a good idea to take her off the ranch," Drury continued. "It's next to impossible to secure all the farm roads and ranch trails, but we've got security measures in place here at the ranch."

Even though it was hard to concentrate, Caitlyn went through the pros and cons of that. Yes. And as much as she hated to admit it, the ranch was the safer option. For now. However, staying didn't accomplish one thing—putting some distance between Drury and her.

But she had to put the baby first.

Drury must have understood because he didn't try to keep selling her on the idea of staying put. He did look at the baby again, though.

"You'll have to name her," he said.

Yes. Caitlyn had held off on doing that because in her mind it would have made it harder to give her up if the DNA test had proved this wasn't her child. Now that she was certain, she couldn't just keep calling her "the baby."

"I did a list a long time ago and wanted Elizabeth for a girl and Samuel for a boy." She looked down at the baby, as well. "But Elizabeth doesn't seem to fit her, does it?"

Drury lifted his shoulder, maybe trying to dismiss any part in this, but then he made a sound of agreement. "What was your second choice?"

"Caroline." It had been her grandmother's name.

He tested it out by repeating it a couple of times and nodded. It was silly to be happy over his approval, but she was.

"Caroline," she verified.

The moment seemed too intimate. Something that parents would do together. And they definitely weren't parents.

Drury must have sensed that as well because he eased away from her. "Too bad Grant died not knowing he would become a father."

Caitlyn figured she should just give a blanket agreement to that and end the discussion. But she didn't.

"Grant didn't actually want a child," she confessed. "I was the one who pushed him to go to Conceptions. He wasn't sold on the idea. In fact, he told me if I had a child that he or she would be just *my* child."

That brought Drury's gaze back to hers, and he cursed. "And you went through with the egg harvesting anyway?"

"I thought he'd change his mind." She paused, shook her head. "*Hoped* he would. And I reasoned that even if he didn't, I'd still have a child." Caitlyn gave a nervous laugh. Definitely not from humor. "Now you know just how desperate I was."

He stayed quiet a moment. "But you didn't stay desperate for long after you found out he was cheating on you."

"No," Caitlyn had to admit. "I decided it'd be better to have him completely out of my life. That included using the embryo at Conceptions. In fact, I was looking into adopting a child right before all of this happened."

This baby was a miracle for her. A miracle that she prayed she could keep safe.

Caitlyn heard the footsteps a few seconds before Lucas appeared in the doorway of the bedroom. At least this time Drury and she weren't in a lip-lock, but that still wasn't an approving look on Lucas's face. Except she thought maybe the look wasn't for her since Lucas was putting away his phone. He'd likely just finished another of the calls he'd been taking and making since they'd arrived at the guesthouse.

"The FBI found a money trail for Ronnie," Lucas explained. "Payments, big ones, that were wired to his account. The surrogate, Nicole Aston, was paid from the same account."

So, it was all connected. Not that Caitlyn had thought otherwise, but it was chilling to hear it spelled out like that. The same person responsible for arranging for her baby to be brought into the world had also arranged for Caitlyn to be killed.

Drury slowly got to his feet, his attention focused solely on his brother. "And did the FBI learn who owned that account?"

Lucas shook his head. "Not yet. It's offshore and buried under layers of false information. But that trail wasn't the only one they uncovered. The FBI found out who received the ransom money."

Caitlyn got to her feet, too. "Who?" she asked.

Lucas looked at Caitlyn. "You."

Chapter Ten

Drury hated every part of what was happening. Caitlyn being accused of orchestrating her baby's kidnapping. Having to take her to the sheriff's office to be questioned by an FBI agent. Having her out in the open again so someone could attack her. But Drury thought all those were a drop in the bucket compared with the final thing about this that he hated.

That Caitlyn was having to leave her daughter after learning the child was actually hers.

Of course, the baby was well protected with two deputies and the ranch hands, but this should be a time for her to savor an hour or two of getting to be with her child instead of being interrogated for something Drury knew she hadn't done.

And his faith in her innocence had nothing to do with the kiss or the attraction between them. This was common sense.

"We'll get this all straightened out," Drury assured her the moment Lucas pulled to a stop in front of the sheriff's office.

Caitlyn looked at him, and he could see the weariness in her eyes. "I didn't do this," she said.

It wasn't necessary for her to tell him that. Drury

knew. No way would she have intentionally put a child, any child, in danger.

As they'd done with their previous visit, the moment Lucas pulled to a stop in front of the sheriff's office, Drury got Caitlyn out of the car and inside. Away from the windows, too. And he immediately spotted someone he recognized.

"You know him?" Caitlyn asked.

"Yeah. FBI Agent Seth Calder."

Seth did his own introductions with Caitlyn. It didn't surprise Drury that they wouldn't want him or one of his cousins to do this interview with Caitlyn. No way could they be impartial, but at least the Bureau had someone whom Drury considered decent and fair.

"Good to see you again, Drury," Seth said before shifting his attention to Caitlyn. "Wish this were under different circumstances, though." He motioned for them to follow him to one of the interview rooms.

Both Grayson and Gage stayed back, following protocol, but it'd take a lot more than protocol to keep Drury out of the room. Thankfully, Seth didn't turn him away when he ushered Caitlyn down the hall.

When they passed in front of one of the other rooms, that's when Drury noticed it wasn't empty. Helen was in there, and she was having a whispered chat with a man who was probably her lawyer.

"Yes, she's here," Seth volunteered. "I'm interviewing her next. Then I'm bringing in Jeremy. He should already be on his way over."

Drury wouldn't have minded talking to Jeremy, but maybe they could dodge the man for Caitlyn's sake. Of course, there was no dodging Helen.

"I want to talk to you," Helen snarled when her attention landed on Caitlyn.

"It'll have to wait," Seth snarled right back.

Seth ushered Drury and Caitlyn into the other interview room. "Arrest Helen if she tries to come in here," Seth told Grayson.

Since Helen had already started to do just that, apparently ready to continue the confrontation, it was a timely order. It got the woman to stop even though she shot a glare at Caitlyn.

Drury glared back at her, and he closed the door behind him as he went into the room with Seth and Caitlyn.

"I'm innocent," Caitlyn said right off the bat.

"Someone is setting her up," Drury added.

Seth didn't refute either of those claims, and once they were seated, he slid some papers toward her. It was a report on the money trail. The one that seemingly led straight to Caitlyn.

Her mouth tightened as she read it. "Why would I take money from Grant's estate to pay myself?"

"Trust me, I had to think long and hard to figure out some possibilities. Maybe so that Grant's family wouldn't try to challenge it, or despise you for having it?"

"They'll always despise me. And Grant's will was written so that they can't challenge it. The money is mine. *Was* mine," Caitlyn corrected. "I used almost all of it to pay for the ransom."

"The ransom that's in an offshore account with your name on it."

"I didn't know anything about that account," she insisted.

Again, Seth didn't dispute that, but he did pause a long time. "I believe you."

Caitlyn released her breath as if she'd been holding it a long time.

"Someone did this to try to get you in legal hot water," he went on. "Not just for this but for the baby itself. The agreement you signed at Conceptions was that neither you nor Grant could use the embryo you stored without the other's written permission."

She nodded. "I did that so he wouldn't be able to use the embryos after we divorced. He wasn't especially thrilled with the notion of fatherhood, not then anyway, but I didn't know if he would change his mind years later."

Seth made a sound of agreement. "Someone in Grant's family could file a civil suit against you, though, if they could prove you took the embryo illegally."

Drury was about to say there was no proof for that, but maybe that's what the bank account was about. If Caitlyn had the money, then she would look guilty.

Well, maybe.

"Even if she had stolen the embryo," Drury said, "why go through with a fake kidnapping and ransom?"

"I'm sure a lawyer could argue that it was to gain sympathy. Or that maybe she has some kind of need for attention."

Caitlyn cursed. A rarity for her. "The only thing I need right now is for my daughter, Drury and his family to be safe."

Drury silently added Caitlyn's name to that list. He didn't want her daughter to be an orphan, and that was just one of the reasons he had to keep her alive.

"Someone else could have access to this bank account," Drury pointed out.

"Yes," Seth readily admitted. "Unfortunately, if someone else did this, I can't tell who. That's where I need Caitlyn's help. The person who created this bank account had access to her personal info. Her Social Security number, for example. That's the password for the account."

"Either Grant's mother or brother could have gotten that," Caitlyn insisted. "For that matter, Melanie could have, too."

Another sound of agreement. "They made it too obvious, though. I mean, why would you open an offshore account using your own name and Social Security number? Yes, it was buried under dummy corporation accounts, but it didn't have nearly enough layers for someone who was genuinely trying to hide dirty money."

Now it was Drury who was breathing easier. He'd known all along that she was innocent, but it was good to hear a fellow agent spell it out. That, however, led him to something else.

"Why did you want to bring Caitlyn in if you knew it was a setup?" Drury asked Seth.

"Because of this." He passed another piece of paper their way. "I didn't want to get into this over the phone, but this was in the memo section of the account. Most people with legit accounts just type in things like what the payment was for. What do you think it is?"

Drury and Caitlyn looked at the paper together. It was the letters *N* and *A* and the word *Samuel*.

"'*N, A,'*" Drury read aloud. Since there wasn't a slash between the letters, it probably didn't mean *not applicable*. He went through all the info they'd collected during this investigation.

Bingo.

"Nicole Aston," Drury and Caitlyn said in unison.

"She's the woman we believe was the surrogate," Drury added to Seth.

Seth nodded. "And who's Samuel?"

Drury started to shake his head, and then he remembered something Caitlyn had told him. "You said if you had a son, you'd name him Samuel. Would Helen, Jeremy or Melanie have known that?"

She stayed quiet a moment, giving that some thought. "Maybe." And she paused again. "But it could be a place. Helen owns an apartment complex, and it's on Samuel Street in San Antonio. I remember because when I first told Grant about my name choice for a baby, he mentioned it."

"Nicole could be there," Drury quickly pointed out. "But if she is, the apartment's not in her name."

Seth was already taking out his phone, and he made a call to get someone to look for her. The moment he was done, he stood.

"You can watch through the observation mirror when I question Helen," Seth said. "For now, I'd rather both of you stay back, but she's clearly got a temper. If she doesn't spill anything useful, I might try to spark that temper by bringing you in to confront her."

Caitlyn and Drury nodded. He wanted Helen to spill all. However, he hated that once again, Caitlyn was going to have to be put through something like this, especially coming on the heels of being accused of having set all of this up.

Drury took her to the observation room and moved her away from the door just in case Helen came barreling out of the interview with plans to confront Caitlyn again. He doubted, though, that Seth would let that happen. Seth wasn't the sort to let Helen ride rough-shod over him.

"If the attackers end up killing me," Caitlyn said, "please don't let Helen get custody of the baby. I know it's a lot to ask," she quickly added. "But I don't have anyone else to turn to."

Yes, it was a lot to ask, but there was no way Drury would refuse. No way he'd let Helen get her hands on the baby.

"You wouldn't have to raise her yourself," Caitlyn went on. "Just make sure she has a good home."

That was it. Drury stopped the gloom and doom with a kiss. All in all, it was a stupid way to stop it, but he didn't want Caitlyn going on about being killed. Even if someone had already tried to do just that.

Drury had intended the kiss to be a quick peck, but it turned into something that fell more into the scalding-hot range. It left them both breathless, flustered and wanting more.

It also distracted them.

Seth's interrogation could turn up something critical, and here he was complicating the hell out of things by kissing Caitlyn again.

Drury forced his attention back on Helen, and he both heard and saw her deny whatever Seth had just asked. Her shoulders were stiff. Eyes, narrowed. And she was volleying glares between Seth and the observation window where she no doubt knew Caitlyn and Drury were watching.

"I didn't arrange to have my granddaughter born," Helen snapped. She jumped up and got right in Seth's face. "But I will be part of her life. A *big* part, without anyone interfering." That was obviously aimed at Caitlyn. "You won't stop that, and neither will my former daughter-in-law."

Seth had his own version of a glare going on, but it had a dangerous edge to it. "You should restrain your client before I do," Seth told her lawyer. His voice was edged with danger, as well.

And it worked. The lawyer took hold of Helen's arm and put her back in the seat. He whispered something to her, probably a reminder that it wouldn't help her case if she managed to get herself arrested.

"Tell me about your bank account in the Cayman Islands," Seth threw out there while he glanced through the papers he was holding.

Of course, there was no proof that it was indeed Helen's account, but the woman didn't know that. Well, if she was guilty, she didn't.

"I have no idea what you're talking about," Helen insisted, but before she could continue, her lawyer leaned in and whispered something else to her. "I have accounts in many places, so you'll have to be more specific."

"The account you used to orchestrate the birth of your granddaughter and the attacks on Caitlyn. You know which attacks I mean. The ones meant to kill her so she wouldn't be in your way." Seth leaned in closer. "On a scale of one to ten, just how upset are you that Caitlyn inherited all your son's money? I'm guessing a ten."

Judging from the way Helen's mouth tightened, she was about to deny the bank account and blast Seth for accusing her of attempted murder. However, Drury missed whatever she said because he heard the commotion in the squad room. Several people were shouting, and one of those people was Grayson.

"Put down the gun now," Grayson ordered.

That got Drury's heart pumping, and he automatically pushed Caitlyn behind him and drew his gun. "Wait here," he told her.

With his gun ready, Drury leaned out from the door, not sure what he would see. After all, who was stupid enough to come into a sheriff's office while brandishing a weapon? And the person did indeed have a gun.

Melanie.

She was in front of the reception desk. Not alone, either. She had a man directly in front of her.

Ronnie.

And Melanie had a gun pressed to his head.

"Melanie," Drury called out.

Caitlyn didn't release the breath she'd been holding. Not yet anyway, but she'd braced herself for an attack. Of course, that would be exactly what this was, though it wasn't Melanie's style to do the dirty work herself.

"Gun down on the floor now," Grayson demanded.

Caitlyn peered out the door for just a glimpse, and she saw a lot in those couple of seconds. It appeared that Melanie had taken Ronnie captive.

Appeared.

But maybe this was the start of an attack after all.

"Be careful," Caitlyn warned Drury when he stepped farther into the hall. He had his gun pointed in the direction where she'd seen Melanie.

"I can't," Melanie insisted. "This is a dangerous snake, and I don't want him to escape."

"We won't let that happen," Drury assured her and went even closer.

Caitlyn had no choice but to stand there and wait.

Pray, too. Because if Melanie started shooting, she might try to take out Drury first.

There was a shuffling sound, followed by some profanity from Ronnie.

"This crazy idiot tried to kill me," Ronnie accused.

"Obviously Melanie didn't succeed," Drury answered, and judging from his footsteps, he went closer to assist Grayson in containing whatever the heck this was.

When Caitlyn glanced around the jamb again, she saw that Melanie had been disarmed and that Grayson was cuffing Ronnie. Good. But she still didn't breathe any easier, not with Helen on one side of the building and now Melanie on the other. Plus, according to what Seth had told them, Jeremy was on his way to the station.

Soon, all their suspects would be under the same roof along with the thug Ronnie, whom one of them had no doubt hired.

"I did your job for you," Melanie bragged. "I found Ronnie and brought him here."

"I'll want to hear a lot more to go along with that explanation," Drury insisted.

"She sneaked up on me and clubbed me on the head," Ronnie jumped to say. It was possible that had happened, but with Ronnie's other injuries from the car accident, it was hard to tell.

"Yes, I clubbed him," Melanie admitted. Her gaze shifted to Caitlyn when she stepped out of the interview room and into the hall. "Still think I'm behind this?" Melanie challenged.

Caitlyn shook her head. "I'm not sure what to think." And she didn't. This could all be some kind of ruse to make Melanie look innocent.

Or to distract them.

Obviously Drury felt the same way because he motioned for her to stay back.

"She had no right to club me like that," Ronnie protested.

No one in the squad room gave him a look of even marginal sympathy. "You're a fugitive," Grayson pointed out, "and you tried to commit murder."

"But I didn't." Ronnie didn't shout exactly, but it was close. "I've been framed. I didn't escape, either. I was dragged at gunpoint from the hospital."

Caitlyn had had enough. "You were in the same vehicle with the person who tried to kill us."

"Because he forced me to be there! Just like this bimbo."

Melanie didn't go after the man for the name-calling, but she shot him a glare that could have melted a glacier.

"I'm not saying another word until my lawyer gets here," Ronnie added.

Gage stepped forward and handed Grayson a piece of paper, and he took over with Ronnie. "I'll put him in a cell," Gage offered.

Grayson nodded, his attention on whatever was on that paper. He didn't turn back to Melanie until he'd finished it.

"Now, explain to me how you found Ronnie?" Grayson prompted the woman.

"I did your job," she snapped.

Drury went to stand by Grayson's side, and the pair just stared at her, waiting for her to continue.

"I had some PI friends looking for him," Melanie went on. "When they spotted him, they called me."

"And why didn't you call the police?" Grayson asked, sounding very much like the lawman that he was.

"Because you let him get away once, and I wasn't

going to let that happen again. Make sure this time you keep him under lock and key. I don't want Ronnie out on the streets where he'll have a chance to kill me."

Drury and Caitlyn exchanged glances. "Why would Ronnie want you dead?" Caitlyn pressed.

Melanie threw her hands in the air. "I don't know. But someone's been following me, spying on me," she quickly added. "And what with the attacks, I figured Ronnie had his sights set on me next."

Caitlyn had to shake her head. "That doesn't make sense. There's no reason for Ronnie to want you dead."

"There is if Helen wants to silence me. She knows I'm not going to just let this drop. She stole from Conceptions Clinic to create a child Grant didn't want. He's not around to fight for what's right, so I'll do it for him."

Caitlyn huffed. "Didn't you try to do the same thing? Or else you claimed to do it."

Melanie pulled back her shoulders. "What do you mean—*claimed*?"

"I got the DNA results. The child is mine and Grant's. Not yours. Not Ronnie's, either. And with only one viable embryo, there's no way Conceptions could have used a surrogate to carry yours and Grant's child."

Melanie opened her mouth, closed it, then opened it again. She seemed genuinely stunned. "Those people at Conceptions duped me," she finally managed to say. But then in a flash the fire returned to her eyes. "Or you're lying. That's it, isn't it? You're lying and so is Helen. She wants me dead."

Caitlyn wasn't sure if the woman was plain delusional or truly believed Helen had a motive to kill her. Either way, Caitlyn didn't have time to press her on the issue because she saw a man making his way to the sheriff's office.

Jeremy.

Drury obviously believed this could be the start of another attack because he stepped in front of her again. "Go back to the observation room," he whispered to Caitlyn.

She hated that once again Drury might have to fight a battle for her, but Caitlyn didn't think this was the time to stand her ground. Especially since it could be a distraction for Drury and Grayson. She hurried back to the room but stayed in the doorway so she could watch what was happening.

"Are you the one who hired Ronnie to come after me?" Melanie asked Jeremy before he'd fully gotten inside.

He drew in a long breath, huffed and shifted his attention to Drury. "Has Melanie been telling you lies about me?"

"I'm not sure," Drury answered. "Did you hire Ronnie?"

Unlike his mother, he didn't have a flash of temper. Not on the outside anyway, but Caitlyn knew the anger was simmering just below the surface.

"No," Jeremy answered after several long moments. He reached into his pocket, prompting Grayson and Drury to go for their guns. "I'm just getting this." He pulled out a USB drive and handed it to Drury. "You'll want to go over what's on there."

"Why?" Drury asked. He passed it to one of the deputies.

"Because it's got everything you need to convict her of these crimes." Jeremy tipped his head to Melanie.

The woman howled out a protest, and she bolted forward as if she were about to rip the storage device from the deputy's hand. Drury blocked her path and turned toward Jeremy. "What's on there?"

"Lies," Melanie insisted.

"Transcripts of conversations that I had with Melanie."

This time Grayson had to physically restrain the woman. "You're a pig!" she shouted, the insult aimed at Jeremy.

Jeremy certainly didn't deny that. "Melanie and I had an affair. A short one," he emphasized. "I recorded our conversations, and in several of them, she says outright that she wants Caitlyn dead."

Melanie called him more names, punctuating it with plenty of ripe curse words. "You'll pay for this, Jeremy. Just wait. You'll pay."

It was hard to hear over Melanie's screeching, and Grayson must have gotten fed up with it because he handed Melanie off to the deputy. "Put her in a holding cell until she calms down."

The deputy carried her away while Melanie shouted obscenities and threats.

"Do you always record conversations with your lovers?" Drury asked once the room was quiet again.

"Always." He tipped his head to the USB drive that the deputy had put on the table. "Somewhere around page thirty, Melanie says she wants to steal the embryo from Conceptions so she could use the baby to get Grant's money from Caitlyn."

Caitlyn's stomach twisted. Was that what this was really all about? A way for Grant's mistress to get his money?

"You said it was transcripts," Caitlyn said, going closer now. "Those can be easily faked. The only way we'd know if it was true would be to listen to what Melanie actually said."

"The recordings were accidentally erased." Jeremy waited until after both Grayson and Drury had finished groaning. "But Melanie mentions a bank account. Offshore. There could be something to help you identify where the account is and if it's the one used to pay off men like Ronnie."

Maybe it was the same account that Seth had found. Of course, maybe Jeremy was just doing this to take suspicion off himself. If so, it wasn't working. Jeremy would stay on her list of suspects.

"Go ahead." Jeremy tipped his head to the storage device. "Read what's on there."

Grayson shook his head. "It could contain a virus to corrupt our files. I'd rather have the FBI check it out. Plus, it could be a waste of my time. And if it is, if you're trying to manipulate this investigation, I can see if obstruction of justice charges apply here."

Judging from the way Jeremy pulled back his shoulders, he didn't like that one bit. Maybe this was an attempt to destroy some evidence by corrupting the computer system. If so, then Grayson would definitely have some charges to file against the man. Too bad those charges wouldn't put Jeremy in jail for long, though.

"Why would you sleep with Melanie?" Caitlyn asked him. "You knew what she was."

He lifted a shoulder. "I blame it on sibling rivalry. I never liked Grant having something I didn't."

It surprised her a little that he admitted it, but then Caitlyn remembered that Jeremy had once hit on her. She'd refused, and she had always thought that was one of the reasons he hated her so much. But maybe it was simply a case of him hating what he couldn't have.

"How did the recordings get *accidentally* erased?" Grayson asked.

Jeremy huffed. "Obviously I'm wasting my time here when I was just trying to do you a favor."

"A favor like Melanie bringing in Ronnie?" Drury didn't wait for an answer. "The only favor we need from either of you is concrete proof to stop these attacks. You got that kind of proof?"

"No," Jeremy said after a long pause and a glare. "But you have to consider that Caitlyn brought this on herself."

Caitlyn tried not to react to that, but she flinched anyway. The memories of the attacks were still too fresh in her mind. Always would be. "I didn't bring this on myself," she managed to say.

Jeremy made a *whatever* sound. "You knew what Grant was before you got involved with him."

It felt as if he'd slapped her. Because it was true.

Jeremy turned as if to leave, but Grayson stopped him. He motioned for a deputy to come closer. "Make sure Mr. Denson isn't armed and then take him to the interview room."

"What?" Jeremy howled. "You're still questioning me even after I bought you the dirt on Melanie?"

"Yes," Grayson said.

Despite Jeremy's protests, the deputy frisked him. No weapons so the deputy led him through the squad room and to the interview room directly across the hall from his mother.

"Jeremy's right," Caitlyn said under her breath. "I should have seen that Grant wasn't who he was pretending to be."

"He's not right," Drury snapped, and he slid his arm

around her waist. "Everything Jeremy says and does could be to cover his tracks."

Caitlyn knew that, but it still didn't rid her of some guilt in this. If she'd never gotten involved with Grant, none of this would be happening.

"You wouldn't have your daughter if you hadn't been with him," Drury said as if reading her mind.

It was the perfect thing to say, and it eased some of the tension that had settled hard and cold in her chest. At least it eased it until she noticed that Grayson was looking at the paper that Gage had given him right before Jeremy had shown up.

"Bad news?" she asked.

Grayson didn't hesitate. He nodded. "SAPD sent someone to Samuel Street to find out if Nicole was staying there."

That got Caitlyn's attention. "Was she?"

Another nod. "The super ID'd her from a photo. The lease wasn't in her name but rather a corporation. One of the dummy companies on the offshore account."

That didn't surprise Caitlyn since Nicole—and Ronnie—had been paid from that same account.

"Nicole wasn't there," Grayson went on, and he handed the report to Drury. "The place had been ransacked, and there was some evidence of a struggle."

Oh, mercy.

"What kind of evidence?" Caitlyn pressed when Grayson didn't continue.

Grayson met her gaze. "Blood."

Chapter Eleven

Blood. Definitely not a good sign.

Especially this kind of blood.

According to the report Grayson had given Drury to read, SAPD had found high-velocity blood spatter on the wall of the living room in the apartment where Nicole had been staying. That meant there'd probably been some blunt force trauma.

Reading that was enough to make the skin crawl on the back of his neck, but there was more. Much more. And that more was something Drury wasn't sure he wanted Caitlyn to know.

"They killed her," Caitlyn said.

That's when Drury realized the color had drained from her face. She also didn't look as if she could stand on her own, so Drury tightened his grip on her.

"We don't know for certain that Nicole's even dead," Drury insisted, and Grayson gave a variation of the same before he went to the cooler to get Caitlyn a drink of water.

"If they didn't kill her, that means they hurt her," Caitlyn amended.

"Not necessarily. It might not be her blood," Drury tried again, though that was reaching.

After all, the person who'd hired her to be a surrogate could want her murdered to tie up any loose ends. Nicole wouldn't be able to ID anyone if she was dead.

Caitlyn's hand was shaking when she took the paper cup of water from Grayson. Her voice shook, too, when she thanked him. That's when Drury knew he needed to get her out of the squad room. Away from the other officers. And especially away from the windows. After all, they had their three suspects under the same roof, and it was possible hired thugs were also nearby.

With the report still in his hand, Drury took her to the break room at the end of the hall, and he shut the door. With Helen and Jeremy just a few yards away, he didn't want Caitlyn to have another encounter with them. Not until she'd steadied her nerves anyway. As much as Drury hated it, sooner or later she'd cross paths not only with Helen and Jeremy but also with Melanie.

"I have to get back to the ranch," she said. "I need to see my baby."

Drury understood that, but the timing wasn't good. "Grayson, Gage and the other deputies are tied up right now. Just hold on a little while longer until we've got someone to drive back with us."

She looked up at him. Nodded. But he could tell the only place she wanted to be right now was with her daughter.

And that would happen.

However, Drury kept going back to the idea that there were probably hired guns nearby, and he didn't want those guns taking shots at them. That meant clearing the area before he took Caitlyn from the building.

Caitlyn shook her head as if she might argue with

that, but then the tears sprang to her eyes. "I'm so sorry about putting you in the middle of all of this trouble."

Drury wanted to snap at her for the apology. It was an insult to a lawman since the only reason he had a job was *because* of trouble. But considering he'd also kissed Caitlyn blind, it was a different kind of insult.

Of course, he shouldn't have been kissing her, either, so he wasn't exactly blameless in the insult department.

She looked at him, their gazes connecting, and even though he hadn't mentioned those kisses out loud, she was likely remembering them.

Feeling them, too.

Drury sure was.

The moment seemed to freeze or something. Well, they did anyway, but it didn't stop the old familiar heat from firing up inside him. Kissing her now would be the biggest mistake of all what with this emotion zinging between them, so he forced himself to look away, and his attention landed back on the report Grayson had given him.

It was several pages stapled together, and Drury made the mistake of flipping to the second page. To the picture that was there. Now the blood spatter was there for him to see.

And for Caitlyn to see, as well.

It'd been easy to sugarcoat the possibility of what had happened, but it was hard to sugarcoat something right in their faces. Along with the blood on the stark white wall, the coffee table and chairs had been tossed over. A lamp was on the floor.

So was a baby carrier. Next to the carrier was a diaper bag filled with supplies.

"Mercy," Caitlyn said, her voice filled with breath. "That's where she must have been holding Caroline."

"Maybe." But inside, Drury had to admit that the answer to that was *probably*. He only hoped the thugs had taken the baby to safety before they'd gone after the woman who'd given birth to her.

"Does the report say how long the blood had been there?" she asked.

Drury glanced through it, hoping that it was recent, as in the past hour or so. That way, it could mean the baby hadn't been around for whatever had gone on. Since there wasn't a body in the apartment, it could also mean that Nicole had escaped and was out there injured but alive. Or better yet, that she'd managed to bludgeon someone who'd tried to attack her.

But no.

"The CSIs will need to test it," Drury explained, "but it appears to have been there for several days." Maybe even as long as a week. That meshed with what her neighbors were saying—that they hadn't seen her in days.

Caitlyn blinked back tears, obviously processing what he was saying. It didn't process well. Because it meant the baby could have been there in the living room when the attack occurred. Caroline hadn't been hurt, but it sickened him to think that she could have been.

"Did anyone hear a disturbance in the apartment? Screams? Anything?" Caitlyn added.

"No." That didn't mean someone hadn't heard, though. The apartment wasn't in the best part of town. It was the kind of place where a lot of people would have turned a blind eye.

Caitlyn took the report from him, glancing through

it, and he saw the exact moment her attention landed on what he wasn't sure he wanted her to see. Her gaze skirted across the lines, gobbling up details that were probably giving her another slam of adrenaline.

"Nicole gave birth in the apartment," she said, her voice thin.

"The cops on the scene are only guessing about that." But it was a darn good guess considering the blood they'd found in the bedroom and adjoining bath.

There'd been evidence of a home delivery, including some kind of clamp that was used for umbilical cords. Other evidence, too, that Nicole hadn't been planning on staying put. They'd also found a plane ticket to California.

"She was taking the baby," Caitlyn whispered.

Everything was certainly pointing in that direction, especially since Nicole had already packed a diaper bag with baby supplies. Her wallet was missing, but Drury was betting she'd had enough cash to live on, for a while anyway.

"Nicole might have found out what was going on at Conceptions," Drury explained. "If she gave birth to the baby before her due date, she might have thought she could escape."

Of course, that meant the woman might have been trying to escape with Caitlyn's daughter, but Nicole might have believed this was the only way to keep the child safe. At least that's what Drury hoped she had in mind. There were cases of surrogates getting so attached to the babies they were carrying that they fled with the infants. No way, though, would the person behind this have allowed that to happen.

Not with a million-dollar ransom at stake.

Obviously, Caitlyn didn't have any trouble piecing together that theory, either, and because Drury thought they could both use it, he pulled her into his arms. She didn't resist even though they both knew this was only going to make things harder when this investigation was over. Still, with that reminder, Drury stayed put and probably would have upped the mistake by kissing her if there hadn't been a knock. Before Drury could untangle himself from her, the door opened.

Because every inch of him was still on high alert, Drury automatically reached for his gun again.

But it was just Grayson.

Like the other time he'd seen Drury close to Caitlyn, Grayson didn't react. He hitched his thumb in the direction of the interview rooms. "You'll want to come out for this," he said. "I think all hell's about to break loose."

"Not another attack?" Drury quickly asked.

Grayson shook his head and motioned for them to follow him. They did with Drury keeping Caitlyn behind him, and they stopped along with Grayson in the door of the interview room. Drury hadn't been sure what he would see once he looked inside. Jeremy was there as expected, but so was Helen, her lawyer and Melanie. It wasn't standard procedure to get suspects together for a joint interrogation, so Drury had no idea what was going on.

Seth was standing at the back of the room, his back against the wall, and he was eyeing their trio of suspects as if they were all rattlesnakes ready to strike.

"You're making a huge mistake," Jeremy said like a warning, and his comment was directed at Melanie.

Drury figured this was just a continuation of the verbal altercation they'd had in the reception area, but then he saw the photo on the phone screen in the center of the table.

"I don't even know why I'm in here," Helen grumbled. "I had nothing to do with that."

Drury went closer with Caitlyn following right behind him.

"That's Jeremy," Melanie announced.

Yes, it was, and the man was in some kind of waiting room. Drury looked at Grayson for an explanation, but Melanie continued before he could say anything.

"That's Jeremy at Conceptions. He was there to try to steal the embryo so he could destroy it."

Drury expected Jeremy to jump to deny that. He didn't.

"Tell them how you got those photos," Jeremy countered.

Melanie hiked up her chin. "I hired a PI to keep an eye on Conceptions. Because I was worried that someone would try to do something dirty. What I did isn't against the law."

"It's not against the law for Jeremy to have been there, either," Helen pointed out.

"Don't defend me," Jeremy snapped.

"I wasn't." Helen's voice was filled with just as much venom as her son's. "I was about to explain that Melanie could have hired that PI to steal the embryo, as well. But these pictures aren't proof that either of you committed a crime."

Everyone turned to the woman. Because that didn't sound like some kind of general statement. It sounded as if she had firsthand knowledge.

"You know something about this?" Grayson pressed.

"I don't know anything," she insisted, "but common

sense tells me it didn't have to be Melanie or Jeremy who took the embryo. Caitlyn has a much stronger motive than either of them. And she couldn't have legally gotten her hands on them because she wouldn't have been able to get permission from Grant."

"That's true," Caitlyn admitted. "But I didn't steal them." She looked at Jeremy. "Did you?"

Jeremy took his time answering. "No." A muscle flickered in his jaw. "But I considered it. Briefly," he quickly added. "And I dismissed the idea just as fast. Frankly, I didn't think you'd want to have Grant's baby, not when you've obviously still got a thing for the cowboy here."

Caitlyn opened her mouth, probably to deny what Jeremy was saying, but since Drury and she had nearly just kissed again, she didn't voice her denial.

"So, if you thought I wouldn't want Grant's baby," Caitlyn continued a moment later, "then why consider stealing the embryo?"

Jeremy gave her a flat look. "You're not the only player in this sick game, Caitlyn. Mommy wants a grandbaby. I think she has hopes of getting it right this time, since she screwed up with Grant and me. But personally I'd like to make sure she doesn't get another chance at motherhood."

Jeremy sounded convincing enough. And maybe he was telling the truth. That didn't mean, though, that he hadn't created an heir to use as some kind of blackmail for his mother and Caitlyn.

"I did the best I could with the likes of you," Helen snapped. "You've always been an ungrateful son."

Jeremy faked a yawn. "Unstable mothers produce ungrateful sons. Am I done here?" he asked Grayson.

"No, he's not done!" Melanie howled. "You need to arrest him."

Grayson huffed. "And I'm sure Jeremy will claim I need to arrest you for what's on those transcripts." He looked at Helen. "You probably want me to arrest both of them."

"I do," Helen verified. "And Caitlyn. I know she had something to do with all of this."

Caitlyn went closer, practically getting right in the woman's face. "I would never do anything that would put my child in harm's way."

Helen stared at her a moment, then shifted her attention to Drury. "Are you the baby's father?"

Well, he sure hadn't seen that question coming. "No." Though he hated to dignify it with an answer.

Helen's stare turned to a glare. "I want to see the baby's DNA results."

"Get a court order," Drury tossed back at her. "If you can."

And he doubted she could since Caitlyn wasn't using the baby to make any kind of claim on Helen's estate. Of course, that wouldn't stop Helen from trying to get those visitation rights or even custody of the baby.

"Am I free to go?" Jeremy repeated.

Grayson didn't jump to answer. He made Jeremy wait several long moments. "Yeah, you can go. Not you two, though." He pointed first to Helen and then Melanie.

Obviously neither woman liked that. Both started to protest, and again Helen's lawyer had to restrain her. That's when Drury decided it was time to get Caitlyn out of there. Seth stepped up to take Helen and her lawyer back to the interview room across the hall. Grayson went in with Melanie, and he shut the door. Jeremy walked out the front of the sheriff's office without even sparing them a glance.

Drury kept his eyes on Jeremy until he was out of sight. "How deep do you think he's into this?"

Caitlyn shook her head. "I don't know, but I just hope they're not all working together."

Drury agreed, though he doubted they trusted each other enough for that, and he was certain there was plenty they weren't telling him.

"We can't leave yet, can we?" Caitlyn asked. He could hear the weariness in her voice and see it in her eyes.

Not with Grayson and the deputies still tied up, but maybe Drury could get some outside help. He took out his phone to call Lucas. Maybe his brother could arrange to bring a couple of the ranch hands with him. Drury definitely didn't want Caitlyn out of the building until he had some security measures in place. However, before Drury could even press his brother's number, he spotted Gage coming toward him. Fast.

"You've got a call through nine-one-one," Gage said, sounding a little out of breath. "The caller says she's Nicole Aston."

Chapter Twelve

Caitlyn tried not to get her hopes up, but that was impossible to do. After everything she'd just read in the report of Nicole's apartment, she had thought the surrogate was likely dead.

And she might be.

This call could be a hoax, designed to make the cops think a murder hadn't occurred. After all, it wasn't as if Drury or she would actually recognize Nicole's voice. Still, this was a thread of hope that didn't exist a couple of minutes ago.

She followed Drury to Gage's desk. The call had come in through the landline, and Gage put it on speaker.

"Nicole?" Drury asked. "I'm Agent Ryland. Where are you?"

"Is Caitlyn Denson with you?" the woman immediately said. Clearly, she was ignoring Drury's question.

"I'm here," Caitlyn answered. "Are you the surrogate who carried my daughter?"

"I am." A hoarse sob tore from her mouth. Too bad Caitlyn couldn't see the woman's face so she could try to figure out if she was faking that agony. "I swear I didn't know what was going on. Not until it was too late."

"Where are you?" Drury pressed.

"I can't say. Not yet. Not until I'm sure I can trust you."

"You can trust us," Drury assured her. "But the real question is—can we trust you?"

"Yes," she said without hesitation. "I had no part in anything that happened. Like I said, I didn't know what was going on until shortly before I gave birth."

"How did you find out what was *going on*?" Drury again.

This time there was some hesitation. Several long seconds of it. "I overheard some things, and I was able to piece together what was happening."

Drury huffed. "I'm going to need a lot more information than that. First, though, I have to make sure you're safe."

It sounded as if Nicole laughed, but it wasn't a laugh of humor. "I'm definitely not safe. Someone tried to kill me in my apartment."

"Yeah, I saw the photos. SAPD is there now. Is that your blood on the wall?"

"No. I hit one of the men who attacked me." Another pause. "God, I was just trying to protect the baby."

Hearing that robbed Caitlyn of her breath. Her daughter had been there with all that violence going on. Well, she had been if Nicole was telling the truth. Caitlyn had so many questions.

So many doubts, too.

"How do I know you're really the surrogate?" Caitlyn asked her.

More silence. "The baby I delivered had a small birthmark on her right ankle."

Bingo.

"She could be lying," Drury whispered to her. "She could have just seen the baby, that's all. Or could have been told about the birthmark."

Yes, and it didn't take Caitlyn long to realize why this woman would lie about something like that. She could be trying to gain their sympathy. Their trust. So she could use that connection to draw them out or find the location of the baby.

"How did you know the baby you were carrying was my daughter?" Caitlyn had so many more questions for the woman, but this might be the start to helping her understand the big picture of what had gone on at Conceptions.

"I knew something was wrong with the surrogacy arrangement," Nicole said. "Too much secrecy, and they were paying me in cash. Each month a man would show up with the money, and sometimes he would move me to a different place."

Yes, definitely secrecy.

"Then about two weeks ago I heard the man talking on the phone," Nicole went on, "and he mentioned your name. I did an internet search. Internet searches on Conceptions, too. All the mess that went on there."

There had indeed been a *mess*. Other babies born just like her own daughter, and all for the sake of collecting a huge ransom.

"Why are you calling exactly?" Drury came out and asked her. "Do you want me to arrange protection for you?"

"I want you to arrest the men who attacked me. Until they're caught, I'm not safe. None of us are safe."

That was the truth. Because even if Nicole was working for the person who'd orchestrated this, it didn't mean her boss would keep her alive. If the attack in her apartment was real, then Nicole would have realized she was a target.

"Give me some information so I can arrest them," Drury insisted.

Nicole sobbed again. "I can give you physical descriptions, but I don't know who they are, and they were both wearing ski masks."

"And they're the ones who took the baby?" Caitlyn asked, though she wasn't sure she actually wanted to hear the answer.

"They did." Another sob. "I swear, I tried to stop them, but I knew if I stayed there and fought them, I'd lose. I'd just delivered the baby, and I was weak."

Drury and Caitlyn exchanged glances, and she saw the skepticism in his eyes. There were holes in what Nicole was telling them. Because if she was indeed so weak, how had she managed to fight off two hired guns.

"What about the blood in my apartment?" Nicole continued. "There must have been blood. Was there a DNA match?"

"Not yet. The CSIs haven't had time to do that. But they will."

"Good. Maybe that'll help you find them."

"You could help with that, too," Drury went on. "You need to tell me where you are so I can send someone to get you."

"No! I can't risk that. Those men could have tapped the phone lines."

"This line is secure," Drury assured her.

"Nothing is secure right now."

Caitlyn couldn't be certain, but it sounded as if the

woman was crying. Maybe for a good reason—because it was indeed possible that nothing was secure.

"Nicole, you can't stay in hiding," Drury continued. "I can arrange protective custody for you with a team I trust. A team you can trust," he emphasized. "All you have to do is tell me where you are."

Silence. For a long time. "All right," Nicole finally said.

The relief Caitlyn felt faded as fast as it'd come when Nicole added, "But I'll do this under my own terms."

"What terms?" Drury snapped. "Because meeting you had better not involve Caitlyn going out in the open so someone can shoot at her again."

More silence from Nicole. "No. I won't involve Caitlyn. She's as much of a target as I am. Maybe more."

"How do you know that?" Caitlyn couldn't ask fast enough.

"I heard one of the thugs mention you by name. I heard a lot of things I shouldn't have," Nicole said in a whisper.

"What things?" Drury demanded.

"I'll tell you all about it when we're face-to-face. Let me find a meeting place. Once I'm sure I'm safe, I'll call you."

Drury groaned. "How long will it take you to set this up?"

"I'll need some time. It probably won't be until tomorrow. I'll call you when I have things in place."

Drury opened his mouth, no doubt to demand some of that info now, but Nicole had already hung up.

"Were you able to trace the call?" Drury immediately asked Gage.

"She was using a burner cell."

Drury cursed, and Caitlyn knew why. There was no way to trace a burner or disposable cell. Obviously, Nicole knew that. It could mean the woman truly was in danger, or it could all be part of a ruse to make them think that.

"You want me to assemble a protection detail?" Gage offered.

Drury shook his head. "I'll get Lucas to do it. You're already spread too thin here."

Gage didn't dispute that, and he stepped away when one of the other deputies motioned for him to go into the hall that led to the holding cells.

"I don't want you to have to wait around here any longer," Drury said, taking out his phone. He fired off a text. "Once Lucas gets here, he can escort us back to the ranch. You can stay there with Caroline while I meet with Nicole. If Nicole calls back, that is."

Yes, Caitlyn was skeptical, too. Even though the woman had reached out to them, it didn't mean she would cooperate.

"Nicole could be part of the dirty dealings that went on at Conceptions," Caitlyn threw out there.

Drury quickly agreed, and he led her back to the break room. Caitlyn was thankful to be away from Melanie and Helen, but she didn't like that troubled look in Drury's eyes.

"Nicole could have also called to pinpoint our location," Drury said.

Oh, mercy. Caitlyn hadn't even considered that.

"We'll just take some extra precautions," he assured her. But she must not have looked very assured because Drury hooked his arm around her waist and led her to the sofa. "I asked Lucas to bring a couple of the ranch hands with him."

"But you'll all still be in danger," she quickly pointed out.

He made another sound of agreement. "It might not be any safer to stay put."

Drury was right. Yes, this was the sheriff's office, but there'd been attacks here before, and the office was right on Main Street, sandwiched between other buildings and businesses.

"Are we safe anywhere?" she asked, but then Caitlyn waved off her question. She already knew the answer. They weren't.

The only silver lining was that, whoever was behind this, they seemed to be after her and not the baby. For now anyway. That could change if and when she was out of the way.

Caitlyn hadn't realized just how close Drury and she were sitting until she turned to look at him again. Too close. Practically mouth to mouth. She glanced away but not before she saw something else in his eyes. Not just worry and concern.

But the attraction, too.

And maybe even something else. Because his forehead was bunched up.

"Are you okay?" she asked, automatically slipping her hand over his.

"I've been having flashbacks," he finally said.

That wasn't what Caitlyn had expected him to say, but she should have. Of course, this would have triggered the horrific memories of his wife's death.

"The sooner you can distance yourself from me, the better," Caitlyn reminded him.

A new emotion went through his eyes. Anger, maybe, but it didn't seem to be directed at her. Judging from the way he groaned, he was aiming it at himself.

"Lily died right in front of me." His voice was a ragged whisper. "Did you know that?"

She nodded and hated that her own flashbacks came. She had seen a man die. Her father. And those were images she'd never forget. It had to be even harder for Drury because Lily had been pregnant. He'd lost his wife and baby with one bullet from a robber's gun.

"Yeah," he grumbled as if he knew exactly what she was thinking. "We've both got plenty of emotional baggage."

They did, and that seemed to be a caution to remind her that neither of them were emotionally ready to have a relationship. And they weren't. That's why she was so surprised when his mouth came to hers.

There it was. That instant slam of heat. The one that could chase away the flashbacks. But that heat could also cloud her mind and body. Definitely not something she needed right now, but Caitlyn didn't stop him. Nor did she stop Drury when he upped the contact and deepened the kiss.

He slipped his arm around the back of her neck, easing her closer and closer. She didn't resist. Couldn't. Drury certainly wasn't the first man she'd ever kissed, but no man had ever drawn her in the way he did.

Caitlyn slid her arm around him, making the contact complete when her breasts landed against his chest. Now she got memories of a different kind. No flashbacks of violence but rather of the times they'd been together.

In bed.

Like his kisses, Drury had her number when it came to sex. She doubted that had changed, but she didn't want this need she felt for him. Didn't want the ache to build inside her. It complicated things and would only lead to a broken heart.

That didn't stop her, though.

She melted into the kiss. Melted into Drury until they were pressed against each other. Until the fire sent them in search of something *more*. And more wasn't something they could have. Not right now anyway.

Drury pulled back, and as if starved for air, he gulped in a deep breath before going right back to her again. This kiss wasn't as deep, but she could still feel the emotion. Could still sense the fierce battle going on inside him.

"I should regret that," he said with his lips still against hers. "I want to regret it," he amended.

"Same here." But she didn't, and judging from the way he groaned, neither did he.

"The baby," he added a moment later.

Caitlyn braced herself for Drury to tell her that he couldn't get involved with her because of the baby. Because Caroline would always trigger memories of his own child that he'd lost. Plus, Caroline would always be Grant's daughter, which would give Drury another dose of memories that he didn't want.

But he didn't get a chance to add more because Grayson opened the door.

"A problem?" Drury immediately asked, and he got to his feet.

"Possibly a solution. Ronnie just said he wants to cut a deal. Information in exchange for reduced charges."

Of all the things that Caitlyn had thought the sheriff

might say, that wasn't one of them. "Why the change of heart?"

Grayson lifted his shoulder. "Maybe he thought his thug cronies wouldn't be able to break him out of jail as easily as they got him out of the hospital."

True, but she was still suspicious, and she definitely didn't like the idea of a man who'd tried to kill them getting a lighter sentence. She wanted him behind bars for a long time.

"What's he offering?" Drury wanted to know.

"The name of the person who hired him."

There it was. Probably the only thing Ronnie could have put on the table that would have made this impossible to turn down.

"Of course, we can't begin to start working out a deal like that until his lawyer gets here," Grayson went on. "And the DA will have to be the one who approves it." He paused. "It could still fall through."

And it could take time. In fact, Ronnie could drag this out so long that there could be another attack. And this time, it might succeed in killing them.

Drury's phone dinged to indicate he had a text message. "It's Lucas," he said, glancing at the screen. "He's just out the back door with Kade. Two ranch hands are behind them in a truck."

Kade was another Ryland cousin. An FBI agent, and while Caitlyn was glad about having three lawmen for protection, that meant less security at the ranch.

"We can hurry," Drury told her as if he knew exactly what her concern was. He stood, helping her to her feet.

"I'll call you with any updates," Grayson assured them while he punched in the security code to disarm the alarm on the back door.

Drury thanked him and got her moving. Of course, he was in front of her and had his gun drawn when he cracked open the door and looked out. Lucas was indeed there, behind the wheel of what appeared to be an unmarked car. Caitlyn hoped it was bulletproof.

"Move fast," Drury reminded her.

He took a single step forward and then stopped cold. For a second anyway. Then he moved them to the side and peered out around the jamb.

Caitlyn couldn't see what had caused him to do that, but Lucas reacted, as well. He, too, drew his gun, and their attention shifted to the park area just behind the sheriff's office. There were clusters of trees and trails back there. Plenty of places for someone to hide, too.

"What's wrong?" Grayson also pulled his gun and joined Drury at the door.

"Someone's out there," Drury said.

Those three words caused Caitlyn's heart to slam against her chest. Please, no. Not another attack.

There were security lights on the back of the sheriff's office. Lights on the trails as well, but there wasn't enough illumination to see the whole area. Even though it wasn't pitch-dark yet because the sun was still setting, it would be easy for an attacker to use that dimness to his advantage.

"Don't shoot," someone called out.

A woman. And it was a voice that Caitlyn thought she recognized.

Nicole.

Chapter Thirteen

Hell. This was not how Drury wanted this to play out. He'd wanted to get Caitlyn out of there before something bad happened. And maybe this wasn't bad, but since it was unexpected, it had the potential to take a nasty turn.

Drury glanced at Caitlyn to make sure she was okay. She wasn't. Her breathing was already way too fast, and it was obvious she was getting another slam of adrenaline. His body was also gearing up for a fight.

A fight that he hoped wouldn't be necessary.

"Please don't shoot," the woman repeated. That voice sure sounded like Nicole's, but that call could have come from someone pretending to be the surrogate.

"Step out so I can get a good look at you," Drury demanded. "And put your hands in the air."

Even though she was probably a good twenty feet away, he could still hear her gasp. "I'm not armed."

"Then prove it. Put your hands in the air." Drury didn't bother to tone down his lawman's voice. Better to be safe than sorry, and he wanted to make it clear to this woman that he would shoot her if she tried to attack them.

"Tell the other men to go away," Nicole bargained. "I don't trust them. And I want to see Caitlyn."

"That's not going to happen," Drury assured her. "Not until I know you're who you say you are. Step out now."

Drury wasn't sure she would. Not with four lawmen's guns trained on her. He figured the ranch hands in the truck behind the car had their weapons drawn, too.

"I don't want to die," Nicole said, her words punctuated with sobs.

"Then come out so I can help you," Drury offered. "You can come inside, and we'll put you in protective custody."

"No. That man is in there."

Drury had to think about that for a few seconds. "You mean Ronnie?"

"Yes."

He waited for Nicole to add more to that, and when she didn't, he asked, "How do you know Ronnie?"

A few seconds crawled by. "He's the one who moved me into the apartment. He works for the people behind all of this, and if he gets the chance, he'll kill me."

Drury had no doubts about that. Well, no doubts if Nicole was telling the truth that is. But she didn't mention Ronnie in their other conversation. Only the two thugs who'd attacked her after she delivered the baby.

"I need to see your face," Drury tried again. "I need to make sure you're really Nicole Aston."

Just as when she was on the phone, there was a long silence. So long that Drury thought the woman might turn and run. He hoped that didn't happen because it could be part of a ruse to divide and conquer. Because at least two of them would have to go after her since she could have critical information to spare Caitlyn from yet another attack.

Just when Drury was about to give up, there was some movement. Not from the trees but rather from some shrubs.

"Stay back," Drury reminded Caitlyn. He wished there was time to move her to another part of the building, but he didn't want her out of his sight. Besides, there could be gunmen at the front of the building by now.

More movement in the shrubs, and finally the woman lifted her head. Not her hands, though.

"I want to make sure you aren't armed," Drury ordered.

She lifted her hands, slowly. No gun. Not one that was visible anyway, but that didn't mean she didn't have one nearby.

Drury picked through the dim light to study the woman's features. She looked like the Nicole Aston in the driver's license photo.

"I told you I wasn't carrying a weapon," Nicole said. "I came to you for help, but if you don't trust me, I'll have to go elsewhere."

"Someone's trying to kill Caitlyn. Maybe trying to take the baby, too. I have to be suspicious of everyone who might be connected to Conceptions."

And Nicole was definitely connected. The question was, just how deep was her involvement?

"Come in so we can talk," Drury tried again.

No hesitation from her that time. She quickly shook her head. "I want to see Caitlyn."

"I can't risk that," Drury said at the same time Caitlyn said, "I'm here."

Drury shot her a glare. He hadn't wanted Nicole to know Caitlyn's position, but then it was highly likely that Nicole had caught a glimpse of her the moment Drury opened the door.

"You need to do as Drury says," Caitlyn called out to the woman. "Come inside. It's not safe out there."

"I know," Nicole answered.

Apparently, she meant that because her gaze was firing all around them. She appeared to be as much on edge as the rest of them because Lucas, Kade and Grayson were doing the same thing. Drury was trying to do that while keeping watch on Nicole. He still wasn't convinced that she wasn't about to pull out a gun.

Tired of this standoff, Drury decided to put an end to it. "Tell me what you came here to say, or else I'm shutting this door."

"I don't want to go to jail," Nicole said.

Once again, she'd surprised him. "For what?"

"I signed a lot of papers when I became a surrogate. A couple of months ago when I heard on the news about what had gone on at Conceptions, I got worried."

She was right to have worried. There'd been a lot of illegal things going on at the clinic.

"When Ronnie came by to give me my monthly payment," she continued, "I told him I wanted out of the deal. I was afraid what they might do to the baby. He said the papers I signed were like a confession. That if I went to the cops that they could use those papers to put me in jail. But I swear, I didn't have anything to do with stealing any embryo."

"I'll want to take a look at those papers," Drury insisted.

She shook her head. "The men who attacked me took them."

Maybe just more tying up of loose ends, but they

also might have taken them because they could implicate their boss.

"That's why I need to talk to Caitlyn," Nicole went on. "Ronnie said the baby's mother could be arrested, too, because she's the one who helped with the plan."

"I didn't," Caitlyn quickly said. "I had no idea what was going on until I got the ransom demand."

"So, Ronnie lied."

Nicole's voice was so soft that Drury barely heard her. But there was something in her tone. Something in the way she said Ronnie's name. Maybe it was nothing, but it seemed as if Nicole might know more about him than she was admitting. Drury really needed to sit her down for an interview. There was no telling what she would reveal when questioned.

"Come inside," Drury pressed. "Caitlyn is in here, and the two of you can talk."

Nicole was shaking her head. Until he added the last part. Obviously, Nicole was very interested in seeing Caitlyn because she stopped shaking her head and made another of those nervous glances around her.

"All right," Nicole finally agreed. "But don't point your gun at me when I come out. I have panic attacks, and I don't want to trigger one."

A panic attack seemed the least of her concerns right now, but Drury glanced at Grayson. Grayson understood exactly what Drury wanted him to do because he stepped to the side, out of Nicole's line of sight.

And he kept his gun ready.

Drury lowered his to his side.

Even though Kade and Lucas were still armed, that didn't seem to bother Nicole. Perhaps because they were inside the car. Or maybe she wasn't able to see through the tinted glass. Either way, she pushed the shrubs aside and started toward them.

She didn't get far.

Nicole made it only a couple of steps before the shot blasted through the air.

THE SOUND OF the shot was so loud and seemed so close that Caitlyn thought for a moment that Drury had been shot. She caught onto him, pulling him out of the doorway, but he was already headed her direction.

Grayson scrambled to the other side.

It wasn't a second too soon because the next shot slammed into the jamb only inches from where they'd both been standing.

Outside, Caitlyn heard a scream. Nicole. Mercy, had the woman been shot?

Even though she wasn't certain she could trust Nicole and that she'd told them the truth about everything, Caitlyn didn't want her hurt. Or worse. Someone could be murdering her right now in front of them.

She fought the flashbacks of her own father's murder. Fought the fear, too, but that was hard to do. The adrenaline was already sky-high, and her heartbeat was crashing in her ears, making it hard to hear. Hard to hear Nicole anyway.

Caitlyn had no trouble hearing the next shot.

It, too, slammed into the doorjamb.

Drury cursed, pulled her to the floor and covered her body with his. Protecting her. Again. She wished she had a gun or some kind of weapon so she could help him, and while she was wishing, she added for the shots to stop.

They didn't.

Two more slammed into the building.

"Can you see the shooter?" Grayson asked Drury.

Drury shook his head. "But I think he's in one of the trees in the park. Somewhere around your ten o'clock."

That didn't help steady her nerves. Because that meant the shooter was in a position to keep firing. Which he did.

"What about Lucas and Kade?" Caitlyn had gotten only a glimpse of them before Drury had pulled her away.

"Still in the car. They won't be able to get out."

No. Because they'd be gunned down. That also meant they would have a hard time returning fire. But at least they were safe. However, she knew that shots could get through a bullet-resistant car.

"What about Nicole?" Caitlyn managed to say.

Another headshake from Drury. "I can't see her, either. I hope to hell she stays down."

Maybe that meant Nicole was still alive. Of course, she wouldn't be for long if they couldn't get her out of the path of the shooter.

Except the gunman wasn't firing at her.

"All the shots are coming into the building," Caitlyn said under her breath.

"Yeah," Drury verified. "It could mean Nicole's in on this. Or…"

He didn't finish that because another shot came at them. One that caused Drury to curse again. And she knew why. Because the angle of the shot had changed. Either the gunman had moved or there were two shooters.

Drury reached up, slapped off the lights and moved her even farther away from the door. Two deputies came in from the squad room, but Grayson motioned for them to get back. Good thing, too, because the shots went in their direction. Clearly, the shooter was pinpointing their moves, and with the lights off it could mean he was using some kind of infrared device.

"The walls and windows of the sheriff's office are all reinforced," Drury said to her. Perhaps he gave her that reminder because she was trembling now and cursing as well with each new shot.

Caitlyn wasn't sure how many rounds were fired, but it seemed to last an eternity. And then it stopped.

Silence.

That was more unnerving than the shots because she knew it could mean the gunmen were closing in on them.

"Stay down," Drury warned her.

He reached in the slide holster of his jeans and handed her his backup weapon. Caitlyn took it, but she had no idea what he had in mind. Not until he started to inch away from her.

Toward the door.

She wanted to pull him back, to try to keep him out of harm's way, but there was no safe place in the room right now. Because if those gunmen got closer, they could start picking them off.

Grayson moved, as well. Both Drury and he stayed low on the floor, but they made their way to the door. Drury lifted his head, listening, and his gaze was firing all around the area. She suspected Kade and Lucas were doing the same thing.

"You can't let them take me," Nicole called out.

Caitlyn had no trouble hearing the terror in the woman's voice, and she instinctively moved to help her.

She didn't move far, though, because Drury motioned for her to stay down.

"It could be a trap," he whispered.

She almost hoped it was. Because a trap like that would fail, and it would mean Nicole wasn't out there with hired killers. Of course, if it was a trap, it meant they had a very dangerous woman on their hands.

After long moments of silence, the sound of the next gunshot caused Caitlyn to gasp. And it didn't stay a single gunshot.

"I see him," Drury said to Grayson a split second before he leaned out and fired.

Caitlyn hadn't thought the shots could get any more deafening, but she'd been wrong. Because Grayson began to fire, as well. And the shooters outside didn't stop. However, even with all the noise, Caitlyn heard Nicole scream.

"No!" she shouted. "Please, no."

Mercy, did that mean she'd been hit?

Caitlyn lifted her head just a fraction so she could peer out the door, but the angle was wrong for her to see Nicole.

However, she saw something else.

She got just a glimpse of a man wearing dark clothes and a ski mask. Obviously one of the shooters. He took aim at Drury.

"Watch out!" Caitlyn warned him.

But no warning was necessary. Drury had already seen the man, and he fired two shots, both of them slamming into the shooter's chest. He made a sharp sound of pain and dropped to the ground.

"I think he's wearing Kevlar," Drury said to Grayson. If so, then the guy might not be dead after all. He could just have gotten the wind knocked out of him, and once he regained his breath, he could try to kill them again.

"You see the other gunman?" Grayson asked.

"No."

Caitlyn figured it was too much to hope that he'd run away. And she soon got confirmation that he hadn't.

"Hell, he's going after Nicole," Drury spat out.

He scrambled to an even closer position by the door, and he took aim, but Drury didn't fire. Neither did Grayson nor the deputies.

"Please, no," Nicole repeated. Caitlyn hadn't thought it possible, but the woman sounded even more terrified than before.

"You want her dead?" someone called out. It was a man, but Caitlyn didn't recognize his voice.

"I want you to let her go," Drury answered.

"No can do. But if you shoot now, the bullet will go into her. Is that a risk you want to take?"

That meant this thug was using Nicole as a human shield, and Caitlyn got a glimpse of that when the gunman moved into her line of sight.

Yes, he had Nicole all right.

The man had his left arm hooked around Nicole's neck. His gun was pressed to her head. And he was backing away from the building. Caitlyn also saw something else.

Another gunman.

The second guy was to the thug's right, and he had a rifle aimed at Drury and the others.

As terrifying as that was, this could also be a different kind of terror for Drury. Because this was almost identical to the way his wife had been murdered.

"What will it take for you to let her go?" Drury tried to bargain with the man. "She's innocent in all of this."

"I don't care. Just following orders, Agent Ryland. You really don't want to watch another woman die, do you?"

So the gunman knew who Drury was. And he knew about Drury's past. Not exactly a surprise, but she had to wonder why the gunmen had made such a bold attack. Plain and simple, it was risky because they'd fired those shots into a building filled with lawmen.

"Why do you want Nicole?" Caitlyn shouted.

That earned her another glare from Drury. Probably because he didn't want the gunman's attention on her and also because he figured the gunman wouldn't answer.

But he did.

"Nicole'll get a chance to tell you all about that," he said. "We'll be in touch soon."

"Don't let him take me!" Nicole shouted.

However, they had no choice but to let the gunman do just that. With his gun still against her head and with his armed partner leading the way, the man took off running, dragging Nicole with him.

Chapter Fourteen

We'll be in touch soon.

The gunman's words kept playing in Drury's head. The words of a kidnapper, not a hired killer. At least it didn't seem as if the guy had plans to kill Nicole. Not yet anyway.

But what did the gunman and his boss hope to gain from this?

Money was the obvious answer. Maybe since they didn't get an additional ransom from Caitlyn, this was a way of making up for that. Of course, this could be some kind of sick bargaining plan to get Caitlyn out in the open.

That wasn't going to happen.

She'd already come too close to being killed, and Drury had to put a stop to it. He also had to put a stop to the other images that kept going through his head.

Yeah, the flashbacks had come at the worst possible moment.

Thank God he hadn't frozen, but that's because he'd had to fight those old images by reminding himself that other lives were at stake. He couldn't go back in time and save Lily.

Hell, he hadn't saved Nicole, either, because the surrogate was in the hands of hired killers.

Drury nearly jumped when he felt the soft touch
on his arm. He'd been in such deep thought what with
wrestling his demons that he hadn't heard Caitlyn walk
up behind him in Grayson's office.

"I wish it were something stronger," she said when
she handed him a bottle of water.

Yeah, they both could have probably used something
stronger, but it would have to do. Especially since they
couldn't go anywhere. The break room was closed off,
now essentially a crime scene, and the building was on
lockdown until Lucas and the other deputies made sure
the area was clear.

"I called the ranch," she added, "and talked to the
nanny who's staying with Caroline. Everything seems
to be okay there."

By *okay* she meant *safe*, but it wasn't truly okay because Caitlyn wanted to be there with her daughter. At
least Caroline was in good hands. There were several
nannies at the ranch, including this nanny, Tillie Palmer,
along with plenty of cousins to help take care of her.

"We shouldn't have to be here much longer," he told
her. Hoped that was true. And because he thought it
would help, he brushed a kiss on her cheek.

It didn't help.

That look was still in her eyes. The look of a woman
who'd just been through hell and back. Hell that wasn't
over now that Nicole was a hostage and two of the gunmen had escaped.

The third was dying.

At least that was what the medic said when they'd
whisked him away in an ambulance. The guy hadn't

been wearing Kevlar after all, and both of the bullets Drury fired had gone into the man's chest. He was in surgery, but it wasn't looking good.

"Your family has really stepped up to help me," she said. "I won't forget that."

Yes, they had stepped up, and Drury wouldn't forget it, either. He, his brothers and cousins had a strong bond, and they didn't forgive easily when one of them was wronged. In their minds, Caitlyn had wronged him, but that hadn't stopped them from doing the right thing.

"You two okay?" Grayson asked from the doorway. He had his hands bracketed on the jamb.

Both Caitlyn and Drury settled for nods. Of course, they were lying, but at least they were alive, and none of his cousins or the other deputies had been hurt in this latest attack. It could have been much, much worse. It sickened Drury to think that Caroline could have been with them.

"Helen and Melanie are still whining about leaving," Grayson went on. "If they keep annoying me, I just might let them."

Of course, if it was one of them who'd hired the gunmen, then that person would be safe. The other could be toast.

"Any news?" Drury asked.

"Nothing on the wounded shooter or Nicole, but Gage just loaded the security footage." Grayson tipped his head to the laptop on his desk. "Kade's going through it, too, but it wouldn't hurt to have another pair of eyes on it."

Drury welcomed the task. Anything to get his mind off the flashbacks and that haunting look in Caitlyn's eyes. She must have welcomed it, too, because she joined him at the desk. Not exactly a good idea, though.

"You don't have to see this," he reminded her.

She dragged in a deep breath. "I have to do something."

He understood. Standing around with too much time to think was the worst way to deal with raw nerves. That said, he didn't want her to watch the actual shooting. Hell, he wasn't sure he wanted to watch that part, either.

Grayson left them, probably to go another round with Helen and Melanie, and Drury had Caitlyn sit at the desk. He stood behind her and pressed the keys to load the security footage. There were four cameras, one on each side of the building, and the screen had the feed from all four. Drury focused on the one at the back.

He fast-forwarded through the footage, not really seeing much until Lucas and Kade pulled to a stop next to the rear exit. No sign of Nicole or the gunmen, though, so he froze the frame and zoomed in on the area where he'd shot the man.

Still nothing.

It took a few more tries before he finally spotted the gunman in the tree. He was well hidden behind a thick live oak branch, and it didn't help that his dark clothes and ski mask camouflaged him.

"I only see the one gunman," Caitlyn said. "You?"

He was about to agree, but then Drury saw the slight movement on the camera that faced the parking lot. It covered just the edge of the park, and he finally saw the second and third gunmen come into view.

And he also saw Nicole.

She was coming from the other side. No car. She was on foot, but it was possible she'd parked a vehicle somewhere nearby. If so, the deputies would find it, and it could be processed for evidence.

Drury continued to watch as Nicole moved closer to the spot where she'd called out to them. She was staying low, looking all around her. Definitely the way a frightened person would be acting, but that didn't mean this wasn't all just that—an act. Especially since Nicole was clearly staying out of Lucas's and Kade's line of sight. In fact, so were the gunmen. That meant they must have scoped out the place beforehand and knew just where to position themselves.

Nicole ducked behind those shrubs, and Drury tried to calculate the angle of the gunmen. The guy in the tree would have definitely seen her. Probably the other two as well, but they hadn't tried to take or shoot her. So, why wait?

Drury didn't like the answer that came to mind, and it twisted at his gut.

Because maybe the thugs were waiting for Nicole to lure Caitlyn out of hiding.

It was less than a minute before Drury saw when he'd opened the door. There was no audio on the feed, but he could tell from their reactions as Nicole had called out for them not to shoot. Seconds later, the shots had started, and Grayson, Caitlyn and he had been pinned down.

"What is that?" Caitlyn asked, pointing to the camera feed from the right side of the building.

Drury had been so focused on the gunmen and all the shooting that he'd missed it. But he didn't miss it now. It was just a glimpse of a man, and like the others he was dressed in black and wearing a ski mask. Skulking along just at the edge of the parking lot, he aimed something at the camera. The screen flickered, and not just a little motion, either. The man had jammed it so that the images were clouded with static.

"Why would he have done that?" Caitlyn looked up at Drury for answers.

Answers he didn't have. It didn't make sense to jam the camera on that side, not when the other camera was capturing the shooters and Nicole.

Drury leaned in, hoping to pick through all the static to catch sight of the man. And he did. Fragments that he had to piece together. The man was on all fours, crawling toward the back door of the sheriff's office.

Maybe.

If he'd come at them from that angle, they wouldn't have been able to see him. Neither would Kade or Lucas. So, why hadn't he attacked?

"He took something from his pocket," Caitlyn said at the exact moment that Drury caught the motion.

It was small enough to fit in the palm of his hand, and it wasn't a gun. Nor was it the same device he'd pointed at the camera. A few seconds later, Drury saw what the man did with it.

He placed it beneath the rear of the car and then scurried back to the side of the building before he stood and took off running. Not toward them. But away from the sheriff's office.

"You think it's a tracking device?" Caitlyn asked.

No. Something worse. "I think it's a bomb."

Caitlyn didn't have much color in her face, and that didn't help. "Stay here," he warned her.

Drury hurried out of the office and made a beeline for the back exit just off the break room. The door was slightly ajar, and Lucas and Kade were back there with a CSI team. So was the car. It was still parked right where his brother had left it when they'd come inside after the attack.

"I think there's an explosive device on the car," Drury warned them.

Lucas cursed, and he quickly relayed the warning to the CSIs. All of them scrambled inside the break room and then toward the front of the building just as soon as Lucas kicked the door shut.

"I'll call the bomb squad," Lucas volunteered.

While his brother did that, they all got as far away from the car as they could while remaining inside.

Hell. Drury thought this was over, and it was possible that it was just beginning. If it was indeed a bomb, it could blast through the building.

Gage went out front, no doubt to make sure the area stayed clear. Both the building and the parking lot were roped off with crime scene tape, but they had to make sure gawkers weren't too close just in case the device detonated.

Caitlyn and Drury went back into Grayson's office and shut the door. Not only in case of a possible explosion but also because Helen was peering out of the interview room. And she was cursing them because she was in danger.

"The gunmen probably intended to set it off once we were in the car," Caitlyn said.

He couldn't disagree with that. But there was an even worse possibility. It could have been timed to go off once they arrived back at the ranch. If so, the baby could have been hurt. Hell, a lot of people could have been hurt.

If that was the intention, then that led him right back to Jeremy.

Jeremy was the only one of their suspects with a strong motive to get rid of his brother's heir. Of course, Melanie might not be too thrilled about it, either. Still, it didn't rule out Helen simply because the bomb might have been rigged to have another go at murdering Caitlyn.

And that meant they were back to square one.

Well, they were unless the wounded gunman somehow managed to stay alive. Then there was Ronnie. Once the bomb threat was taken care of, Grayson would no doubt figure out if Ronnie was blowing smoke or if he truly had something to make a deal.

All of those thoughts were racing through Drury's mind, but he hadn't forgotten about Caitlyn. Now that the adrenaline was wearing off, it wouldn't be long before she crashed. There was an apartment on the second floor. More of a flop room, really, but if they ended up being stuck here for a while, he might be able to coax her into getting some rest.

Alone.

With all the energy still zinging between them, it definitely wouldn't be a good idea for him to get close to her right now. Caitlyn had a different notion about that, though. She stood, slipping right into his arms, and she dropped her head against his shoulder.

"Don't you dare apologize," Drury warned her. "Because none of this is your fault."

"This is my fault," she argued, and Caitlyn glanced at the now-close contact between them.

Yes, it was, but that still didn't cause Drury to back away from her. No way could he do that because this was soothing his nerves as much as he hoped it was soothing hers. It wouldn't last, of course. Because he knew the comfort would turn into so much more.

Even now he wanted her.

Hell, he always wanted her, and he couldn't seem to get it through his thick skull that being with her could complicate his life in the worst possible way. Drury wasn't sure how long they stood there, but the sound of his phone buzzing had him finally breaking the contact. He expected to see his brother's name on the screen, but his chest tightened when he saw that the caller had blocked his identity and number.

Caitlyn saw it, too, and she sucked in her breath. "Put it on speaker," she insisted.

Drury did, but he would have preferred to buffer any bad news, and he figured this would fall into the bad news category. He hit the answer button but waited for the caller to speak first.

"Agent Ryland?" a man said. Drury couldn't be sure, but it sounded like the same person who'd fired shots at them. The one who'd taken Nicole at gunpoint.

"Where's Nicole?" Drury snapped.

"Alive for now. If you want her to stay that way, then I'll be needing some cash. Lots of it. I know she's not Ryland kin. Hell, she's probably not even someone you're sure you can trust, but hear this, I will kill her if you don't pay up."

The caller was right about Drury not being certain that he could trust Nicole, but there was something in this guy's voice. Something to let Drury know that he would indeed kill the surrogate.

"How much?" Drury asked.

"I'm lettin' you off cheap. A quarter of a million. Chump change for folks like you and Caitlyn."

"Caitlyn's already drained her accounts paying the ransom for the baby. And why should I pay? The surrogate is nothing to me."

It was a bluff, of course. She was something to him. Not just because she was a human being who probably needed protection, but also because Nicole could perhaps give them answers that would put this thug and his boss in jail for the rest of their miserable lives.

"You'll pay," the man answered, "because you're one of the good guys. A real cowboy cop with a code of honor and junk like that. I, however, have no such code. Start scraping together the money, and I'll call you back with instructions on how this drop will happen."

"I want to talk to Nicole. I want to make sure she's all right," Drury countered.

"She's all right," the guy snapped.

"Then prove it," Drury snapped right back.

The guy cursed, and a few seconds dragged by before Drury heard something he didn't want to hear.

Nicole.

Screaming.

Chapter Fifteen

No matter how much she tried to shut it out, Caitlyn couldn't stop Nicole's scream from replaying in her head. Couldn't stop the fears she had about the woman's safety, either.

She could be dead.

They had no way of knowing because right after that scream, the kidnapper had ended the call. It was possible that he'd killed her on the spot, but Caitlyn was praying that he'd only frightened Nicole into making that blood-curdling sound. After all, if Nicole was dead, he wouldn't get the quarter-of-a-million-dollar ransom. Maybe that alone would be enough for him to keep her alive.

She sank down onto the bed of the small second-floor apartment where Drury had told her to wait. It was definitely bare bones, a place for the cops to rest when pulling long shifts.

Like now.

All the Silver Creek lawmen, including Drury, were scrambling to remedy this nightmare, and she figured they wouldn't be doing much sleeping until they made an arrest.

Whenever that would be.

She finished the sandwich that Drury had brought

her earlier. Not because she was hungry. She wasn't, and her stomach was still in knots. But she didn't want to give him anything else to worry about since he'd insisted that she eat something.

The bone-weary fatigue was catching up with her fast, so Caitlyn went to the small bathroom and splashed some water on her face. It didn't help, but nothing would at this point. Well, nothing other than the person behind this being caught so everyone could try to get on with their normal lives.

For her, though, it'd be a new normal.

Since Grant's death, she'd been working again as a CPA and had a full list of clients. That would have to change since she wanted to spend as much time as she could with Caroline. She was looking forward to that.

Not looking forward, though, to dealing with the fallout from Drury.

And there would be fallout. Caitlyn wasn't sure how she was going to get over this broken heart. Nor was she sure she could stop herself from falling in love with him. Talk about stupid. But it was as if she had no choice in any of this.

She wiped away a fresh set of tears when she heard someone coming up the steps that led to the apartment. As Drury had instructed, she'd locked the door, and she didn't jump to open it. Not until she heard Drury's voice, that is.

"It's me," he said, and he relocked it as soon as she let him in. It was just a precaution, he'd assured her, but Caitlyn knew he had to be concerned about another attack. She certainly was.

"Bad news?" she asked.

He shook his head. "Nothing from the kidnapper

anyway. But the bomb's been disarmed. No one was hurt."

Good. There'd been enough people hurt. "Was the bomb on a timer?"

"No, it was rigged with a remote control, and there weren't enough explosives to blow up the car, only to disable it."

It took Caitlyn a moment to process that. "You think they wanted us stranded on the road?"

"That's my guess. That's why Grayson's having all the roads and ditches checked between here and the ranch. It might take a while, though." He paused. "That means we might have to stay here all night."

Part of her had already figured that out, but it didn't hurt any less.

He brushed a kiss on her cheek, got the laptop from the desk and brought it to her. He sat down on the bed next to her. "I thought maybe you'd like to see the baby. Tillie is setting up the video feed. It should be ready any second now."

Drury had managed to make her feel as if she were melting when he kissed her, but this was a melting feeling of a different kind. Caitlyn was so touched that she kissed him even before she knew she was going to do it.

It was a good thing that the movement on the screen stopped the kiss before it had a chance to catch fire. A good thing, too, because Caitlyn soon saw her precious baby on the screen.

"She had a bottle about ten minutes ago," Tillie said. She wasn't on camera. Only Caroline, who was sleeping in the bassinet that one of the Ryland brothers had brought over, was.

"Has she cried much?" Caitlyn asked.

"Hardly at all. And she's got such a sweet disposition. So calm. Unlike Mason's boys. Those two can run you ragged pretty fast."

"They can," Drury agreed. "Max and Matt. When they team up with Gage's boy, Dustin, all the nannies at Silver Creek Ranch have to join forces just to keep them out of trouble."

Caitlyn smiled through the happy tears. The conversation was something that families had all the time, and since she'd lost both her parents when she was young, she'd missed this. Missed having the support system that Gage and Mason clearly had.

Drury, too.

"Thank you for watching her," Caitlyn said. "I know you have plenty of other things you could be doing."

Tillie went to the side of the bassinet so that Caitlyn could see her. "She's no trouble at all. Besides, we're in between newborns at the ranch right now. A rarity, I can tell you, and newborns are my favorite."

Caitlyn was thankful for that, but she still wished she was the one there taking care of her.

"Soon," Drury whispered, slipping his hand over hers.

Caitlyn wasn't sure if Tillie could see the gesture, but she smiled. "Lynette's coming over to get some cuddle time and to spend the night," she went on. "That's Gage's wife."

"Yes, I remember her." She owned the town's newspaper. "Uh, is it safe for her to be outside, though?"

"The ranch is under heavy guard right now. Mason even hired some private security to patrol the fence. Don't worry, Lynette will be careful. We'll all be careful," Tillie added.

Caroline squirmed and made a face, and Caitlyn

watched as the nanny scooped her up in her arms. "I think it's time for a diaper change. Tell you what, if you're still stuck in town come morning, we'll have another computer chat over her morning bottle."

Caitlyn thanked the woman again, blew her daughter a kiss and watched until the screen went blank. Almost immediately, she felt the loss. Mercy, these were the moments she should be spending with her daughter.

"I'm sorry," Drury said, putting the laptop aside. "I thought it might make you feel better."

"It did." She wiped away the tears. "Seeing her helped."

"You're sure about that?" He used his thumb to brush away a tear on her cheek that she'd missed.

She tried to force a smile. Was sure she failed. Was also sure she shouldn't start this conversation, but Caitlyn did anyway.

"Do you think of Lily when you see the baby?" she asked.

Drury looked away, dodging her gaze for a couple of seconds, and she was certain the answer was yes. It cut her to the core to think what this was doing to him.

"No," he said.

Oh. And she added another "oh" when their eyes met again. That wasn't the look of a man dealing with the old memories.

"Sometimes, it'd be easier if I did think of her," he added. "Because then I wouldn't feel this guilt that I'm forgetting her."

"You'll never forget her," Caitlyn assured him.

He made a sound that could have meant anything and then groaned softly. Caitlyn was sure he would find an excuse to leave so he could deal with these feelings that were causing chaos inside him.

But he didn't leave.

Drury stared at her. "If you're going to stop this, stop it now."

She knew exactly what he meant by *this*. Sex. They'd been skirting around it for days. Heck, for years. Now the fire was burning even hotter than ever, and the walls they'd built between them were crumbling fast.

Caitlyn shook her head, almost afraid to trust her voice. "I'm not stopping it."

She couldn't tell if that pleased Drury or not. But he must have accepted it because he slid his hand around the back of her neck and pulled her to him.

DRURY DIDN'T ALLOW himself to consider that this was a mistake. Everything he did with Caitlyn seemed to fall into that category, and he was tired of fighting this attraction. This need. Tired of fighting with himself, too.

Apparently, Caitlyn felt the same way because she moved right into the kiss. Before his mouth touched her, all Drury had felt was the spent adrenaline and the bitter taste of what would be regret.

The kiss erased them both.

Caitlyn somehow managed to rid him of the remaining doubts along with heating up every inch of his body. He didn't believe in magic or miracles, but she could weave some kind of spell around him. She'd always been able to do that.

She slipped her arms around him and pulled him closer. Not that she had to urge him to do that. Drury was already heading in that direction anyway. And he continued moving, continued kissing her until there was no way for them to get any closer. Well, not with their clothes on anyway.

"Don't stop," Caitlyn warned him.

A good man would have. Or at least a sensible one would have. But Drury wasn't in a good, sensible place right now. He was in an apartment, the door was locked, and even though they could get interrupted, he'd go with this and try to put out this raging fire they'd started.

He took the kisses to her neck and got the exact reaction he wanted. Caitlyn made that silky sound of pleasure. He knew there were other places where he could get the same reaction from her, and Drury wished he had time to rediscover them all. But there wouldn't be much time for foreplay tonight.

Maybe next time.

That thought didn't give him much comfort. Because there might not be a next time, and even if there was, next times came with even more complications. Sex couldn't be just sex with Caitlyn.

He shoved up her top and went even lower with his next round of kisses. To the tops of her breasts. She repeated the sound, kicking the heat into overdrive. Apparently kicking up her own need, too, because Caitlyn kissed him right back. On his neck. His chest.

That sure didn't slow things down.

Along with the raging need, Drury could feel everything speeding up. Not just for him but for Caitlyn. Her hands were trembling, hurried, when she took off his shoulder holster. Drury helped. Helped with his shirt, too, though he didn't manage to get it off, only unbuttoned.

Because Caitlyn went after his zipper.

"Please tell me you have a condom," she said.

"Wallet," he managed to answer.

She rummaged around for that while Drury pulled off her top. Then her bra. No way could he pass up her breasts, so he dropped some kisses there despite the fact that Caitlyn seemed hell-bent on finishing this off now.

Drury hated that this felt like some kind of race. Hated that it would only cool the fire temporarily. But that hate vanished in a split second when Caitlyn peeled off her jeans and underwear. Then his. Seeing her naked was a way to rid him of any doubts he had about this. A way to rid him of every thought that had been in his head.

He took her.

Drury pulled her back onto the bed with him with only one thought in mind. Finish this. So that's what he did.

Their bodies automatically adjusted, and he eased into her. He had to take a moment, to rein in his body. To settle himself. But he also took a moment just to enjoy the feel of her. Always pleasure.

Always something more.

The *more* fueled him. Not that he needed anything else now. He had plenty of motivation.

The years melted away, and they fell right into the old rhythm. The one that would end all of this much too soon. Drury tried to hold on to each sensation, each sound that she made. The taste of her.

Each moment.

He kissed her when she shattered and gathered her close. That was all he needed.

Just Caitlyn.

Drury held on to her and shattered right along with her.

Chapter Sixteen

Caitlyn had been certain that she wouldn't be able to sleep. Not with the insanity that had been going on. And especially not with Drury in the bed with her. But when she woke up and looked at the clock, she realized it was already past midnight.

Four hours of sleep might not sound like much, but it was the most rest she'd gotten since this whole ordeal had started.

She could thank Drury in part for that.

The sex had calmed her nerves along with giving her the pleasure that she knew Drury was plenty capable of giving. The trouble was she wanted more of that pleasure. She wanted more of him.

He was still next to her in the small bed. A surprise. Though he was no longer naked. Sometime after she'd fallen asleep, he'd gotten dressed. Probably because the building was full of Ryland lawmen. That reminder was her cue to get dressed as well.

Caitlyn tried not to make a sound, but the moment she moved, Drury's eyes flew open.

"They'll knock first before they try the door," he said, sounding very wide-awake. "And the door is locked."

Yes, she knew that. "If they knock, I don't want them to hear me scrambling around in here for my clothes."

Of course, she also didn't want to climb out of the bed naked and dress with Drury watching her.

"They'll know we've had sex," Drury added. "I don't know how they'll know, but they will."

Caitlyn didn't doubt that. There seemed to be a deep connection between Drury and his cousins and brothers. She'd witnessed many instances where unspoken things had passed between them with just simple glances.

She nodded, and despite the being-naked part, she got up anyway, gathered up her clothes and took them to the bathroom so she could freshen up and dress. Caitlyn figured she was in there only five minutes or less, but when she came back out, Drury was not only up, he was making a fresh pot of coffee and was looking at something on the laptop.

"Did something happen?" she asked.

The corner of his mouth lifted for just a moment, and Drury glanced at the bed.

"Did something happen other than the obvious?" Caitlyn amended. "I know what went on there."

Now Drury's gaze came to hers. "Do you? Because I'm still trying to figure it out."

This seemed like much too deep of a post-sex question, so she went to the coffeepot and poured them both a cup.

"I, uh, don't want you to think this means something," she said. "I mean, it does mean something. To me." Mercy, she was babbling. "I just don't expect you to have to feel the same way. In fact, you don't have to feel any way at all."

Yes, definite babbling.

Drury's expression didn't change even though he was staring at her, and just when Caitlyn thought he was going to sit there and let her keep talking, he stood, brushed a kiss on her mouth.

A kiss so hot that it could have melted chrome.

"It meant something to me, too," he said in that hot and cowboy way that only Drury could have managed.

But she didn't get a chance to ask him what he meant by that because there was a knock at the door. When Drury opened the door, she saw Mason standing there. Since he was only a reserve deputy these days, it meant Grayson had to be plenty busy to call him out, and Mason didn't look very happy about it. Of course, Mason wasn't the looking-happy-about-anything sort.

"The roads are clear," Mason greeted. "No guarantees, of course, but there are no signs of the kidnappers or idiot clowns who want to shoot at you. That means you can head back to the ranch, unless you're busy..." He glanced at the unmade bed. Then he turned those glances on Drury and her.

Yes, Mason knew all right.

"You ready to leave?" Drury asked her.

"More than ready. I want to see my daughter."

"I figured you would." Mason started down the stairs, and they followed him. "Gage had to leave. Lynette's having labor pains. Somebody's always having labor pains at the ranch," he added, though he didn't seem upset that it had caused him to be called into work.

However, Drury's forehead bunched up. "Isn't it a little early for Lynette to be having the babies?"

Mason shrugged. "The doc said twins can come early."

Drury didn't exactly seem comforted by that. Maybe

because it brought back memories of Lily. The sex upstairs wouldn't have helped with that, either, and Caitlyn suspected it wouldn't be long before he would feel guilty. Almost as if he'd cheated on his wife.

"Is Lynette having boys, girls or one of each?" Caitlyn asked.

"Boys," Mason answered. "No shortage of those at Silver Creek Ranch." He looked back at her. "Having your little girl there is a nice change. Not just for Drury but for all of us."

Caitlyn couldn't be sure, but she thought maybe that was some kind of hint that she was welcome there. Or maybe even more than that. Was he matchmaking?

No, she had to be wrong about that.

When they made it to the squad room, Caitlyn immediately spotted the car parked right outside the front door. "It's not a cop car," Drury explained. "It's one of Mason's."

"Is it bullet resistant?" she quickly asked.

He nodded. "Mason had it modified, and I'm hoping that since it doesn't look like a cop car, we won't be followed."

She hoped that, as well.

Drury didn't have to tell her to move fast. Every second out in the open was a second they could be gunned down, so she hurried into the backseat of the car with Drury following.

However, Mason didn't join them. Deputy Kara Duggan was behind the wheel, and Dade was riding shotgun. The moment Drury and she were inside, Kara took off.

"We need to take the long way," Dade informed them. "Just to make sure no one is following us."

As much as Caitlyn hated spending any more time away from Caroline, this precaution was one she welcomed. She definitely didn't want to lead those armed thugs back to the ranch.

Dade glanced back at Drury. "The safe house is finally ready. Just as you requested, first thing in the morning the Rangers will be taking over the protection detail for Caitlyn and the baby."

That brought on an uncomfortable silence. Drury had made those arrangements before, well, *before*, and maybe he wasn't regretting them now. Or not. He could want some space so he could sort through everything that'd happened.

"Of course, I can cancel the Rangers if you'd rather keep them in your protective custody," Dade added.

Even in the darkness, Caitlyn had no trouble seeing Dade's half smile. So maybe he wasn't totally opposed to Drury being with her. But that didn't mean the Rylands would welcome her with open arms. Heck, it didn't mean Drury would, either.

"Was there some kind of family meeting about Caitlyn?" Drury came out and asked.

"Some things were mentioned," Dade admitted. "The wives got involved."

And with that cryptic comment, Dade turned in the seat to look at her. "They seem to think we've all been too rough on you. Of course, there's the part about you drop-kicking Drury's heart, but the *suggestion* I got was that everyone deserves a fresh start."

Drury opened his mouth but didn't get a chance to answer because his phone buzzed. Caitlyn was close enough to see the blocked caller on the screen, and her stomach dropped. No. Not another call from the kidnappers.

"I'll record it," Dade offered, and he pressed the button on his phone to do that just as Drury took the call and put it on speaker.

"Drury?" she heard the caller say.

It was Nicole.

"Are you okay?" Drury immediately asked.

"For now. I escaped, and I stole the kidnapper's phone so I could call you. You have to help me, Drury. You have to help me now."

Drury groaned softly. Not because he wasn't relieved that Nicole was alive, but because he didn't want to do this with her in the car.

"Where are you?" Drury demanded.

"Nearby. Pull over right now."

Caitlyn glanced around. They were at the end of Main Street where there was only a handful of businesses. All closed for the night.

"Should I stop?" Kara asked.

She could practically see the debate going on inside Drury and Dade, and like her, they were trying to pick through the dimly lit street.

And Caitlyn finally saw her.

Sweet heaven.

Nicole staggered out from between two buildings, and Caitlyn got just a glimpse of the woman's bloody, battered face before Nicole collapsed onto the ground.

"DON'T YOU DARE get out of the car," Drury warned Caitlyn when she reached for the door handle.

She was probably running on pure instinct to help an

injured woman, but it was possible that Nicole wasn't even hurt.

Or if she really was hurt, she could be bait.

Either scenario wasn't good because it meant someone was going to try to ambush them.

"I'll call Grayson so we can get some help out here," Dade said, taking out his phone.

"Please help me," Nicole begged. At least she sounded as if she were begging, but Drury wasn't about to trust any of this.

"Where are the men who kidnapped you?" he asked.

Nicole didn't answer right away. All he could hear was her ragged breath, and she lifted her head, only for it to drop back down again. It twisted at him to think she could be truly injured and that he was just sitting there. But he didn't have a lot of options here.

"I ran from them," Nicole finally said. "They were going to kill me after they got the ransom. I heard them say it. They were going to kill both Caitlyn and me."

"Why Caitlyn?" Drury pressed.

Nicole lifted her head again. Shook it. "I don't know, but I think they want the baby. Please don't let them have the baby."

"I won't," Caitlyn quickly assured her. That's when Drury realized she was trembling. Of course, she had a good reason to do that since she'd just heard that someone was out to kill her. If they were to believe Nicole, that is.

"Grayson's on the way," Dade relayed when he ended the call.

Both Kara and he already had their guns drawn. Drury, too. And they had them aimed at Nicole. Like the others, Drury also continued to look around to make sure no one was trying to sneak up on them. As soon as backup arrived, he wanted to get Caitlyn out of there.

"Watch the tops of the buildings," Drury told Dade, and Drury turned his attention back to Nicole. "How bad are you hurt?"

"Bad. I think one of the thugs broke some of my ribs. I'm in a lot of pain." She moaned again.

"Why did they only hit you?" Drury pressed. "If they wanted to kill you, they could have just shot you." He heard his own words and mentally cringed. Definitely not kid-glove treatment, but he had to treat her like a suspect until he was positive that she wasn't.

"They were holding me just a few blocks from here, and I ran when they stepped away to make a phone call. They caught up with me, and the big guy tackled me. Then he punched me. He would have killed me, but I kicked him between his legs and ran. I came here because I need you to help me."

Yeah, she'd made that clear. "Help is on the way."

She lifted her head, looked at him. He expected her to demand that he allow her in the car. Something that would give her or those thugs easy access to Caitlyn. But she didn't.

"Thank you," Nicole said, and she lay her head back down.

Dade's phone rang, the shrill sound shooting through the car and causing Caitlyn to gasp. Obviously she was as much on edge as he was. Dade didn't put the call on speaker, maybe because he didn't want the call to drown out any sounds they might need to hear.

Like footsteps.

But only a few seconds into the conversation, Dade

cursed, and Drury knew they had more trouble on their hands.

"Grayson said someone set fires on Main Street," Dade told them, and now he pressed the speaker button so they could hear the rest from Grayson himself.

"It's a wall of flames right now in both directions," Grayson went on. "I have no way of reaching you, except on foot."

Hell. That was not what Drury wanted to hear. It meant backup couldn't get to them, and he figured that wasn't an accident. No. This was all part of someone's sick plan to get to Caitlyn.

"My advice is to get out of there," Grayson went on. "Fast. I'll get to Nicole as soon as I can."

Which might not be very soon. Or in time. Because if she was truly innocent in all of this, she would be easy prey for the kidnappers to finish off.

"Someone's on the roof," Kara said, and she pointed to the building across the street. "And he's got a gun."

"Get down on the seat," Drury told Caitlyn.

Because of his position, he had to lean down to see the shooter on the roof. He was in the shadows, but Drury had no trouble figuring out where the guy was aiming. Not at the car.

But rather at Nicole.

Oh, man. This thug was going to gun her down. Nicole must have seen him, too, because she managed a strangled scream and got to her feet. She staggered toward the car.

There was no time for Drury to debate what he had to do. No time for anything because the first shot rang out and blasted into the sidewalk, just a few inches from Nicole.

Nicole kept coming toward the car. Kept screaming for help, too. And knowing it was a decision that he could instantly regret, Drury opened the door. He took hold of Nicole's arm and pulled her inside.

"Go now!" Drury shouted to Kara.

The deputy sped off as the bullets slammed into the car.

Chapter Seventeen

Caitlyn's heart went into overdrive, but she figured she wasn't the only one in the cruiser with that reaction. The bullets were coming right at them, and it was possible they'd just let one of their attackers into the car.

"Go faster," Nicole insisted. "They'll kill us all."

Nicole certainly sounded terrified. Looked it, too. Caitlyn peered around Drury so she could see the woman. And she saw her all right. Nicole's face was a bloody mess, and judging from her ragged breath and wincing, she was in a lot of pain.

Kara did hit the accelerator, and the tires of the cruiser squealed as the deputy turned off Main Street. Caitlyn couldn't tell where she was going, but she prayed they could outrun whoever was attacking them.

"I have to frisk you," Drury told Nicole. "Put your hands on your head and don't make any sudden moves."

The woman didn't object. Nicole just nodded and did as he'd instructed. Drury kept himself positioned between Nicole and her while he checked the surrogate for weapons.

"She's not armed," Drury told them after he'd finished.

Caitlyn released the breath she'd been holding, but

she didn't feel much relief. Since Nicole wasn't armed and she was injured, it meant she'd likely been telling the truth. It also meant she needed medical attention.

"Call the hospital," Drury told Dade. "If the shooter isn't tailing us, we'll take Nicole to the ER."

It was necessary, but Caitlyn knew it wouldn't necessarily be safe. For any of them. After all, an armed thug had gotten into the hospital to take Ronnie, and while that particular kidnapping had been fake, it was a reminder of just how easy it would be for a gunman to get inside.

If one wasn't already there.

In fact, those thugs could have injured Nicole as a way to lure them all into a trap.

Caitlyn looked at Drury to tell him that, but judging from his expression, he already knew.

"We've got a tail," Kara warned them.

Even though Drury pushed both Nicole and her lower on the seat, Caitlyn managed to get a glimpse of the SUV that was coming up fast behind them. It was too much to hope that it was someone from the sheriff's office who'd made it through that fiery roadblock.

"Something's wrong with my phone," Dade said. "I'm not getting a signal."

Caitlyn hoped it was just a matter of them being in a dead zone. There were some places in Texas where you couldn't use a cell phone, but they were just outside town where that shouldn't have been a problem.

While still volleying his attention between Nicole and that SUV, Drury took out his phone and handed it to Caitlyn. "See if I've got any bars."

Her stomach sank when she saw no signal on the screen. She shook her head. "Nothing."

Several seconds later, Kara verified the same.

No. Now they had no way to get in touch with Grayson and the others to tell them where they were heading. Once they knew where they were heading, that is. Right now, their only goal was to escape before this attack escalated.

"Maybe the SUV's got some kind of jamming device aimed at us," Dade suggested.

That didn't help with her nerves. "Is that even possible?"

A muscle flickered in Drury's jaw. "Yeah. I've seen devices that can shut down services for up to a mile. Any chance you can put some distance between us and the SUV?" he asked Kara.

"I'll try." She slowed, only so she could make another turn, and gunned the engine again.

The problem with getting away from the SUV, though, was that they were heading farther and farther away from town. And they couldn't go to the ranch. Not with possible gunmen in pursuit. At least the men weren't shooting at them.

Not now anyway.

But Caitlyn figured that probably wouldn't last. Added to that, the men probably had their own backup all over the area. There weren't that many roads in this part of the county, and they could have someone stashed on each one of them. Of course, that meant those *someones* had stayed hidden when Mason and the others had been checking the roads.

Drury glanced at Nicole again. "Did the men who kidnapped you have you in that SUV?"

She dragged in a long breath and looked back at the vehicle. "I think so, yes. But I didn't see any kind of equipment in it that could jam phones. They had a lot of guns, though."

"Think hard," Drury pressed. "Is there anything about them that will help us out of this situation?"

She started shaking her head again but then stopped. "One of them is injured. He fell when they were chasing me, and he hurt his shoulder."

It wasn't much, but maybe it would be enough if it came down to a face-to-face showdown. Of course, maybe there were more than two men in that SUV.

Drury tipped his head to his phone that Caitlyn was still holding. "Keep checking the phone to see if we get a signal, but stay down."

The words had no sooner left his mouth when Caitlyn heard a sound she definitely didn't want to hear.

A gunshot.

The bullet crashed into the back windshield. The glass held, but it cracked and webbed.

Another shot.

Then another.

Both tore into the glass even more, and Caitlyn knew it wouldn't be long before the bullets made it through.

"Hold on," Kara said a split second before she slammed on the brakes so she could take another turn.

Caitlyn was wearing her seat belt, but she still slammed against Drury, and Nicole hit the window and door, causing her to make a sharp sound of pain. She obviously needed to get to the hospital, but that couldn't happen until they lost the goons behind them.

"Still no phone signal," Caitlyn relayed to them after she checked the screen again. She'd hoped that the turn Kara had made would have been enough to lose the jammer. But no such luck.

She got proof of that when the next shot bashed into the window.

"The shooter's leaning out the passenger's-side door," Dade said, looking in the mirror. "Let me see if I can do something to stop him."

"Be careful," Drury warned him, and he looked at Nicole. "I need you to move next to Caitlyn so I can try to take out the driver from this window. So help me, you'd better be an innocent victim in all of this."

"I am. I swear, I am."

Drury apparently didn't take that as gospel because he took out his backup weapon and handed it to Caitlyn. "Watch her," he said.

Caitlyn would, along with keeping an eye on the phone screen, but now she had a new distraction. Drury was putting himself right in the path of those bullets, and there wouldn't be any glass to protect him.

Drury maneuvered himself around Nicole, putting the woman in the middle of the seat, and he lowered the window. Leaned out. And fired.

From the other side of the car Dade did the same.

Both got off several shots, and that seemed to do the trick of stopping the gunman from continuing to fire. Now if they could just get away from them and regroup.

"Hell." Drury added more profanity to that. So did Dade. Both of them quit shooting and dropped back in their seats.

And Caitlyn soon figured out why.

The SUV rammed into the rear of their car.

DRURY HAD SEEN the impact coming. Had tried to stop it from hurting Caitlyn and Nicole, but he failed. The jolt slung them around like rag dolls, and even though

Caitlyn was wearing a seat belt, her body still snapped forward.

Nicole yelped in pain. Heaven knew what this was doing to her if she truly did have broken ribs. An impact like that could puncture a lung.

And worse, it didn't stop.

The driver of the SUV plowed into them again. Then again.

Drury glanced back, hoping like the devil that the collisions were tearing up the front of the SUV, but it must have been reinforced because he couldn't see any damage at all.

Unlike their car.

The back end was bashed in, and the windows were holding by a thread. The SUV and the bullets were tearing the vehicle apart. Which was no doubt the plan. After that, these thugs could pick them off one by one.

"Still no signal on the phone," Caitlyn said, though he wasn't sure how she managed to speak. Especially not when the SUV rammed into them again.

This was obviously a well-thought-out plan, and they'd been waiting for Caitlyn and him to leave the sheriff's office. In hindsight, that was a mistake. Of course, there could be an attack going on there, too. With Ronnie in the building, his comrades might try to break him out of jail.

"I'm turning on Millington Road," Kara told them. She was fighting with the steering wheel, doing her best to keep them out of the ditch—where the SUV driver was apparently trying to force them to go.

Just when Drury thought it couldn't get any worse, it did.

After the SUV rammed them again, the shots returned. The shooter was barely leaning out of the window, and he started sending a spray of bullets into the back windshield.

"Oh, God," Kara said.

Drury's gaze whipped in her direction to see what'd caused that reaction, and he soon saw it. A fire just ahead. And it stretched across the entire width of the farm road. Drury hadn't seen the fires that Grayson had described near the sheriff's office, but he suspected this one was identical to those.

Set by the same people.

People who clearly wanted them dead.

Kara slammed on the brakes, and even though they were still a good forty feet from the fire, the wind was whipping the smoke in their direction. They couldn't see far enough to know how deep those flames extended, which meant they were now officially sitting ducks.

The SUV braked, too, but it wasn't nearly enough. It slammed into them again. The hardest impact of all, and this time it didn't just send them flying around. The car jolted.

Because it wound up in a ditch.

The car immediately tilted, the tires on the passenger's side sinking deep into the ditch. Drury figured these thugs weren't just going to drive off and leave them there. They also had help nearby because after all, someone had set that fire.

"Keep watch around us," Drury warned them.

They did. Caitlyn, too. She still had his phone in her left hand and continued to check it for a signal. Which they likely weren't going to get out here. No jamming equipment needed since this spot was far away from any houses and not close enough to the tower for them to have service.

Part of this sick plan, no doubt.

But the question was—how would they get out of this?

They were probably outnumbered, but there were two cops and an FBI agent in the car. Plus, Caitlyn was armed, though he hoped it didn't come down to her having to shoot.

However, the men in the SUV didn't get out.

Maybe Nicole had been right about one of them being hurt. Or they could be just waiting for the rest of their thug crew to arrive.

"We can't just sit here," Drury said, talking more to himself than the others.

He looked around to try to figure out how to do this, but there weren't many options. They couldn't get out on the driver's side because that would mean they'd be on the road. With the SUV right there, they'd be gunned down the moment they stepped from the car.

That left the ditch.

Both doors were blocked on the passenger's side because of the way the car was wedged in, but there was another way out.

"We can crawl out the windows," Drury suggested. "Once we're out, we can use the ditch for cover." Actually, it was more than a suggestion. It was their only option.

Caitlyn and Dade didn't waste any time lowering the windows, but while Drury kept watch of the SUV, he scrambled across Nicole and her. No way did he want them going out there first. He snaked his way through the window but didn't go toward the front of the car that he could use for cover. Instead, he needed to provide some cover for Caitlyn and Nicole.

Dade got out as well, and he moved back to make room for Caitlyn. Once she was out, Dade hurried her to the front.

Of course, there were no guarantees that there weren't other gunmen on that side, but at least they wouldn't be coming up the road that way because of the fire. Unfortunately, there was plenty of pasture and even some woods for killers to hide.

Kara got out, helping him with Nicole. He could tell from her labored breathing that each movement only caused her pain to spike, but there was nothing he could do about that now. This was their best chance of making it out of here alive.

Drury kept volleying glances back at the SUV, and he tried to steel himself for the bullets to start flying. But the goons didn't shoot.

Why?

Maybe because they wanted at least one of them alive? But again, he had to ask himself why.

There was a cluster of huge trees only about fifteen feet away from the ditch. Close but that would mean plenty of time out in the open. Still, if they could make it there, they could perhaps then go into the woods. The creek was less than a quarter of a mile away, and they could follow it either to the ranch or back into town.

"We could just wait here and see what they decide to do," Kara said.

"Or we could make it to those trees and use them for cover," Drury countered. The darkness and smoke would help some with that. Still, it was risky. Everything was at this point.

"Hell," Dade spat out. "We've got to move now."

Drury glanced back at the SUV, and he, too, cursed. The passenger's-side window was down now, but it wasn't a gun that the thug had aimed at them. It was some kind of launcher. Drury didn't know if it held a grenade or a firebomb, and he didn't want to find out.

"Stay low and move fast," Drury ordered. "Get to those trees." He fired a shot at the SUV with the hopes of getting the guy to duck back inside the vehicle.

It worked, but he knew their luck wouldn't hold out for long.

Caitlyn crawled out of the ditch, dragging Nicole with her. Kara helped, and while they scrambled toward the trees, Dade and Drury continued to send some rounds in the SUV. The bullets weren't making their way through the windshield, but they were holding the guy with the launcher at bay.

At first anyway.

But then the barrel of the launcher came out again. Not the shooter, though. He stayed protected behind the reinforced glass.

And Drury knew Dade and he didn't have much time.

"Run!" he shouted to Dade.

They did. They took off, heading for the trees. Not a second too soon.

Because the firebomb ripped through the car.

Chapter Eighteen

The sound of the blast roared through her, but Caitlyn didn't look back. She tightened her grip on Nicole and just kept moving as fast as she could.

She prayed, though, that Dade and Drury hadn't been hurt.

They'd stayed back, to protect the rest of them, but that could have cost them their lives. Still, Caitlyn tried not to think about that, tried not to give in to the fear that had her by the throat.

With Kara on one side of Nicole and Caitlyn on the other, they made it to the trees and ducked behind them. Caitlyn got her first good look at the effects of the explosion then.

There was nothing left of the car.

It was nothing but a ball of fire.

Of course, it created even more smoke, and this was thick and black, and it took her several heart-stopping moments to look through it and spot Drury and Dade.

Alive.

Thank heaven.

They were running toward the trees, and just when Caitlyn thought they might make it, she saw something else. Something that caused her fear to spike even more.

The thug who'd launched that firebomb was leaning out the window again, and this time, he had a gun.

"Watch out!" she shouted to Drury and Dade.

But it was too late. The shot slammed through the air.

The scream wouldn't make it past her throat. It was jammed there, stalling her breath, causing the panic to rise. It didn't help when the thug fired off another round of shots.

Caitlyn couldn't tell if either had been hit, but she couldn't just hide there and watch them get gunned down. She leaned out from the tree, took aim with the backup weapon Drury had given her.

And she pulled the trigger.

She wasn't sure where the shot landed, but it must have been close enough to the shooter that it got him to duck back inside. From the side of another tree, Kara fired off a shot as well, pinning down the gunman enough so that Dade and Drury could scramble in beside them.

"Stay down," Drury immediately snapped, and he pushed her out of the line of sight of the thug in the SUV.

Not a second too soon.

Because he fired off more rounds, each of them slamming into the spot where she'd just been. It stunned her for a second. Then terrified her. Because those bullets could have hit Drury, too.

"Keep watch all around us," Drury instructed, and he glanced at Nicole. "How's she doing?"

Nicole managed to nod, though she was holding her hands over her stomach and chest. "Just stop these monsters, *please*."

Caitlyn knew that Drury and the others would try to

do that. So would she. But they didn't know what they were up against.

She glanced around at their surroundings. The night. The smoke. And way too many places for backup thugs to hide and ambush them. It sickened her to think that Drury, Kara and Dade were in grave danger because of her. These men were clearly after her. Probably Nicole, too, since she might have witnessed something while captive that could be used to identify them.

Nicole moaned, drawing Caitlyn's attention back to her. She knelt down beside her and tried to see if there was anything she could do to help her. There was a gash on her forehead that was bleeding, but it wasn't enough to be life threatening. However, the woman could have internal injuries.

"Caitlyn?" someone called out. It was the man in the SUV. The one who'd been shooting at them. "You can make this easy on your boyfriend and the cops if you just give yourself up."

"That's not going to happen," Drury shouted before she could say anything. "It's not," he repeated to her.

Caitlyn knew that Drury wasn't going to want to hear this, but she had to try anyway. "You could use me to draw them out. Then we could maybe take the SUV and get Nicole to the hospital."

As expected, Drury was shaking his head before she even finished. "They'll gun you down the second you step out into the opening."

"Maybe. But they might want to take me to the person who hired them."

Drury cursed. "That isn't helping to convince me. In fact, nothing will convince me to let you go out there."

Caitlyn went closer to him. "It could save you. It could save the others. At least consider it."

Drury's next round of profanity was much worse. "You're not going out there. Do you want to make your daughter an orphan, huh?"

It felt as if he'd slapped her. No, she didn't want that, and going out there could indeed get her killed. It ate away at her to think of her baby growing up without a parent, but this was eating away at her, too.

"We'll find another way out of this," Drury insisted. He tipped his head to the phone. "Keep checking for a signal." Before she could continue the argument, he switched his attention to Kara. "You keep watch on your right. Dade, look for anything coming up from behind. Caitlyn will make sure the left side stays clear."

Judging from the way Drury barked out those orders, there wouldn't be any compromises or debates. The glare he shot her only verified that. He knelt down by the side of the tree and pinned his attention to the SUV, so Caitlyn did the same. Except she looked in the area he'd assigned to her.

Nothing.

Well, nothing that she could see anyway. There was another cluster of trees about only ten yards away, and it was plenty thick enough for someone to be hiding there.

"Caitlyn?" the thug called out again. "Maybe this will convince you that it'll be a good idea to come with us."

The barrel of a rifle came out from the SUV, and the shots started. A string of them. The bullets slammed into the tree and sent a spray of splinters all over them. Caitlyn and the others had to shelter their eyes. Worse, the wind shifted, and the smoke started drifting their way. It wouldn't kill them, but it would be hard to aim if they were coughing.

Even though the bullets were deafening, Caitlyn volleyed her attention between the phone and the area to their left. At least she did until a slash of light caught her attention. Not coming from the trees but rather the road.

Mercy, had Grayson or the deputies found them?

She held on to that hope for several seconds. Until she heard Drury curse again. Caitlyn glanced at the SUV and saw the black car pull to a stop behind it. Since the thugs weren't shooting at the vehicle, it meant this was probably more hired killers.

"What the hell are they doing?" Dade asked.

Drury shook his head, and Caitlyn tried to follow his gaze to see what had caused that reaction. Someone stepped from the car. Yes, definitely another thug. He was dressed in all dark clothes and was wearing a ski mask.

He also had the launcher aimed at them. It wasn't the same size as the other one had used. This one was much smaller.

Caitlyn's heart slammed against her ribs because she thought it might be a grenade or another firebomb, but when it hit the ground, there wasn't a blast. Instead, it began to spew out a thick cloud of smoke.

"Are they trying to get us to run?" Kara asked.

Neither Dade nor Drury answered. They continued to keep watch. Not just on the smoke but all around them.

With everything going on, it was a miracle that Caitlyn remembered to glance down at the phone, but when she did, she saw a welcome sight.

"We have a signal," she said. "It's a weak one, but I can try to text Grayson."

"Do it," Drury insisted.

Caitlyn's hands were shaking, and it took her a few seconds to steady them. However, she'd barely gotten the message started when Drury caught onto her arm and pulled her to her feet. He immediately pivoted and took aim in the direction of the SUV.

"Run!" Drury shouted.

Dade picked up Nicole and started running, too, with Kara racing right along behind him. Caitlyn glanced back but all she saw was the milky smoke.

At first anyway.

Then she saw the man. Maybe the same one who'd fired at them from the SUV, and he had the big launcher. And he fired.

The firebomb came right at them.

Chaos.

That one word kept repeating through Drury's head.

He fired two shots at the goon with that launcher, but couldn't stop him in time. Now, all hell was breaking loose.

"Run!" Drury repeated to the others, and he hoped like the devil they were doing that.

He ran, too, toward the other cluster of trees that was nearest to them, but he also pulled up, pivoted and fired at their attacker. Maybe, just maybe, Drury could stop him from shooting another firebomb. Or even regular shots. At this range, the gunman would be able to pick them off.

It didn't take long, mere seconds, for the smoke to get so thick that Drury couldn't see. Plus, there was the heat from the fire.

He couldn't stay put, not out in the open like this, because those gunmen could come from that wall of smoke at any second. He also didn't want to leave the others alone any longer than necessary since they'd probably already made it to the trees. That twisting feeling in his gut let him know that this could get even uglier than it already was.

"Get behind cover now and stay down," Dade called out to them.

Drury tried to do just that, and he hoped Dade had eyes on whoever was coming after them. Drury raced to those trees, dropped down and took aim. He immediately saw one of the thugs who was positioning himself to shoot what appeared to be another firebomb.

Right at them.

Drury double-tapped the trigger, sending two shots into the guy's chest. He fell, but Drury couldn't tell if he was dead or not. He hoped so because he didn't want the idiot to get another chance to use those bombs. Of course, that didn't mean there wasn't someone else ready to take the downed thug's place.

The seconds crawled by while Drury waited for someone else to come at them. There could be a half dozen or more in the SUV and car. Heck, there could be more in these woods, and that's why Drury glanced around to get his bearings and to make sure they weren't about to be ambushed.

Kara was about three yards behind him, watching their backs. Dade had taken up position two trees over, and he was looking all around them. Nicole was flat on her back and moaning in pain.

Drury hated that he couldn't do anything to help the woman, but maybe Caitlyn had managed to send that text to Grayson so that he would have their position. Grayson wouldn't be able to get an ambulance in here, not with the possibility of shots still being fired, but he and the other deputies could help them deal with the attackers.

He glanced around to ask Caitlyn about that text.

And his breath stalled in his throat.

She wasn't there. He frantically looked around while also trying to keep watch for the attackers, but there was no sign of her.

"Where's Caitlyn?" he asked Dade and Kara.

They, too, glanced around, and Drury could tell they didn't have a clue. His first instinct was to call out to her, but that would give away their position, so he dropped back and began to search behind every tree. Hard to do that, though, with the thick underbrush covering the ground and the smoke. It was getting even thicker now.

Hell, was Caitlyn hurt?

That revved up Drury's pulse a significant notch. In all the mayhem of them running for cover, one of the thugs could have shot her. Or maybe she hadn't made it out at all.

With his stomach twisting, Drury looked back at the other set of trees. The ones that were on fire now. If she was in the middle of that, then… But he didn't even want to go there.

Caitlyn couldn't be dead.

He heard the sound to his left. A snap of a twig maybe, and the relief flooded through him.

But not for long.

It was Caitlyn all right, but she wasn't alone. Nor was she all right. There was someone behind her. One of the ski mask–wearing goons. And he had his left arm clamped around her throat in a choke hold.

He also had a gun pointed at her head.

"Surprised to see me?" the man taunted.

That immediately caused both Dade and Kara to pivot in his direction, and they took aim just as Drury already had. But none of them had a clean shot. The man had ducked down and was using Caitlyn as a human shield.

"I'm sorry," Caitlyn said. "I didn't see him in time."

Drury hated that she felt the need to apologize. Hated, too, that look in her eyes. Fear, not just for herself but for all of them.

"You probably know what you have to do next," the man continued. "You gotta all put down your guns just like Caitlyn did."

"I didn't put mine down," she snapped. "He knocked it from my hand."

"Just doing my job, and my job includes killing her right here, right now if you don't put down those guns. Same for the bimbo on the ground. My friend wants me to give her a little payback for hurting him. Of course, she won't like my version of payback."

Drury didn't recognize the guy's voice, and it definitely wasn't one of their suspects. However, it was obvious he was connected to the men who'd taken Nicole from the back of the sheriff's office.

"Who are you working for?" Drury demanded.

The man tightened his grip on Caitlyn's throat. "What part of my order didn't you understand? I mean, it was simple enough. Guns on the ground now!"

Drury hated to surrender his weapon because he didn't have a backup. He'd given it to Caitlyn. But Kara and Dade almost certainly had some other weapon stashed away. Weapons they would no doubt need to get all of them out of this alive.

Dade was the first to drop his gun. Then Kara. Drury finally did, too, while he continued to fire glances around them. It would be a good time for other attackers to swarm in and take them all, and if that happened, their chances of survival would drop considerably.

"Now kick the guns away so you can't get to them," the man ordered.

They did, but Drury kicked his in Nicole's direction. It was a risk since there was a slim chance she could be working with these clowns. But he doubted it. And even though she was clearly in a lot of pain, maybe she'd be able to use his gun if it came down to it.

"So, what now?" Drury asked the goon when he just stood there.

"Waiting for the boss. Shouldn't be long now."

Drury doubted the boss had anything good in mind for Caitlyn. For any of them really.

The moments crawled by, and when the wind shifted, Drury saw someone walking through the smoke. Not just one person but three. Two men both dressed in black and wearing ski masks. They were armed.

But not the person in the middle.

Hell.

So, this was the *boss*.

Chapter Nineteen

Because of the way the goon had her standing, Caitlyn couldn't see the reason Drury had cursed. But she figured it couldn't be good.

Nothing about this was good, and they'd need plenty of luck to get out of it alive.

Since Dade, Kara, Drury and even the thug holding her now had their attention focused in the direction of the road, Caitlyn considered trying something. Maybe like elbowing the guy or dropping to the ground. It might cause him to shoot, but at least his gun was still aimed at her.

Mercy, she didn't want to die. But she doubted whoever was coming would spare any of them. This way, there might be a scuffle. One that Dade, Kara and Drury could maybe win.

But why hadn't the goon already killed her?

That was the question racing through her head when Caitlyn finally saw the people making their way toward them. Two more hired guns.

And Melanie.

The woman wasn't a hostage, either. Dressed as if ready to attend a business meeting, she was walking beside the men, and even though she wasn't armed, she didn't need a gun. Not with those two hired killers.

"I got her just like you said," the goon holding Caitlyn relayed to Melanie.

"Good." Melanie barely spared the others a glance. Instead, she kept her stare on Caitlyn.

Except it was a glare.

Even in the near darkness, Caitlyn had no trouble seeing it. Melanie hated her, and while she hadn't exactly kept that hatred under wraps while they were at the sheriff's office, this was pure venom that she was now aiming at Caitlyn.

Melanie's glare was still in place when she made a sweeping glance around them. "Couldn't get your lover out of this, huh?" she directed at Drury.

"The night's not over," he countered, matching her glare for glare.

Melanie smiled as if all of this were a done deal. It wasn't. Somehow they had to fight their way out of this because if Melanie and those hired killers eliminated them, they might go to the ranch next.

"Is she still alive?" Melanie asked when she looked at Nicole.

"Yeah," the goon behind Caitlyn verified. "Wasn't sure if you wanted her kept alive or not."

"No. She's worthless to me now that I can't get any money for her."

There it was—Melanie's motive all spelled out for them. Well, her partial motive anyway. She wanted Grant's money.

"Is that why my baby was born, because you wanted me to pay for her?" Caitlyn asked. She didn't bother to contain the anger in her voice and wished she could blast this idiot to smithereens.

"Of course," Melanie readily admitted. She glanced at the others again. "And I guess you know that means it's bad news for all of you. Well, bad news for everyone but Caitlyn."

Caitlyn replayed the words to make sure she'd heard her correctly. "Why would you keep me alive?" But she immediately thought of the answer. "You want me to drain all my bank accounts and give the money to you. There isn't much left."

"I want every penny of it." Caitlyn hadn't thought Melanie's venom could get any worse, but it had. Melanie fanned her hand over the thugs. "Grant's money paid for all of this."

"And you put that money in an offshore account with my name on it," Caitlyn snapped.

Melanie shrugged. "It seemed the easiest way to cover my tracks, and there's no way you could have gotten your hands on it because you didn't know the security code I set up."

And by covering her tracks, Melanie had also tried to make Caitlyn look guilty. It hadn't worked, but she hadn't needed it to work since she had the upper hand here.

"Grant's money will pay for a whole lot more since there are some loose ends that need to be tied up," Melanie added. "And what it doesn't cover, Helen will pay for. My personal living expenses, nannies and private schools for the baby."

Everything inside Caitlyn went still. "Are you talking about nannies and private schools for my daughter?"

"She's Grant's daughter, too, and I plan to raise her

as my own. That way I'll have a part of Grant. If Helen cooperates with me, then she'll get to see the child. Not here, of course. I won't be able to live here."

If the thug hadn't held her back, Caitlyn would have gone after her. "You're not getting my child."

Melanie shrugged. "We'll see about that, and I'm sure Helen will pay up when she realizes I have her granddaughter."

"Is Helen in on this?" Drury asked.

Melanie made a you've-got-to-be-kidding sound. "No, this was my plan and my plan only, but since you didn't take the bait when I planted evidence against Jeremy and her, it means you sealed everyone's fate."

Drury shook his head. "What did you do?"

Melanie actually smiled. "Jeremy deserves what he gets. Do you know he killed Grant?"

"Got any proof of that?" Drury countered.

"Jeremy talks in his sleep," Melanie said under her breath. "No way could I let him get away without being punished." She motioned toward the goon holding Caitlyn. "Come on. Bring her to the car. Kill the rest," she added to the other two. "No need to do a cleanup. I'll have the kid and will be out of the country before any of these Silver Creek lawmen figure out it's me. They'll be too busy chasing Jeremy."

She'd obviously set him up somehow, but Caitlyn didn't care about that. "How do you think you're going to get my baby?"

Melanie tipped her head to the fires. "Plenty of those. In comparison to the rest of this, firebombs don't cost much at all, and I figure if we land enough of them on the Silver Creek Ranch, the Rylands will give her up to save their own."

Clearly, she didn't know the Rylands. They'd never give up the baby. But that didn't mean plenty of them wouldn't die or get hurt trying.

It felt as if someone had clamped onto her heart and was squeezing it hard. The rage bashed at her like a violent storm, building and building until Caitlyn knew where she needed to aim that rage.

At Melanie.

Melanie turned to walk away, and the goon started moving, dragging Caitlyn along with him. Leading her to where she would no doubt be tortured and eventually killed. Of course, Drury and the others would be targets long before that. They'd die within seconds if Caitlyn didn't do something now.

She latched onto all that rage she was feeling and let it and the adrenaline fuel her. Caitlyn bashed the back of her head against the goon's face, as hard as she could. So hard that she could have sworn she saw stars. She pushed aside the pain, though, and dropped to the ground. The goon didn't drop with her, nor did he let go of the gun. He was cursing her now and latched onto her hair.

That's when all hell broke loose.

Drury lunged at the thug. Dade went after the other two, and Kara scooped up Drury's gun off the ground. She probably didn't have a clean shot, but at least one of them was armed, and maybe she could stop Melanie from getting away.

"Kill them!" Melanie screamed.

Her thugs were certainly trying to do just that. Caitlyn's attacker still had hold of her hair and was using his fierce grip to sling her around to block Drury from slugging him. Drury didn't give up, though, and he finally managed to bash the guy right in the face.

It was enough to get him to stagger back and let go of her hair.

Drury pushed her away and went after the guy, plowing right into him and sending him to the ground. Caitlyn frantically looked around for the goon's gun, and her breath stalled in her throat when she saw that he still had hold of it. Worse, he was trying to aim it at Drury.

"Do your jobs and kill them." Melanie's voice was a screech, followed by some ripe profanity. She sounded insane. And probably was.

Since Melanie wasn't armed and wasn't running, Caitlyn tuned her out for a moment and tried to help Drury.

"Stay back," Drury warned her.

He probably didn't want her to be anywhere near that gun, but she wasn't just going to let him fight this alone. Caitlyn kicked at the goon's legs. And she continued to kick until the sound of the shot stopped her cold.

Oh, mercy.

Had Drury been shot?

It seemed as if time slowed to a crawl, and the sounds in her head were a series of loud echoes. She couldn't lose Drury. Especially not like this, while he'd been trying to protect her.

Caitlyn clawed at the goon, hitting any part of him that she could reach, but that's when she realized Drury hadn't been hit. The bullet had come from behind her.

Kara.

The deputy had put a bullet in one of the thug's heads. Lifeless, he dropped to the ground.

One down, but Dade and Drury were still battling

the other two attackers. She couldn't tell if either was winning, but at least Kara had a gun, and the deputy hurried closer, waiting for a shot that Caitlyn was sure she would take if she got the chance. Maybe they'd actually get out of this alive.

But that's when Caitlyn saw something she didn't want to see.

Melanie was running. Getting away. And if she reached the car or SUV, she could escape. Maybe she would even try to get to the Silver Creek Ranch and try to take Caroline.

Caitlyn went after her.

It wasn't easy. She'd burned a lot of energy hitting the thug, and the smoke didn't help. It wasn't as thick as it had been, but it cut her breath. Still, that didn't stop her. Nothing would at this point. Not even Drury shouting out to her.

"Caitlyn, come back."

He was probably concerned that there were other hired killers who would come to Melanie's aid. And maybe they would, but Caitlyn couldn't let Melanie make it to the road.

Behind her, there were two shots. She hoped they'd come from Kara or that maybe Dade and Drury had managed to get hold of a weapon. Part of her wanted to go back and see, but she had to stop Melanie.

Melanie was running a lot faster than Caitlyn thought she could, and she made it all the way to the thug whom Drury had shot before Caitlyn caught up with her. Caitlyn dived at her, catching onto Melanie's waist and dragging her to the ground.

That's when Caitlyn saw the gun.

Melanie must have grabbed it from the dead guy, but she lifted her hand, taking aim at Caitlyn.

Caitlyn didn't think. She only reacted. She hit Melanie's hand just as the woman pulled the trigger.

The shot roared through the air.

Caitlyn couldn't tell where the bullet had gone, but she prayed it hadn't hit Drury or the others. Prayed, too, that she could stop Melanie from firing again. She latched onto the woman's wrist, and even though Melanie outsized her by a good thirty pounds, Caitlyn had something to fight for.

Her daughter.

If the woman escaped, there was no telling what she might do.

Behind her, there were more shots. Caitlyn had no trouble hearing them, but she couldn't look back and see if Drury was okay.

Melanie cursed her, calling her vile names while she fought like a wildcat. She kicked and dug her fingernails into Caitlyn's hand. She drew blood, but Caitlyn drew blood, too, when she rammed her forearm against Melanie's face.

She howled in pain, cursed even more and tried to bash Caitlyn against the head with the gun. Caitlyn dodged it and dropped her weight onto the woman, pinning her arms to the ground. That didn't stop Melanie from screaming and fighting, and just when Caitlyn wasn't sure how much longer she could hold her, she heard the movement behind her.

Since she hadn't been able to look back and see what was going on, Caitlyn didn't know if this was friend or foe approaching her. Worse, there was nothing she could do because if she let go of Melanie, she would pull the trigger.

The fear rose inside Caitlyn as the hurried footsteps got closer and closer, but she tried to steel herself for whatever might happen.

"It's all right," someone said.

Drury.

The relief nearly caused Caitlyn to go limp. Temporary relief, anyway. She still wasn't sure he was okay.

He wrenched the gun from Melanie's hands and moved Caitlyn off her so he could flip Melanie onto her stomach. He restrained her with some plastic cuffs that he took from his pocket.

Caitlyn pulled in her breath and held it. Until Drury finally turned and looked at her. He had some blood on his face. No doubt from the fistfight with the hired gun, but he was all right.

"You shouldn't have done that," he said, his breath gusting. "She could have killed you."

"She didn't," Caitlyn managed to say, but she could see from the stark look in Drury's eyes that this had almost certainly triggered some flashbacks of Lily's death.

Even though Drury didn't exactly have a welcoming expression, Caitlyn leaned in and kissed him. A very quick one because his attention went back to where she'd last seen Dade, Kara, Nicole and those other goons.

Caitlyn snapped in that direction, too, and she spotted Dade hurrying toward them. He had Nicole in his arms. Kara was right behind him, and she was still keeping watch all around them.

"What happened to the gunmen?" Caitlyn asked.

Kara shook her head. "All dead."

It was hard to feel any grief over the deaths of hired killers, but Caitlyn also knew that if they'd managed to keep at least one of them alive, then he could perhaps spill details they might not get from Melanie.

"You think this is over?" Melanie snarled when Drury hauled her to her feet. She looked back at Caitlyn, and the raw hatred was all over the woman's face. "It's not over. You'll never see your daughter again."

Chapter Twenty

"Hurry," Caitlyn insisted.

Though she really didn't have to remind Drury to do that. He already was in the "get there fast" mode and hadn't even waited for backup to arrive. Instead, Caitlyn and he had taken the car that Melanie and her thugs had used. It was a risk since there could be some kind of tracking device on the vehicle, but Drury weighed that risk against an even greater one.

Not getting to the baby before there was an attack at the ranch.

"Do you have a signal yet?" he asked, tipping his head to the cell phone she was holding.

Caitlyn shook her head. Cursed. It was frustrating, all right, but they'd be out of the dead zone soon, and she should be able to call the ranch. And Grayson. Drury had no idea what was going on with him, and it was entirely possible that Melanie had had another team of attackers go after the lawmen in the sheriff's office.

As Drury continued to do, Caitlyn glanced all around them. Watching for more of those hired guns. He was certain that Kara and Dade were doing the same thing. They'd taken the SUV so they could get Melanie to jail and Nicole to the hospital.

The surrogate was yet another concern.

Her injuries could be life threatening. Of course, Melanie was high on his list of worries, too, because she could have arranged for more gunmen to be positioned on the road. He didn't know how many hired killers that the million dollars of ransom money would buy, and Drury didn't want to find out.

"What do you think Melanie did to Jeremy?" Caitlyn asked.

Drury hadn't had time to give it much thought, but he didn't need a lot of thinking time to know that it probably wasn't something good. Melanie had been plenty riled over Jeremy's rejection and betrayal, and she'd no doubt set him up somehow to take the blame for all of this.

He took another turn onto a farm road, heading toward the ranch, but they were still a good ten minutes out. Drury figured it would seem more like an hour before they got there.

"Finally," Caitlyn said, looking at the phone screen. Her hands were shaking when she pressed Grayson's number.

Drury hoped that his cousin would answer on the first ring. And he did.

"You two okay?" Grayson immediately asked.

"Yeah, but Melanie might have sent someone to attack—"

"I just got off the phone with Dade, and he told me. I've alerted the ranch hands, and Nate, Mason and our cousin Sawyer are heading down to the road now to make sure no one is there."

Caitlyn's breath rushed out from relief. They weren't out of the woods yet, but there was no way his cousins would let Melanie's thugs get close enough to do any real damage.

"I told Ronnie that we had Melanie in custody," Grayson went on, "and he's ready to spill all for a plea deal."

Drury had to shake his head. "If Ronnie was working for Melanie, why did she bring him at gunpoint to the jail?"

"Ronnie says that's the plan they worked out. That she'd pretend to turn him in, and that he'd take the fall in exchange for his kids getting a ton of money. He figures there won't be a payoff now that Melanie's being arrested."

No, there wouldn't be. In fact, Melanie's accounts would be frozen, and Caitlyn would get back any portion of the ransom money that Melanie hadn't spent on these attacks. Of course, that was probably the last thing on Caitlyn's mind right now. She just wanted to see her baby and make sure she was all right.

"Let me call you back after I've finished talking with the DA," Grayson continued. "Oh, and be careful when you make it to the ranch."

Drury would be, but he doubted he was going to be able to hold Caitlyn back. She had such a grip on his phone that she would probably have bruises. Bruises to go with the ones on her face.

It turned his stomach to see them. To know just how close he'd come to losing her.

"After this is done," he said, "I intend to chew you out for going after Melanie like that."

"You would have done the same thing if you'd been me."

He would have. "But I'm an FBI agent trained to

do things like that." He paused, huffed. "That doesn't trump motherhood, though."

She made a sound of agreement. Followed by a helpless moan. "Please just hurry," Caitlyn repeated.

Drury did, taking the final turn. When the ranch finally came into view, he saw something that had him hitting the brakes.

There were men clustered around the cattle gate at the start of the ranch road, and someone was on the ground.

Hell.

Drury hoped he hadn't driven Caitlyn into the middle of another attack. Just in case, he turned off the headlights and eased closer. While he was trying to get a better look at what was going on, his phone buzzed, and he saw Mason's name on the screen.

"Is that Caitlyn and you in the car?" Mason growled.

Drury felt some of the tightness ease up in his chest. If Mason could call them, then he was okay. Well, maybe.

"Yes. What happened?" Drury asked.

"This dirthead we've got on the ground thought it would be a good idea to try to shoot something at the ranch. Trust me, he knows now it wasn't a good idea. We're about to haul him off to jail."

"Is Caroline okay?" Caitlyn asked.

"She's fine. Josh and Bree are with the nanny and her."

Josh, his other cousin, and Bree, who was Kade's wife and had once been in law enforcement. Caroline was in good hands. Better yet, she was safe.

Caitlyn's breath rushed out again. And the tears came. Tears of relief, no doubt. The happy tears would come once she had her baby in her arms.

"Was the hired gun alone?" Caitlyn asked.

"He was," Mason verified. "But we've got the hands patrolling the area just in case. They found the clown's car just up the road, and there are no signs that anyone else was in it."

Maybe because Melanie had thought one firebomb shooter was enough. Or perhaps the woman had just wanted to save a little money.

"The gate and the fences are all armed, though," Mason went on. "So the alarm will sound if there are any stragglers who try to get onto the grounds. Someone's also monitoring the security cameras."

Good. It was a lot of security, but it had obviously worked since they'd caught this guy before he'd managed to do any damage.

He watched as Nate and Sawyer got the hired gun to his feet and started moving him toward a car that was nearby.

"Is it okay for me to drive Caitlyn to the guesthouse?" Drury asked Mason.

Mason kept his glare on the man being arrested. "Yeah, because if this dirthead moves even an eyelash, he's going to pay and pay hard. It's too late to be testing my patience."

Drury wondered if it was ever a good time to test Mason's patience, but he didn't say that to his cousin. He drove onto the ranch.

"By the way," Mason said just as Drury was about to end the call. "Have you fixed things with Caitlyn yet?"

Since they were on speaker, Drury hesitated before he said anything. "Fix things?" he settled for asking.

Mason cursed. "Have you told her you're in love with her? And no, the question isn't for me. It's because I know when I get back home, Abbie will ask me how the personal stuff worked out for you two."

Drury glanced at Caitlyn, who seemed a little shell-shocked. Maybe because of the whole ordeal she'd just been through. Maybe in part because of Mason's *you're in love with her* comment.

"I'll keep you posted," Drury answered, and he didn't bother to take out the sarcasm.

There was a ranch hand at the main entry gate, and he ushered Drury in, closing the gate behind them. Yet another security measure that Drury appreciated.

When Drury approached the guesthouse, he parked as close to the front porch as possible, and the moment he stopped, Caitlyn hurried out. He didn't try to stop her. No chance of doing that. So, he just raced in after her.

With all the chaos that'd gone on, being in the quiet room seemed a little surreal. The baby was asleep in her bassinet. Josh was sitting next to her, guarding her, and Bree was at the kitchen table quietly looking at the feed from the cameras.

"She's okay," Bree assured Caitlyn. Maybe because Bree was a mother herself, she no doubt figured Caitlyn would want to hear that right off.

"Thank you," Caitlyn said, and she repeated it several more times while she scooped up the baby. She pressed a flurry of kisses on her cheeks and held her close. Drury wondered if she'd ever let Caroline out of her sight again.

"She's a quiet baby," Josh added. "Unlike mine and most of the others on the ranch."

That was true. There were several contenders for the loudest Ryland kid, and Josh's was one of them.

"You think you two will be okay without us?" Bree asked. "Lynette had the twins, and I'd like to go to the hospital to see her. If Kade will let me off the grounds, that is."

Kade probably wouldn't allow that for a while, not until they were positive all was well.

"Are Lynette and the babies all right?" Caitlyn asked.

Bree nodded. "Gage sounded downright giddy when he called and said that the C-section went well. The boys are little, only four pounds each, but otherwise healthy. I could hear them crying in the background."

Great. More criers. More kids. But Drury found himself smiling at that thought. He'd never wanted to live on a quiet ranch anyway, and there was something comforting about knowing there'd be another generation of Rylands to run the ranch. Some of them might even follow in their footsteps and become cops.

"We'll be fine here," Drury assured Bree. Then he looked at Josh. "You can head home, too. The thug that Mason and the others caught is on his way to jail. Melanie, too." In fact, she was probably already there.

Caitlyn and Drury thanked them both again. Josh and Bree gathered up their things, both of them kissing the baby before they headed out. Drury locked the door behind them and armed the security system.

"It's just a precaution," Drury said when he saw the renewed concern in Caitlyn's eyes.

"Good. I don't want to take any more chances."

That sounded a little unnerving, as if she weren't just talking about security now. Maybe she wasn't ready or willing to take a chance on, well, him.

He eased down next to her on the sofa and was prepared to tell her how sorry he was that all of this had happened. But he didn't get a chance. That's because Caitlyn leaned over and kissed him. It wasn't a peck, either. This was an honest-to-goodness kiss, not of relief, either. This felt more like foreplay.

"The adrenaline," he said, ready to offer an excuse so she'd have an out. If she wanted an out, that is.

Apparently she didn't.

"I didn't kiss you because of the adrenaline," she insisted. "Or because we were nearly just killed." She paused. "Okay, maybe it did have a little to do with nearly dying, but things got crystal clear for me tonight when I thought I'd lost you."

Drury had experienced some of that clarity himself. "Yes," he settled for saying.

She stared at him, maybe waiting for more, and since Drury wasn't sure what more to say, he just kissed her right back. At first he thought she might be disappointed that they hadn't continued what could be the start of a promising conversation, but she moved right into the kiss. As much as she could anyway, considering that she still had the baby in her arms.

"You're very good at that," she said with her mouth still against his.

"I think it's just because we're good at it together."

Caitlyn eased back, met his gaze, and again she seemed to be waiting for him to say something important. Something that didn't have anything to do with what had just happened.

Drury finally managed to gather some words that he hoped made sense. "I realized tonight that life's short. And there are no certainties."

She frowned but nodded. "You're talking about Lily now."

It was Drury's turn to frown. "No." And he wasn't. "I was talking about us." He had to stop and try to figure out how to say this. "I don't want you to leave. I want Caroline and you in my life."

At least she didn't frown, but Caitlyn did continue to stare at him. That wasn't the response he wanted, so Drury kissed her again, and he kept on kissing her until they were both breathless.

When they finally broke for air, she looked down at the baby. "She'll always be Grant's biological daughter."

He lifted his shoulder. In the grand scheme of things, DNA didn't seem important. "She'll always be *your* daughter. And I get what you're saying. Or maybe it's what you're asking. Can I accept her? Can I accept any of this?"

Caitlyn nodded.

Drury nodded, too. He could definitely accept it if Caitlyn was willing to stay and give them a chance. However, he didn't have time to spell that all out for her because his phone buzzed, and he saw Grayson's name on the screen.

Hell, he hoped something bad hadn't happened.

"Put it on speaker," Caitlyn insisted, and she eased the baby back into the bassinet as if preparing herself for one more round of the nightmare that they'd thought was finished.

"Are you two all right?" Grayson asked the moment Drury answered.

"Yes," they both answered cautiously. It was Drury who continued. "Did something else go wrong?"

"Not here. Why? Did something go wrong there?"

"No." Drury looked at Caitlyn. But everything wasn't all right just yet. He still needed to tell her so many things. First, though, he had to get through this call with Grayson.

"Dade just called me from the hospital," Grayson explained a moment later. "Nicole is being examined now, but the doctor doesn't think her injuries are life threatening."

Drury could see the relief in Caitlyn's eyes. Could hear it also in the slow breath she released.

"I've already got the approval from the DA for a plea deal with Ronnie," Grayson went on. "Don't worry, he'll still get plenty of jail time, but in exchange for testifying against Melanie, he won't be charged with murder."

"Murder?" Drury and Caitlyn asked at the same time.

Grayson paused. "Jeremy's dead. I've only spent about ten minutes with Ronnie, but according to him, Melanie set it up to look like a suicide, and in the note he confessed to killing Caitlyn and you. Grant, too."

"Melanie said Jeremy did murder Grant," Drury explained. "No proof, of course. And at this point we might never know for sure since Jeremy's dead."

"You're right. And I don't believe everything in this fake note. In it, he claims that Helen is responsible for stealing the embryo from Conceptions."

"But she didn't?" Caitlyn said under her breath.

"No, it was all Melanie, and Ronnie even has some proof. Guess he didn't completely trust his boss because he recorded some conversations that he says will prove Melanie was scheming to get both the baby and the ransom money. The recordings won't be admissible in court, but Ronnie can testify against everything on them."

That would tie everything up. Well, except for Helen

and Jeremy. Jeremy was dead, and Helen had lost another son. Even though they obviously weren't close as most mothers and sons, Drury figured she'd still feel that loss. That didn't mean he had much sympathy for the woman.

"Helen's not getting Caroline," Drury insisted.

Caitlyn had a new look in her eyes now, one of thanks for backing her up. Drury intended much more than playing backup for her, though.

"Can't see how Helen would have a claim," Grayson agreed. "Caitlyn doesn't have as much as a parking ticket, and none of what happened was her fault. When I tell Helen about Jeremy, I'll remind her that if she ever wants to see her granddaughter, then she'd better try to mend fences with Caitlyn."

That might work, and if it didn't, Drury would have a chat with the woman. After everything that Caitlyn had been through, he didn't want her to have to deal with the likes of Helen.

"What about Nicole?" Caitlyn asked. "Other than being the surrogate, please tell me she didn't have any part in this nightmare."

"According to Ronnie she didn't. I asked. He said Nicole didn't have a clue what was going on, not even after Melanie decided to have her kidnapped and held hostage. I'm sure Ronnie will give us a lot more info on how that all went down."

Yes, it sounded that way. Which was a good thing considering Melanie's other hired guns were all dead and wouldn't be able to spill their guts the way Ronnie was doing.

"Guess you heard that Lynette had the babies?" Grayson continued a moment later.

"Bree told us," Drury answered. "She said Lynette and the babies were doing okay."

"They are. Gage maybe not so much. He's crazy happy, but I figure it'll soon sink in that he's not going to get much sleep for the next few years what with twin boys in the house. By the way, has anyone mentioned that the females are seriously outnumbered on the ranch?"

Drury was instantly suspicious. "Mason said something about that. Any reason you're bringing it up?"

"You're a smart man. You figure it out." And with that, Grayson hung up.

This was Grayson's attempt at matchmaking, and he sucked at it. He was about as subtle as all the Ryland kids piled into the same room.

He put away his phone, checked the baby to make sure she was okay. She was. Then he looked at Caitlyn.

Not okay.

She was frowning again, and after all the good news they'd just gotten, that expression shouldn't be on her face. Especially since the frown was paired with a determined look in her eyes.

"I'm in love with you," she said as if it were a declaration of war. "I know that's probably not what you want to hear, but I can't undo my feelings for you. That doesn't mean you owe me anything—"

Drury stopped her with a kiss, one of those long ones that did more than rob them of their breaths. The heat slid right through him.

"I don't want you to undo your feelings for me," he assured her. "And having you say you love me is exactly what I want to hear."

She blinked. "Really?"

"Oh, yeah. Because I'm in love with you, too."

Finally, that got the frown off her face and erased the doubt in her eyes. She smiled. Kissed him until he was certain if they kept kissing, it was going to lead them straight to the bed.

Or the sofa.

Smiling in between the kisses, Caitlyn eased him back until his head was against the sofa's armrest. She didn't stop there, thank goodness. She slid her body on top of his.

"So, where do we go from here?" Caitlyn asked, glancing down at their new position.

Drury didn't think she was just talking about sex, and neither was he. "Everywhere. I love you, Caitlyn."

"And I love you," she repeated, pulling him to her.

* * * * *

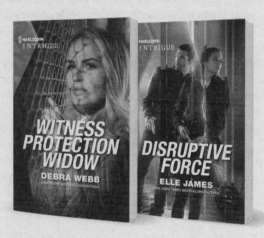

He was challenging her already and they hadn't even really
started working together, but if they were going to survive
several weeks of training, honesty was going to be the best
policy.

"My husband was a marine," Piper said, but didn't make
eye contact with him. Instead, she whirled and started
walking back in the direction of the outdoor training ring.

He turned and kept pace beside her, his gaze trained on
her face. "Was?"

Challenging again. Pushing, but regardless of that, she
said, "He was killed in action in Iraq. Four years ago and
yet..."

Her throat choked up and tears welled in her eyes as she
rushed forward, almost as if she could outrun the discussion
and the pain it brought.

The gentle touch of his big, calloused hand on her forearm stopped her escape.

She glanced down at that hand and then followed his arm up to meet his gaze, so full of concern and something else. Pain?

"I'm sorry. It can't be easy," he said, the simple words filled with so much more. Pain for sure. Understanding. Compassion. Not pity, thankfully. The last nearly undid her, but she sucked in a breath, held it for the briefest second before blurting out, "We should get going. If you're going to do search and rescue with Decoy, we'll have to improve his obedience skills."

Rushing away from him, she slipped through the gaps in the split-rail fence and walked to the center of the training ring.

Shane hesitated, obviously uneasy, but then he bent to go across the fence railing and met her in the middle of the ring, Decoy at his side.

"I'm ready if you are," he said, his big body several feet away, only he still felt too close. Too big. Too masculine with that kind of posture and strength that screamed military.

She took a step back and said, "I'm ready."

She wasn't and didn't know if she ever could be with this man. He was testing her on too many levels.

Only she'd never failed a training assignment and she didn't intend to start with Shane and Decoy.

"Let's get going," she said.

Don't miss
Decoy Training *by Caridad Piñeiro,*
available April 2022 wherever
Harlequin Intrigue books and ebooks are sold.

Love Harlequin romance?

DISCOVER.

Be the first to find out about promotions, news and exclusive content!

f Facebook.com/HarlequinBooks

y Twitter.com/HarlequinBooks

⊙ Instagram.com/HarlequinBooks

℗ Pinterest.com/HarlequinBooks

YouTube YouTube.com/HarlequinBooks

ReaderService.com

EXPLORE.

Sign up for the Harlequin e-newsletter and download a free book from any series at
TryHarlequin.com

CONNECT.

Join our Harlequin community to share your thoughts and connect with other romance readers!
Facebook.com/groups/HarlequinConnection

HARLEQUIN

Heartfelt or thrilling, passionate or uplifting—Harlequin is more than just happily-ever-after.

With twelve different series to choose from and new books available every month, you are sure to find stories that will move you, uplift you, inspire and delight you.